THE WRECKAGE

Michael Crummey

The Wreckage

A Novel

DOUBLEDAY CANADA

Doubleday Canada and colophon are trademarks.

LIBRARY AND ARCHIVES CANADA CATALOGUING IN PUBLICATION

Crummey, Michael
The wreckage / Michael Crummey.

ISBN 0—385—66060-X

I. Title.

PS8555.R84W74 2005   C813.'54   C2005—901694—9

Jacket image: © Hulton-Deutsch Collection/CORBIS
Jacket and text design: CS Richardson
Printed and bound in the USA

Published in Canada by
Doubleday Canada, a division of
Random House of Canada Limited

Visit Random House of Canada Limited's website: www.randomhouse.ca

BVG 10 9 8 7 6 5 4 3 2 1

FOR HOLLY ANN

And General Yamoshito, when American troops marched into Manila, remarked "with a broad smile," the radio said, "that now the enemy is in our bosom."

RUTH BENEDICT, *The Chrysanthemum and the Sword*

He was never dry.

Every day they abandoned field guns mired in mud. The tires and axles of ammunition carts disappeared in sludge and the shells for the guns still with them were carried by hand. Half a dozen men at the front of the column slashed a trail with machetes, the rainforest so densely organic, so humid and rank, it felt as if they were forcing their way through the tissue of a living creature. Soldiers lost their footing on exposed roots, on the slick ground, and they collapsed under their packs like marionettes cut free of strings. There was only river water to drink, and everyone in the company was miserable with dengue and with dysentery, men stepping out of the column to relieve themselves in the bush. Nishino thought the reek alone would be enough to give away their position.

Animals he would never see or know by name called and cawed in the trees. Only the birds came into view, hallucinatory flashes of colour dipping through the branches. The parrots picked up words and phrases from the soldiers and mimicked them. *Hikoki hikoki* sent the entire company face down into the foliage, listening for American planes.

They'd out-marched their rice rations and the soldiers were fed a little dried fish and crackers and hard candy at midday. Nishino sat beside Ogawa as they ate, and they picked through each other's hair and clothing for fleas and biting ants and chiggers. Then Ogawa lay his head in Nishino's lap and slept until the officers ordered them on.

He heard a voice calling "Yes sir!" and crouched defensively, swinging his rifle up to his waist, staring left and right.

Ogawa tilted his head. "Are you all right, Noburo?"

He heard the phrase repeated twice more before he realized it was a parrot calling from the forest. He let the rifle come down by his side and looked around at the other soldiers.

"Noburo?"

No one else had noticed. "Never mind," he said.

At the end of the day's march he went to Lieutenant Kurakake, who was sitting under a fold of canvas with maps spread across his thighs. The charts glowing with a yellow bioluminescent substance smeared on the surface for light. He stood to one side at attention.

"Yes?" the lieutenant said finally.

He hesitated. Bowed deeply. "I heard a parrot," he said.

Kurakake looked up at him. "We have all heard them," he said. "Endlessly," he said.

"It was an English phrase I heard, Lieutenant."

"English?"

"Yes. I am certain of it."

"What is your name, Private?"

"Nishino, sir. Noburo Nishino."

"And what did this bird say to you, Private Nishino?"

"It said, 'Yes sir.' Several times."

The lieutenant nodded slowly. He called to a company sergeant and ordered him to double the number of soldiers on sentry duty through the night. He nodded up to Nishino, dismissing him.

All the way back to the spot where Ogawa lay sleeping, he could feel the officer's eyes following him.

Shortly before dark the next evening the soldiers crested a hill, breathing in open air blowing off a long grassy ridge a hundred feet below. The officers walked through the ranks, whispering, ordering them to dig in.

Nishino woke to the sound of the Americans talking among themselves below, their conversation carried up to him on the wind. Ogawa was still asleep, and Nishino lay quiet next to him, trying to pick words from the drift. Eased away from the boy finally to relieve himself in the trees. Covered his face as he crouched, shivering uncontrollably, his skin slick with sweat as the stink ran from him.

Lieutenant Kurakake was standing over Ogawa when Nishino came back. "Lieutenant," he said and bowed.

He could smell a hint of something sweet in the air, something refined and so foreign to the place and condition he was in that he sniffed the air like a dog. Lieutenant Kurakake smiled at Nishino's confusion, brought his hands from behind his back and passed across a small crystal bottle.

"My wife's perfume," Kurakake told him. "I wanted to have something of her with me."

Nishino nodded, unsure what to make of the revelation, wary of the unexpected intimacy. Kurakake's hair was greying at the temples, the bags under his eyes so dark they were almost black. He was older than any other officer in the field with them.

"You are not married," Kurakake said.

Nishino shook his head.

"There is a woman at home? Someone is waiting for you?"

He looked briefly into Kurakake's face, shook his head again. He returned the bottle of perfume.

Kurakake watched him a moment. "A story for another time," he said. He looked down at Ogawa still motionless on the ground. The young man's face even more childish in sleep. The officer made a dissatisfied noise in his throat. "This boy," he said. "Chozo. He depends on you."

"We help one another."

Kurakake nodded dismissively. "What is it that is wrong with him?"

"I don't know," Nishino said. Though he understood exactly what the officer meant. There was something simple about Ogawa that made him seem younger even than his age.

The lieutenant made the same dissatisfied noise and nodded. Then turned and left them.

Nishino dozed half an hour more, waking occasionally to shift on the ground. Catching the faintest scent of perfume every time he brought his hands near his face.

The soldiers were given the last of the company's food that afternoon, one can of sardines for every two men. He and Ogawa cleaned the oil from the can with their fingers. Nishino was hungrier after eating than before, and he felt the hunger sharpening an edge in him.

Ogawa stared down at the Americans. They moved about in the open, wearing only undershirts. Sunlight glinting off the dog tags around their necks. "I wonder what they're saying." He shook his head in disgust. "Sssss ssss sss. That's all it sounds like to me."

Nishino had removed his shoes and socks, splashing his feet with river water from the canteen and wiping them dry with his shirt. All but two of his toenails had blackened and fallen off. He said, "They're too far off to make anything out." Quickly added, "Even if you could speak the language."

Ogawa smiled. "We'll hear them up close soon enough," he said.

The drone of aircraft billowed in off the ocean, and men on both sides paused to scan the horizon. Japanese bombers. A scurry of movement among the soldiers below, orders shouted. The planes dropping their payloads on the grassy ridge to soften the American defences.

Two nights later, the Japanese began their advance through the forest toward the American positions. Soldiers fixed a criss-cross of white cloth to their backs to help those behind stay with them. Lieutenant Kurakake doused himself with his wife's perfume. "Follow your noses," he told his men.

Just after nine a floater plane released flares overhead, destroyers and field guns using the light to fix on their targets. The whine of mortars made Nishino's ears hum and then he registered them lower, a rippling thump that vibrated in his intestines. Return fire started up immediately, the ground shifting beneath him. Ogawa wandered off to the right and Nishino was yelling at him to stay close when a shell exploded behind them, throwing him into the air. He floated a moment, turning slowly as if suspended in water, before landing hard on his back. He lay motionless, trying to get his breath. Calcium flares and explosions lit up the sky, but the sound of it all was submerged in the massive ringing in his ears. There was a peculiar numbness the length of his torso, but nothing seemed seriously wrong when he finally got to his feet.

He started down the hill shouting for Ogawa and was ambushed by an overwhelming urge to shit, the cramps like a twisted length of barbed wire being hauled through his bowels. He crawled behind the nearest tree and dropped his pants, pushing against the waves of pain, but nothing came of it. The noise of the artillery broke through the ringing in his ears and he covered them with his hands, swearing into the racket until the cramps subsided. He hauled angrily at his trousers, and started down the hill again.

He caught sight of Ogawa on his knees, waving wildly, as if trying to flag a taxi on a busy street. When Nishino came up to him, the boy wrapped an arm around his legs.

"Water," Ogawa said. "Do you have water?"

The boy's head was bare and there was something odd about his posture that Nishino couldn't place. He grabbed at Ogawa's uniform, yelling "Get up," but the boy slipped lower and turned onto his back, still clutching Nishino's legs. And he saw clearly the right arm was torn clean from Ogawa's body at the shoulder.

"Water," Ogawa called again.

The cramps struck Nishino a second time and he shuffled away, struggling with his uniform, sure he would soil himself before he could undo the belt. He leaned a shoulder against a tree trunk as he crouched, both arms folded over the spasms in his gut, but there was no movement, no release, and he fell sideways to the ground, lying there until the pain lifted as suddenly as it had hit him. He got to his knees, pulling the trousers awkwardly to his waist. The intensity of the cramps drained him of any sense of urgency, though the gunfire and shouting and rumbling carried on. He took long, measured breaths through his nostrils, tucked his shirtfront into his pants. Reached behind to do the same at the back and felt the wetness soaking the material. When he looked at his hand in the light of the flares it seemed to have been blackened with oil. He brought it to his face to smell the cold iron smell. He touched his back gingerly through his shirt but there was only the peculiar numbness and the wet of his own blood.

"I'm bleeding," he said. "Chozo. I'm bleeding."

But by the time Nishino turned back to him the boy was dead.

The retreat began three days after the initial engagement. Every able-bodied soldier was engaged to carry the wounded. There were no medics and there was little in the way of medicine among them. Dozens died on their stretchers and were abandoned on the side of the path hacked through the rainforest during their approach. Nishino moved past the dead without looking down. The numbness in his back had subsided and the intermittent cramping had eased enough that he was able to walk through it, leaning heavily on a walking stick. He refused to be carried.

Even burdened by the injured, the company made better time without the heavy guns and shells and other munitions. Nishino fell behind each day and was forced to walk hours to catch up after the others had stopped for the night. There was no food, and he sucked juice from vines and ate betel nuts and weeds to calm his stomach.

Three days into the retreat, Lieutenant Kurakake ordered his men to throw grenades into the river. They waded in afterwards to gather up the fish killed by the concussion, their bodies floating belly up on the surface. The men ate them raw and nothing was wasted, not the eyeballs or the skin or the intestines.

It was after dark by the time Nishino reached them. He talked aloud to himself to avoid being shot by the sentries as he approached, repeating passages of General Tojo's *Field Service Guide* he had memorized while in training. "Faith is strength," he told the trees. "He who has faith in combat is always the victor."

He used his walking stick to ease himself onto the ground at the outer edge of the circle of sleeping soldiers, still talking. "Do not live in shame as a prisoner," he said. "Die and leave no ignominious crime behind you." Only when he closed his eyes did he think of the explosions he'd heard earlier that evening. But he was too exhausted to sit up and ask for an explanation.

In the morning he was nudged awake by Lieutenant Kurakake. He forced himself up onto his elbows and Kurakake crouched beside him.

"I didn't expect to find you here this morning," the officer said.

"I'm holding you back."

He shook his head. "There are at least three more days ahead of us. You won't keep up much longer." Kurakake looked around, pursing his lips. There was no one else awake in the camp but the soldiers on sentry duty. "Perhaps now is the time for that story," he said.

Nishino stared at him.

7

"The woman. Is there someone you would like me to send a message to?"

"There is no woman."

Kurakake stared at the forest, still dark and without definition. "There is always a woman," he said. He reached into a pouch at his side and pressed a packet into the soldier's hand.

Nishino unwrapped the paper, found a fillet of raw fish.

Kurakake got to his feet and stared down at him. He said, "Where did you learn to speak English, Private?"

The smell of the fish was making Nishino's hands shake. He felt as if his throat had closed over.

"Where did you learn this?" Kurakake repeated.

He swallowed several times, trying to find his voice. "In Kitsilano," he said finally. "In Canada."

1940

—

WISH

—

1.

HE LOVED HIS TIME ALONE in the church and fishermen's halls before afternoon shows. Even on the hottest mornings of a summer the halls were shadowy, cool, which made them seem private and sheltered, like the gardens of the merchant houses on Circular Road in St. John's. He'd carried the generator up from the harbour last and was sweating with the weight by the time he set it down. He stood the door open for the extra light and the breeze. Walked off two dozen paces from the Victor projector and set the movie screen down, raising the white sheet of it like a trap skiff sail. The surface catching what little sunlight came in the few windows and the open door. His shoulder brushed across the screen as he turned, the crushed-glass sparkle coming off in a powder on his shirt.

By this time word would have reached every household on Little Fogo Island that the shows were in on the coastal boat, whole families loading into punts and trap skiffs and bully boats to make way for the hall. By mid-afternoon fifty souls would be crammed into the room, sitting on the chairs or stools or wooden

11

crates they'd carted with them. The heat of so many bodies so close together rising to the rafters, the air's sweetness adulterated by the smell of kelp and sweat.

For now, though, he was alone with the machinery and the shadowy light. He threaded the celluloid from the front reel directly to the rear to revise it, letting the movie play backwards through his thumb and forefinger, checking for nicks or cuts from the last screening. He had his back to the open door, humming tunelessly to accompany the drone of the gas generator outside, and it took him a while to notice the change in the light, the slight darkening of the shadows in the hall. To look finally toward the figure in the doorway. He had no idea how long she'd been watching. The sun directly behind her made it impossible to distinguish any of the girl's features, though her dress and the length of her hair were clearly outlined. He knew right away who it was, and though he'd arrived in the Cove hoping to lay eyes on her, he felt foolish to have been spied on.

"You're too early," he said. He almost shouted at her. "Come back after you haves your dinner."

"Sure I was only having a look."

"You're too early," he said again.

The girl and her mother had come across to Fogo with another family to see the shows the previous fall, his first trip out of St. John's with Hiram. She and Wish hadn't spoken a word together, though they caught one another's attention. Hiram had leaned in close to him during the movie. "You're going to wear out your eyes looking at that young one," he said.

Wish walked across the hall to shut the door, still embarrassed and feeling peculiarly exposed. She stepped back from the doorsill into the light, and he could see she was more than just a girl now, all of sixteen at least. She wore her light brown hair long, unlike most every other woman on the shore, and tied it back in a ponytail. There was a suggestion of extravagance in the uncommon length of it, a hint of vanity. That her hair might be fine enough to be worth the trouble. A flower-print dress with a belt knotted loosely at the waist so he could make out the curve of her hips and her breasts under the material. Nearly a woman already.

He expected the girl to keep backing away as he approached but she only stood there, watching him come. Hands clasped demurely behind her back and everything else in her manner like a dare.

"What's the show this afternoon?"

"*The 39 Steps.*"

"What's it about?"

"Don't want to ruin it for you now, do I?"

"I only wants a hint."

"It's about a Canadian gets in trouble with spies in England."

She drew her head back skeptically. "A Canadian?"

"He's from Montreal," Wish said and she nodded, as if that fact was almost enough to sway her disbelief.

Her eyes were set so deeply the colour was hidden from a distance and he was surprised now by the emerald shade of them. Green as sea-glass. She was wearing yellow bobby socks and leather patent shoes with a buckle. She turned the toe of one foot over on the ground, the opposite hip jutting out slightly, and he started at the motion.

"No law against looking," she said when he glanced away. She stepped toward him and brushed the powdery residue from his shoulder where he'd grazed the screen, then stepped back. She smiled up at him in exactly the way he remembered. As brazen as a cat.

It made him feel childish and uncertain of himself to have her touch him that way. He raised his hand to close the door and she said, "Could I watch what you're at in there?"

"No," he said and he nudged the door shut on her.

Her voice then, raised so he could hear it inside. "Don't be such a sook," she said.

She came late to the show with her mother and father and a young man who was older than her by several years. *Brother*, Wish assumed, and that assumption confirmed the feeling he'd tried to ignore all afternoon—watching, then not watching for her through the door where Hiram sat at a table with a moneybox open in front of him. He'd become increasingly agitated as the room filled with bodies and chairs and no sight of her among them. Men in long garnsey sweaters and salt-and-pepper hats left their seats to stand at arm's length from the projector, pointing at the reels and the lens and the mechanical innards and asking him endless questions about how the thing worked. Invariably one of them turned his attention to Wish and to his unfamiliar accent. "Now where do you belong to?" he was asked.

Renews, he told them. On the Southern Shore of the Avalon, outside St. John's.

"Catholics down that way, is it?"

Yes, he said. Good deal of Catholics on the Southern Shore.

"We got a few up this way," one man admitted. "Most of them across in Tilting."

He hadn't been to Tilting, he told them. Hiram used to stop there but he'd heard talk of an army base, some kind of warning squadron, about to set up in Sandy Cove. Which would mean a different movie screened every week at the cookhouse. Which meant his audience over there was about to dry up. Hiram decided to come to Little Fogo Island this year, far enough to guarantee a decent audience even after the base went in. They didn't stop on that side of Fogo at all this trip, Wish admitted.

"Missed your chance at confession then," the same man said, smiling and nodding at the projector. Clive, his name was.

14

Wish allowed he wasn't that great a sinner to be worried about missing the opportunity.

No one spoke to him of the war or asked what he thought of the latest news or whether he might end up overseas himself, although it was obvious he was old enough to think about signing up. Was it hard to operate the machine, they wanted to know. How did he end up knocking around with Hiram Keeping? How many times could he show a film before it wore out? Did he fish at all, or was Hiram paying enough he could make a go of the shows alone? Did Hiram know he was a mick before he was hired on?

They shook their heads at the improbability of the match.

It was Wish's second time along the northeast coast and he'd gotten used to the interrogation. Most days he paid no attention to it, had his answers by rote and could carry on the conversation without thinking. But he was too riled up this afternoon to settle and was about to head outside to escape their curiosity when the girl stepped up into the doorway again.

Her father leaned over the table and counted out a handful of coins into Hiram's palm, and the four of them carted their chairs into the hall, setting up in the only space still unclaimed, near the projector at the back of the room. She didn't look in his direction or acknowledge him in any way, and he could feel the pull of that deliberate inattention, as if someone had hooked a cod-jigger to his sternum and let the lead weight of it hang there. The man who paid their way in might be her grandfather now that Wish had a closer look at him, a stringy wattle of flesh beneath the chin, the grizzle of unshaven whisker mostly grey. The mother had the girl's green eyes and slight build. Her face had an anxious, almost angry quality to it, as if she was newly blind and uncertain of each step ahead. The man touched her shoulder occasionally, encouraging her, cajoling her forward, and she shot him a look back that he simply smiled at. An old conversation between them, Wish could see. A dailiness to it that said marriage. April and September.

Wish glanced across the room to Hiram, who was watching him and rubbing a knuckle along both sides of his moustache in turn. He was trying to suppress a smile and Wish looked away from him. *Randy old fucker*, he thought. When Wish had described her approximate age and her height and hair and green eyes earlier in the afternoon Hiram had looked to the ceiling, puffing his cheeks full of air, considering.

"Sixteen, you think is it?"

"Give or take. She was over to Fogo last year, came across with her mother."

Hiram said, "You're not going to be looking for trouble here tonight, are you?" He was already three parts drunk, his face red with the alcohol. He'd left the set-up and running of the projector to Wish and had been off all afternoon drinking swish or shine or dandelion beer, swapping gossip with the locals in a twine loft down on the landwash.

"I'm just asking," Wish told him.

"Sadie Parsons you saw. Lives up the south side a ways, past Earle's wharf."

Wish repeated her name under his breath.

Hiram shook his head. "You know what they'll do to a Catholic boy sniffing around the women out here," he said. He was smiling, wavering slightly on his feet. An air of anticipation about him. "Don't say I haven't warned you."

The girl sat straight in her chair between her mother and brother—he was certain it was a brother. He sat with his legs crossed and hands folded in his lap exactly as the mother did beside him, and there was something of the mother's hard way about the young man's face. He and Sadie ignored one another completely and casually, out of long habit. Which was different altogether than how he sensed her ignoring him.

The Victor had an automatic trip mechanism when the film began to tear or jam, shutting down to keep the celluloid from snapping or being set alight by the heat of the bulb. The trip stopped *The 39 Steps* half a dozen times and the audience shouted and whistled through each interruption. The longer it took him to clear the jam and rethread the film safely through the projector, the uglier the mood of the crowd. All of them standing or shifting to turn to him, yelling abuse. But Sadie didn't move her head to the right or left through the length and breadth of the afternoon. And she left the hall without so much as a glance in his direction when it was done.

They were staying at Mrs. Gillard's, a widow who took in the occasional visitor to the Cove. After their supper Hiram sat for a while in the parlour with his pipe. Wish stood at a small shelf of books over the fireplace mantel, taking them down one at a time to leaf through the pages, waiting on Hiram to set things in motion. The largest of the set was covered in green baize with laminated gold lettering. *A History of Art.* Colourless reproductions mostly, paintings by men with names he couldn't pronounce.

Hiram came across the room and looked over Wish's shoulder. "This is what people had before there were movies," he said. "Poor buggers." He stooped to knock pipe ash into the fireplace. He said, "How about a little stroll?"

The evening was uncharacteristically still, the harbour almost glass. They walked along a path rutted by carts near Earle's wharf, nodding and saying hello to the few men they passed. They started up the hill on the harbour's south side where only a handful of houses stood, their heads bowed under busy clouds of blackflies. The cart path narrowed to a walking trail, and Wish slipped behind the older man. Cows and sheep grazed on the hillside, and Hiram stopped occasionally to cluck stupidly at the animals. The man was a townie, born and raised in St. John's, which to Wish's way of thinking was a kind of ignorance in and of itself.

When they came to the house farthest out on the hill, Hiram stood a minute looking at it. The front of the two-story building was whitewashed and trimmed with green, though the sides were covered in red ochre, like every other house in the harbour. There was a false door nailed to the clapboard between the downstairs windows. Its only function was aesthetic, set there simply to make the front of the house look complete. From where they stood, the place looked empty. They walked along the side of the house to the back kitchen and stepped inside the porch, scraped their boots on the porch rug as Hiram called into the room.

A man's voice shouted, "Come in, come in."

The rafters were so low that both men had to duck their heads. It was still light outside but already dark enough in the small room to mask details. Wish could see four of them sitting about the kitchen—the father splayed out on the daybed, the mother at the table. Sadie was beside the stove, where a fire offered the only light through the grate. She was sitting in a rocking chair fashioned from an old flour barrel. A girl younger than Sadie sat on a mat directly in front of the stove. And then a figure Wish hadn't seen stepped away from the doorway leading deeper into the house. The young man from the afternoon. Wish could smell a heavy tide of cologne rising off him.

"We're not interrupting?" Hiram said.

"Not at all," the man said. "The young courter is just on his way."

Sadie got up from her rocker and kissed him on the cheek.

"Give up that foolishness and let him go," the mother said.

Two chairs were offered to the new visitors. Wish sat heavily and looked to the fire in the stove as the young man went out the door. A slow collapse carrying on inside his chest after he came up hard on the seat. Not her brother, then.

Her father said, "We heard you coming out the path."

"Where's the young fellow off to?" Hiram asked.

18

"Hardy didn't have his last forkful in his mouth, he was upstairs getting dandied up. Gone along the shore after Willard Slade's youngest."

"Is that right?" Hiram said.

"Can't keep his mind on the fish long enough to bait a hook. We'll starve to death the winter if he don't soon marry the girl and have it done with."

Wish glanced at Sadie, who was watching him steadily. He looked away again, hoping she wasn't able to register his look of relief in the dim.

Her mother said, "You'll have a cup of tea."

"Grand, yes," Hiram said. "We would."

She stared at Wish a moment. "And you," she said. "Do you have a tongue in your head?"

Sadie said, "He did this afternoon."

She looked across at her daughter. "We know you've got tongue enough."

"Now Helen," her husband said.

"This is Aloysious Furey," Hiram announced, as if it had just occurred to him to make introductions. "From Renews, on the Southern Shore."

Helen sat back slowly in her chair. And it seemed to Wish that everyone else in the room shifted away from him in much the same fashion. Wish looked from Sadie to her mother. They had likely never had a Catholic sit in their kitchen before, he knew. Some people on the northeast shore had never met a Catholic before encountering Wish and it was always hard to say how things would go. Hiram appeared to be oblivious to the sudden change in the room, taking out his tobacco and papers to roll a cigarette. Though Wish knew he was paying attention and enjoying himself. Hiram took some kind of pleasure from observing the flustered civility, the consternation, the outright hostility of people unexpectedly confronted by Wish's religious affiliation.

He said it was like throwing two strange dogs together to see how they'd get on.

He offered a cigarette to Aubrey, who got up to take it, then went to the stove and held a shovie through the grate until it was alight. He lit his cigarette from it and passed it along to Hiram. Aubrey sat back on the bed and lay with an arm behind his head, the hand holding the cigarette propped above his chest. Hiram took a long drag and leaned forward to tap ash into the wide cuff of his trousers.

Helen was staring at Wish, taking harsh little breaths through her nostrils. He put his hand into his pocket and fingered his mother's rosary beads, considering whether or not to make a show of them.

"I'll say this much for the Romans," Aubrey said. "They got nothing against a scuff on the dance floor, or a drink." He waved the cigarette he held. "Or a smoke. Not like we Methodist crowd."

"Being Methodist don't seem to have stopped you," his wife said.

"I'll let the Good Lord take it up with me when my time comes."

"Don't be tempting," Helen said softly. "It's all bad enough without that."

A woman's voice began calling from inside the main house. Helen turned to her daughters. She said, "Would one of you go see to her?"

"She doesn't want anything," Sadie said.

"Go on, Sade," her father said.

Wish watched her as she went down the narrow hallway to the parlour. Agnes got up from the floor and settled into the vacated seat.

"That's your mother, is it, Aubrey?" Hiram asked.

"It is."

"She must be getting on."

"Ninety-two. And three, providing she lives to September month. But she haven't been well, is the truth of it. She's lost her mind, most days. And can't get up out of the bed to make water. Be a blessing to everyone when she goes," Aubrey said to the ceiling. "For Helen especially, not having to watch after her every moment of the day and night."

Wish was still watching down the hallway toward the parlour, set up as a sickroom to spare the old woman the stairs. Sadie came out of the dark finally and stood in the doorway. "She wants you," she told her mother.

Helen stood up. "Make these folks a cup of tea, would you?" She stared at Wish a moment. "And see if you can't drag a word out of this one before he leaves."

He smiled at the woman but she didn't notice or chose for some reason not to return it.

When Sadie set the tea in front of them she sat in her mother's chair, close enough that Wish could smell the soap from her skin. Hiram tipped his cup to fill the saucer and blew on the surface to cool the tea, then drank from it in small noisy sips. The sun was well down and the room settled deeper into pitch, but no one moved to light a lamp, content to sit and talk in the dark.

Hiram said, "Have you lost many boys to overseas, Aubrey?"

"A scatter one is gone into St. John's to join the Newfoundland Regiment." Aubrey was into a second cigarette and it seemed that the man's voice was coming from the red dot glowing in the corner of the room. "Clive Reid's oldest is gone across to Halifax to join up with the Canadians. Wanted to get on with the air force."

Wish said, "He can do that?"

"We're citizens of the Commonwealth," Hiram told him. "A fellow could go to Britain and join up there if he had a mind to."

"If it weren't for Will Slade's girl I don't know but we might have lost Hardy to it. By and by, we won't have anyone left around here to fish. Is it as bad across the pond as the newsreels make it out, I wonder?"

"Be a job to make that stuff up."

"I don't know what it is keeping the Americans out of it so long."

Hiram said, "They're overrun by the Irish down there, is what's wrong. But it's only a matter of time. The Yanks already got their eyes on the land for a base in St. John's, down along Quidi Vidi Lake. Canadians over on Buckmaster's Field. All of them in uniform. Local boys haven't got a chance with the girls any more. Have they, Wish?"

Sadie leaned over the table to bring her head closer to his. "Are you going overseas?"

He tried to picture her face again, to connect it to the sound of her voice. He couldn't tell from her tone what she might prefer as an answer. "I don't have plans," he said.

Helen came back down the hall, one hand coasting the wall as a guide. "Is anyone going to light a lamp here this evening?" she said.

She shooed Sadie from the table and the girl sat herself on the mat in front of the stove.

"More tea?" Helen said.

"I think we'll be off," Hiram said.

Wish looked back to Sadie as he left, one side of her face in firelight. She was staring into her lap, as if listening intently to a conversation in another room.

Aubrey followed them to the door. "I'll step out a minute, walk you a ways." When they'd found the path and started down he said, "When do you push on?"

"The coaster comes back through day after tomorrow."

"You'll be getting back to St. John's before long, will you?"

"A week or so, I'd say."

"Back this way one more time before the winter settles in?"

"If the weather doesn't turn early."

"Sadie came on sixteen a couple of months ago," Aubrey said. "Promised her a new dress if I lived to Christmas. Doubt I'll see St. John's before then though, alive or dead. Was wondering if you could stop into Ayers on Water Street. Get her something decent."

"You don't know what size she wears, do you, Aubrey?"

He fished in his pants pocket and hauled out a length of knotted string. "I was going to drop by with this before you left," he said. He shook the string and held it at one end. "Double knot on this end," he said. "Here to the first knot is shoulder to wrist. To the second knot is shoulder to waist. Second to third is the circumference of the bosom, third to fourth is her waist. No concern about the length, Helen can put that to rights when you carries it up."

"Any particular colour she's fond of?"

"Well now. Never stopped to think of that."

"I'll ask Mr. Golfman at Ayers what he recommends."

Aubrey clapped his hands. "Cracker jack," he said. "I'll settle up the bill when you brings the dress along."

He turned back then and wished them both a good night. Hiram continued down the hill and when he was sure Aubrey was out of earshot he fingered the knots in the string. "Second to third," he said as he measured the distance, and he let out an appreciative whistle.

He balled the string and passed it along to Wish. "I imagine you'll take more care with this than me."

Wish said, "I don't think her mother thinks much of me."

"Well now, Mrs. Parsons is already taken, isn't she," Hiram said. "Unless you're more reckless a man than I know."

The morning dawned as breathless as the night before. Wish woke in darkness to the sound of men on the wharf and the rhythmic plash of oars as dories rowed out to the schooners anchored offshore. Engines of the trap skiffs coming alive in the distance, one after another, a muffled drone like bluebottles caught between the panes of a window. He drifted off again and slept until well after the sun was up. Not a sound in the house as he lay there, coming to himself, remembering where he was. The bedroom window was propped wide but the curtains didn't stir.

He dressed and made his way to the kitchen, where the kettle sat warm at the back of the stove but no one was about. Hiram was still in bed asleep and could easily spend the better part of the morning there. Under a napkin on the table Wish found a plate of buns and cheese, which meant Mrs. Gillard didn't expect to be back anytime soon. He added a scoop of coal to the fire and wandered around the downstairs waiting for the kettle to boil.

After he ate, Wish walked down past Earle's wharf. Not a soul about, the men already out on the fishing grounds. The houses were strangely quiet as well, no movement through the windows, the air nearly clear of wood or coal smoke. It was almost as if the Cove had been abandoned between his first waking moment in the dark and the time he crawled out of bed. He did his best to keep his mind clear of his destination until he stopped outside Sadie's house, and he stood there, watching it awhile. The front windows were open to the fresh air and he heard the old woman calling for Helen.

He walked around to the back kitchen, where the porch door was propped open with a broomstick. He stepped inside and cocked his head to listen. Just the old woman's voice. No dishes on the table. The walls bare but for two small pictures, a portrait of Queen Victoria on her diamond jubilee, a line drawing of some ancient monarch fording a river on a horse. He walked up close to read the inscription. *King William III Crossing the Boyne.* King Billy. Prince of Orange, King of England. Driving the Catholic King James out of Ireland. Hiram used to amuse himself in St. John's by bringing home anti-Catholic literature being passed out on the downtown streets, quoting them aloud to Wish. The pamphlets called Catholics enemies of social order and deluded slaves of despotism. "The simple institution of Christ is not to the taste

of the ignorant multitude that form the serfs of the Popedom."
Wish had seen the Orangemen parading through the streets in
bowler hats and salt-and-pepper caps, sashes draped over their
coats, singing Protestant hymns. Catholics making their way
indoors before the parade reached them, lowering the window
shades so as not to have to watch them go by.

He walked to the stove and placed his hand along the top to
feel the warmth. Not cold, but an hour and more since a fire had
been laid there. He looked around the kitchen and placed both his
hands on his hips. "Hello," he called.

"Aubrey?"

He walked down the hall and stood in the doorway to the parlour, looking in on the sick woman. She was lying on a cot wedged
in among a chair and a settle. The covers were tucked up to her
chest despite the warmth of the morning. She faced the wall she
was calling through, a long grey braid of hair across her shoulder.

"Hello, missus."

Her cheeks were sunken, and the skin where it stretched over
the forehead and cheekbones was unnaturally white and smooth.

"I wants Helen," she told him.

"Have they gone and left you alone?"

"I'm all mops and brooms today," she said. She patted a spot
on the bed without taking her eyes from his. She took his hand in
her own when he sat beside her. Her eyes were pale blue and dis-
coloured with tiny flecks of darkness, as if old paint had flaked
away from them. The room smelled faintly of urine and oil soap
and lavender. "You're Jenny Reid's youngster."

"I'm not from around here," he said. "Where have they gone
and left you?"

She smiled up at him sweetly. "Am I dead?" she asked. "Is
this heaven?"

Wish felt his stomach turn and he leaned away from her but
she refused to let go of his hand. "Is Sadie not around?" he asked her.

25

The old woman's face darkened and she spoke something in a whisper.

"What did you say?"

"The little slut," the old woman repeated. And in another tone altogether she said, "Can I get up out of the bed now?"

"No, Nan. You can't get up out of the bed."

Wish looked to the doorway, where Sadie's younger sister stood with her arms folded across her chest.

"I must be in hell, then," the old woman said.

"I come by and there was no one about," Wish told the girl. "She was calling for your mother." He pried his hand from the old woman's grip and stood up.

"I was only out back for a few minutes." The girl turned away toward the kitchen, meaning for him to follow her.

He started for the door, glanced over his shoulder before stepping out into the hall. The old woman said, "It's a good life if you don't weaken."

The girl was standing by the stove, her hands held behind her back. A child's body, thin as a stick. Hair cut short and parted on the side. Eyes like her sister's, though not as deeply green and quicker—they settled on nothing for long, darting up and down him and then away like a skittish school of fish. He couldn't recall her name.

"She's not herself," the girl said. And after a pause she said, "Don't mind a thing she says."

He didn't know whether the girl had heard what the old woman had said about Sadie and didn't see how he could ask.

"Can I get you anything?" she asked him. "A cup of tea?"

"Just had breakfast. Where's everyone gone today? There's not a soul about."

"All the women are over in Gooseberry Cove after the winter's berries. They won't be back before dark. I had to stay behind to watch out for Nan."

"How far is Gooseberry Cove?"

The girl looked up at him from under the frill of bangs that fell to her eyebrows.

Wish smiled at her. "Can you tell me how to get there, do you think?"

"Sure it's only the women goes over after the berries."

"Maybe it's only the women I'm wanting to talk to." Her eyes darted away from him again. *Agnes*, her name was. "Can you tell me how to get there, Agnes?"

She smiled to herself, not looking at him.

"Agnes?" he said, wanting her to hear her name aloud a second time.

"Do you know the Washing Pond?" she asked him. "Out past the Spell Rock?"

"The big rock on the other side of the cove?"

She nodded.

"I know it," he said.

The women were spread out across the bare hills on the far side of Gooseberry Cove, bent double, filling the metal dippers they carried with them, emptying those into pillowcases when they were full. He stopped on the ridge where he came in sight of them and picked out Sadie among the group, and her mother working a little higher up the hill. On the beach an older woman was tending pots over a driftwood fire. Mrs. Gillard.

She glanced up at him as he approached. "You must be lost."

"Just out for a wander."

She looked at him as if to say she wasn't as stunned as all that. "Did you and Hiram manage all right for breakfast?"

"I had a bun and a bite of the cheese you put out for us. There was no sign of Hiram before I left."

She bent over the pot of baked beans. "How a hangashore like that keeps body and bones together is a mystery to me."

27

MICHAEL CRUMMEY

There was something in her assessment of Hiram that Wish felt was directed at him. As if Hiram's habitual laziness had a spiritual as well as a physical side and this explained his keeping company with Romans. Wish said, "I'd kill for a drink of water."

Mrs. Gillard straightened and poured a glassful of warm water from a container, then stood beside him as he drained it.

He glanced up the hill. "Have you got a spare dipper?"

"What do you want with that?"

"I thought I might try to make myself useful. Seeing as I'm here."

Wish walked up the hillside toward Sadie, bending now and then to throw a handful of blueberries into his pot. A low murmur moving among the women as one after the other took note of him there, though no one raised their heads to say hello. It was like swimming in a pond on the barrens, striking spring-fed pockets of water so cold they stole his breath. He saw it as if from a height then, a slow pan of the cove. A young Catholic boy set loose among a group of Protestant women grazing for berries. *The trap of priest-craft*, Hiram's pamphlets said, *the trickery of Satan*. No man of theirs for miles.

For a moment he considered turning back the way he came. But knew he would only look more the fool for that. He settled in at a likely-looking berry bush across from Sadie and began picking in earnest. He could feel the attention of everyone on him as he worked. Only Sadie seemed not to have noticed his arrival. He worked his way up the bush to have a fairer view of her. Hair over her shoulder, her face and neck red from bending forward. A halo of blackflies danced around her head in the stillness and she waved a hand absently to clear them from her eyes. The curve of her breasts down the front of the blouse.

She said, "How did you know to find us out here?"

"Just luck," he said, turning back to the berries. "Took a walk out past the Washing Pond."

28

Sadie sat back on her haunches to look at him, pushing the hair out of her face, waving the blackflies away. "You went up to the house, didn't you. Talked to Agnes."

"Maybe I did." He smiled to tell her he wasn't about to admit more than that, and she smiled back.

"Who knit you, I wonder? I never seen the gall."

One of the women across the hill stood up and shouted across to them. "Have he got his bottom covered, Sade?"

There was a scatter of laughter, though most of the women didn't seem to see anything funny in the situation.

Sadie reached across and tipped his dipper far enough she could see into it. "Mostly leaves," she shouted back. "Leaves and green berries."

Her mother stepped between them. "He's a dab hand at picking, is he?" Helen looked down at him without smiling and turned to her daughter. "Go on and give Mrs. Gillard a hand setting out the dishes."

Sadie opened her mouth but Helen cut her off. "Go on like I told you," she said.

Sadie dumped her berries into the pillowcase and walked down toward the beach. Helen took the dipper from Wish's hand and glanced into it.

"I don't have the woman's touch with this," he said.

"No," she said. "I expect you're all man."

He half expected her to tell him to push off, could see her weighing her instincts against common courtesy. She went back to the berries finally, didn't bother returning the dipper he'd been using. He looked down to the beach after Sadie. Weighing his options in much the same way.

He sat on the sand, holding his ankles, watching Sadie take stacks of plates and cutlery out of a hamper.

"Aloysious," she said.

"Most people calls me Wish."

"Wish," she repeated. He could tell she liked it, the feel of the word in her mouth, its connection to him. "You're from the Southern Shore."

Mrs. Gillard lifted out a platter of tea buns wrapped in towels. She handed it to Sadie, who offered the tray to Wish. He took one but didn't taste it, only held it as they talked. It was still warm with the heat of the oven though it had been sitting wrapped in the basket for hours.

"I'm from Lord's Cove, over Burin way. Moved across to the Southern Shore when I was a boy."

Three crows pitched on the shoreline ten yards from the fire, and Wish crossed himself three times. Looked up to see Sadie and the older woman staring.

"Can't be too careful," he said.

"Where did you get that mark?" Sadie asked him. "On the nape of your neck."

Wish reached to touch himself there reflexively, surprised she'd taken note of it. She seemed not even to glance his way when he was stooped near her, picking berries.

"It looks like you were burnt," she said.

"It's only a birthmark."

"Can I have a look?"

Before he could answer, Mrs. Gillard said, "Finish what you were at, Sadie." A moment later she said, "Watch yourself around that one." She was speaking into the pot of beans and Wish couldn't tell if the warning was meant for Sadie or for him.

By the time the women came down to their dinner the sun was directly overhead, and even on the shoreline the heat was stifling. Mrs. Gillard said grace before ladling food onto the plates, and Wish crossed himself when she Amened, knowing it was expected of him. Everyone sat well away from the remains of the fire, where a blackened kettle steamed. The group of them tired and subdued, quieter than Wish expected a gathering of women to be. He leaned toward Sadie and whispered as much to her. She slapped his shoulder. "You saucy black," she said.

Wish smiled at the girl. It was the same word they used for Protestants on the Southern Shore. *Blacks.* It was the state of their souls they were referring to.

Mrs. Gillard said, "What did you do in Renews before you hooked up with Hiram Keeping?"

"Ran a list for Gooderiche's store when I was a youngster, setting out cod to dry. Spent a couple of summers on the Banks after the fish with Tom Keating. A bit of salvage." He shrugged. "I'll take St. John's over all of it any day."

"What's St. John's like?" Sadie asked him. She quoted the crofter's wife from the movie she'd seen the day before. "Do all the ladies paint their toenails?"

"Have you never been to town?"

"Gooseberry Cove is as far as I've been. Except for the one trip to Fogo last fall to see the shows."

Wish tried to recall his first sight of the place, coming through the cliffs of the Narrows on Tom Keating's bully boat. Long flat flakes for drying cod built over the Battery, a crowded row of finger piers on the north side of the harbour moored tight with schooners. Up the hill behind them the bustle of buildings set among thick stands of trees. The Kirk, the twin towers of the Basilica looking down to the sea. A handful of young Salvation Army officers were witnessing to a crowd on Water Street, red epaulettes on their dark uniforms. The place stank to high heaven, salt fish and rot and maggots, exhaust and coal smoke. It smelled to Wish like life at work.

He glanced at Sadie. He didn't want to belittle her or the world she knew so he said, "St. John's isn't much. Horse shit and taverns, mostly."

"And which one is it keeping you there?"

31

He looked at her, surprised. And then he said, "I'm not about to tell any tales."

"Then why am I sitting here talking to you, I wonder?"

He leaned slightly in her direction again without saying a word.

"What kind of things did you bring in," Helen asked him abruptly, "salvaging?"

"Just about anything under the sun," he said.

"Name some for me."

"Doors and windows. Lumber. Jam and fruit and meat. Cans of ketchup. Soap. We came into a load of twenty pound hams once, bobbing around the wreck, had to use casting nets to get them aboard. A wheelbarrow, shovels. Copper pipe. We got a few Portugee coins one time and we drilled them out for washers. There was a statue off a Spanish boat, Jesus on the cross, all in bronze and big as life. A couple of alky wrecks."

"Alky wrecks?"

"A schooner full of Black Horse beer out from St. John's. They put the constable on that one where she went aground, to keep an eye on her. We got paid so much a dozen to bring the beer ashore. There was an English boat loaded down with gin. Sold most of it up in Ferryland, although we kept a little to help get us through the winter."

"Alcohol," Mrs. Gillard said, "is the milk of the devil."

Wish nodded, doing his best to look contrite. Half the people on the northeast shore were teetotallers. Hiram carried his own emergency supply to avoid being caught dry. Drank on the sly at the boarding house. Wish said, "I expect the devil don't mind a drop now and then."

"Makes you wonder," Sadie said, "why the Lord's first miracle was turning water into wine."

"Sadie," her mother warned.

"Hard to know whose side He was on there, isn't it?"

"Mercedes," her mother said and she got to her feet, started collecting empty plates.

Mrs. Gillard shifted noisily, her lips moving, as if she was singing a hymn under her breath.

Wish watched Sadie out of the corner of his eye. The voice of the Salvation Army preacher on the St. John's street corner chimed in his head and he leaned toward her. "The wisdom of God is foolishness in the eyes of the world," he said, quietly enough that only she would hear him.

"Amen to that," she whispered.

They wandered back up to the hills after the meal was cleared away. The heat seemed to rise from the ground beneath them and not a breath of wind for relief. Wish stayed near Sadie but not as close as her mother, who seemed determined to keep by her daughter's side for the rest of the afternoon. Sadie told her to clear off and find her own bush to pick but Helen ignored her.

It was clear he was making no friends by staying. "Got a bit of a walk ahead of me," he said finally. "Best be on my way."

Sadie said, "We can carry you back when Sam Rose comes across for us in his boat."

Helen turned a look on her daughter.

"I'm all right," Wish said. "Don't mind walking."

"You leave tomorrow?" Sadie asked.

"Heading over to Twillingate."

"Do you stop in on your way back to St. John's?"

"If the coaster comes in this way."

"Why don't you and Hiram drop over this evening?"

Helen handed her dipper to Sadie. "I'll walk you along a ways," she said.

They went down to the beach together and past Mrs. Gillard at the fire. They climbed up the ridge he'd crossed over earlier that morning and Helen said, "How old are you, Aloysious?"

33

"Eighteen."

"You don't so much act eighteen," she said.

He didn't know what she meant by that but was afraid to ask.

"Sadie is a headstrong girl."

"I know it."

"She likes the look of you."

He nodded.

"She don't know anything outside the Cove, haven't been anywhere to know anything. She looks at you, all she sees is a door."

"A door to what?"

"She haven't got a clue. Maybe that's why she likes the look of you."

They went on without talking then until they topped the ridge, where Helen stopped, letting Wish walk a few yards down the opposite side before she spoke again.

"Aloysious."

The sun stood behind her head and he had to shade his eyes with his hand.

"You seem a fine young man." Helen took a breath and looked away out over the ocean. "My daughter is not going to take up with you," she said. "Or anyone of your kind."

"My kind."

"You know what I mean," she said. "You oughtn't to come by this evening."

The sun made his eyes water and he had to look away.

"It don't have anything to do with yourself or how you are," she said.

He walked away from her, not looking back until she called to him. She was still standing at the height of the ridge.

"Safe trip," she shouted. He stood with his hands on his hips, watching until she disappeared down the opposite side of the hill.

Silence all around him then. The sky cloudless and the

surface of the ocean as smooth as a tablecloth below him. Blood pounding across his ears.

2.

THE COASTER CAME BACK into the Cove nine days later. A Sunday morning, the church service under way, and there was no one on the wharf to greet them as they came ashore. After they settled their things in at the boarding house, Hiram announced he was off to visit Mrs. Jones about a horse. He'd likely be half an hour or more in the outhouse, humming aloud to keep himself company. Wish went out the front door and looked up and down the path, relieved to be free of the man.

They hadn't gone over to the Parsonses the night before they left the Cove, getting quietly pissed together instead at the boarding house after Mrs. Gillard went off to bed. Hiram had seemed altogether put out by Wish's lack of interest in seeing Sadie.

"You had no chance with the likes of her anyway," he said, trying to goad him. "A dirty little mick like you."

"Leave off," Wish said sourly.

They'd had much the same conversation the night before the coaster came back into the Cove from Twillingate, and it escalated into an exchange of taunts about balls and guts and nancy-boys that made Wish feel half his age.

Fucking Hiram.

Wish walked up toward the church, which stood on a small plateau above the harbour, backing onto the only trees left standing for miles in any direction, a stand of stunted spruce, the tops all trained toward the harbour by the prevailing wind. He heard the strains of the foot-pump organ, the nearly tuneless effort of the congregation as they made their way through "How Great Thou Art." He walked along the side of the church and up the hill past

the cemetery among a grazing herd of sheep, the animals complaining as they stepped out of his way. He went nearly to the ridge
of the hill and sat until the service ended, watched the congregation file into the sunlight. Picked out Sadie and her family making
their way toward the south side. Agnes wasn't with them, left at
home to watch the old woman, he assumed. Sadie looked back
occasionally, scanning up and down the cove as if she hoped to
catch sight of something in particular.

He had no desire to go back to the boarding house and sat on
the hill until he saw the minister leave the building. Walked down
to the vacant church. He had never been inside a Protestant
church before and it felt like a lonely place to him, empty of the
saints and their rows of votive candles. He sat in a pew at the back,
taking in the smell of polished wood and cured leather. An altar
on a low dais at the front, an embroidered purple banner hanging
there. A plain wooden cross high on the wall behind it. There was
no one nailed to the cross, just the naked arms of the wood. It
seemed almost to miss the point of the whole thing, to his mind.
He pictured his aunt then, stretched out on the floor of her little
hovel like a crucifix of flesh and blood, the otherworldly look of
transport on her face. Not peaceful, but fierce. The look of someone confronted with the inexpressible.

He'd never met his aunt Lilly before he was sent to live with her
in Renews. A Presentation Sister was waiting for him as he came off
the boat down at Gooderiche's wharf and led him up to her house.
Lilly was standing in the middle of the larger room, as if she had been
waiting there for hours or days. He could see nothing at all of his
mother in the woman and he found this a relief for some reason.

After their supper, Lilly knelt on the packed-earth floor near
the stove to say the rosary and he joined her there without waiting
for an invitation. It was a Tuesday evening and they were meditat-
ing on the sorrowful mysteries. Wish was using his mother's rosary.
She had been dead eleven days. Sorrow and mystery. Lilly prayed

in the language the priests used in church, her face alight with some Godly thing he couldn't feel in himself.

"I've learned this much about God," Lilly once said to him. "He doesn't trust us with the truth. He makes us work for it, so we don't squander what comes to us."

Wish had no idea what she meant by that. God was too much for people, is what he thought. Some wanted more than just to wet their feet and they walked out of their depth and drowned in Him.

He walked back up to the ridge, avoiding the horseshoe of buildings altogether, cutting down to the Gooseberry Cove path out beyond the Washing Pond. He hadn't eaten since breakfast and stopped along the way to pick handfuls of partridgeberries and blueberries. He went as far as a pond halfway to Gooseberry Cove where he stopped to drink and lay awhile on the bank. He took Aubrey's knotted string from his pocket and worried it mindlessly, wrapping it around his wrist, looping it through his fingers. He counted off the knots over and over as if they were beads in a rosary. He looked out over the low-lying hills, the moss and berry bushes, the humps of pale stone raftered above the soil. A steady wind had come up and clouds scudded across the face of the sun so that the landscape shifted in and out of the light like some distressed creature that could not settle where it lay. When he closed his eyes he felt the same roiling in his gut. He was ravenously hungry and he thought of the feeling as hunger, though there was more at the root of it than that. Some furious little engine at work in him.

The Monsignor had come to St. John's to visit the Archbishop in the spring and he'd called on Wish at Hiram's place. "Lilly asked me to look in on you," he said. Wish took him to his rooms on the second floor and made him tea while the Monsignor offered a little sermon on the creeping evils of all things ecumenical. "Don't think," Father Power told him, "there is no danger to your soul in living under the roof of a Protestant."

"No, Father," Wish said.

"It's the humiliation of the Holy Mother Church they preach," the Monsignor said. "And the degradation of every child of the Church is their goal."

Wish could feel the priest watching him and he tried not to fidget.

He said, "Exposure to the diseased imagination of the followers of Luther can blight even the purest constitution."

Wish stared down at his hands.

Father Power took off his glasses and polished the lenses with a silk handkerchief. "There are those that are lost to God," he said. "And that makes them capable of anything."

"Hiram, you mean?"

"Hiram Keeping and his kind." The Monsignor replaced his glasses. "Remember who you are, Aloysious. Remember who you belong to."

It all sounded like so much bullshit to Wish but the conversation unsettled him, made him fearful and angry. As if the truth of what the priest said was simply beyond his understanding, that his failure to fully comprehend the danger he was in somehow proved the Monsignor's argument. And those words came back to him fresh at odd moments like this, filled him with the same humiliation, the same irritation.

He called up Sadie to push it all aside, imagining the girl's hands under his waistband. He stripped out of his clothing, kneeling up on the moss with his legs spread, his head tipped back. Lifted her skirt over the white of her bare thighs where she bowed away from him, that dark cleft offered up, her face covered by a long veil of hair. Reached to grab a fistful as he slapped against her. Fell forward to catch his breath after he came, wiping his hand clean in the thick nap of the moss. That furious engine still running full-belt inside him.

———

The evening service had begun by the time he made his way back from the pond, the congregation's singing reaching him over the sound of the wind. He expected that Agnes would be at church this evening and Sadie left home to watch her grandmother. He stood outside the back-kitchen door and called to her. The sun had dipped beneath the moving raft of clouds and was nearly below the hill behind him, the face of the house stained with the last light of the day, the windows reflecting gold. Three outbuildings stood in the back, a stable and a workshed and a cool house where milk and vegetables were stored. All three were painted with a mixture of red ochre and oil, all three surrounded by a riddle fence woven out of alder sticks. Two goats in the enclosure, cropping grass, a dozen chickens in a wire run behind the stable.

When Sadie didn't answer him, he called again. She came to the door finally and stood with her arms crossed over her breasts. Her hair done up in plaits and tied into a bun at the back of her head. She said, "I thought maybe you were dead." In the bronze light her skin looked tanned, as dark as cinnamon. Even the green of her eyes seemed another colour altogether, some shade between copper and rust.

"Delayed is all," he told her.

"You'll want to come in, I guess."

"I was hoping." He shifted on his feet, as if he was out in the cold of winter and freezing.

Sadie went back to the kitchen, leaving the door open, and he followed her inside.

"Have you had your supper?"

"Haven't eaten anything but berries since breakfast."

She went off into the pantry and returned with a plate of cold roast beef and pastry and sliced cheese that she set on the table. "A cup of tea?"

"If it's not too much trouble."

"And what if I said it was?"

39

It hadn't occurred to him that she might be angry. "I don't know," he said. "I'd have a glass of water, I spose."

"You would, would you?" She busied herself making tea. He took off his jacket and folded it carefully across the back of the chair. He'd been planning on the same eagerness he'd seen in her at Gooseberry Cove, the reckless streak it hinted at. The delicacy of things between them made him uncertain how to act. He sat in front of the food but didn't touch it, waiting instead for Sadie to sit beside him. He said, "How's your nan?"

"You've seen her." A note of accusation in her voice again. "She's off her head."

"*Capo perduto*," Wish whispered. He thought of what the old woman had said about Sadie. Considered telling her something about his aunt Lilly but stopped himself. "What did your mother say to you the other day?" he asked. "Out at Gooseberry Cove, when she was trying to keep you quiet. Mer-something."

"That's my name," she said.

"What is?"

"Mercedes. I only hears it when Mother's upset with me. Not another soul calls me anything but Sadie. Sade."

"What kind of a name is Mercedes?"

"I don't know. What kind of a name is Aloysious?"

"I haven't ever heard of it before, not even in town." He thought her mother was just the type to christen a child something so grand, so foreign sounding. It was probably a boat from overseas gave Helen the fancy, they all had names like *Mirandella* and *Amarante* and *Maria Christina*. He said, "It's not Portugee, is it?"

She glared at him. "Do I *look* Portuguese to you?"

"Outside just now," he said. "The way the light was." He smiled helplessly. He said, "I was on a Portugee boat one time, out on the Cape Ballard Banks. The *Dona Amelia*, she was called. The crew only knew a few words of English so there wasn't a lot said, mostly about the fish. The size of them and where they were keeping to. Never offered us a morsel of food but they had three casks of wine in the galley and we had as much of that as we could hold. I was fine while I was sitting down," he said. "But when I stood up."

She folded her arms and looked at him as if to say, *Do you have a point?*

"A few of those fellows had pictures of their wives they took out to show us. They all talked about how beautiful the women were back home in Portugal."

It was a convoluted attempt at a compliment and he wasn't sure if it had come across that way or not. He could see the girl thinking it through. "I like your name fine," he said. "Mercedes."

"Why didn't you come by the house before you left?"

"I don't know."

She got up from her chair and took his plate into the pantry. Still furious, he could see. It wasn't at all how he had imagined things happening between them, that there'd be so much finagling. When she came back to the kitchen he said, "I didn't think I'd be welcome. Your mother," he said.

She sat back in her chair and looked at him, the anger still there though he could see it shifting away from him.

"When she walked me off in Gooseberry Cove. She told me not to come by." He waited a moment to let her sit with it. He said, "I'm going to join up when I gets back to St. John's."

"Join up?"

"I'm going to quit Hiram. Go overseas."

"You can't."

"I turned eighteen this year," he said, as if his age had been the only obstacle.

She seemed not to know what to say to him. She excused herself suddenly and went down the hallway and up the stairs. He listened to her footsteps overhead, was on the verge of taking his jacket and leaving altogether when he heard her coming back

41

down. At the foot of the staircase she stopped to look in on her grandmother. He could see she had taken out the plaits to let her hair hang straight to her shoulders.

When she came into the kitchen she went to the windows and began closing the curtains. "We'll light a lamp," she said.

With the curtains down the kitchen seemed smaller and separate from the world outside. They might be sitting in the cabin of a boat miles from shore, he thought. She lit a kerosene lamp on the table and turned down the wick. Then she leaned over him and kissed him full on the lips, her mouth open. He reached up to touch her but she backed away quickly and sat in her seat. There was no shyness in her, just the same brazen look he'd seen from her in the doorway of the church hall.

"Where'd you learn to kiss like that?"

"I've seen it," she said. "In the movies."

"I hope you're not done."

She shrugged, in a way that made him think she hadn't yet decided.

"You look fine, Mercedes," he said. "With your hair."

"Can I see your birthmark?"

She got up from her chair to stand beside him. She placed her hand at the back of his head, tipping it forward, then pulled the collar of his shirt gently away from his neck as if lifting a bandage away from a wound. She turned him in his chair to have more of the light. The mark was just below the hairline, smaller than the palm of a hand and scald red. He could smell her skin, that and a hint of vanilla that she must have dabbed behind her ears while she was upstairs. She was leaning against his arm, her breasts brushing his shoulder through the fabric of their clothes, and his cock was immediately, painfully erect. He shifted against the discomfort.

"Hold still," she said. "Can I touch it?"

"All right."

She brushed her fingers lightly over the patch of skin. "Does it hurt?"

"No. No, not a bit."

He could feel her tracing the outline of it with the tip of one finger. He raised a hand toward her but she backed away enough to make him think better of it. He was afraid she might sit back in her chair altogether. "What does it look like to you?" he asked her.

"I don't know. Not much."

"It doesn't look like the head of a horse to you?"

He felt her shrug against him.

"Maybe," she said. "It could be a horse." She didn't seem to like the idea at all.

"My mother always said it looked like a horse. You never heard tell of the burning horse, have you? Down on the Southern Shore?"

"No."

"When Mother was expecting me she shipped over to Renews to stay with her sister. Father had a berth on a sealing vessel and was away on the ice fields and they both thought it would be best if she wasn't left alone. She was some size with me and I woke her up one night, kicking. She shifted around a while, trying to settle, and finally give it up. Hauled Lilly out of bed and the two of them went for a walk on a slide-hauling trail in over the mash."

The girl laid her hand flat against his neck as if there was heat rising off the mark that she wanted to hold there. And he carried on talking to keep her where she was.

"It was nearly a full moon that night. And they felt the hoof-beats coming up through the ground, same as Mother could feel me kicking inside. They turned back to look and the horse was driving up from the shoreline, all aflame and going full gallop, burning along the length of her back. Half-mad by then trying to outrun the fire and she barrelled past them, trailing the stink of burnt hair and kerosene. Mother said it was like something out of the Bible, like a sign of the world coming to an end. She fell back as the mare went by, grabbed the nape of her neck going down. In the same spot where that mark is under your hand."

She trailed her fingers back and forth over the birthmark. "Why would anyone do that?"

"Some sort of a grudge, is the way I hear it. Someone settling a score. I was born with that mark."

"Does she live in St. John's? Your mother?"

He looked down at his hands. "She's dead this years."

She sat back in her chair. "What happened to her?"

He hesitated, unsure how it would change things between them, how it would alter the arc of the conversation to tell her. "Diphtheria," he said. "They quarantined us in the house. Used to pass food into us through the side window with a scarf tied over their faces. There was only the one woman would come by to look after Mother, Mrs. Roche. She was a widow, I spose she thought it made no odds if she got sick herself. She stayed with us until Mother died. Boiling up stuff all the time, dogwood and cherry bark, Indian tea, juniper. She used to give it to mother off a spoon. Made me drink it too." He looked around himself a moment, then back at his hands. "They flew a doctor down from St. John's near the end. This was the middle of winter, January. We still had the tree up from Christmas when she first got sick with it. I watched the plane land on the pond from my bedroom window, first time I'd ever seen a plane, that was. And this young fellow, he didn't look old enough to be a doctor, that's what I thought of him. He come up to the house and gave Mother some medicine, but she was all but gone by then. She'd got the croup and blood coming out her nose. She couldn't swallow proper or catch her breath. And her skin was gone blue. Like a baby born dead is what Mrs. Roche said. The doctor wasn't out of the house three hours when she died."

He lifted his hands and set them back on the table.

After a moment, the girl got up and poured them both more tea. He was thinking it was the wrong thing to have told her, that it had ruined his chances altogether, when she put her hand back on the nape of his neck. He looked up to her and she kissed him again. When he reached for her she backed off, just as she'd done the first time. He watched her a moment. Reached into his pocket for the length of string Aubrey had passed to Hiram.

"Your father give me this," he said. "I'm meant to get you a dress in St. John's." He stood up beside her and spread his arms wide, the string looped loosely across his hands. "I thought I should check to see if these measurements are true."

He could see she knew the truth of what he was after but she spread her arms to mirror his own. He started at the double knot, running the string the length of one arm to her wrist. He set the second knot on her shoulder and let the string drop to the floor, his free hand moving lightly down to the third knot, pressing it a moment, feeling the jut of her hipbone through the fabric of the skirt. He looked her in the eye to be sure of her before he went any further. He could hear the sound of her breath through her nostrils and her arms wavered slightly but she didn't look away from him.

He reached around her back, bringing the rope forward from both sides, his loose fists brushing against her breasts as he brought the knots together. Their faces were nearly touching. "All right," he said. She lifted her face to kiss him and he let the string drop, circled his arms around her waist, moved his hands along the length of her back. His fingers slid beneath the waist of her skirt, the band of her underpants, and she pushed her hips against him when he touched skin. He reached with one hand down to her bare thighs and then up into the startling heat and wet of her.

Her head snapped back a moment and she sank her face into the crook of his neck. "Wish," she said.

It was a hesitation in her and he tried to kiss her again, to keep her from speaking anything more, but she pushed away

45

suddenly and held him at arm's length. She wouldn't look at him and he leaned to one side, trying to catch her eye.

"Sadie," he said. "Mercedes."

She shook her head, then smiled up at him for a second. She said, "Don't make a whore of me."

His mouth opening and closing. She took his hand still wet where he'd touched her, pressed it to her lips. She stepped toward him, her mind made up he could see, but he fell back into his chair. He felt unhinged, as if he had been drinking Portuguese wine all evening and the effects were just striking him.

"I'm sorry," she said. "I didn't mean."

He tried to settle properly in the seat at the table. "It's all right."

She turned her back to him and stood still a few moments. "I'm going to look in on Nan," she said.

He watched her go down the hallway and tried to collect himself. He picked the knotted string up off the floor and folded it away in his pocket. His head felt waterlogged, he couldn't wring sense out of a single thought. Her parents were at the door before he registered them coming and he jumped up, surprised, taking his coat off the back of the chair and folding it across his arm.

Helen was first through the door and she stopped when she saw him.

"Evening," Wish said and he bobbed his head.

"Well," Aubrey said, standing behind his wife. He smiled at the younger man. "You come by after all."

"Where's Sadie?" Helen asked.

"She's looking in on her nan."

Helen called out, "Mercedes." Her husband had to squeeze by her to get into the kitchen.

Aubrey said, "You've had a bit of a lunch, have you?" He noticed the lamp beside the plate on the table then and said, "Who closed these curtains?" He looked at Wish and back at the lamp.

"I'm just on my way," Wish said.

The girl came into the room with her hair tied back into an untidy ponytail. "How was church?" she said.

"Don't you ask us about church," Helen whispered.

"Hiram's expecting me," Wish said. "Over to the boarding house." He glanced at Aubrey, but the man had turned his back to try and hold his temper. Helen still hadn't moved and Wish couldn't figure how to get by without coming into contact with her. He kept the hand he had touched Sadie with under the folded coat, as if the sight of it alone might give him away.

"You got no right," Helen said fiercely.

He half expected the woman to slap him. She stepped to one side finally but held his eyes the while. He nodded awkwardly to the room. "Night all," he said.

He sat in the dark outside Mrs. Gillard's house until he was sure everyone inside was asleep, crept up to his room with his shoes in his hand. He didn't light the lamp and left the curtain up so he could watch the sky. Managed to doze off when first light sketched in the barest details of the bureau and washstand across the room.

The wind woke him, gusts driving against the side of the house so the frame clenched and complained, the panes shaking in the windows. Out the window he could see that the coaster had come in sometime during the morning and anchored at the mouth of the shallow harbour. She wasn't due to leave the Cove before noon and he skipped his breakfast, staying to his room until near eleven. When he came downstairs with his bag, Hiram was sitting in the parlour with a pipe.

"How did things go with the Parsons girl?"

"Shut up, Hiram."

"Well now, that doesn't sound very promising. I figure if you'd managed to get your little dick wet, you'd have come knocking on my door first thing."

Wish left the room and walked off toward the kitchen. Hiram got up out of his chair to follow.

"Where's Mrs. Gillard to this morning?" Wish asked him. "I'm gut-foundered."

"Haven't laid eyes on her since she stepped out around nine." He looked out the window, where a bare washing line was being whipped about in the wind. "She's caught out in the weather down the road somewhere and holed up with a cup of tea, I'd say."

Wish found a loaf in the breadbox and began cutting off slices on the counter.

Hiram came up close to him. "You must have got caught," he said. "Is that it? Someone walked in on you? Is that why you're so contrary this morning?"

Wish took the knife to the loaf to cut another slice of bread. He said, "I'm quitting you, Hiram. When we gets back to town. I'm quitting this racket."

"Now Wish, I'm only after having a bit of fun with you. You know now, all I got left to me is that. A drink and a bit of fun."

"Maybe I had enough fun to last me a while." He was working to hold back the tears.

"Are you in trouble here, Wish?"

He shook his head. "I'm quitting you, is all."

"And what the hell are you going to do with yourself? Go back fishing?"

"I don't know. Join up, maybe. Go overseas."

"Overseas?" Hiram said. "You?"

"I mean it."

"Jesus Christ, Wish. What's got into you, at all?" He went to the cupboard and took down a tumbler, poured himself a shot of whisky from the flask he kept in the inside pocket of his coat. The wind whipping at the loose panes of the windows. He took a sip and held the edge of the glass against his chin. "Do I owe you any money?"

Wish pointed at him with the knife. "Fuck off, Hiram," he said.

———

By the time they were loading their gear into a dory to be ferried to the coaster, most of the trap skiffs and small schooners that had gone out early that morning were coming in, two and three at a time, straggling into the Cove against a wind blowing hard northeasterly. The day had come up fine with no indication of this turning and the fishermen would have been taken by surprise on open water. Forced to haul up their gear or set the traps loose, starting their engines to try and outrun the storm. The local men on the wharf stood and watched the ocean, counting boats as they appeared, rhyming off the names of those aboard, checking them against the list in their heads. Clive Reid said, "You'll not likely get away today."

"We'll as well pass the time on board as onshore, I expect," Hiram said. "They've got the saloon at least."

When they reached the coaster, they had trouble transferring themselves off the dory to the ladder fixed to the side. It rose and fell beside them like the piston of some enormous engine. They perched on the gunnel and reached for the rungs as the man at the oars rowed hard to keep them steady in the lun of the ship.

"You'll have a fine day of it out there, I imagine," he shouted to them as they made their way up to the deck.

Wish and Hiram shared a cabin with a single set of bunk beds. The boat hadn't even weighed anchor and they were forced to hold on to the bunks to steady themselves. Finally Hiram said, "If I'm going to stagger like this, I may as well be drunk," and he went out the door to make his way to the saloon.

Wish turned in a circle several times, as if he'd been locked into the cabin and was taking the measure of the tiny room. He was furious with everything around him, with Hiram, with the featureless white walls, with his clothes, with the sound of the wind howling outside.

He removed his shoes and stripped down to his undershirt and lay on the bunk, playing over the previous night, jumping

49

from one sensation or fragment of conversation to another in time to the rocking motion of the ship. Sadie coming into the kitchen with her hair down and vanilla dabbed behind her ears. The smell of her still on his fingers. Her mother's stare in the door. The burning horse and her fingers trailing back and forth across the nape of his neck. Sadie holding him at arm's length after he had touched her. The smell of her still.

He picked up one of his shoes, heaved the weight of it against the cabin door. "Useless fucking shoes," he said.

He picked up the other and heaved it after the first.

The wind moderated enough by early afternoon for the coaster to weigh anchor, and she got under way just after two. The change in the motion of the ship woke him and he turned onto his side, blinking, trying to orient himself. He didn't know how long he'd been asleep, couldn't remember where Hiram had gone. A knot of anxiety in his stomach but he couldn't identify the source of it. He sat up and looked out the porthole.

Sadie. Mercedes.

That peculiar name. Portuguese or Spanish, he was certain, French. Maybe Norwegian. He tried to recall some other country whose vessels he'd come across on the fishing banks but couldn't think. The Cove was still in sight behind them, distant and about to disappear behind the headland. He pulled on his shirt and shoes and found his coat. He headed out on deck, pushing the weight of the door against the wind. A heavy sea running across the foredeck as the coaster crested each successive wave. Wish walked unsteadily toward the stern, going hand over hand along the length of rope fastened to the wheelhouse wall. The spray was bitter and he turned up his collar against it, stood watching Little Fogo Island recede.

He was just about to give in to the cold when he felt a shudder running the length of the vessel as she went into full reverse. He ran back toward the bow where several men had already come down from the bridge and were at one of the ship's boats, stripping off the tarp, lowering her to the level of the deck on her chains.

"What's going on?"

"Men in the water," one of them said. "Out to starboard."

Wish stood up on the railing to get a better look but couldn't see anything in the shifting expanse of water. "Did they go aground?"

"Trap skiff gone over. A couple of fellows hanging on."

Three men had stepped into the boat and were setting the oars into their locks. Someone shouted, "Let her go," and the boat dropped down the side.

By the time the boat came back to the coaster all hands were at the rail. Two men went down the ladder to guide the survivors up to the deck. They were wrapped in woollen blankets and they moved like decrepit old men as they took the hands reaching to help them out of the boat. One of the two was Mercedes' brother, Hardy. The other an older man Wish didn't recognize.

The captain was at the rail as they came aboard and he ordered them carried to the saloon and stripped out of their sodden clothing. He shouted down to the men in the boat. "How many more?"

"They said there was two others, Skipper. Carried off hours ago now."

Mercedes' father, Wish knew.

The captain looked up at the horizon. "A few hours of light yet," he said. "Let's get those other boats in the water. We'll carry on with the wind a ways before we turn back to the Cove." He shouted to the men below. "Head in close to shore. Maybe God landed one of them on solid ground. We'll pick you up on the swing around before dark."

Wish volunteered to go out with the boats and took his place at the oars, hauling against the wind to keep her from going abroad of the sling of each wave. They went by bits and pieces of gear floating free in the water and then passed the over-turned skiff.

"Not a soul could swim far in this," the man on the opposite oar shouted.

"They might of got hold of something to keep afloat," Wish said.

The man beside him looked across. "You knew them, did you?"

Wish came back hard on the oar. He was soaked to the skin by the salt spray. "One of them," he said.

A third man stood in the bow as a spotter, staring out at the water ahead of them. He started in on a hymn that Wish didn't know, singing it out over the wind.

It was gone to dark before the coaster had finished her turn and come back to pick them from the water. They had to light a lamp and set it aloft on an oar so as not to be missed. The wind had gone down with the sun and they had no trouble bringing the boat aboard. Wish saw the Parsonses' trap skiff gleaming white on the foredeck and leaning hard to one side, like she was in open water and about to go over again. He ran his hand along the gunnel, as smooth as glass and dry.

They were brought to the saloon for rum and tea and a hot meal. The stoves had been kept humming and the room was sti-fling with heat. Hiram was sitting alone at a table beside one of the stoves. He raised his hand.

"No luck?"

Wish shook his head.

"Got some dry stuff for you," Hiram said, pointing to a pile of clothing on a chair.

The barman went around the room with a tray of rum and he set a glass on their table. Wish tipped back a mouthful before he stripped off his soaked clothes.

"It was a fellow Slade in the skiff with them," Hiram said. "The father of the one Hardy's been courting. Slade's youngest was out with them. Eleven year old."

"Where are they?"

"Put them to bed," Hiram said. He waved to the bags and blankets stacked along the wall on the far side of the stove. "They were going to set them up here, but I volunteered our cabin."

"Your dream berth, Hiram. Bunking out in the saloon."

He smiled. "Died and gone to heaven."

The mention of death sobered them again and they sat quiet a few minutes. "We're heading back to the Cove, are we?"

"We'll put in by nine or ten, I expect," Hiram said. "You should stay aboard when we get in, Wish. That might be best for all concerned."

The barman came back to the table with a plate of fish cakes and fresh bread. Wish was so hungry he felt nauseous. He took another mouthful of the rum to calm his stomach.

"You still got it in your head to quit me?"

"I'm already gone, Hiram."

The older man nodded. He'd been hard at the liquor since boarding the ship at noon and he was drunk, though a stranger might not see it in him. He leaned onto the table and looked down into his glass. "I should've known better than to open my door to a goddamned mick," he said.

Wish gathered his few belongings together to head in to shore at first light the following morning. As he was going over the side to the dory waiting below, Hiram gave him five dollars, which was enough to keep him at the boarding house awhile and pay his way back to town besides. Wish tried to refuse the money, but Hiram insisted.

"What's your plan, Wish? Swim back to St. John's, is it?" He was viciously hungover and belligerent. "I have a feeling I owe you the fiver anyway."

Wish decided it would be simpler to take the money and repay it later than to argue with him now. Mrs. Gillard set him up in the same room he'd been in two nights before and she served him breakfast, then Wish made his way down to the landwash. Most of the boats in the Cove were already out on the water. Only Clive Reid and his two sons still tied up, trying to start a contrary engine. Wish walked along to their stage and put one foot on the gunnel of the boat.

"You've missed your trip home," Clive said.

"Thought I might stick around, see if I can't help out. The more eyes out there the better."

"They've been all day and all night in the water," Clive said. "I don't expect we'll find anything pretty." His bottom lip was distended by a wad of chewing tobacco. He spat over the side of the boat. "Won't do much looking anyway if we can't get this bastard of a thing to turn over."

Wish stepped down into the skiff. "Mind if I have a look?"

The inboard stuttered alive half an hour later, an explosion of black smoke rising out of the housing before the engine settled into a steady chug. Wish closed his eyes a moment, listening. He was grease up to his elbows.

"That'll do her," he said. "She'll get you out and home, anyway." And then he said, "Would it be all right if I come out with you today?"

"More eyes the better, like you said."

As they made their way to open water Wish sat aft, looking back at Mercedes' house behind them. The blinds drawn over the windows.

He said, "Do you know what happened out there yesterday, Clive?"

"According to Hardy, they were already making for home when the weather turned. They'd had a good morning at the fish, nearly a full load aboard of her. Hit the heaviest wind when they came around the backside of the island, the seas coming over the rail and the engine swamped. They tried to get the sail up, but they made a fuck of that in the wind and couldn't keep the skiff face on. They were trying to pitch the fish back over side but it was too late by then. Went broadside to the waves with all that weight in her. No way she could right herself."

"What time was that?"

"Sometime after noon. They never saw the youngster after they went over. Just disappeared, they said. Hardy got ahold of his father and hung on to him a few minutes. But the seas tore him loose. Couldn't swim a stroke." Clive stared straight out over the water toward the headlands. "Faster going down, I guess," he said.

Wish glanced at the two boys in the boat with them. The youngest, David, not much older than eleven himself.

Three days the Cove's boats went along the coast beyond the headland to look for the missing. The searchers used fish finders and glass-bottomed buckets, leaning over the gunnels and holding them in the water to search the rocks and seabed in shallow areas. Wish and Clive's two boys took turns at the glass while Clive drove the boat slow along the coast.

The missing boy was found early on the third day, his clothes snagged on shoal rock fifteen feet below the surface. Clive noticed boats gathering near the shoals, like bluebottles hovering over a garden composted with capelin. He nudged Wish's shoulder and pointed.

As they came up close, Wish could see that two men had lines over the sides, using the metal hooks of a cod-jigger to grapple and haul the body free. One of the men straining at the lines was

Willard Slade. The body was brought up to the side of the skiff, Willard and another man gripping the clothes to hoist it over the gunnel. All Wish saw of the boy was one of his hands at the end of its cuff, the skin as white as salt. Willard Slade bawling hard as he set his son's body down in the skiff.

They headed back to the Cove in a small convoy. Wish and Clive sat at the stern, talking in whispers. Clive said it was most likely Aubrey had drifted out into deeper water and been driven off to God knows where by the Labrador current.

"I allow he's gone and gone," he said.

"You think that's it then? Will they give it up now?"

Clive shifted against the tiller. "That's three fine days of fishing lost," he said. "I'm glad we got the youngster. That'll be a comfort to his mother. But I wouldn't want no one wasting their time out here after me as long as this."

Wish nodded.

"What about you now?"

"What about me?"

"You going to set yourself up at that boarding house for good?"

"Not hardly."

"It's Sadie you're hoping for, I spose. Staying on in the Cove. Out here all hours, fishing for strangers. Got to be a woman at the root of that."

Wish didn't answer him and Clive settled back at the tiller, taking his silence as answer enough.

Wish hadn't gotten up the nerve to go by Mercedes' house since coming back into the Cove. Hardy had been on the water every day and made note of Wish in Clive's boat, though they hadn't exchanged a word. He'd been hoping Mercedes might find a way to come to him at the boarding house or down to the wharf to see the boats off in the morning.

"You'll want to step careful," Clive said.

Wish looked at him.

"I'm only saying. It's a hard time. And you being from away. Don't make a spectacle of yourself. Folks won't stand for it."

Wish looked ahead to the skiff that carried the boy's body, his father sitting over it in the bow. "What was his name?" he asked.

"Willard," Clive said. "Same as his father. Little bugger used to steal rhubarb out of the garden. Don't know why. They always had plenty of rhubarb over at Slade's." He spat into the wake of the boat. "Always sweeter if it don't belong to you, I guess." And he smiled across at Wish, his teeth the colour of dried peat.

After his supper he went up to his room and stripped down to his undershirt. He filled the basin and scrubbed his face and neck and his arms up to the elbows. He wet his hair enough to comb it flat and buffed at his shoes with a rag. He put on his one clean shirt and buttoned it to the neck. Then he walked across to the Slade house where the boy was being waked.

The back kitchen was busy with people, though strangely hushed. Willard Slade got up from his seat and came across to greet him. "Appreciate you coming along," he said. He introduced Wish around to the few people he hadn't already met—Willard waved into the pantry, "The wife and Ruthie," he said, but neither woman looked at them—and then brought him in through to the parlour. Clive was standing near the window and he raised his glass to Wish.

The plain wood coffin was against the far wall, set on two chairs at opposite ends. The casket was closed and the room smelled of camphor and lime. Wish ran his fingers across the top of the coffin briefly, as he'd run them across the gunnel of the trap skiff several nights before. Both made by the same hand more than likely. He crossed himself as he stepped back and became immediately aware of being watched by everyone in the room. Mrs. Slade came up behind him with a glass of syrup and a tray of fruitcake.

"Thank you, missus," he said. "I'm sorry for your troubles."

She seemed to look through him and made no response except to wave the fruitcake at him until he took a piece. Then she went back out to the kitchen.

Wish took a mouthful of the syrup. It was thick and sickly sweet. Everyone in the house was stone sober. Clive came across the room and stood beside him.

"This is it, is it?" Wish whispered.

"Not what you're used to, I imagine." He had shaved off the grizzle of beard and his face looked misshapen without the plug of tobacco under his lip. "There's a flask handed around outside now and then, if you need a drop to get you through."

Wish lifted his glass again and smelled the syrup but didn't taste it. "I only wanted to pay my respects," he said. "I think I should be on my way."

"She haven't been along yet," Clive told him. "If that's what you're wondering."

Wish nodded sheepishly. "Have you got the flask on you, Clive?"

They set their glasses on a sideboard and went back out through the kitchen.

"On your way already?" Willard said.

"Taking the young fellow out for a smoke," Clive told him. Before he closed the door he leaned back into the kitchen. "Bloody Catholics, hey?"

They went out into the dark of the yard and Clive took the flask from an inside pocket. He passed it along and Wish swallowed a mouthful before he knew what he was getting himself into. Potato shine, gut-rot and raw. It cut his wind going down and the vapours sifted up through his head like some miracle cure for congested sinuses. He held the flask at arm's length as if trying to fend it off. He shook his head violently and straightened up. He passed the flask back to Clive. "Fine stuff," he said.

They heard footsteps coming up the lane and fell silent as the new visitors came around the side of the house. It was a clear night and Wish could see their silhouettes against the horizon, but it wasn't till the door opened that he saw her in the spill of light from inside. Hardy was with her, and Agnes.

Clive tapped Wish's arm with his forefinger. He called to the girl and she stopped on the doorsill, looking over her shoulder into the darkness. "Come over a second," he said.

"Who's that?" she said. "Clive?"

"Come here, I wants to talk to you."

Hardy appeared in the doorway again.

"You go on," she told him. "I'll be right in."

She came across the uneven ground toward them, a hand over her brow like she was shading away sunlight. Clive squeezed Wish's elbow. "You be a gentleman now," he whispered. "For Aubrey's sake." He stepped away into the dark.

"Clive?" she said as she came closer.

"Hello, Mercedes."

She stopped, still ten feet from him.

"I'm sorry for your troubles," he said.

"Where's Clive?" She walked closer to him and he could just make out her features in the dark.

"How is your mother holding up?"

She said, "You were going to go off to St. John's without saying goodbye, weren't you."

"I didn't," he said. "In the end."

"Hardy said you were with them when they found young Will."

"I was along with Clive. The youngster was some mess when they—" He stopped himself. He could hear Mercedes draw a breath.

"Has everyone given Father up, then?" she asked.

He could see she'd started to cry though she didn't make a sound. He felt his cock begin to harden, inexplicably, and he tipped his head back to stare up at the constellations. "Jesus, Mercedes," he whispered.

She moved into him and put her arms around his back and they held one another. And just as inexplicably the urge drained away from him.

"I like how you say that," she said when she'd recovered herself.

"Say what?"

"My name."

"Mercedes," he said again. There was something illicit in using the mother's name for the girl, making it their own. A private thing between them, a stolen intimacy.

She said, "You smell nice."

He looked down at her, surprised. "It's just soap, Mercedes."

"No. I can smell the soap. It's something else altogether."

"What is it, then?"

"It's you. Cinnamon. Moss. I can't say exactly."

He had no idea what she was going on about but his scalp prickled and a queer sensation of vertigo came over him. The world seemed to be moving too quickly for him to keep his feet.

The door opened behind them and the dull rectangle of light fell across the ground. Agnes stepped over the doorsill. "Sadie," she called quietly.

She stepped away from Wish. "I'll be right there."

Agnes came toward them, her head ducking against the darkness. "Mrs. Slade is asking after you."

"I'm coming." She looked up at Wish and whispered, "Are you coming back in?"

"I don't think I better." He saw Hardy step out behind his sister.

"Sadie," Hardy said sharply.

"Oh for the love of God," she said. "I'll be there directly."

Agnes was beside them and she said, "What are you doing out here with him?"

"Who is it you're talking to?" Hardy said. He hadn't moved beyond the patch of light from the door.

"I'm coming," she said. "Go on, Agnes," she told her sister. "Go *on*." She began walking backwards toward the house. "Can you meet me tomorrow?" she whispered to him.

"Where?"

"The Spell Rock. After the boats go out."

"Yes," he said.

He watched her shoo her brother and sister into the house. She looked back into the yard where she knew he was still standing in the dark and waved before closing the door behind her.

Just after sunrise he left the boarding house and went across to the Spell Rock, where he watched the fishermen leave the harbour. A low fog rolled over the hills from Gooseberry Cove and settled thick on the land and the water, and he lost sight of the boats before they'd made open seas. He sat beside the pink granite stone and hauled his coat tight against the chill of the fog. Eventually he drifted asleep.

He dreamt of the dead boy sitting up in his coffin at the wake. The youngster was eyeless and mouthless and held a glass of syrup, he lifted a salt-white hand to greet mourners as they entered the room. His entire body seemed to be constantly in motion, a slow undulation, as if he was still trapped underwater and stirred by ocean currents. Mercedes came into the parlour and leaned into the coffin to kiss the corpse full on the dark hole where his mouth once was. She looked over her shoulder at Wish and said, "Don't make a whore of me."

He didn't know where he was when she woke him.

"I've only got a few minutes," she said.

"I fell asleep." Trying to clear his head of the clinging accusation in those words.

She was kneeling beside him and he pushed himself up to a

sitting position. She touched his shoulder. "Sorry I had to run off last night."

He wiped at his face with both hands.

"Hardy was at me all evening to say who I was talking to."

"Did you tell him?"

"Not a word. He can stew till his bones go to mush. And I told Agnes to mind her mouth around him too."

"You don't mind much, do you, Mercedes?"

"I minds what bears minding. The rest won't ever hurt me to ignore."

"I like that in you."

"You like it now," she said, smiling back. "It won't wear so well once you're stuck with me."

She leaned forward to kiss him but he tilted his head away.

"It don't seem right," he said. "What with your father."

"You didn't mind when he was up at the church saying his prayers."

"That was different."

She wrapped the woollen shawl around her shoulders and studied him a moment. She said, "It wasn't just me you come back for, was it."

"It was you," he said.

"But that wasn't the only thing."

"What makes you say that?"

She looked down a second. "Aggie says there must be something," she said.

"Your sister?"

"She says there must be something in all that's going on to have brought you back. And keep you here."

He sat up straighter against the rock. There was a tinny buzz across his ears and the taste of Clive's alcohol came back into his mouth, the burn of it right up through his head.

She only waited for him.

"I was born in Renews," he said. "But we lived over in Burin. In Lord's Cove. We lost everything in '29, in the tidal wave, stage and the skiff. The house."

"I heard of it."

"Mother had an uncle living on his own in Calvert and we shifted over to stay with him. But we had nothing much to bring with us and we had a hard winter of it. Father and Mother's uncle walked into St. John's in March for a berth on one of the sealing vessels heading out to the ice." He looked away again.

"You lost him," she said.

"He was out with a crew in slobby ice. Blowing hard and snow coming up. They were making their way back to the vessel to get in out of it, all in single file. Everyone with their heads down and running to stay afloat on the pans. Father was at the end of the line when they started back. But when they got aboard the ship." He made a helpless little motion with his hand. "We never did get him. His body. I thought I might help spare your crowd some of that."

"Are you going to go overseas, Wish? Like you said?"

He took her hand. He opened his mouth to speak and closed it again. Finally he said, "I told Hiram I was quitting him."

She watched him as if she expected something more to follow, but he sat quiet.

"They're expecting me home," she told him.

Before she left him she pushed the shawl off one shoulder and slipped the hand she was holding inside her blouse, beneath the white shift to her naked breast. She watched him as he touched her there, the skin soft as down and the nipple against his fingers like a knot of wood.

She removed his hand and set it against him like some creature she was being careful not to wake. "Tomorrow," she said. "Same time."

"All right."

63

He watched her go, cradling his hand in his lap. He called out, "You're some beautiful, Mercedes," and she looked back, her expression almost angry, he thought. "You don't mind me saying."

"You've said it before," she said. "To other girls."

"I never really meant it though. Not like I means it now."

"Then I don't mind you saying."

Clive's skiff came back into the Cove around ten o'clock that morning, and Wish made his way down to the stage to meet them. Clive and his two boys were plunging the long tines of their fish-forks into the black-backed roil around their legs, heaving the cod up onto the lungers.

"You had a good trip," Wish said.

"The fish was maggoty out there this morning."

"You'll want a hand getting through them before dinner."

"An extra hand wouldn't go astray."

Wish was set up cut-throat, passing the blade under the gills and down the length of the white belly. He sent the opened bodies along the table to Eli, who took off the heads, scalloped tongues from the mouths, separated livers from the offal and pushed them into a tub. Clive splitting at the end of the table, his knife flicking the spine clear, not an ounce of flesh on the bone. Their movements practised and casual, so effortless it looked as simple as buttering toast. David washed and stacked the fish meat at the end of the line, reaching elbow deep into a puncheon of sea water to scrub it clean. He was born with one hand smaller than the other, the fingers folded in on themselves like the claws of a bird's foot.

Wish said, "He don't mind I took his spot?"

Clive glanced toward the boy. "He hates all this. Rather be up at the school or home reading a book."

Wish slipped his fingers into the gills of another cod, lifted it to the table. The knife through the seamless skin envelope making a sound like a piece of fabric ripped cleanly. He'd always hated making the fish himself. It was part of what he felt he was escaping in St. John's. But he found the unremitting activity a blessing this morning. There was little talk, just the cold, ugly work of heading and gutting and time ticking him closer to seeing Mercedes at the Spell Rock the following morning. The thought of her like a kettle kept warm at the back of the stove.

They sat together on the water side of the Spell Rock, to be out of view of women hanging their washing or looking out their windows at the harbour. Mercedes between his legs and leaning back into him.

"Do you still miss them?"

He shrugged against the weight of her. "Sometimes. Yes."

"Where do you feel it?"

He laughed into her hair. "Don't be talking so much bloody foolishness."

She reached around, touched an index finger to his shoulder. "There?"

"No."

She touched his earlobe. His nose, his hip, the fly of his trousers.

"No," he said.

She laid her hand flat against his breastbone.

"There."

He held her eye to avoid looking down, afraid he would see her hand buried up to the wrist in his chest.

The first night he slept in his aunt Lilly's house she'd stopped in the door of her little room to look back at him on the daybed. "There will come a day," she said, "when everything that's happened to you will seem purposeful." The light of the lamp threw dark shadows on her face and she looked vaguely sinister. "If you keep your heart open to it," she said, "the time will come. I promise."

He felt himself on the verge of something that unlikely now, something that potent.

Mercedes said, "I'll never not miss him, will I."

He pulled her into his chest, wrapped both his arms around her.

"Don't let go of me," she said.

He held on to her without saying a word, which felt like promise enough.

He spent the rest of the day down on Clive's stage and went back to Mrs. Gillard's for his supper. Stepped out for a walk just as it was coming on to dark. He and Mercedes had kissed before she left him that morning and he let his hands drift over her, knowing she would have let him touch her anywhere he chose. And it was touching her he had in his head as he walked down behind Mercedes' house to sit beyond the riddle fence. She wasn't expecting him and he had no plan other than hoping to steal a word with her if she made a trip to the outhouse before bed, to bury his face in her neck, to let his hands wander.

He'd distrusted that urge their first morning at the Spell Rock but it felt pure and proper now, almost chaste. It was her father gone missing and wanting to offer solace that altered his sense of it. Recognizing the girl's grief in himself made him believe in his ability to love her, made the physical attraction between them seem true.

Someone came through the back kitchen door and walked toward him. Outline of a long skirt, a woman's gait. Too tall to be Agnes, so it was Mercedes or her mother stepping up into the out-house, closing the door. When the woman came outside again he stood up and crossed himself. "Mercedes," he whispered.

The woman froze.

"It's Wish."

She spun on him, furious with relief. "Don't you *ever*," Mercedes said.

"I was only wanting to say goodnight."

66

She rushed back to the outhouse, clapped the door shut, and he didn't know what to make of that until he heard her peeing again from the fright. He jumped the riddle fence and was waiting when she came out the door. They walked awkwardly to the side-wall holding each other and kissing and he leaned her against the rough lumber. He could feel her heart against his chest. He lifted the skirt of her dress in handfuls until he was underneath it, fingers touching bare skin, the fine bristle of her pubic hair, and it came into his mind then to kneel in front of her.

It was something he'd only heard spoken of drunkenly or as a lewd joke and it was always meant to demean a man's reputation, as if only a fool would put himself in such a position. And it was true he felt ridiculous, dropping to his knees, holding her skirt high with his hands. It was an act of surrender, a kind of penance he thought the girl was owed. She had her fingers in his hair and was trying to pull his head away, but he kissed her there. Her cunt. Salt and the tang of urine and folds of skin as smooth as. He didn't know as smooth as what. He felt foolish and willing, and he saw it as a measure of proof, the willingness. He slid both hands under the cheeks of her ass and kissed her until she came down on top of him. Lay pinned beneath her in the long grass, so out of breath with certainty that he was dizzy.

He woke with the taste of her still in his mouth. Skipped his tea and breakfast, wanting to hold on to it as long as he could. Walked down to the Spell Rock and waited, but no fishing boats went out of the Cove and Mercedes didn't come to meet him.

A bully boat he didn't recognize came into the harbour mid-morning and tied up at Earle's wharf. Two men stepped off and they reached back to help a third up onto the dock. The minister over from Fogo for the funeral.

Willard Slade's youngest boy was buried in the graveyard in the meadow above the church that afternoon. Wish didn't attend the service but he stood outside the fence as the mourners filed into the cemetery and watched while they prayed over the coffin. The minister read from the 23rd Psalm, *Thy rod and thy staff, they comfort me.* He thought briefly how Mercedes found something of that same comfort in his company, though he couldn't avoid thinking of his cock in connection with *rod* and *staff,* and he wound up having to push the entire thing from his mind to keep the stupid grin from his face.

The coffin was let down into the earth, four men with ropes dropping the boy hand over hand, just the opposite of how he'd been salvaged from the ocean. After the interment the entire community passed by Wish again. Willard and Mrs. Slade and their other children in various states of undone. Mercedes wiping her face with a handkerchief and holding his gaze until she was past him, Agnes staring hard too, as if there was a riddle to him she might be able to figure just by looking. Their mother stone faced on Hardy's arm, both of them refusing to acknowledge Wish.

Clive was one of the last out the gate and he stopped to talk, his eyes bloodshot and his mouth working hard. "Miserable old racket," he said.

The minister came by them and nodded hello to Clive. He had one walleye that seemed directed toward Wish as he passed and its peculiarly wandering attention struck the younger man as malevolent.

Clive said, "How are things with the little miss?"

Wish was watching after the minister as he walked toward the church. "Things are fine with the little miss. The old miss, now. That's a different quintal of fish."

Clive smiled. "She's as hard as a box of nails, that one. Hardly heard a civil word out of her mouth in all the years she's been in the Cove."

"She's not from here?"

"Aubrey hooked up with her down on the Labrador one summer. She was working with a crew in Domino Run, cooking and cleaning, helping to make the fish. Not more than fifteen then and some says already in the family way when she got here with Aubrey. Not what you'd expect of the old bugger. But you know what men are like."

Wish studied his feet to hide the flush coming into his face.

"Don't even know for sure where she's from," Clive went on. "Somewhere in Conception Bay, I hear. She left all her people behind to come to the Cove with Aubrey and never shed a tear as far as I can tell. Although you can't ever say what goes on behind closed doors."

"She don't think much of me or mine."

"Being from the opposite side of the house, you mean?"

"She said as much."

They both looked back at the gravesite, where two men were spading dirt into the hole. "Bloody old foolishness in the end. Don't matter to that one who's throwing the dirt down into his face, now, does it?"

Wish wasn't sure that argument held where marriage was concerned. But he didn't want to insult Clive by disagreeing.

"A mother won't think much of any man sniffing around the daughter, I guarantee you that. It's in her nature. But you be civil and keep the girl happy. Helen will settle."

"I got me doubts about that."

Clive grinned at him. "Would be no sport to it at all if you had no doubts."

He was waiting for her at the Spell Rock three days later when he saw Clive's trap skiff coming around the headland on its way back into the Cove. The engine's raw racket travelling over open water and echoing back off the hills above the Cove. They'd been out barely long enough to get to their cod traps and she was riding too high in the water to have a load of fish aboard. Clive was sitting in tight against the tiller and both his sons were sitting aft as well, as close to the stern-board as they could get. Wish headed for the wharf at a run. Mercedes was on her way to meet him when they crossed paths.

"Where's Agnes?"

"I made her wait behind on the path."

"Take Agnes and go on up to the house," he said. "Send your mother down."

"What is it?"

He went down to the stage where Clive's trap skiff was drifting in, the engine cut. As the boat came abreast he saw the bundle of canvas in the bow. Wish took the lines thrown to him from the skiff and fastened her to the pilings. Clive facing away from him, gathering up gloves and a jacket and his hat, then looking up to Wish standing above him on the wharf.

"What a fucking mess we got there," he said.

Wish and Clive and the two boys carted the body up to the church hall, each holding a corner of the canvas shroud. David holding the bottom lip of his full, feminine mouth between his teeth. Clive told Wish the body had drifted into the leader of their cod trap and they'd found it there as soon as they tried to haul up the door.

By the time they reached the church, Mercedes and her mother were coming down the path toward them. Clive said, "Get him inside before they gets here."

They shuffled awkwardly through the door and set their load in the middle of the floor, for some reason wanting to keep it as far from the walls as possible. They threw open the windows and then hurried back outside, away from the ballooning stench. Clive caught Helen and wrapped his arms around her to keep her from going inside.

"Now, Helen," he said. "There's nothing for you to see in there."

"Is it Aubrey?" She was looking over one of Clive's shoulders and then the other, as if trying to glimpse someone in a crowd. "Is it him?"

"Couldn't be anyone else, Helen."

"He was wearing his yellow garnsey and red vamps. He couldn't ever keep his feet warm, you know how he was, Clive, wore his vamps winter and summer."

"There weren't a stitch left on him, maid," he whispered. "He been out there a week. And hauled around something fierce it looks like."

"He had his initials engraved," she said. "On the inside of his wedding band."

Clive shook his head. "The left arm," he said. "The whole thing."

"Blue eyes?"

Wish stood holding Mercedes a little off to the side. Sea lice would have taken the eyes, he knew. But neither he nor Clive had the heart to say it. Mercedes had buried her face in his chest and was wailing.

Clive said, "Get the child back up to the house, Wish. For the love of Christ Jesus."

He sat Mercedes in her rocker and stood back as Agnes knelt in front of her and the two sisters held each other and wept. Then he did the only thing he could think to do. He put the kettle on the stove. He took down mugs and sugar and hunted about for tea. When he found everything he needed he stood by the door, waiting for the water to boil. The old woman started calling out from the parlour and he went down the hall to look in on her. She was lying in the exact same posture as before, shouting through the wall. He took her hand as he sat on the edge of her bed.

"I thought you might be Aubrey home," she said.

"No, missus." He had no idea how much she knew of what was happening.

"Is he dead and gone, then?"

"I'm sorry to say he is."

"And gone to hell," the old woman said. "To judge by the company he kept." She looked toward the window and said, "What *is* that noise?"

There wasn't a sound that he could hear. "What noise?"

She glared at him, as if an unpleasant odour was emanating from his body. "Where do you belong to?"

"St. John's."

"You're not from town. Where's home?"

"I should go see to the kettle."

She held his hand fiercely. "You're a *Catholic*."

He had to stop himself from laughing, caught off guard by the force of her disgust, by the bizarre fluke of being named for what he was. She was trying to sit up and he thought she'd go for his throat if she could find the strength. He shushed her back down into the bed. "Don't be so foolish. *Catholic*," he said. "Sure a Catholic wouldn't be caught dead in this house, would they? They'd be struck down before they got in the door."

She was out of breath and had lost her train of thought altogether, the fury evaporating as quickly as it had overtaken her, and she reached up to pat his face. "You're a good boy," she said. "You're Jenny Reid's boy, are you?"

"Can I bring you a cup of tea?"

By the time he came back into the kitchen, Helen had returned with several other women. She was at the windows, closing the curtains.

He said, "I'm sorry for your troubles, Mrs. Parsons."

For a moment it seemed she might begin crying but she reined herself in.

"The missus was calling," he said, "so I looked in on her."

"I hope she was civil to you."

As civil as I've come to expect of the women of the house, he thought. But he only said, "She wanted a cup of tea." And then he added, "If there's anything I can do."

She carried on at the blinds, ignoring him.

Mercedes was still in the rocker, her face red and bloated with crying. He said, "I'll be on my way, I guess."

She looked to her mother. "Can't he stay awhile?"

"We got to get the house ready for your father, Sade."

Wish said, "I'll see you again before long."

And Helen stepped away from the door to let him pass.

For the second time in less than a week, he stripped to the waist in front of the washbasin and scrubbed himself. He put on his one good shirt and cleaned his shoes.

He fell in with a sparse column of people heading to Aubrey's wake, picking their way along the path in the dark. Inside the house he was offered a glass of syrup by Agnes and then he walked down the hallway to the parlour. The coffin stood where the old woman had been lying that afternoon. He guessed she was carried body and bed to one of the upstairs rooms where she'd stay until she died. Near the covered window Helen sat beside Mercedes, holding her hand in a fashion that suggested restraint more than comfort. And Hardy stood over them both, glaring across the room at Wish. Offering his sympathies would only make things worse, he knew, so he went to the casket instead.

Clive was sitting near the head of the coffin. "Looks pretty bleak for you across the room," he said.

"I hope you got that flask with you."

Clive set down his glass of syrup and got to his feet. As they walked out into the hallway there was a muffled commotion in the parlour. Wish went back to the door, saw a crowd of bodies in the centre of the room, all bending forward as if they were looking down a well.

73

Willard Slade put his hands up to Wish's shoulders and backed him into the hall. "She's only after having a little fainting spell."

"Sadie?"

"She's all right, Wish. You best go on out of it."

Clive grabbed him by the sleeve and hauled him toward the kitchen and out into the night.

"You sure she's all right in there, Clive?"

"She's overcome is all, leave her be awhile."

They walked into the enclosure of outbuildings away from the house and passed the flask back and forth between them. Clive told him how they'd strewn the body with lime and then sewed up the canvas it had been carried in. "They'll have to bury him tomorrow, I allow. He's fair to gone already. Can't be waiting to get the minister back across from Fogo."

"I got no chance with her mother," Wish said. "Her mind is set."

Clive said, "Back in my father's day, there was a young one from over in Tilting came courting a girl on the other side of the islands. A few of the locals got together and lay for him down on the landwash and they put the boots to him. Father said the fellow had one eyeball hanging out on his cheek when they were done with him. Blood everywhere."

"Jesus, Clive."

"All I'm saying is, Wish, it's not like it was."

Wish let out an angry little laugh. He could feel the liquor seeping into his head and he took another mouthful. He thought of the picture in the back kitchen of King Billy crossing the Boyne. That army still on the move. He said, "Would you take us as far as Fogo? If she was willing?"

Clive reached for the bottle. "Maybe you've had enough for tonight."

Wish hauled it free of his hand and glared at him.

"I'm going inside," Clive said. "You take that flask and go on back to Mrs. Gillard's."

Wish tipped the bottle up to his mouth but never took his eyes from the man.

He emptied the flask before he made his way back to the parlour, reeling off the narrow walls of the hallway. Feeling drunker by the second. Helen and Hardy were still sitting across the room but there was no sign of Mercedes. Everyone else staring at their shoes to avoid catching his eye. *Fuck them*, he thought. Mrs. Gillard sitting him alone at the table for his supper and the minister over from Fogo with his walleyed stare and the crazy old woman lying upstairs in her own piss and fuck King Billy crossing the Boyne out in the back kitchen. Every soul in the Cove stood against them. And Wish was struck by a moment of drunken clarity, seeing that truth made so plain there in the parlour. A line had been drawn that the girl wouldn't be hard enough to cross once it came clear to her. And he had no right to ask her to cross it.

He stepped into the room, fishing the rosary from his pocket. He knelt in front of the coffin and began praying aloud. "Hail Mary, full of grace; the Lord is with thee: blessed art thou among women, and blessed is the fruit of thy womb, Jesus."

He could hear the rustle of people standing and leaving the room behind him and he raised his voice to be heard over the noise. Expecting any moment to be grabbed by the hair and thrown out the door. "Holy Mary, Mother of God, pray for us sinners, now and at the hour of our death. Amen." He went on praying until he was sure the room was empty and then he stood and put the rosary away in his pocket. Disappointed not to have provoked a decent fight, a shoving match, the tiniest bit of cursing. *Fucking Protestants*, he thought.

"You're a devout one, Aloysious," Helen said.

He spun around to see her sitting where she'd been before he knelt down. He bowed slightly in her direction, not sure where he'd picked up such a formal gesture but feeling it was right all the

75

same. The proper mixture of deference and defiance. He thought for a moment she might understand what he was up to. But she only watched him, and he bowed again, drunkenly, before he went down the hallway. The people he'd driven from the parlour were packed into the back kitchen. Not even Clive was willing to look Wish in the eye as he pushed by to get through the door.

He was lying in his bed at Mrs. Gillard's an hour later, a fierce pulse in his temples. He heard the door to the back kitchen open and footsteps track through the house, up the stairs to his door. "Mr. Furey."

He didn't answer, and Mrs. Gillard hammered at the door impatiently. "I knows you're in there."

He sat up on the side of his bed. "Come in," he said.

She swung the door open and stood just inside his room. She was carrying a lamp and the light held below her face made dark holes of her eyes.

"Evening, Mrs. Gillard."

"I give you a room in my house," she said. "I fed you from my table."

"At very reasonable rates."

Mrs. Gillard straightened her shoulders. "I'll be staying at the Slades' tonight rather than sleep under the same roof as you. You feel free to make yourself some breakfast. I expect you to be gone by the time I gets back tomorrow."

She closed the door before he could ask what time that might be and he sat on the bed with his hands in his lap, listening to her go back down over the stairs.

He was woken by the sound of the back kitchen door opening again and he lay still listening to the footsteps coming up the stairs. He had no idea how long he'd been asleep and he went to the window, peeking past the curtain to see the barest glimmer of first light on the horizon. He called to Mrs. Gillard before she knocked on his door.

"You can't expect a man to have his breakfast eat by this time in the morning," he said. He hadn't undressed at all, falling asleep with his boots up on the bed. He hauled at his shirt and pants, trying to straighten his clothes. "I'll be gone in an hour."

The door opened without a knock and a figure much larger than Mrs. Gillard stood there.

"You got a few minutes to pack your things," Hardy said.

Wish was struck by the bulk of him. Not as tall as himself but broad across the shoulders and thick through.

"I got the boat ready to go," Hardy went on. "I'll take you across to Fogo and you can catch a coaster into St. John's from there."

Wish scratched at his head and looked around himself, then back at Hardy. "You'll miss your father's burial," he said. He didn't understand exactly what Hardy was doing there.

Hardy took a step into the room. He reached into his pants pocket and pulled out a small handful of bills and coins. "There's enough here to get you to St. John's and keep you a little while."

Wish looked from the money to Hardy's face. "You maggoty prick."

"You don't touch it till I cut you loose in Fogo."

Wish stood still. So furious he couldn't get his breath. That they could think a lousy little bribe would be enough to send him off.

"Are you going to pack up your materials," Hardy said, "or do you want me to do it for you?"

Leaving was his plan but he wasn't about to let her mother think she'd forced him into it. He said, "I think I'll have myself a bite of breakfast."

He stepped past Hardy and started down to the kitchen. Hardy hesitated in the room behind him but came after Wish before he'd gotten halfway down the stairs, leaning out over the railing to grab the collar of his shirt.

"Fuck off," Wish shouted. He reached up and hauled Hardy by the arm, tipping him full over the rail on top of himself. And the two of them fell arse over kettle onto the landing below.

He chugged into Fogo in Aubrey's trap skiff before noon and tied up at the stage farthest from the main wharf. Two boys were fishing for conners off the end and he asked them if they knew the Cove on Little Fogo Island and how to get there. The smaller of the two said yes, everyone knew the Cove. Wish took one of the bills from his pocket and held it in the air for them to see. "Would you be able to take this skiff to the Cove today?"

"We can leave right now if you want," the smaller boy said.

"When's the next coaster heading into St. John's?"

They both pointed into the main wharf. "Earle's got one about loaded and ready to go."

Wish nodded. The Railway boats that Clive travelled on stopped in at every harbour and cove on the coast but Earle's would sail straight into St. John's. He put the dollar bill in the boy's hand.

"Whose skiff is it?"

"Parsons'," Wish said. "There's a girl," he said. "Mercedes. Sadie. Sadie Parsons."

The boys both looked at him, waiting.

"Never mind," he said. "Go on. Plenty of fuel to get you there."

Earle's coaster made St. John's at five the following morning. He'd bunked down in steerage for a while but couldn't sleep, his head travelling circles and he couldn't take a decent breath. He came out on the deck finally and stood at the rail the rest of the trip, staring blindly at the water. The headlands of the Avalon as they neared St. John's black against the night sky, like the dark height of that tidal wave coming after him years ago in Lord's

Cove, he could almost feel the tunnelling roar of it coming in over open water behind them. Glancing back as they ran, a long line of black on the horizon, travelling hard.

Wish stood at the rail of the coaster as they sailed toward the Narrows of St. John's with that same panic churning in him. A voice in his head shouting *Run. Run. Run.*

MERCEDES

—

1.

THERE HAD BEEN A TREMOR earlier that evening, Wish told her. Just before supper. The house quivering so that all the dishes shimmied off the table and the Sacred Heart pitched from the wall. His father said, "Signs and wonders before the end of time." His mother picked up the Sacred Heart and put it back in its place.

After they ate, he and his father went down to the stage to see what damage had been done there. It was coming on to dark and his father opened the stage-house doors onto the water for the last of the sunlight and lit up two torches. They found a mess of nets and gear that had dropped out of the rafters and set about clearing it away. And then the water went out of the harbour, the same as if someone had taken the plug from a sink. Wet rock and thick beds of seaweed. Skiffs and a two-masted schooner sitting on the harbour floor, still on their lines. Quiet then, every creature on God's earth gone silent.

His father turned to Wish and said, Run. Get your mother, he said, and run. He kept shouting that: Run, run, run. He'd hauled his boat up behind the stage weeks before and put her under a load of boughs for the winter and he started clearing those off, trying to get her back over on her keel, wanting to haul her far enough up the shore to save her. But he saw it was useless and gave it up, following after Wish toward the house. They met his mother on her way down to find them and looked back to the shoreline. Water sluicing into the empty harbour ahead of a dark wall bearing down on them. They lit out for the high ground among the trees, trying to outpace the roar smashing up over the wharves and houses and gardens.

She woke early to the sound of someone talking aloud in the room next to her own. Three nights in a row now she'd dreamt of the tidal wave Wish described to her—something about the blind surge of it had taken hold of her—and each morning she woke with the same amorphous sense of dread. She pushed it aside, trying to identify the sound coming through the bedroom wall.

Her grandmother.

The old woman seemed rarely to sleep at night, only drifted somewhere further off the shore of consciousness and sense. Her soliloquies indecipherable and relentless, like the burble of a rattling brook. When the old woman was in her bed downstairs it was a low murmur that was almost soothing. But through the wall beside her now it was persistent as a toothache.

It took another moment to piece together why the sound was coming from her parents' bedroom rather than downstairs. She remembered getting up from her chair when Wish left the room with Clive and all the blood draining to her feet. A smell of ammonia in her nostrils before the blackness swamped her. And now she was in bed, her grandmother mewling away in her parents' room.

Her father flashed to her mind, boxed up in the parlour, and she covered her mouth with her hand to keep from crying out. A hint of lime and putrefaction crawling in under the door. She pressed her face into her pillow to escape the smell and to muffle the sound of her crying, trying not to wake Agnes beside her. It seemed obscene to have forgotten, even those few moments after waking, that the man was dead and about to be set in the ground.

She hadn't seen Wish arrive for the wake the evening before, though she knew he'd entered the room by the pressure of her mother's hand ratcheting hold of her. Like she was about to dangle her daughter over a cliff edge. Mercedes looked up to see him across the room by the casket, having a quiet word with Clive. Hardy stood straighter beside her like some guard dog, edging sideways to block her view, and she had to fight an urge to give him a good smack in the crotch.

Mercedes had stumbled upon Hardy early on the morning after young Willard Slade's funeral. She almost fell over him in his chair as she came out the bedroom door on her way to the outhouse, his arms folded across his chest, his head crooked into the wall. She thought it was her father asleep there at first and in the few seconds it took to recognize Hardy her heart hammered oddly in her chest, as if it was operating in an empty cavity. She shook Hardy by the shoulder and called his name.

He came to his feet with a start, grabbed her by the arms. "Where are you going?" he said.

"To the backyard. To the outhouse. Where do you think I'm going this time of the night?"

He settled back, trying to overcome the startle she'd given him.

"I thought you were Father for a second."

"Didn't mean to frighten you."

"What in God's name are you doing asleep in the hall?"

"Nothing," he said. He sat back in the chair and looked up at her. "Don't you be too long out there."

It started to come clear to her then. "What are you doing here, Hardy?"

Her mother came to the door of her room in her nightdress. "Hush up Sadie. Leave your brother alone."

"This is your doing, is it?"

"Don't wake your sister."

"How long are you planning on having him stand guard on the door?"

"As long as it takes."

Mercedes felt the tears welling up and she slapped Hardy's shoulder. "He was sound asleep out here," she shouted. "I had to shake him awake. A lot of good he is to you."

"Shut up, Sadie," Hardy said.

"I could be over to Wish's place now with half my clothes off. And he'd still be sound asleep there with his mouth hung open."

Her mother said, "Go back to your room, Mercedes."

"I'm going to the outhouse."

"You got a chamber pot to take care of your business."

Hardy stood to block the way downstairs.

"Are you going to empt it for me, Hardy?"

He didn't answer. She looked back and forth from her mother to Hardy, then went into her room and slammed the door. Squatted over the pot, her legs shaking with rage. Agnes up on her elbows to see what the racket was about. Mercedes carried the honey pot out into the hall, said, "This belongs to you, does it?" and dropped it in Hardy's lap.

Hardy threw his hands up to his shoulders as if she'd set a feral cat on him. Mercedes went back into her room and slammed the door again.

Next morning at the Spell Rock she told Wish about her *confinement*.

"It's a wonder they let you out alone at all if you're as wild as that."

"Agnes is supposed to be with me. I talked her into waiting back off the path a ways. Promised I wouldn't be gone long enough to get into trouble."

She could tell he was surprised by her wilfulness, and pleased by it, by her willingness to sneak him into her life.

"I thought Hardy was my father for a second," she said. "I saw him in that chair outside the door once."

"Your father?"

"The night he went missing." She looked at him shyly. "Nan was calling for water downstairs and I got up to look in on her. And Father was sitting in the chair outside the door."

"Did you tell your mother about it?"

"I haven't mentioned it to a soul, till now. He was soaking wet, Wish. Every stitch of clothes he had on was dripping water."

"Did he say anything?"

"I tried to talk to him but he was gone after a second."

He surprised her by smiling then, although there was nothing dismissive in it. He had a strangely attractive face, large soft eyes, a long lower jaw and the chin just off centre. There was something vaguely equine about it, about the way his head moved as he listened, sudden sideways motions, an exaggerated lifting of the chin when she said something unexpected. Mercedes was uncomfortable around horses, she distrusted their size and slow walk, the crooked limb of their cocks almost touching the ground as they grazed, their wet eyes that seemed bottomless. She couldn't explain why the look of Wish calmed her.

She said, "That was Father's fetch, wasn't it? He's dead, isn't he?"

"I expect he is."

She realized she was crying and wiped at her face with her hands, then they sat with their foreheads touching. She loved the smell of his breath, the changing layers and undertones in it. Tobacco and ginger. Sugared tea. Raisins. She adjusted her breathing to take in his exhalations as they sat there, as if there was some strength she could draw from it.

She tried to recall that smell now with her face pressed into her pillow, trying not to wake Agnes beside her, not wanting Hardy to hear her outside the door. A tremor shook through her that she couldn't name. Grief, for certain, and wanting to touch Wish and have him touch her, anger and fear and anticipation, exhaustion, she couldn't separate the different strands and felt them corkscrew through her as one thing. She had never felt more alive.

When Wish and Clive left the parlour during the wake, she knew they were heading outside for a smoke and a mouthful of shine. Her mother yanked her back by the arm when she stood to follow them.

"Not while your father lies there," Helen had whispered to her. "Don't you dare."

She was stung by the accusation in the woman's voice. Felt for the first time that Helen's decision to stand between her and Wish was somehow a dismissal of Mercedes' love for her father as well. She pulled her hand free, intending to follow Wish out the door. And that sour stench of ammonia struck her, rising up through her head before she passed out on the floor.

It felt like a failure of nerve, a kind of cowardice to have fainted away when so much was at stake. She got up from the bed quietly and dressed. A line was drawn and she'd been too fearful to cross it. But she promised herself she wouldn't waver after her father was buried.

When she opened her bedroom door Hardy was not in the chair. She stood and looked at it awhile, picturing her father there in his soaking clothes, his hair plastered flat against his head. He had nodded at her and half smiled. She had spoken his name aloud, and the sound of her voice in the empty hall had spooked her. She'd glanced over her shoulder toward her parents' bedroom and he was gone.

She made her way downstairs and found her mother alone in the parlour, sitting at the head of her father's casket. She was dressed in the same mourning clothes she'd been wearing the evening before and seemed not to have slept at all.

"Where's the prison guard this morning?"

"Stoke up the fire, would you, Sadie? I'm dying for a cup of tea."

"That's not an answer."

Her mother looked into her lap. She said, "You know it would never work, Mercedes. That boy here in the Cove."

"It wouldn't break my heart to leave."

"You'd just wind up in another cove. No different than this one."

"It would have him," she said.

Helen smiled. "You're just a child, Mercedes. I won't let you throw yourself away."

A panic kicked up in her stomach. "Where's Hardy?"

"The boat went out of the harbour an hour ago."

She spun away from the woman. "You *witch*," she said. She went to the kitchen and straight out the door. A handful of men at the wharf nodded as she hurried past. Her father's trap skiff gone from its mooring beyond the stagehead.

She burst into the back kitchen at Mrs. Gillard's to find Hardy at the table, his head propped on one hand. He didn't look up when Mercedes came in.

"What did you do to him?" she shouted.

Mrs. Gillard was standing over against the stove. "Sadie," she whispered. She nodded at Hardy. "He was lying on the floor dead to the world when I come in. Couldn't get a rise out of him before I put the salts to his nose."

"What did you do to him, Hardy?"

"Sadie?" he said. It seemed to cause him pain to move even that much and he grimaced against it. There was blood on his mouth.

"That laddio of yours tried to kill Hardy," Mrs. Gillard said.

Mercedes ignored her and leaned in close to Hardy at the table. "The boat is gone from the mooring."

He turned his body to face her more directly. "What boat?"

"The trap skiff. She's not on her mooring."

Mrs. Gillard said, "He stole your father's boat?"

"Hardy?"

Her brother's face was blank and his eyes wandered about in an unfocused way. "He must have decided to go out after a few fish," he said.

Mercedes thought he was making fun of her. She was so furious she felt light-headed. A rush of ammonia in her nostrils and she grabbed Hardy's shoulder to keep from falling. "You did this," she shouted.

Mrs Gillard said, "He pushed your brother down those stairs, Sadie. And he stole your father's boat and run off."

She was already at the door.

"He tried to kill your brother," Mrs. Gillard insisted.

"I only wish," she said.

They had to take out the parlour window to carry the coffin from the house. A horse-drawn cart was waiting on the path, the piebald mare stamping her feet as the casket was settled aboard. Mercedes kept a little apart from her mother and Hardy, who walked arm-in-arm toward the church, the entire community in procession behind them. They'd delayed the funeral until Hardy was well enough to keep his feet and even now Helen appeared to be holding him upright against a persistent list in his step.

Mercedes had been watching from her bedroom window when Hardy was helped home late that morning and saw her mother run out to meet him. She greeted him with a stream of questions that Mercedes couldn't make out, though the urgency and surprise in them was obvious. Hardy mostly shook his head and looked confused about what his own name might be.

Agnes wept all the way to the church and through the funeral, where Willard Slade led the hymns and Mrs. Gillard read from the Psalms. She was still crying now as her father was set into the ground, the casket scraping at the earth walls, the

weight of him arching the backs of the pallbearers as they lowered him down. Mercedes felt strangely empty of emotion
herself. She looked down across the scrabble of houses and sheds
and stages of the Cove, the buildings balanced over bald rock on
wooden pilings and stilts. None of it looked substantial enough
to stay upright in a decent wind. If a wave swept them away, she
thought, there wouldn't be so much as a foundation to leave a
mark on the place.

As they filed out of the cemetery she saw her father's trap skiff
come into the harbour, a rowing punt attached by a line at the
stern. There were two figures aboard of her but she knew in her
heart that Wish wasn't one of them.

In the days after the funeral Hardy slept a good part of every day
and complained of headaches and became nauseous at the slightest physical exertion. Helen sat beside him on the daybed and
catered to his every need, but Mercedes wouldn't so much as bring
him a glass of water. She refused to ask either of them what had
happened or where Wish had ended up, though at night she plied
Agnes for whatever information she might have.

"They don't tell me anything, Sadie. You know that."

"You must have overheard something, Agnes, for God's sake,
have you got ears?"

"I'm only in the same house as you."

"You've never heard them mention his name?"

Agnes turned onto her side away from her sister.

"I knew it," Mercedes whispered. "I knew it." She grabbed
Agnes by the shoulder and shook her. "What did they say?"

"He took some money off of Hardy."

"What money?"

"I don't know, Sadie."

"What was Hardy doing over to Mrs. Gillard's that morning
anyway?"

"He was supposed to take Wish to Fogo. But he don't remember anything after going upstairs at Mrs. Gillard's to get him out of bed."

Mercedes rolled onto her back and lay there with her hands folded over her chest. "Why did he take the boat and go on his own?"

"I don't *know*," Agnes said, almost in tears.

"I wasn't talking to you. I was only thinking."

Agnes wormed all the way to her edge of the bed. "Think in your head then, would you? Not out loud."

After supper the next evening, Mercedes walked across the Cove to Clive's house. She found Clive's wife at the dishes in the pantry.

"Come in, my love," Jenny Reid said. "Come in."

"Where are your boys?"

"Down at the Spell Rock, I imagine. Looking for trouble."

"I was after Clive. Is he not around either?"

Jenny wiped her wet hands in her apron. "Clive is up at the still."

She went along the path that ran between the neat square of outbuildings and on up to a tiny shed beyond them, half hidden in a swale. She found Clive stoking a fire under a large copper pot held together with rivets. When he caught sight of Mercedes in the door he glanced past her a second. A look something like dismay crossed his face when he realized she was there to see him alone. But he waved her toward a low bench set against the wall. She didn't speak, letting him carry on at the fire.

Clive stood straight after a few minutes. He said, "There's nothing I can do for you, Sadie."

"I got no one else to ask, Clive. You were good to him."

"He was a nice young fellow, you wants my opinion."

"Do you know where he got to?"

"Went back to St. John's, I'd say."

"But *why*?" She slapped her thigh to emphasize the word.

89

"You're afraid he give up on you."

She nodded.

"He didn't strike me as someone who turned that easy."

She had been holding her breath and let it out suddenly. "So whatever sent him away," she said, "will keep him away."

"I imagine."

"What should I do?"

Clive stepped to the door, looked down the path and then out across the hill toward the opposite side of the Cove. "The walls have got ears around here," he said. He smiled at her a moment, but couldn't hold her eye.

It was the first time they'd been alone in one another's company since the previous fall, a soft September evening when they crossed paths near the Spell Rock. He'd been drinking, but only enough to feel giddy with it. He'd bowed to Mercedes and called her Missus, danced her in the grass, singing a few lines of "The Tennessee Waltz." She could hardly stand for laughing at him. He stopped suddenly, still holding her, and the way Clive looked at her made Mercedes want to pull away. He leaned down to her face. Smell of alcohol and chewing tobacco, a rough brush of whisker. He backed off and they stood watching each other another moment before he stepped in again, kissing her for real this time. Mercedes opened her mouth to him as he seemed to want, slipping her arms around his neck. His tongue touching hers and she was surprised and appalled and afraid she might buckle to the ground if she let go.

Clive came up for air finally, hauling her arms from his shoulders. "Jesus, Jesus," he said. He walked away from her, his gait intent and peculiarly hunched, as if he was trying to disguise a wound. Mercedes stood watching him go, her belly a wasps' nest. She spent weeks afterwards wondering if she liked being kissed by Clive. Decided eventually she did not, though she had to admit it was Clive and not the kissing itself she had reservations about.

They'd never spoken of the incident, though it coloured every word that passed between them. She could see now that Clive had been relieved to see her with Wish. As if it might absolve him of some responsibility or debt.

She said, "I have to get to St. John's."

He took up a wooden ladle, poking half-heartedly at the liquid in the pot. "The minister was up to see me after we buried young Willard Slade. He warned me off interfering."

"Tell me how I get to St. John's. That's all I'm asking."

"I got to live here after you go, Sadie."

"Please."

He walked to the door and stood looking out at the Cove as he spoke. "You have to get across to Fogo. Steal the boat is your best bet, same as Wish."

"I don't know how to get to Fogo, Clive."

"You come over with us to the shows last summer. It haven't moved anywhere. Make way round the headland for your father's trap berth. Keep her steady sou'east from there and you'll hit Fogo Island by and by. Keep close to the shoreline, first place you'll see is Barr'd Islands at the head of a bay, next along after that is Fogo. Someone over that way can bring the skiff back. You'll need money to get a coastal boat into town."

"How much?"

"A dollar fifty for steerage, last I heard. But it could be more by now. Everything's gone to hell since the war. Do you know anyone in St. John's, Sade?"

"I knows Hiram."

Clive looked at her. "Jesus loves the little children," he said.

That night she confessed her plan to Agnes. She suspected her sister was a little in love with Wish herself and decided to trust her on that possibility alone.

Ag lifted up on one elbow. "How are you going to get to town?"

"Leave that to me. But I need your help, Ag. In the morning when they miss me, tell them I went off to Gooseberry Cove before light."

"Why would you go there?"

"I was in a state, tell them. Woke up from a bad dream. Just wanted to be off on my own awhile."

Agnes lay back on the bed and snuggled into her sister's shoulder. "They'll miss the boat, Sadie. First thing."

She was about to deny the boat was part of the plan but knew it was useless. It was always a surprise to her, that the girl was smarter than she was.

"You could head out on a Sunday," Ag suggested. "That'll give you an hour or two longer before anyone is likely to be on the water. No one might take note till after church."

"Sunday," Mercedes said. "That's when it'll be."

"Have you got any money, Sade?"

"Shut up, Agnes," she said.

"What's wrong with you, child?"

Mercedes had thought her grandmother was asleep or drifting in her own world and she looked up quickly at the sound of her voice. They hadn't exchanged so much as a hello since she sat down with the pan of warm water and untied the ribbon at the front of the old woman's nightdress.

"Nothing's wrong," she said.

"You're a shocking liar."

Mercedes tipped her head to the ceiling a moment. "S'pose I am."

"What's your name, my duck?"

"Sadie," she said. "Mercedes."

"Mercedes," Sarah repeated and tossed her head at the strangeness of it.

She could feel her grandmother watching her as she carried

on washing the pale grey arms. The body in her hands was limp, lifeless, and it seemed as if the old woman had for the moment retreated entirely into the unblinking blue eyes.

Sarah said, "I knows what's wrong with you."

"What's that now?"

"You're in love."

"You think so, do you?"

"You're like a waterlogged punt, you are. Plemmed tight with it."

There was sometimes a disconcerting coherence to the old woman's delusions. She mistook family for strangers or thought herself decades younger than her age and yet somehow managed to be uncommonly lucid and perceptive, almost by way of compensation.

"You don't let it go by," she said. "That's my advice to you. Look at me now. I knew love, though you'd never say it by the sight of me." She dipped her chin toward her naked torso, the breasts gone away almost to nothing, the dark nipples facing opposite points of the compass. "You'll lie here one day too," her grandmother said, "guaranteed." It was a simple statement of fact she was making and there was nothing self-pitying in it. "Don't let love go by if it's close enough to grab ahold to."

Mercedes looked behind herself to the bedroom door. "I need some money," she said. "I have to get to St. John's."

"Is that where your man is to?"

She nodded.

"Does he treat you right?"

"Yes."

"Is he willing to marry you?"

"I think he is," she said. "Yes, he is."

Sarah smiled at her. "This was our bed, you know. Mine and Gasker's. I stayed in it years after he died. Until Aubrey got married." She looked up over her head as best she could, toward the

93

wrought-iron frame. She pointed unsteadily to the left bedpost. "You have a look up there."

The knob came free, and stuffed in the hollow bedpost was a parcel tightly wrapped in brown paper. Her grandmother tapped the covers. "Set it here," she said. "Take off the string."

Inside was a roll of Newfoundland bills, ones and twos, a five. A handful of coins in wax paper. The wedding ring her grandmother had taken off the day her husband was buried and never wore again.

Sarah looked at her with a coy pride. "I adds a note or two whenever I manage to scrounge one."

Mercedes imagined the old woman was happy to keep this one piece of her daughter-in-law's marriage bed to herself, that it gave her some perverse pleasure to claim a piece of that privacy. Her grandmother's dislike for Helen was exhaustive. She disapproved of her cooking, her dress, her manner with company, her lack of attentiveness in church. Helen was no limp rag of a woman and even Sarah had to credit her on that account: she never whined. But she was a newcomer to the Cove, and even after years in the community Mercedes could sense that her mother kept to herself in some significant way. It was her solitariness that made her seem vulnerable, and her grandmother picked at that scab relentlessly. Until the illness overtook the old woman and her mind shifted. Almost overnight she began demanding Helen's attention and was dissatisfied with other company. She could turn on anyone else without warning, using a tongue so foul that Agnes would run from the room in tears.

"That woman is possessed, is what she is," her mother said one evening while they sat in the back kitchen, Sarah shouting obscenities through the wall.

"Don't be talking any papist foolishness in this house," her father said.

"I'm only saying."

Mercedes couldn't help but agree with her mother when the old woman was in one of her states. But this morning she was sanguine, buoyant, eerily reasonable. She pointed at the roll of bills by her side on the bed. "You take what you needs," she said. "And the ring. You tell your man who give it to you. Sarah Parsons, you tell him. From Little Fogo Island."

Mercedes counted out ten dollars—seven in bills and three in change—and returned the rest of the roll without counting how much was there. She turned the ring over in her hand—a simple gold band, engraved with her grandmother's initials.

"Try it on," Sarah said.

"Are you sure you want me to take it, Nan?"

"What did you say your name was, child?"

"Mercedes," she said. "Sade. Your granddaughter. Don't you know me?"

"When I gets up out of this bed," Sarah said, "I'm going to have some feed of potatoes."

"Nan?"

But the old woman was somewhere else already. Mercedes tucked the ring into the bundle and set it all in the hollow of the bedpost where she'd found it. Then she took her handful of money and the pan of water off the floor and left the room.

It was hours to daylight still when she walked out on the stagehead and brought the trap skiff in off her mooring, hauling the wet twine hand over hand. Not a whisper of wind, as if the Cove was holding its breath for her. A sliver of moon on its back overhead, one star hung beneath it like a hook drifting on a line. She couldn't start the engine before she cleared the Cove, put out the oars instead and pulled against the weight of the boat, taking her head around and moving for open water. The skiff was a fourteen-footer and not built for a single hand to row. But for the tide being with her she'd have made no headway at all. It felt to her like the world's slowest escape.

She had gone up to the cemetery the previous afternoon to visit her father's grave, to say a second goodbye in the space of a week, and it surprised her by feeling more final. "I'm going," she said aloud. "I'm leaving the Cove." As if she had to give him a chance to show some sign he objected. Her father had never offered Mercedes much in the way of advice on any subject. Her grandmother gave enough of that to do them both. As a rule, he made his views known with the subtlest change in his posture, inching a mug of tea right or left on the table in front of him, tipping his head, pursing his lips.

There was only one occasion when Aubrey had given her a talking to. He'd come home drunk after the rest of the house had gone to bed. Mercedes was still awake and waited to hear him come up the stairs. Went down to the back kitchen finally to see what was keeping him. He was on the daybed, still in his coat and boots, snoring softly. She had never seen him drunk before, could smell the alcohol on his breath as she hauled the boots off his feet. He woke when she lifted him forward, trying to get his coat free of an arm.

"My darling girl," he said.

"Be quiet a minute, I gets this coat off."

His head drooped on his shoulders as she hauled at the jacket.

"Where were you tonight?"

"Down at Clive's stage." He giggled. "Having a chat."

It wasn't two weeks after Clive had kissed her and the mention of his name made her blush. She said, "You'd best sleep here tonight."

"I'll have a word." He sat straighter, taking his coat off himself. "Before I sleep, I'll have a word."

"As long as it's a quiet one."

He rambled on a few minutes then, without ever stating his subject clearly. "You keep a fellow with that business on his mind at arm's length," he told her. "A man will say anything to a woman to get it, as sure as there's shit in a cat. And the sweeter the words out of his mouth, the darker the hole they comes from. Mind I don't know," he said.

He stopped there awhile and his head drooped forward again.

"All right," Mercedes said, thinking he was finished. "Lie back now."

He lifted his head and said, "Don't let a man make a whore of you, Sadie."

She was a young woman before she began to see how effective her father's more subtle approach had been, noticing how often she asked herself what her father might think before she made any decision, picturing how he'd bob his head to indicate approval or doubt. When she made up her mind to leave the Cove, she felt almost as if it was a choice she'd made in consultation with the man, with his blessing. But that certainty left her in the cemetery, standing over the mound of fresh dirt.

She faced the houses and stages as she rowed away from them, all of the buildings hunkered in the black of night, only the barest outlines visible to her. When she reached the mouth of the harbour she set the oars along the tauts and took a moment to catch her wind, the boat rocking on the heavier swell of open water. She stared hard at the south side where the house she'd grown up in stood, hoping for a last glimpse. But it was buried completely in the dark and already lost to her.

She stood over the trap skiff's engine and set it running, the sudden noise of it in the stillness almost knocking her over. Sat at the tiller and steered into the open air away from the shoreline, making for the headland lying southeast.

2.

IT WAS PELTING IN ST. JOHN'S, the rain falling in drifts against the buildings on Water Street. She stood under a store awning that offered only intermittent protection. The shop window crowded with fresh apples. Inside she could see wood stoves, dishware, the rafters hung with cast-iron pots and buckets. Cars and trucks rattled past in both directions, throwing up showers of water onto the sidewalks. A coal cart stood nearby, the horse tethered to a light post, the blinkered animal shying from the rumble of the streetcar as it passed. A group of soldiers came half running along the sidewalk, their heads bent against the rain. No one paid her the slightest mind.

She'd marked the twin towers of the Basilica on the north side of the harbour as the coaster followed the pilot through the Narrows. Planned to use it like a compass in the city, taking her bearings from the spires, but it was invisible to her now. Clive had offered some rudimentary directions to Hiram's storefront from a trip he'd made years before—straight up the hill from the water, he'd said, a little jog east from the Kirk, if you come up against the Basilica you've gone too far. They were exactly the kind of directions he'd given her to Fogo but they seemed useless by comparison.

She couldn't see anything north or south but the buildings on either side of the street and she felt as blinkered as the horse beside her. All along Water Street roads rose away from the harbour. They couldn't all lead to Hiram. Even if she found his place on her own there was a chance that he might be off on one of his trips along the coast and gone a week or longer. And Wish likely with him.

"Now, Mercedes," she said aloud. She clutched her bundle of clothes to her chest. The shops full of people and for the first time in her life she was too shy to say hello to a soul. "What have you got yourself into here?"

She was too cold to stand still any longer and stepped out from under the awning, walking east simply because there was more of the street ahead in that direction. Her head down against the rain. She glanced up the hill at each cross street until she caught sight of the Basilica above her and turned up the steep grade. There was a massive red-brick church in sight that she assumed was the Presbyterian church, and she turned east again as she came near it, walking to a corner where half a dozen streets came together in a twisted clover. Rain ran out of her hair and she wiped at her face to keep her eyes clear. Cars stuttered through potholes beside her, soaking her already soaked clothing, the filthy rainwater flooding into her shoes. The maze of streets made no sense.

A man wearing an officer's hat stood changing the lone traffic signal in a booth at the centre of the clover. She made several false starts out into traffic before she finally ran between the moving vehicles to reach him.

"You'll get yourself killed like that," he said.

"I'm looking for Hiram," she announced. "He runs the movies along the coast."

"Hiram Keeping?"

"You know him?"

"Everyone knows Hiram," he said.

His directions made no sense to her. He was pointing and naming streets, intersections. "Your first time to town, is it?" he asked. He changed the lights, and cars began moving around them from opposite directions. He looked past her, frustrated. Called to a young woman hurrying along the sidewalk. "Amy," he said, waving. "Amy, come here, I wants you."

She was wearing a headscarf against the rain. Black hair and brown eyes. A hint of something foreign in the face, in the colour of her skin, which made Mercedes apprehensive.

The man in the hat said, "This young one is after Hiram Keeping. Drop her by his place, would you?"

Hiram's shop was a house-front in Georgestown. There was no sign to say what the place was. A fusty acid smell inside, a permanent gloom from the barred windows. Mercedes could see a counter strewn with film canisters, several box cameras on tripods. A small office through a doorway beside the stairs, a crowded desk.

Hiram came down the stairs in a rush, looking like he'd woken from a nap. "Hello, Amy," he said.

"I brought someone wants to talk to you, Hiram."

"Who would that be now?"

"It's Mercedes, Hiram." She stepped forward. "Mercedes Parsons."

Hiram dipped his head and began tapping his pants pockets front and back as if he was looking for glasses or tobacco. "Mercedes Parsons," he said without looking up at her.

"Sadie. From Little Fogo," she said. "Is Wish here with you? He run off in Father's trap skiff as far as Fogo and got on a coaster for St. John's. This was a week ago now. I come looking for him."

Hiram walked through to the office. Mercedes followed after him and stopped in the doorway, watching as he poured a finger of whisky. She heard the water from her soaked clothes raining onto the hardwood floor and a clacking noise it took her a moment to recognize as her teeth chattering.

"Anyone else come down here with you, Sadie?"

"I come on my own."

"I don't know where he is." He looked at her directly. "I'm sorry for your loss. But I can't be no help to you where Wish is concerned."

Mercedes was trembling with the cold.

"I haven't got a thing to tell you," Hiram said.

Amy came down the hall and took Mercedes' arm. "Let's go," she whispered.

Mercedes pulled free. "Wish didn't come to see you at all? He's not upstairs, is he?"

Amy tugged at Mercedes' arm again, headed to the front door holding the sleeve of her coat.

"I didn't mean no harm to anyone," Hiram called after them.

The two girls stood outside, the rain still coming down hard. Mercedes looking up and down the nameless street.

Amy said, "You don't know a soul in town, do you."

Mercedes shook her head.

Amy took her arm and headed back the way they'd come. Mercedes was aware of being led and paid no attention to their route, asked no questions. They walked to the back entrance of a dry-goods shop that led straight up to the kitchen and Amy sat Mercedes in a rocking chair beside a coal stove. Amy shooed away two children at the table and she followed them upstairs.

The kitchen was dominated by a table that seated eight or more. The air close with heat and the smell from a pot simmering on the stove. Mutton, though she couldn't identify any of the spices that accompanied it. She rocked in her chair. She didn't know what it meant that Wish hadn't returned to St. John's or had returned without visiting Hiram. Or that Hiram had lied to her. She'd imagined a straightforward reunion with Wish and had no clue what to do now.

A middle-aged man came into the kitchen from the storefront and stopped when he saw her. A large moustache and hair darker than any Mercedes had ever seen, so black it seemed to gleam. She was sodden, her hair loose, long strands of it lying flat against her forehead and cheeks.

"A terrible day," the man said.

The way he said "terrible" struck her, it was as if there was something lodged under his tongue. The jet-black hair. There was something vaguely threatening in his manner, his peculiar accent.

"You must have come far," the man said.

She nodded.

He shouted up the stairs in a language not English. He said, "Where do you live, miss?"

"Little Fogo Island."

The man's eyebrows lifted in surprise.

"I left," she said by way of explanation. "I ran away."

The girl and another woman came down the stairs. Amy was carrying a towel and an armful of dry clothes. She exchanged a few incomprehensible words with the man, who turned to Mercedes and said, "This is my niece Amina," as if a formal introduction was required.

"That coat is sopping," Amy said. Pure Newfoundland in her accent. "Strip it off."

"She has run away," her uncle announced. "A refugee, yes?" he said to Mercedes, smiling at her.

"What's your name?" the other woman asked her.

"Mercedes Parsons."

Amina was on her knees, wrenching off her shoes. Mercedes leaned forward and whispered, "Is he a Portugee?"

"We're from Lebanon," she said. She smiled up at Mercedes, her hands squeezing one foot to bring some warmth back into it. "This is my uncle Sammy."

"It is not quite," Amina's uncle said. He wrote letters in the air. "S-A-M-A-R," he said. "Samar. But in your country it is Sammy."

At intervals children of various ages came into the kitchen to watch her where she sat.

"Are they all yours?" Mercedes asked the woman.

"Four of them are ours. The rest are nieces and nephews."

"We hope for more," Sammy said.

"*You* hope for more," his wife said. She was a strikingly tall woman, the same height as her husband. She was fair-skinned and nearly blonde, and though she spoke Arabic with her husband and Amina, her English was differently accented again.

"It is God's will for us, Maya," he insisted.

"Let God do some of the work, then."

They were both smiling as they argued.

"I should have known better," Sammy said, "than to marry a Jew."

"An Irish Jew at that," Maya added, to emphasize the severity of his mistake.

"It was the music," he said. "I married my wife for these. You know these Irish songs?" he asked Mercedes. He sang the opening lines of "Carrickfergus" in a high, sweet tenor and every trace of his accent disappeared.

The smell of the room struck Mercedes again, the strangeness of it in relation to the music. Her grandmother had told her once that Catholic saints were identified by the sweet smell rising off the body after death. She'd meant it as another example of how ridiculous a faith it was, something to set alongside the notion of transubstantiation and limbo, all that kneeling and crossing yourself and dousing the church with holy water. But there was something in the idea that seemed true to Mercedes. That the soul of a thing existed in the scent of it. It was one of the ways she judged everything she encountered, the sense she trusted most. She was always lifting things to her nose to smell them, to place them.

The aroma from the stove was sweet and sour at once and altogether foreign to her. And that foreignness overwhelmed her suddenly. As if she'd surrendered her world for one so utterly different she would never understand it. She started to cry, and Sammy broke off mid-verse, his hands held in the air.

"You," Maya said, pointing at him, "leave us women alone."

And he went out the door to the storefront, muttering in his own language.

By the time they had dressed her in dry clothing and wrapped her in a blanket by the stove, the room had begun to fill with other adults, all with the same black hair, all speaking Arabic. She was introduced to each of them as they arrived, the men returning from the shipyard at the west end of the harbour, the women from custodial jobs at the Canadian army base. They greeted Mercedes as if they'd been expecting to find her there. They were all physically striking. Their skin seemed to shine as if they'd been dipped in oil.

Amina's parents were both slender and fragile looking, though there was a palpable air of energy about them that contradicted that impression. Tony Basha was nearly bald and sported a pencil-thin moustache.

"This is the girl you reduced to tears, Sammy?" he asked.

Rania sat beside Mercedes and held her hand in her lap while Amina gave an account of her presence in the house. Amina seemed hardly more than a few years older than her daughter.

"You are here all alone?" Rania asked.

Mercedes nodded.

"How old are you?"

"Sixteen, miss. How old are you?"

Rania smiled. Her top teeth looked too large for her mouth, Mercedes thought, and they protruded slightly. But this fact didn't alter the beauty of her face. "Such a rude question to ask a lady."

Before she thought to hold her tongue Mercedes said, "You asked me."

"So I did. I asked you. You had the right. But I won't be foolish enough to answer." She looked intently at Mercedes, her face serious. "I think," she said, "you are in trouble. With this boy, Wish. Is that right?"

Mercedes looked from Rania to Amina.

Rania said, "Wish has gotten you into trouble and run away from you."

"No."

Rania started over. "He left before you knew about your trouble. And you have come to tell him."

"No," Mercedes said. "Nothing like that."

The two women beside her exchanged glances. Rania said, "What will you do if you find this boy?"

"We'll get married."

"And what will you do," she said, "what will you do if you don't find him?"

Mercedes said, "I—" Realized she'd never allowed herself to consider the possibility. She said, "I'll wait for him."

Rania nodded. "I hope, in that case, that you find him. I would hate to see you waste your life waiting."

The crowd at the supper table was raucous; they talked with their hands and shouted. Mercedes couldn't say from one moment to the next if they were arguing or joking. She barely touched her food. She felt completely wrung out and was still shaking with a chill. Her father dead and buried and she couldn't possibly go home. She bowed her head over her plate and began crying again.

"You see," Sammy said, gesturing with both hands. "I did nothing."

"Shut up, Samar," Maya said.

Rania and Amina took Mercedes up the stairs and tucked her into a single bed. Amina sat beside her until she settled, drifted mercifully into sleep.

The house was quiet when she woke. Sunlight through the window where the curtain was drawn back. The peacefulness of it lulled her a moment. She turned over and nearly dozed off again until she placed herself. She threw the bedsheets off. Still wearing the dress they'd given her after stripping her out of her own clothes.

Amina and Maya were hanging laundry off the back bridge when she came downstairs. Rows and rows of clotheslines weighted down with laundry behind the houses. Drift of coal smoke, the steady noise of traffic.

Mercedes watched them until they took note of her there. She said, "I think I'll take a walk."

"Where to?" Maya asked.

She shrugged. Could just see the nub of Signal Hill above the line of laundry. "Up there," she said. Just to have a destination.

Maya said, "Amina will show you the way."

Mercedes had been hoping to sneak off alone but didn't know how to say so without insulting their generosity. "That would be nice," she said.

The road to Signal Hill was surprisingly steep and meandering. Military vehicles lumbered past them. Soldiers waved and whistled from the bed of a truck struggling against the grade and the girls had to slow their pace to put some distance between them. The mid-morning sun lit up the houses clinging to the Battery. The bare rock as red as wet clay.

"My mother says this light is the closest she'll ever get to Lebanon," Amina said.

"Where is Lebanon to?"

"Do you know where Jesus is from?"

"From Bethlehem. From Galilee."

"It's over that way."

"The Holy Lands?"

Amina nodded her head.

"Why did you leave the Holy Lands for this place?"

"We're Christians."

"That don't seem reason enough."

"Things were bad for us there. That's all I know. I was just a baby."

They didn't say another word until they reached Cabot Tower and looked back out over the city. The harbour crowded with steamers and navy vessels, two-masted schooners with their sails raised to dry in the sun. Mercedes had always thought of the Holy Lands in the same way she imagined the Garden of Eden, a real place but lost in time now. Inviolable, inaccessible to living, breathing human beings. Things were bad in the Holy Lands, Amina had said. It made Mercedes' own troubles seem trifling and altogether hopeless.

"What are you going to do now?" Amina asked.

"I don't know," she said. She wished she had Agnes to talk to, to suggest a way forward. All around them red-rock cliffs sheered hundreds of feet to the ocean and she felt the dark tug of that drop. It was a momentary notion but altogether compelling.

Amina put her hand on Mercedes' arm, as if she saw the thought pass across her face. She said, "Wish isn't from town, is he?"

"No," Mercedes said. "He's from Renews." It was a moment longer before she saw what the girl was suggesting. "You think that's where he went?"

"Someone might have news at least."

"I don't," Mercedes said, still trying to take in the simple common sense of the idea, "I don't know how to get there."

"Let me talk to my mother."

Rania set her folded hands under her chin, her eyes on a point over the heads of the two girls. Everyone else around the table gone silent while she considered.

"It isn't right to let a girl run wild around the country," she said.

Amina put a hand on Mercedes' arm to keep her quiet.

"Has Wish got family out there?" Rania asked.

"His parents are dead for long ago," Mercedes said. "He lived there with his aunt for a while after his mother passed on." That was everything she knew of Lilly. It made her suddenly apprehensive, seeing how deliberately Wish had neglected her in their conversations, looking ahead to meeting the woman.

Rania nodded. Said, "Let me think about it."

Mercedes bit her lip. Looked to Amina, who was smiling down at her plate. "But," she said.

Amina pinched her thigh to shut her up. When Mercedes reached to push her away they locked hands under the table, Amina glancing sidelong to warn her, reassure her. Bullying in exactly the same fashion Mercedes would have treated her younger sister.

"I'll think about it," Rania said again.

Amina squeezed Mercedes' hand once more and got up to clear the table.

The men left the house in a group while the dishes were being done. They carried black cases so oddly shaped that Mercedes could not begin to guess what they held.

"Do you like to dance?" Maya asked her.

The dance hall was the largest room Mercedes had ever been inside. She could just see a stage at the far end over the crowd. A drifting fog of cigarette smoke hung in the air and it looked as if the band was standing behind a gauze curtain. Most of the men in the room wore uniforms of one kind or another, Canadian or British, a handful of Americans. A table was cleared for them at the front, just below the stage where the Basha men stood in white tuxedos and black ties. Their hair was pomaded flat against their heads. The bass drum read *The Basha Orchestra*. Sammy nodded at them over his guitar.

Amina had done Mercedes' face before they left the house, applying blush and eye shadow and lipstick in front of a dresser mirror. Mercedes had never worn makeup and she was startled by the change. No one from the Cove would recognize her, she was sure. And the physical transformation seemed to suit her circumstances.

Rania ordered soft drinks and leaned across to shout into Mercedes' ear. "If you want to dance, I will find a gentleman to take you out."

Mercedes didn't recognize the music or the choreographed motions of the dancers. The crowded room made her feel claustrophobic. The coloured lights and smoke put her in mind of the hell her grandmother was fond of describing. She said, "I don't want to dance."

"You say that now," Rania said.

The song ended and Tony Basha spent a few moments talking to the audience. Mercedes strained to make out what he was saying, but the amplified muffle of his voice was indecipherable through the noise of the crowd. Tony extended an arm to a corner of the stage and a young man in uniform walked across to join the band, a trumpet held at his thigh.

She leaned into Amina. "Who is he?" she asked.

"Johnny Boustani. He's an American."

Rania said, "He's a good Lebanese boy."

Johnny Boustani looked completely out of place in his drab uniform, standing sideways to the microphone so he looked not part of the band or the audience but in a world all his own. He was smiling to himself and he waited as the song rolled ahead without him, the trumpet held loosely at his hip until the second before he started to play.

Mercedes knew nothing of music beyond the hymns she'd heard in church and the scatter ballad sung *a cappella* in the back kitchen. She had no idea what to call the sound coming from Johnny Boustani's instrument. Listening to him reminded her of the first time she'd tasted an apple when she was five years old, a minor sensual epiphany. The music was that sweet and clean.

When he finished his set with the band, Johnny Boustani came to the table. "From Pennsylvania," Rania said and she repeated her earlier assessment. "A good Lebanese boy."

Johnny nodded and smiled without saying a word. He looked much younger than Mercedes had first thought and he sat with his shoulders hunched high as if he was warding off a chill.

"Johnny is here with the U.S. Army Engineers," Rania said. "To put in the base."

"Communications," he said. "I'm just a communications officer." He was being self-effacing out of habit, Mercedes could see.

"I have a proposal for you, Johnny Boustani," Rania said.

"Yes, ma'am."

"You have some leave available?"

"Things are always pretty slow down at Communications." He couldn't help himself.

"How would you like to chaperone two young women on an overnight trip to the Southern Shore?"

"Which young women would I be chaperoning, exactly?"

"She will insist on going," Rania said. "But I won't allow her to go alone." She turned to Mercedes. "Amina will go with you. And Johnny Boustani, if he agrees"—she smiled at him—"will accompany you both."

Mercedes sat back in her chair, trying to disguise a look of consternation. *Who are these people?* she wondered. And beneath the worry, a growing sense of relief to be so unexpectedly watched over.

Johnny Boustani arrived to collect them in full uniform. Green melton jacket, cotton shirt and green woollen tie. The buttons on his jacket were polished and his boots gleamed black. But the army hat looked a little like an overturned dory on his head. It made him look like a boy playing at being a soldier. Rania offered a list of instructions to him on demeanour and comportment as they went out the door. Johnny nodded and said "Yes, ma'am" to every one.

They stood at the railing as the coaster sailed through the Narrows into open water. The girls both wore overcoats against the first real chill of the fall. Johnny wore only his army jacket.

"You must be cold," Amina said to him. "Go on in out of the wind."

He said, "How could I be cold in the company of two beautiful women?"

"You're not going to make a liar of my mother, are you, Johnny?"

"Absolutely not. No." He cleared his throat. "Anyone going to tell me what this trip is all about?"

Mercedes said, "How long have you been playing the trumpet, Johnny Boustani?" She couldn't bring herself to separate *Johnny* from *Boustani*. It was the childishness of the rhyme she liked, how perfectly it seemed to suit him.

"I learned from my father. Can't remember a time when I didn't play."

"You're really good."

His cheeks went red and he nodded self-consciously. "So are you," he said. "What I mean is—" He turned away from the girls. "You're real nice," he said.

"You should go inside awhile," Amina told him.

"Okay, sure. Here I go then." He put his hands in his pockets and walked off toward the lounge.

When he went through the door, Mercedes said, "Is he in love with you?"

"Johnny Boustani falls in love with everyone," Amina said. "Just so's you know."

There was a low bank of cloud skimming the headlands as the coaster turned into the harbour at Renews. A scatter of ragged rocks in the water, a low cliff face on the north side, juniper and dwarf spruce and club moss clinging to the highest rocks. The foot of the harbour coming into view behind it and then the houses of the north side, the white clapboard church. The storehouses at Gooderiche's wharf.

Dozens of barrels of salt fish lined the dock, ready to be loaded aboard a ship for Europe or the Caribbean. Men staring at the three strangers as they went by, nodding at Johnny's uniform.

"So," Johnny said. "What's next?"

"I don't know."

Amina said, "Maybe you should go talk to the priest."

The church stood beside a small brook running toward the harbour. The windows on all three stories were pebbled glass, red and gold and white. A handful of votive candles alight inside the sanctuary, the high altar castled with spires, the tabernacle rising highest in the centre, winged angels perched on both sides. Amina and Johnny both genuflected before the altar and Mercedes mimicked them. Johnny walked to a door behind the altar and called into a room at the back of the church.

A young nun came to the doorway and looked them up and down.

"We're looking," Johnny said. He turned to the girls. "Who are we looking for?"

"The priest," Amina said.

Mercedes said, "We're trying to find Lilly Berrigan. I knows her nephew. Wish Furey. I was hoping."

"The Monsignor isn't here at the moment."

The nun's face was framed by her wimple so that nothing of her hair showed, her ears and her throat below the chin curtained behind white fabric. There was something about the arrangement that made the woman's face look like an infant's, Mercedes thought, and it was unnerving to be stared at so intently by her, to hear complete sentences come from her mouth.

"Father Power is at the rectory," she said.

"Is Lilly still in Renews?"

"You'd best speak to the Monsignor," the nun said. "Come." She went past them to the front doors.

"Thank you, Sister," Johnny said, following after her.

She took them across a narrow footbridge over the stream, the banks reinforced with shale. Mercedes looked up the hill to where it ran down from a grotto behind the church—a high, mortared wall of shale stone, a marble statue of a woman placed out of the weather in an alcove.

"Who is that supposed to be?" Mercedes asked and Amina gave her a look.

They waited in the hall while the young nun spoke to Father Power behind a closed door.

"Do I have to bow when I sees him?" Mercedes asked.

"What?"

"Like what you did at the church."

"Let me do the talking," Amina said.

The nun beckoned them into the parlour, where the priest was standing beside the fireplace. He was dressed in black robes with a sash around his waist that served to draw attention to his massive belly.

"Come in, come in," he said impatiently, motioning with both hands as if he was trying to scoop water onto his clothes. They lined off in front of him and he put his hands behind his back. His wire-rimmed spectacles caught the light coming through the window in such a way that they couldn't see his eyes.

"Thank you, Father, for seeing us," Amina said.

"Sister Marion tells me you are looking for Lilly Berrigan."

"We're looking for Wish Furey," Mercedes said.

Amina jumped in quickly. "We were hoping his aunt might be able to tell us where he is."

The priest turned to Johnny Boustani. "Who are you to these girls?"

"I'm meant to be their chaperone, Father."

"Are you related?"

"He's a friend of the family, Father," Amina said.

"You two are sisters?" He sounded skeptical on the matter.

"No, Father."

"Which one of you is it is looking for Aloysious?"

"I am," Mercedes said.

The priest looked over their heads a moment. "If I might inquire," he said, "what is it you want with him? Has he done harm to someone?"

"No, Father. He's—" Amina looked at Mercedes quickly, then back to the priest. "He's engaged to Mercedes here," she said.

"Engaged?" Johnny Boustani said.

"Engaged?" Father Power repeated.

"Yes, sir," Mercedes said. "Father, I mean."

The priest stood completely still a moment and then made a sound that seemed involuntary, as if he'd touched an open sore in his mouth with his tongue. "Where are you from—Mercedes, is it?"

"I'm from Little Fogo Island."

He wiped a finger under his nose. He turned to Johnny Boustani. He said, "Would you excuse us a moment, Mr. . . . ?"

"Boustani, Father. Lieutenant Johnny Boustani."

"Boustani," the priest repeated.

"It's Lebanese, Father," Johnny said. "But I'm from Pennsylvania."

"If we could have a moment alone, Lieutenant."

As Johnny left the room the priest rose up on his toes and rocked back a number of times, as if preparing to break into song. He looked from one girl to the other. "Are you with child?" he asked Mercedes.

"No, sir."

"Father," Amina whispered.

"No, Father," Mercedes said.

"But he's run off on you."

"He was drove out of the Cove, Father. Being as he was a Catholic."

"Ah," the priest said. A look of consternation came over him a moment before he pushed it aside. "Your parents did not sanction the engagement."

"My father," Mercedes said, "is dead."

The priest bowed slightly forward. "Your mother, then."

"I come into St. John's to find him, Father, but he isn't there. I thought he might have come back to Renews."

The priest turned to face the empty fireplace. "I have a delicate question for you, Mercedes. Has there been"—he reached a finger to touch the cast-iron poker in its stand—"has there been a union of the flesh between yourself and Aloysious?"

"A what?"

"No, Father," Amina said.

"No, Father," Mercedes repeated.

The priest watched Mercedes to see if he could gauge the truth of the matter from her expression. "I know it may seem a cruelty to you," he said. "But you are very young to be entering into holy matrimony."

"I'm the same age my mother was when she married."

"Still and all. Perhaps as things are in—" he paused, "as things are at such a preliminary stage, it may be that your mother is not wrong to oppose a union such as this."

"I need to talk to Miss Berrigan."

"I'm afraid that's impossible. Lilly Berrigan is cloistered."

"Father?"

"In seclusion. She sees no one but the Sisters." The priest smiled at them, which seemed an unkind thing and made Mercedes dislike him more intensely.

"He used to live," Mercedes said, and she took a moment to call up the name, "with Tom Keating. Do you know where he lives?"

"Twenty-five years," Father Power said, "I have been parish priest in Renews. I know everything there is to know about the people here. Including your," he paused over the word, "—fiancé."

"Would you be so kind," Mercedes said deliberately, "as to tell me where Tom Keating lives?"

"I can show them the way," Sister Marion offered. Everyone turned to where she stood against the wall by the door. They had all forgotten she was in the room.

"Oh all right," Father Power said angrily. "Take them." And he made the same strange scooping motion he'd ushered them in with, but in the opposite direction.

They went down a path pointed out to them by Sister Marion, toward the water, travelling along the harbour edge. Past each house they added a dog or curious youngster to the caravan following behind them. The Keatings' saltbox house stood beside a salmon river that ran into the tidal flats at the foot of the harbour. Tom Keating's wife, Patty, saw the troupe coming and met them at the door. Her hair grey and blonde hauled back into a bun, the skin of her forehead and face criss-crossed with lines deep enough to funnel rain. A black-and-white dog with orange markings over its eyes sniffed at their shoes.

She said, "You must be after Tom."

"Is he about?" Mercedes asked.

"Depends why you're after him." She looked Johnny up and down. "You fellers carry guns?"

He lifted his hands away from his body. "No, ma'am."

"How in hell's flames you planning to beat the Jerries, you don't carry guns?"

"I'm trying to find Wish Furey," Mercedes said.

Patty Keating held her eye a moment. "You might as well come in. You crowd looks half-starved."

She sent one of the youngsters who had followed them off to find Tom. Inside she set out a plateful of molasses buns. "Supper won't be ready before five, you'll have to tide yourself over with these. Where are you staying tonight?"

"We don't know," Amina said.

Johnny bit into a bun, looked at it curiously as he chewed. Pale chunks of something greasy and unidentifiable in the dough.

"Room here if you don't mind a crowd," Patty said. "Pork fat," she said to Johnny. "Make a meal of those buns if you need to."

He nodded, his mouth still full. And started surreptitiously feeding the bun to the dog under the table.

Tom Keating arrived with a young man about the age of Wish.

Patty put a hand on her husband's arm, said, "She's here looking for Wish."

"I'd love a mug of tea," he told her. "Now," he said to the group at the table, "which one of you is—?"

"I'm not pregnant," Mercedes announced.

Johnny Boustani's head jerked in her direction as if he'd been slapped.

"We're engaged," Mercedes went on. "Me and Wish."

"Signs and wonders," the younger man said, "before the end of time."

Eleven people sat at the table when supper was served, adult children and their husbands and wives and grandchildren of various ages, along with the three guests. A handful of children stood outside, trying to get a glimpse of the strangers through the windows. Various conversations went on across the table, and people moved from one to another without seeming to miss a word.

"I'll say one thing for Wish Furey," Tom said. He had just turned from a discussion of how long it would take to mend a cod trap torn by drift ice. He was cleaning his plate with a piece of bread, swivelling it with his hand to cover the entire surface. "He knew how to make a drop of shine. Best ever I tasted. I never bothered with more than a few potatoes or molasses myself, but Wish used to pick the juniper berries down by Aggie Dinn's Cove. Went down honey-sweet, his brew."

"He could turn his hand to anything," the younger man said. His name was Billy-Peter. "Wish could put the arse in a cat."

"Where do you think he might have gone?" Mercedes asked.

Tom Keating watched her. "Couldn't say, my love. Haven't laid eyes on him since he run off in St. John's."

"What do you mean, he ran off?" Johnny Boustani asked.

"We were sailing in this bronze statue we took off a Spanish wreck," Tom said. "Christ on the cross, it was. This was just after the war started. The Archbishop got wind of it and asked the Monsignor if we would bring it to town. Not much money in it and two days lost to the trip, but it was the Church asking. Me and Billy-Peter and Wish took it in."

"And he ran off?"

Billy-Peter said, "We went out on the town after we got the statue off the boat. Me and Wish. He never bothered to come back to the harbour."

"It was his first time to town," Tom said. "Should have known by the look on his face he was gone. He always had a restless streak to him, that one. Couldn't settle." He looked at Mercedes apologetically. "What with losing his folks. And things with his aunt being the way they were."

"She got the second sight, Lilly have," Patty said. "She've told women they're pregnant before they knows it themselves."

"I wanted to see her," Mercedes said. "But the priest says she's . . . she's . . ."

"Cloistered," Amina said.

"Locked up, is what she is," Tom said. "Father Power got her tied to a stake up at the convent."

Patty leaned toward Mercedes. "I might be able to help you," she said.

———

The house was gone to bed when Patty roused Mercedes. They went out along the main road and turned onto a path that went steeply uphill, travelling above the houses on the water. Off to their left Mercedes could make out a field of pale shapes stretching back into blackness. The graveyard chill drifted through her, goosebumps rising on her skin, and she walked closer to Patty.

"Not a soul in there going to do you any harm."

Mercedes said, "Why did Wish come to live with you and Tom?"

"He was more or less living with us months before Lilly was brought to the convent."

"They didn't get on?"

"You know she was going to be a nun?"

"No."

"Entered the convent when she was sixteen, left again within the year. Moved into a little place here used to be a goat barn. Taught up at the school, worked as the priest's housekeeper. A mystery why she give up the nuns. She was asked to leave, is what I heard. Not even the Sisters knew what to do with her."

"It's true what Tom said, is it? She's locked away?"

Patty said, "Lilly belongs to another world than this one."

They passed behind the church and Patty stopped in front of the low concrete wall at the grotto, crossing herself before the statue of Mary. There was a room beside her with a large window just above ground level where a row of votive candles were burning. In the light of them, Mercedes could make out the face of Mary in her portal.

"The Ocean Star," Patty said. "She'll watch out for us tonight."

They went on past the rectory to the convent, which was completely dark. They walked around to a side door that led down to a room in the basement. Mercedes could tell from the heat and the smell of vegetable must and dishwater that they were in the kitchen. Patty said, "I cooks for the sisters when they have special events at the convent."

They were standing close in the pitch. Mercedes could smell the older woman, an unpleasant, oddly metallic odour carried on the heat of her body. Patty felt her way to a table and scuffled around a moment until she found an oil lamp. "Leave your shoes by the door," she said, "and stay close to me. Not a word from here on."

They went down a long corridor, keeping one hand to the wall as a guide. At the end of the corridor they went up a staircase to the third floor, then back along the corridor with Patty counting doorways as they went. At the fourth door they stopped, and Mercedes could hear the muffled jangle of a key ring being taken from a coat pocket.

"Where did you get those?"

"Tom found them up at Lilly's place after she was brought over here. She used to have the run of the convent when she cleaned for them."

"He stole them?"

"Salvage, my love," Patty said. "Salvage."

She was trying one key after another in the door, without success. She stood straight and took a deep breath, then went back to it. The right key finally thunked in the lock and Patty pushed the door open. She struck a match inside and lit the lamp, turned the wick back and placed the globe over the flame. When they turned to the illuminated room Lilly Berrigan was sitting up on the side of her bed, watching them. The tiny space was bare but for a nightstand and a crucifix on the wall over the bed.

"Hello, my duck," Patty said.

Lilly smiled at them. Mercedes had been expecting a raver of some description, something that only a barred door would hold. But the stillness of the woman was just as disconcerting. Blonde hair close cropped to her head, a face so pale she looked as if she'd just recovered from an illness. A light to her skin that might have been the aftermath of a fever.

"She don't eat enough to keep a bird alive," Patty said, talking to Mercedes as if Lilly was a child too young to understand. "Lilly," she said, "I brought you a few lassie buns."

"Who's this one?" Lilly said, still smiling.

"This is Mercedes."

"Hello, Miss Berrigan."

"You're here after Wish, is it?"

Mercedes glanced quickly at Patty.

Lilly patted the mattress beside her. "Sister Marion told me you were by the church and talked to Father Power."

Mercedes sat next to her while Patty set the lamp and buns on the nightstand. Lilly put an arm around Mercedes' waist.

"Now," she said. "Who do you belong to?"

"I'm a Parsons, miss. From up Little Fogo way."

Lilly leaned away to have a better view of her. "Parsons," she said. "That's a Protestant name."

Mercedes nodded uncertainly. She said, "Do you know where Wish is to?"

"Sister Marion tells me you're in love with Aloysious," Lilly said quietly.

For no reason she could identify Mercedes said, "Is that a good thing, Miss Berrigan?"

"Where is your family, Mercedes?"

"They're all home in Little Fogo."

"They must be worried about you."

She didn't answer.

"What is it you want from me, Mercedes?"

It seemed a ridiculous question for someone with the gift of second sight to ask. A hint of dismissal in it no different than the priest earlier in the day. No different than her mother. "Wish haven't told you where he's gone?"

"I'm sure you know," she said, "how close Wish keeps things."

"You don't know anything at all? Is he even alive?"

Lilly pushed the girl's hair over her ear. "I'll pray for you," she said.

Patty said, "You couldn't ask for anything more in the world than to have Lilly praying for you, Mercedes."

A heavy sea was running on their trip home the following day, the coaster rolling to port and starboard in languorous arcs like a metronome keeping a slow, relentless beat. The colour drained from Johnny's face as soon as they hit open water and he was forced to stretch out on his coat in steerage and lie on the floor. His face had a greenish hue that reminded Mercedes of the palest colours of the northern lights. He blinked up at her and said, "I wish I was dead."

"You don't know anything about it," she said dismissively.

"It's not my business to say, Mercedes. But I think a girl like you could do better."

"You mean someone like you, Johnny Boustani?"

"Maybe," he said. He smiled his stupid smile in spite of his misery.

"Yes, you're some prize, you are. Is your poor little stomach all right, Johnny? Want something to eat?" She pushed one of Patty Keating's molasses and pork fat buns under his nose. "Have a bite, my love."

He heaved himself to his feet, one hand covering his mouth as he staggered outside to the rail.

"That was mean," Amina said.

Even over the steady murmur of the engine they could hear him retching.

"He sure can play that trumpet, can't he?"

She was surprised at how angry she was, how Johnny called it up in her so quickly. He had the hapless innocence of people who bore the brunt of others' anger all their lives, and at the moment Mercedes felt capable of just about any cruelty. She thought of her mother suddenly, sitting at the head of her father's coffin, calmly telling her the skiff left the harbour an hour before. The flash of recognition made Mercedes' stomach turn. Love at the root of that ruthlessness. It made her wonder about God, to see it so plain.

When they got off the boat in St. John's harbour, Johnny was too weak to walk on his own and the girls stood on either side to steady him as they made their way up Prescott Street. They had to stop halfway up the incline to let him catch his breath. Mercedes did her best to avoid feeling sorry for him and simply couldn't help herself.

Rania was waiting for them when they came through the door of the shop. She took Mercedes to one side, told her Hiram Keeping was there to see her. "He's been in the kitchen all afternoon," she said.

Mercedes found him in the chair beside the stove. He had his handkerchief in his hand, blotting it across his forehead and neck. "Hello, Hiram," she said.

"Jesus, Sadie. You didn't tell me he was alive."

She stepped back toward the doorway, putting a hand on the frame.

"Your brother," he said. "You didn't tell me he was still alive."

"What are you talking about?"

"Jesus Christ," he said, mopping at his forehead. "Wish said he'd killed him. He told me Hardy was dead."

"You've seen him," Mercedes said. "I *knew* it."

Hiram's entire body clenched, as if a cramp passed through him. "He come to the shop and dragged me out of bed when he got to town. Said Hardy was dead and he'd killed him."

"Where is he, Hiram?"

"I don't know. He came by yesterday. Said you'd run off after Wish and he was looking to bring you home."

"Not Hardy," Mercedes shouted. "*Wish.* Where's Wish?"

"Jesus Christ," he said.

"Hiram."

"In Halifax," he said without looking at her. "In Canada."

Lieutenant Kurakake visited Nishino several times after the retreat from Guadalcanal, before the company shipped back to the front. The officer arrived each time with two bottles of sake, one of which he left unopened with the injured soldier. He placed a small table over Nishino's midriff on the hospital berth and set out two porcelain cups, filling them with the rice wine. There was always a protracted period of silence between them as they drank to Nishino's recovery, before Kurakake put his first question to the soldier.

His inquiries weren't antagonistic and followed no set pattern, but there was a sense of interrogation about their time together. The man's rank and the gifts of alcohol compelled Nishino to make limited confessions of one sort or another.

Kurakake set down his cup and folded his arms. "Tell me, Private Nishino. Why did you keep this to yourself? Your English?"

"I am Japanese."

"Of course." Kurakake rocked slightly in his chair, thinking. "It's a valuable thing to the Imperial Army to have soldiers with this skill."

Nishino didn't respond.

"You preferred to serve in other ways. You wished to fight."

"Asia for the Asians," Nishino said, sitting up slightly in his bed.

Kurakake smiled down at his feet. The inclination of his head suggesting this sentiment embarrassed him although Nishino had heard the phrase used by every officer he'd encountered.

"Still," Kurakake said. "It seems unnecessary to have been entirely secretive in this matter."

"I am Japanese," he said again.

"We have established as much."

"I would not allow others to doubt that."

Kurakake tilted his head to one side. "Tell me, Nishino," he said. "How old were you when you arrived in Canada?"

"I was five."

"And you moved with your family."

"My mother. My father was already there. He went to Hawaii long before he married. He spent a year there, then moved on to British Columbia."

"The Golden Door."

Nishino looked at him.

"It was how people referred to British Columbia years ago, when I was a boy. The Golden Door. He worked in the sawmills?"

"And the salmon rivers. Eventually he wrote his parents to ask them to arrange a wedding for him. He came home to Japan for six months and then went back to Canada."

"Your mother was expecting you when your father left."

Nishino said, "He wanted to own a piece of land before his family arrived."

"It took him five years?"

"To buy it and clear it and build a house."

A medic was working on the jungle sores of a soldier at the other end of the makeshift field hospital, scraping under the skin at the edges of the ulcer with a kitchen spoon, cleaning away pus and rot to try to stop the spread. The soldier grunting through the treatment, a harsh staccato rasp.

"The name again, please," Kurakake said.

"Kitsilano."

"Kitt-su-sa-ra-no," Kurakake said. And he nodded to Nishino in the way he would to a musician waiting for permission to begin playing.

When he left British Columbia, Nishino's intention had been to wipe the place from his mind. A scorched-earth program, slash and burn. He joined the Imperial Army in a northern country district where his mother's people originated, claiming he had spent his years away in Taiwan. The soldiers in his unit had coarse accents and rougher manners. They were fervently nationalistic, fatalist, brawling, and he aspired to the same conditions for himself. He tried to bury every conscious verbal and social tic that would mark him as an outsider, but he was often taunted for his city-fied accent, for his barely definable but undeniable separateness. Found a level of acceptance among the other soldiers finally by enduring a drunken company beating without uttering a sound. Kept their trust with a vicious disregard for his own safety in combat. He fully expected to be killed during the war to liberate Asia and wanted nothing more for himself than that.

And still Kitsilano surfaced in his sleep, in moments of near delirium brought on by exhaustion and lack of food. Summer days on the farm where they grew strawberries and tomatoes to sell to the canneries in New Westminster and to stalls in the market along the river. The long seasons of public school with its mix of whites and Japanese, Chinese and Sikhs, Jews, Portuguese, Scots. The afternoon Japanese-language school where Mr. Yawata taught them about the samurai and the old wars against China and Russia. On special occasions the students saluted the Japanese flag and Mr. Yawata led them in singing the *kimiga yo*. Most of the other students were Nissei, born in Canada, and they knew only rudimentary Japanese. They ridiculed Mr. Yawata, who was in his fifties, absent-minded and partly deaf and spoke no English at all. He lifted his eyeglasses to his forehead to write on the chalkboard and minutes later was rifling through his pockets and desk drawers, muttering to himself, trying to find them. He had to cup a hand behind his good ear to hear his students and they tormented him by speaking in whispers or simply mouthing words. The one obligation trumping all others in their lives, Mr. Yawata insisted, was their obligation to the emperor.

In Vancouver and Steveston and Kitsilano there were restaurants that would not serve Japanese. Most movie theatres required they sit in the balcony. On Alexander Street in Vancouver white men handed out leaflets that said "Get Rid of the Japs" and "The Rising Sun Must Set," accusing the teachers in the language schools of being navy reservists sent to teach naval tactics or to spy.

Mr. Yawata read aloud to them from the *League of the Divine Wind*, a book about an uprising during the Meiji era when two hundred patriots attacked a garrison of two thousand soldiers. The kamikaze rebels wore short *hakama* over their everyday dress with two swords held in their sashes. They wore headbands of white cloth and bound up their sleeves with strips of white cotton, and every man wore a white shoulder strap bearing the word "Victory." Mr. Yawata walked as he read, stumbling into his desk, the trash can. The rebels were adherents of the Ukei shrine, of the gods of Japan before the invasion of Buddhism and the Christian missionaries from the West. "How did the men of the League prepare for combat?" Mr. Yawata read. "Most of all, night and day alike, by imploring the blessing of Heaven." They fought to return Japan to the rule of His Glorious Majesty with only swords and spears and halberds. After their defeat, the survivors of the league committed the ritual disembowelment of seppuku in fidelity to the emperor. Mr. Yawata leaned over to grab awkwardly at the fallen trash can without taking his eyes from the book in his hand.

A handful of boys in Nishino's class could pass gas at will and they formed their own League of the Divine Wind, belching and farting through the halls of the school, shouting "Kamikaze!" as they went. They sat outside the classroom and performed mock seppuku with their pencils. It was all a bizarre joke to them. Two of the boys slipped into the classroom early one afternoon and removed the screws from Mr. Yawata's chair and it collapsed underneath his weight the moment he sat down. He lay there, sputtering among the wreckage, his glasses fallen across his face. And Nishino felt as if the fate of all things Japanese in the new world lay there with him.

Lieutenant Kurakake sat with his arms folded. They had finished most of the bottle of sake as Nishino spoke through the worst heat of the afternoon. He had never talked of these experiences to anyone before. As soldiers they were required to ignore the protocol of hints and innuendo and formal politeness that otherwise governed interactions between people of such different station. But more than this, Kurakake clearly felt he owed Nishino something. Something unspoken between them, something related to Chozo Ogawa allowed Nishino to talk as freely as he did.

He was fighting the drowse of the late afternoon and for a few moments he thought the officer might have drifted off. But Kurakake looked up suddenly, as if someone had shaken him by the shoulder. "Your father," he said.

Nishino looked away. He said, "Words are the root of all evil."

Kurakake smiled, acknowledging the proverb, and they were silent a long time afterwards as if to honour it. Finally the officer said, "You left your family in Canada, Nishino? No one returned with you?"

"I came alone."

"You have no contact with them?"

"I have no one now but Japan."

The officer poured the last of the sake into their cups and lifted his. "Then we will drink to what you have," he said.

He slept a drunken sleep after Kurakake left him and woke in the early evening with a fierce headache. He got out of bed and made his slow way to the latrines behind the ward. He was unable to piss when he got there, breathing hard against the tide of pain that ran the length of his back, waiting for it to subside.

He didn't know what he would have said to Kurakake if there had been more questions about his parents. He would have lied or simply refused to answer, he was certain of that. Once he made it back to his cot he sipped at the sake to deaden the throb in his back and to fog the memory of his mother that Kurakake's interrogation provoked. But she stayed with him all evening.

He had never witnessed a single instance of physical affection between his parents. There was no meanness or cruelty, just a constant remoteness that he took to be the natural state of affairs between a man and a woman. They spoke to each other only of practical matters. Nishino never heard his mother talk about the future beyond what the next morning held. She bore five other children after arriving in Canada, a girl who died at three weeks old, then two sons and another daughter. She travelled to the Japanese consul in Vancouver to register the name of each child after they were born.

She was a remarkably tiny woman, and her stature made her steadfastness seem more heroic to Nishino. She rose each morning at five and bathed outside in all weather, soaking her naked torso with dippers of cold water to "harden" herself. Her attention was absorbed by each successive task she undertook, and there was something in her diligence and single-minded concentration that made her seem smaller still. As if she was disappearing in whatever work she was doing at the time. She smiled only in those moments after she had completed a job, putting the kitchen to rights before going to bed, setting the last basket of strawberries onto the truck. The only affectation of luxury she allowed herself was to serve even ordinary meals in bowls of Ninsei porcelain that she'd received as a wedding gift.

She had no interest in the world outside the family home and nothing of the new country touched or stained the woman she was when she arrived. She was all he had of the real Japan they'd left behind. And while she was alive, that was almost enough for him.

The last time Kurakake came to see him, Nishino was sitting in a wooden chair beside the bed. The officer opened the first of the two bottles of sake. "We have much to celebrate," he said. "The company will be moving back to the front very soon."

"I will be ready."

Kurakake said, "You will never be a field soldier again, Private."

And nothing more was spoken between them for a while.

"I have been thinking about Chozo Ogawa," the officer said finally. "He was not meant to be a soldier, that boy. Do you agree?"

Nishino looked away down the aisle. He didn't understand what the officer was looking for and didn't know how to answer.

"He was refused by the army when he first tried to enlist," Kurakake went on. "Did you know that?"

"No, I didn't," he said defensively. "I did not know that."

"Unfit for duty, is what they said. You noticed of course, not right in the head somehow. His father was a friend of mine, an officer from the service who died a number of years ago. His oldest son contacted me and asked if I could help find a place for Chozo. And, naturally, I did what I could. I saw it immediately after he came into the ranks. He wasn't fit. And yet I couldn't be seen to be favouring him." Kurakake raised and lowered his hands in a helpless gesture. He took a sheet of paper from an inside pocket of his uniform coat and turned it over without unfolding it. "What I am trying to say," he said. "I think his father would have been thankful for the way you watched out for him. He would have wanted to show his appreciation."

"We helped one another," Nishino said.

"Yes," Kurakake said. "I have your orders, Private Nishino." He raised the sheet of paper. "You will be transferred back to Japan, to Kumamoto. There is a camp being constructed there."

"A guard for prisoners?"

Kurakake smiled at the look of disgust on the young man's face. "Not a guard exactly. You will act as an interpreter for the camp commandant, Lieutenant Sakamoto. We served two years together in Manchuria. I have already written to let him know you will be joining his staff."

Kurakake stood and handed the folded sheet of paper to Nishino.

Nishino looked away from the officer to hide the tears in his eyes, recognizing that the war was over for him and he had no choice now but to submit. He stood and bowed.

"Good luck to you, Private Nishino."

"Thank you, Lieutenant."

1945

WISH

—

THE THREE PRISONERS CLIMBED into the back of the open truck and sat awkwardly, all of them out of breath from the exertion. They were wearing standard prison-issue uniforms, short-sleeved shirts and shorts, though the April weather still edged toward a chill. Wish turned his face to the sky, white stars pinging in his peripheral vision.

The guard slapped his palm against the cab of the truck and they lurched up out of the valley. They drove past Nagasaki Station, the surface of the harbour on their left salted with sunlight. The water was a dark blue but for a line of black at mid-strait where a tidal current ran. Past the long dock of the shipyard they turned away from the city centre that lay out of sight among the maze of hills, travelling toward the outskirts. Wish closed his eyes, letting his head rock with the movement. Twice a month he accompanied Major McCarthy and a Dutch officer on this excursion. They were transporting the cremated ashes of POWs from the scatter of camps in the area to the French Temple, where the urns were stored in a crypt beneath the church. Wish looked forward to these trips. It was a rare pleasure to be stationary and in motion at the same time. It was almost hallucinatory, like a dream of flying.

He turned to the civilian guard who was standing against the cab and solemnly watching the road behind them. "Mr. Osano." He patted the floor of the truck bed. "*Chakuseki,*" he said. "Have a seat."

The guard smiled briefly and raised his hand. The same offer and refusal every time.

"You work too hard, Mr. Osano," Wish told him. Knowing the man understood little or nothing of what he said.

"They all work too hard for my liking," McCarthy whispered. He was an Irishman but had finished his education in England, where the sharpest crags of his accent had been ground down. He nodded toward the box of urns. "Who have we got here today?" he asked.

There were four, each marked by the name, rank and serial number of the dead. Wish lifted them out in turn. "Australian. Australian. American," he said. He looked across at Captain van der Meulen, holding the last urn. "Dutch," he said.

The captain spoke English but not fluently and he said very little on these trips. He came with them largely because he was Catholic and it was a chance to spend a few minutes inside a sanctuary, among the candles and stained glass and the saints. It was being Catholic himself that had gotten Wish the assignment from Major McCarthy shortly after their arrival in the camp.

The French Temple was an ornate wooden building with two slope-roofed wings framing the main hall where portal doors stood below three large stained-glass windows. It had been constructed by European missionaries centuries before. A marble statue of the Blessed Virgin stood on a pedestal in the central entrance, a high narrow steeple above it topped with a cross.

The first time Wish had come to the church he stood outside a long time. "Who does it belong to?" he asked. "I mean, who goes to it?"

"Japs, I expect," McCarthy said.

The Blessed Virgin looked out over the square with the same blank, beatific expression as the Ocean Star at her grotto in Renews. Wish was amazed to find her here, in the heart of Japan. He'd have been less surprised to hear an animal speak.

McCarthy crossed himself and whispered, "Nuestra Señora de las Mercedes."

Wish looked at the officer. "What did you say?"

"It's Spanish. Nuestra Señora de las Mercedes."

"Mercedes?"

"It means compassion or tender mercy. The Spaniards call Mary Our Lady of Mercies."

Wish watched him until McCarthy said, "One of the Sisters at school was from Salamanca. Sister Concepcion."

Not Portuguese after all. He came to think of the statue of Mary as Mercedes and every time he came to the French Temple he crossed himself before her and touched her marble feet for luck, bringing his hand to his lips.

They carried the four urns past her into the cool air of the church, up the central aisle. There was no one else in the sanctuary, but votive candles and a red oil lamp were burning near the altar, where they placed the ashes. They knelt at the rail and McCarthy and Wish led the rosary in English, van der Meulen responding in Dutch. Then Wish recited the Pater Noster in Latin, McCarthy and the Dutch officer joining in on the phrases they remembered.

"I love hearing those old words," McCarthy said.

The soldiers left the urns at the altar to be moved into the crypt by a prelate or a priest and they started back down the aisle.

"It's strange, isn't it," McCarthy said, "how there's never a soul about when we're here?"

It had never really occurred to Wish there might be people in the building to see, priests or nuns or parishioners. And he realized he was happy to have it empty, that it made the place seem completely theirs somehow. Sacrosanct. Unspoiled.

Osano never stepped inside the sanctuary, waited for them at the open doorway. All three soldiers bowed as they filed past him into the sunlight and he bowed in return. At the truck Osano took a lighter from his pocket and lit cigarettes for them. Then they hoisted themselves into the truck bed for the trip home to the camp.

When he finished his smoke, Wish took a folded sheet of paper from his shirt pocket. It was the first letter he had received from her in England and the one letter from Mercedes he had carried with him through all his time in the Pacific. He unfolded it carefully, taking out the black-and-white picture that had come with it. The photograph was taken in the shop in Georgestown, Hiram's name and address stamped on the grey backing. It had taken him a moment to recognize her, Mercedes standing in a black dress, her once straight brown hair sporting tight curls. He had no idea how she'd managed to do that. She was wearing makeup as well, lipstick and dark eye shadow, and she looked like someone out of the movies. She seemed much older than he remembered, more a woman. As if she'd made up her mind to put away childish things. His bunk-mate, Anstey, peeking over his shoulder to get a look at her the afternoon the letter arrived. "How come you've never mentioned her before?" he asked.

After Earle's coaster docked in St. John's that morning, Wish had picked his way up the steep streets from the harbour to Georgestown. Hammered hard at the door of the shop to wake Hiram and nearly knocked the man over in his rush to get in.

He'd said, "I killed him, Hiram."

Hiram took Wish by the arm and led him into the office at the back of the shop, settled him into a chair. Coaxed the story from him.

"What happened after you fell?"

"I backed off till I come to the wall and waited for him, couldn't see a thing in the black. By and by, I went into the kitchen and found a candle." Wish's face screwed tight and he bent over his lap, rocking and moaning. "He had blood coming out his mouth. And his head gone sideways against the wall."

"It was an accident," Hiram told him. "It was self-defence." And he stopped in mid-thought, leaning back in his chair. "Wish," he said. "How did you get back to St. John's?"

"I took the Parsonses' trap skiff over to Fogo, caught the coaster from there."

"You stole their boat?"

"I sent it right back with a couple of youngsters."

"You oughtn't to have run, Wish. It doesn't look good."

He sat silent a moment, his mouth half open.

"What is it?"

"There was some money, Hiram. He'd brought some money with him to send me on my way. To bribe me into leaving."

"Jesus, Wish, you didn't take it off him?"

"I had hardly a cent left."

"You stole money off a corpse?"

"I didn't know how else I was going to get on a coaster. Or get the skiff back to the Cove."

Hiram stood up out of his seat and turned his back. He was barefoot and his suspenders hung loose at his sides. He took a deep breath and touched his head delicately with both hands, thinking. He said, "We'll have to get you out of the country."

"What?"

"We'll get you on the train to Port aux Basques. Next one leaves at six this evening. You can get a berth on the *Caribou* from there across to Canada." He pulled the suspenders up over his shoulders and reached under the desk for a bottle of dark rum. "I'll loan you enough for the fares," he said.

"What will I do with myself over there, Hiram?"

The older man sat back in his chair. "You were planning on joining up, weren't you?"

"The army?"

"Overseas," Hiram said.

Hiram told me everything about you and Hardy, Wish. Hardy was only knocked senseless and is up and around same as if nothing ever happened to him. I wish you'd only come and talked to me before you run off and —there was half a line scribbled out here that Wish had spent hours trying to decipher, holding the page to the light to guess at letters and words, with no luck—*everything would be all right now. I have left the Cove for St. John's and will wait here till you get home again, no matter how long.*

He could feel the speed in the writing, letters running into one another in her rush to finish and mail it to him, as if there was still a chance to turn things around, to bring him back. He was in the middle of basic training by the time it arrived. He'd sent Hiram the money he owed him with a note saying how he'd found his way to England. And Mercedes had written back.

Please write to me care of Hiram when you get this. Hardy come to bring me home to the Cove but I told him we are engaged and are going to marry when you come home, whenever that might be, I will be waiting if you will have me. And there was a long Bible verse written out as a kind of P.S. at the bottom of the letter. *Intreat me not to leave thee, or to return from following after thee: for whither thou goest, I will go; and where thou lodgest, I will lodge: thy people shall be my people, and thy God my God.*

Hardy was alive and fine. The relief of that flooded him like the light of revelation. The Salvationist on the St. John's street corner had shouted out over the crowd: "Ye must be born again." Amen to that.

Wish was stationed in England for the better part of a year, waiting to be sent into action. He and Mercedes wrote back and forth, the regular letters from St. John's a relief from the endless parade drills and rifle exercises and early-morning calisthenics. He had been wrong about Mercedes, about how ruthless love could make her. There was no smell to the paper other than the smell of his own hands anymore but he lifted it to his face each time he read it.

In October of 1941 they sailed out of England with no word of their destination. Ten days later he sighted the rocks of Cape Race, the ship skirting the southern coast of Newfoundland on its way to Halifax. A heavy sea and he could just make out the white line of surf where it rode up the foot of the cliffs.

They had a week on leave in Halifax, and on November 8 they were ordered aboard the *Wakefield*, a former passenger liner refitted as a U.S. Navy troop ship. They departed on the tenth, part of a large convoy of American vessels transporting British soldiers, sailing south. Wish wrote to Mercedes, *I thought joining the infantry would at least keep me off the water.* Rumours had them heading for Australia or Singapore or Malaysia. The Pacific, either way, which meant the Japanese and jungle fighting.

The convoy ran dark with hatches secured from half an hour before sunset, which made the overcrowded quarters stifling. They were under U.S. Navy regulations and the ship was dry. Wish managed to jerry up a still with potato skins and sugar and water in a garbage bag that he kept hidden in a latrine, the alcohol passed around in metal cups after lights out. Major McCarthy turning a blind eye as long as none of the liquor got into the hands of American sailors.

The entire battalion was made up of green soldiers. None of them knew a thing about how the war was going in the region and they made do with rumours and crackpot theories that were passed around quarters in the dark. The Japs couldn't see at night because of their slant-eyes, they were genetically predisposed to seasickness. They were an army of lady-boys with tiny cocks, they held hands as they marched. They cut off the heads of civilians and raised them on stakes, they used women and children for bayonet practice. Except for the lurid relief of war gossip, there was nothing in the way of distraction.

We have half an hour of exercise before breakfast, rain or shine, Wish wrote. *A sing-song on weather decks after supper. A couple of fellows in blackface doing show tunes. The rest is just waiting.*

The convoy refuelled in Trinidad and from there went on to South Africa. Wish and Harris and Anstey mailed letters at each stop, as if they were marking a path they could follow home after the war. Wish's last note to reach Mercedes found its way from the Maldive Islands where the *Wakefield* put in for fresh water. He knew by then that Singapore was their destination, though he couldn't say as much. HMS *Prince of Wales* and *Repulse* were sunk off the coast of Malaya in December. The Japanese had travelled south through the supposedly impenetrable jungle of that country as far as the island of Singapore in less than two months. General Percival, the commanding officer of Fortress Singapore, had sent an urgent request for all available reinforcements. Or so the stories went.

They reached Singapore on January 30. The naval base across the strait from Malaya was abandoned by then and the *Wakefield* put in at Keppell's Harbour on the southern shore. The soldiers and their equipment were offloaded between Japanese bombing raids, and the *Wakefield* departed with thirteen hundred civilians aboard, bound for Batavia, where more refugees were waiting.

Their unit was ordered to establish a perimeter defence along the Lornie, Adam and Farrar roads. He dug in with Harris and Anstey, and the three men sat on the packed earth to wait. Wish wrote a short note to Mercedes each of the next fifteen days in

Singapore. He knew the letters would never be mailed but found some comfort in the sense he was talking to her directly. *Am certain of seeing action any moment and feel it's about time,* he told her, *sick of drills.* And knowing there was something false in that sentiment, he added, *They sounds like the real sonsabitches when the game is on.*

Conjecture and reports and scuttlebutt passed back and forth along the line. They heard that the Japanese had crossed the strait by the thousands in collapsible boats at night.

"I thought the fuckers were blind in the dark," Harris said.

"They get seasick in the bath too," Anstey said. "Don't forget that."

The causeway to the mainland, which had been dynamited at the beginning of January, was already repaired and Japanese tanks were crossing into Singapore. The defending force had retreated as far as Bukit Timah at the centre of the island. They were told that General Percival had refused to deploy barbed wire or mines along the Singapore coast before the Japanese attack because the preparation of such defences was bad for morale.

Wish wrote to Mercedes, *I feel I am living in a made-up world.*

The city was bombed daily, with no Allied planes in the air to offer resistance. The Japanese took Bukit Timah, which left open road to Singapore City. On February 14 the city's water reservoirs were lost. Wish could see the fighting now, rifle and machine-gun and mortar fire pressing toward their trenches, inexorable as weather. It was like being trapped aboard a punt in heavy seas, the ground shifting as the shockwave of each explosion broke over them, their little gravel boat about to capsize and spit them into the storm. Anstey said, "I'll bet every one of those bastards is hung like a horse." Wish kept having to piss, turning his back to relieve himself against the wall of the trench.

On February 15 General Percival walked out to the Japanese command post in the Ford motor factory on the Bukit Timah road carrying a Union Jack and a white flag. Wish was taken prisoner along with the seventy thousand other Allied soldiers on the island. He hadn't fired a single shot.

Thousands of the Allied soldiers were herded into Changi prison on the northeast shore of the island, where they were stripped of their clothes and boots and left with only a loincloth for cover. They were sent out in work groups, clearing away the dead in the streets of Saigon City, cleaning up after the halfhearted scorched-earth program undertaken at the naval base before the surrender. Dock cranes tilting on their bases, the huge oil tanks burnt out and blackened. The capsized hulls of vessels visible on the ocean floor.

The prisoners were issued a booklet of English-to-Japanese translations that they were supposed to memorize, numbers and days of the week and months of the year. Basic orders such as *Start eating, Go to toilet, Begin work, Stop work.* There were also odd lists of specific objects. *Mine timber* and *coal tub, intake* and *out-take shaft, rock drill. Cement bag, rail track, tie, explosives.*

"Not hard to guess," Wish said, "what they've got in mind for us."

Beatings were a daily occurrence, most often with a four-foot-long stick dubbed "the bamboo interpreter" that the guards depended on to get their message across when all else failed. Most of the prisoners were sick with dysentery and fevers. Wish returned from the dock one evening running a temperature and by morning he was half out of his mind. Harris and Anstey carried him to the hospital before heading off to join their work group at the docks. He lay in that delirious state for the better part of two days. And it was a week longer before he was well enough to leave the hospital.

Wish had heard stories about malaria as they headed into the tropics, how people went mad with hallucinations. At the time he'd imagined visual monsters of some sort, spiders the size of tanks, rock falls, nightmarish creatures. His own delusions turned out to be subtler though no less terrifying. He was convinced he had to eat the hospital and spent hours feverishly trying to deal with the logistics of the task. The thatched straw roof was the obvious place to start, but the walls were concrete. What would he do once his teeth cracked and fell out? How would he manage to shit it all from his system without causing serious damage? Even the memory of that ludicrous belief and the absolute certainty with which he held it made his stomach turn.

He passed his recovery time in the hospital writing notes to Mercedes and studying the Japanese wordbook, practising his pronunciation on the guards and hospital orderlies. Much the way he'd learned Latin from his aunt Lilly. He found two empty pages at the back of the book and began pointing to objects around him—bed, window, cup, book—writing out phonetic versions of the Japanese words. Rifle, uniform, doctor. Sleep, sick, tired, hungry.

He got himself yelled at and slapped occasionally for his interest. Even the Japanese who were most cooperative barked the words at him, as if they were about to start gnawing on his leg. Not a one of them smiled easily, if at all. He wrote, *I thought you Protestants were a sour crowd Mercedes but I never seen the like of these.*

His company was transported to Japan six weeks later. When they arrived at Nagasaki #14 they were given permission to send a forty-word card home. In the three years he'd been incarcerated, he'd received four letters from Mercedes, all of them a year or more out of date. Each offering the same message as the first. *I will be waiting if you will have me.*

Osano spoke to him. The guard was sitting with his back against the cab of the truck, his arm draped over the urn box, which was carrying a slightly different cargo now, Wish knew. He smiled and flashed the picture of Mercedes in his hand. Wish pointed at Osano, touched the pocket he'd taken the letter from, then pointed again. Osano fished a small leather billfold from his pocket and took out a photograph of his own that he held toward the prisoner. They traded the photos carefully, like an exchange of hostages. The woman in Osano's photo stared straight ahead, dark eyes and hair cut sharply at the jaw line. The picture was badly taken or overdeveloped, her features barely visible in the washout.

"Some beautiful," Wish said, as he did every time. "*Kirie.*" The guard spoke briefly then, shaking the picture of Mercedes to show what he was talking about, before returning it to Wish.

McCarthy said, "You sure he doesn't speak any English?"

"I'd be dead for long ago if he did, sir."

"What have you got on him?"

"Sir?"

"You wouldn't trust that picture in the hands of someone who didn't owe you something, is my guess."

Wish shrugged. Some debt or obligation was obvious in the man's behaviour, something related to the first time they'd exchanged these pictures, though more than that Wish couldn't say.

The truck struggled up the steep incline past the shipyard, gave an audible mechanical sigh as they crested the hill and coasted toward the camp gates. As they drove closer the driver reached out his window to slap the cab roof three times. Osano got to his feet quickly, to make a show of watching over the prisoners.

Three large trucks with covered beds were parked near the guardhouse and a group of prisoners stood at attention in the square, at least a hundred of them, all strangers. They were mostly barefoot and so thin it was clear they'd been living in camps for an extended time.

"Looks like we have newcomers," McCarthy said.

McCarthy was summoned to the commandant's office as soon as he stepped from the truck. Inside the urn box in the truck bed was a bag of empty liquor bottles, stowed there by Osano while the men were inside the church. There was too much activity in the camp to try shifting them to the still or the barracks. Wish tried to guess from Osano's face what they should do but the guard refused to look in his direction, shouting to dismiss him and the Dutch officer. They walked off to join a handful of other prisoners who were watching the newcomers from the shade.

Harris said, "They've been shipped in from Mushiroda Camp."

Anstey nudged him with his elbow. "They look like they could use a drink, Wish."

He made a face, thinking of the bottles in the truck. The moonshine operation and the location of Wish's still were an open secret in the camp. He'd begun making liquor within a week of arriving at #14 and occasionally, discreetly, offered it to guards as a bribe or payment for some small favour. Both parties acting as if no transaction was taking place between them. Even when Osano first approached Wish through the civilian interpreter, the conversation was oblique, barely decipherable. "There are many shortages in the city due to the war," Mr. Haruyama translated, while Osano bowed to Wish. "Many people are suffering the lack of luxuries they once took for granted." He carried on this vein for a long while before he said: "Mr. Osano worked as a liquor distributor in Nagasaki for many years before the war. It was a job at which he excelled." Wish feigned ignorance at the time, though he was careful not to be discouraging. Over a period of months the two men made their arrangements through trial and error, with offhand comments about equipment and payment passed through Haruyama, with grimaces and nods. It was like a lengthy, clandestine courtship.

As long as the enterprise operated beneath the strictly ordered surface in the camp, as long as it did nothing to disturb the appearance of complete submission to rules and regimen, the guards acted as if it didn't exist. Many of them purchased liquor from Osano themselves. But that didn't mean there was no risk involved. Wish didn't doubt he'd be beaten, maybe even shot, if he was seen trying to sneak those bottles from the truck.

The commandant came through the door of his office ten minutes later, accompanied by McCarthy. The two officers were trailed by a Japanese soldier Wish didn't recognize. A tall fellow for a Jap, almost the height of Harris. There was a barely perceptible hiccup in his gait. He stood beside the commandant as Koyagi addressed the newly arrived men, translating for him.

"You will be treated with respect if you earn respect," he said. "You will be under the command of the senior British officer in camp, Major McCarthy," he said and he gestured toward the Irishman. "Exercise commences at 0500 hours. Breakfast at 0530, followed by a fifteen-minute smoking period. Work crews depart at 0600 hours. Tardiness will not be tolerated. Laziness will not be tolerated. Insubordination will not be tolerated." He smiled as he translated. Not a trace of an accent in his words.

"Where's Haruyama?" Wish asked.

The prisoners looked at one another. No one knew where the civilian interpreter was hiding himself. But it was obvious he'd been supplanted by the newcomer.

"Something's wrong with his leg," Anstey said. "He's got a limp."

"His leg or his back," Wish said.

The camp guards were a mix of Koreans, who weren't permitted to join the Imperial Army, and civilians and Japanese soldiers assigned to the camps because of injuries that made them unfit for front-line duty. It was a game for POWs to guess at the less obvious afflictions, to pinpoint their weaknesses.

Wish said, "Where did he learn to talk like that, I wonder?"

"The Great Japanese Empire," the interpreter was saying, "will not try to punish you all with death. Our goal is to bring the blessing of freedom to the people of Southeast Asia. Those obeying all rules and regulations and cooperating with Japan in constructing the New Order of the Greater Asia which leads to world peace will be well treated."

Koyagi was watching the interpreter with a startled, slightly offended look. Wish looked back and forth between the two. A moment later the commandant interrupted the little sermon being tacked on to his comments to dismiss the new prisoners. The younger soldier bowed curtly to his superior and walked off to the guardhouse.

"We got a true believer there," Wish said.

"Jesus Henry Christ," Harris whispered.

They didn't know what to make of the new arrivals. It might have been a simple administrative shuffle. It might even be a consolidation made necessary by American advances. But the POWs had so little say in the world of the camp that any change put them on edge, a reminder of how fragile and erratic their fortunes were.

"You'll have to get the bottles after lights out," Anstey said as they walked to the kitchen for their evening meal.

"The guards'll be more watchful than we're used to with the new ones in camp," Wish said. "I'm not tore up about getting myself shot for a dozen liquor bottles."

With the exception of sporadically distributed Red Cross parcels, the prisoners ate boiled rice supplemented on occasion with sweet potatoes or cabbage or seaweed. The rice was infected with weevils and maggots that floated to the surface as it was boiled. *Little friends*, they were called, and were skimmed off and cooked separately in a broth.

The line-up was a hundred men longer than they were used to. The new prisoners were all Brits and they swapped stories with the English soldiers at #14, trading names of their regiments and hometowns. There was almost a festive air to the queue that for some reason made Wish feel more contrary. As if he was the sober one at a drunken party.

The three men took their bowls away from the square, sitting on the ground between two barracks. Harris and Anstey used spoons, but Wish picked out his rice with chopsticks, one grain at a time. Just to make it last. He glanced at his friends as they ate. It was something about the unfamiliarity of the new arrivals that made Harris and Anstey look so pathetic, dressed in rags and their faces staved in with hunger.

During their enlistment physicals there was a full-size anatomy skeleton in the corner and the bare bones looked wrong in comparison to the naked men in the room, as if a child had drawn them out of scale. Both Harris and Anstey had that sense of disproportion about them now, their emaciated limbs seeming too long for the frames they were attached to.

En route to Singapore, the *Wakefield* had put in at Mombasa to give the troops a few hours shore leave on Christmas Day, 1941. They anchored at the mouth of the Duruma River just before noon and the servicemen were let loose on the city. Open-air restaurants and small taverns overrun by British soldiers and American sailors. Wish and his two buddies wandered around with half a dozen others from their company through the afternoon, drinking and singing Christmas carols, flipping shillings and American nickels to the youngsters following them in packs. Brazen sunlight, the clothes of the men and women in the street red and gold and ocean blue. The heat so close it felt as if the air was wearing a pelt of oil and fur.

They found a deserted hole-in-the-wall restaurant early that evening, the proprietor drunker than they were and unable to get out of his seat to serve them. They poked through the kitchen and cooked up a haunch of meat, goat or some animal native to the place, along with sweet potato and carrots and onion. The owner held out his empty glass periodically and they filled it for him, shouting questions as they ate. He was in no shape to answer with much more than monosyllables but they managed to learn his name (Charles) and age (fifty-two), that he was married but his wife was dead, that he was a Christian. He didn't drink, he said, holding out his empty glass again. The meat was dark and gamey with just a hint of rot in the flesh and none of them managed to finish what was on their plate. Anstey cleared the table before they left and Harris tucked a two-dollar bill into Charles' shirt. "Merry Christmas, old man," he said. And he leaned in drunkenly to kiss his cheek.

It was a sweet gesture, that kiss. Something out of another world altogether, Wish knew. It wasn't just their bodies that were wasting away in the camp. He didn't doubt they'd kill Charles for that piece of rotten meat now. They'd turn on any one of the newly arrived prisoners if there was a decent meal to be gained.

Wish didn't think much of the army in basic. It all came down to charts and grids and rank and formations, which felt childish at the time, a ridiculous little game. But he could map his world in one simple diagram now, a hierarchy of concentric circles with Harris and Anstey in the ring closest to him, then McCarthy and the men in their unit. The other Brits they'd arrived with next and beyond them the Americans and the Dutch. Then Osano and Haruyama and the one or two others who Wish had some sway over. Next, the guards who were decent, followed by those who were hard-line but impersonal. And way out among the farthest planets, somewhere beyond the human, he placed the handful of sadists who seemed to love their work.

Harris had finished his food and lay splayed on the ground, half asleep. Anstey was turning his empty bowl in his hands to lick it clean. Wish's inner circle. The Brits in their unit made no distinction between the two Canadians and the Newfoundlander, lumping them into one indistinguishable category. They arrived at the same time from somewhere in the colonies. They had the manners of savages. They added milk to their tea after it was poured. They butchered the English language. They were known within the ranks as the Three Stooges. The ragging from their fellow soldiers was mostly good-natured but it created a sense of shared persecution that solidified them as a unit.

They were still hanging on to one another now and Wish felt a surge of affection for them both, though the affection was tainted, already edged with regret. There was a limit, he knew, a breaking point beyond which one of them would turn on or away from the others. It was simply a matter of chance whether they ever reached it.

For weeks, "latrine rumours" in camp suggested the war in Europe was all but over. Two Korean guards were overheard discussing the fall of Iwo Jima and a fight for Okinawa going badly. There were increasingly frequent American bombing raids on the areas around Nagasaki, including the shipyard, where a detail of POWs was deployed as slave labour. The aircraft carrier Wish had spent months working on as a riveter was destroyed in a raid before its keel ever touched water. He spent his days now clearing up the debris. "If the Yanks don't kill us," Harris said to him, "we might get home alive yet."

Wish had nearly given up on that notion. But the possibility of it seemed so certain these days that it was like a new feeling altogether. Like falling in love after a lifetime of feeding simple animal lust.

After they left the restaurant in Mombasa, Harris and Anstey bartered with a man for the favours of a woman he was parading on the street. Harris tried to talk him down to half his asking price but the man refused to budge. She was his wife, the man said, she knew how to take care of a man. Harris shook his head. "She's *fat*," he said, using both hands to mime a full moon over his belly.

"Never mind," Anstey said. He was drunkenly counting the bills in his hand. "I like a bit of meat on a woman."

"Look at the hips on it, Ants. You'll fall body and bones into a cunny that size."

"You in on this, Wish?"

"Count me out."

"Don't be such a goddamn saint," Harris said.

"It's *Christmas*, Wish."

152

Wish had only been with a prostitute once, on leave in London with Harris and Anstey, before Mercedes' first letter reached him. The three soldiers had spent most of an afternoon drinking and Wish lost his companions on the city streets shortly before dark. He'd spent every cent he brought with him and had no idea how to get back to their hostel. He stopped a woman to ask directions and she looked him up and down. She was wearing so much makeup he found it impossible to guess her age.

"You a soldier, love?" she asked.

Wish was in uniform and simply nodded.

She did another slow measure of him. "You seen any action?"

"On leave from basic," he said.

The woman smiled at him. Her top teeth leaned in one direction like trees bowed by a prevailing wind. "That's not the sort of action I meant, dearie," she said. "You look awful young, is all."

"I don't have a cent on me," he told her.

She tipped her head to one side. "I don't mind doing my bit," she said. "For the war effort."

She took him to a tiny bedsit just large enough for a cot and a coal stove and an ancient loveseat covered with a thin sheet. The woman was on her period, or claimed as much, and she simply removed her blouse and bra, sitting in front of him on the cot to take down his trousers, clamping his half-erect cock in her unshaven armpit. There was a rancid smell of fried sausages in the bedsit (*bangers*, the English called them, which Anstey and Harris found endlessly amusing), grey flowered wallpaper that he stared at while stroking against her. Her head turned demurely to one side as if it was a solitary activity Wish was engaged in and she wanted to avoid invading his privacy. His head ached and he knew he would be bawling drunkenly in some alleyway before the night was through and the evening fell steadily around him in the tiny room. It felt as if he was bringing it down on himself, fucking his way into the dark.

Wish backed away from the ongoing negotiations to lean against the wall of Charlie's restaurant. He watched the woman standing at her husband's shoulder with a half smile on her face that could have meant anything. She was wearing a wide collar of roped beads and a dress of patterned cloth, a line of script along the border at her knees. Most of the women he'd seen on the streets had a phrase foreign to him sewn onto the material of their clothing, and he pointed to it, interrupting the negotiations.

"What does that say?" he asked.

The husband looked to see what he was pointing at. "*Usisafirie nyota ya mwenzio,*" he said.

"What does it say in *English?*"

"Don't set sail," the husband translated, "by someone else's star."

He nodded then. He was loaded drunk. And never wavered for a moment.

The light from headquarters was sent around at 6:30 in the evening, and the prisoners sat against the walls of the barracks, smoking their last official cigarette of the day. Wish was keeping a close eye on the truck, which hadn't moved from the spot where it was parked that afternoon. Osano was off duty and gone.

One of the newcomers strolled across the grounds toward them. "Which one of you is Furey?" he asked.

"Who wants to know?" Harris said.

"Ronnie Matthews," the soldier said, extending a hand to Harris. "18th Division."

Harris simply looked at him.

"Sherwood Foresters," he said. "We shipped out of Halifax on the *Mount Vernon.* Taken in Singapore."

"Spent some time in Changi prison, I imagine?" Harris said.

"Are you Furey?"

"No," Wish said. He was sitting several spaces down the wall. "I am."

"Just the man I'm after."

He was trying to guess Matthews's age. The soldier's hair had gone completely white but the face said early twenties at the most.

"We had a long trip in," he was saying. "Some of us would welcome a little refreshment. We were told you were the man to speak with."

"I could be," Wish said. He lifted himself to his feet, using the barracks wall to hold his weight on the way up. He stood still a moment to let the dizziness pass.

"We've put together a few dollars. Some cigarettes."

"We're old prison mates," Wish said. "A special price for you."

He and Harris and Anstey waited just inside the barracks entrance. Matthews arrived to the minute. McCarthy always said you could count on that in an Englishman, they were punctual. It was part of their formality, it gave them the same satisfaction as wearing the right jacket to dinner, tying a tie just so.

"Right then," Matthews said. "What do I do?"

Wish pointed out the truck, still sitting near the guardhouse. "There's a box in the back, you'll find a cloth bag inside."

"You're not going to get me shot, are you, Furey?"

"They don't pay much mind to us after dark," he said.

"Why don't you go get it yourself, then?"

Harris said, "Do you want the goddamn liquor or not?"

"Right," Matthews said. "I'm on my way."

Wish opened one of the bottles he had with him and handed it across. "One for the road," he said. Matthews drank and passed the bottle back. From the doorway, they watched him skulk along the line of barracks, then scramble over the open ground to the truck. A muffled clinking of bottles all the way back.

"You didn't tell me it was going to make such a bloody racket."

Wish held up two corked bottles. "This is good stuff," he said. "Lots more where it come from." He handed them to Matthews

155

and then said, "What about the Jap come over with you? The interpreter."

"We were hoping to be rid of him in the transfer."

"Hard case?"

"Lefty was strictly by the book when he first showed up at Mushiroda. No messing about. But he pretty much ran the show by the time we left. Owned the Red Cross storeroom. Heavy into the black market."

"No wonder he smiles so much," Anstey said.

"We got a ration of Red Cross beef at Mushiroda last year, just a tin per. Someone handed them out without consulting Lefty. As soon as he got wind of it he had them recalled. Don't know what he had over Sakamoto to get authorization for that. There was one fellow in the camp didn't return his ration. Lefty had his kit turned out, found the tin. Went at him with a bamboo stick while he lay in bed. Blood all over the place."

A shock of white hair, Wish was thinking. It had never struck him before, that phrase. Matthews had a shock of white hair. He said, "I had the interpreter pegged as a true believer."

"Oh he's all of that and then some," Matthews said. "Whatever's good for Japan is good for Lefty. I guess he decided the opposite must also be true."

"Why do you call him Lefty?" Harris asked.

"Here's hoping you never have cause to know," Matthews said. "You'd do well to stay clear of him if you can."

The camp buildings stood two or three feet off the ground on wooden posts. Their barracks was backed into a corner of the prison fence, as private a spot as the camp offered, and Wish had dug out a shallow trench underneath the far end to house the still and store the liquor. He used anything that came to hand to brew the shine, sweet potatoes and rice too rotten to eat, carrot and turnip tops, yeast that the Dutch soldiers in the cookhouse set aside for him. The unrefined sugar and soybeans and bottles were supplied by Osano, who took half the product to sell in Nagasaki. Left to stand two weeks in the bottle, the liquor was 90 proof. Wish hadn't tasted anything as foul since his first mouthful of Clive's shine in the Cove. But it got the job done.

After Matthews left them, they carried the bag to the rear of the barracks and crawled underneath. Along with the bottles, the bag contained a box of matches. The bottles were bad enough, but possessing matches could get a man shot. Harris said, "I think we'd best head back inside tonight. What with the new fellows about."

Wish was still feeling too contrary to listen to common sense. "I'm having a drink and a smoke before I call it a night," he said. "Lefty or no."

"Anstey?"

"I can't leave him out here alone, now, can I?"

"It's your funeral," Harris said. And he left them there.

Wish opened a bottle and lit up two cigarettes. "Miserable bastard," he said.

"Matthews spooked him. He's just trying to watch out for us."

Wish had fallen in with the two men his first evening in Halifax. When he cleared the vessel that afternoon he tried to find his way to an enlistment office, following the partial and contradictory directions of people he approached on the street. Spent hours crossing and recrossing the same intersections, as if there was some vast conspiracy among the citizens of Halifax to keep him from joining up. The office was closed by the time he found it and he carried on wandering the streets awhile. Drifted into a tavern after dark to order a beer. Harris and Anstey were at the bar and already halfways drunk. They got up from their seats periodically to salute one another, march in formation through the tables to the toilets. Boys at the outset of some grand adventure. They saluted Wish and every other drinker in the room as they passed, called them all *soldier*.

There was something Abbott and Costello-ish about the pair. Harris a good head taller than his companion, a straight man's seriousness about him even in his cups. Anstey thin as a rake but hissing with energy like a gas lamp. Ants, the bigger man called him. Antsy.

Wish got drunk watching them carry on. Found out they'd hooked up at the same enlistment office he'd spent the afternoon searching for. The two of them fell to talking as they waited, Anstey said, decided to head across the pond instead, join the British army.

"Citizens of the Commonwealth," Wish said.

Harris raised his glass. "The Brits pay better money," he said. He was the schemer of the two, the instigator.

Anstey said, "We'll see action a lot sooner than the crowd signing up here ever will." So jacked up with the thought of what lay ahead he could just sit still on his stool. He looked at Wish and said, "What about you, soldier?" Saluted again.

The extra money made no odds to Wish, but the thought of getting as far from Newfoundland as he could was incentive enough.

Wish watched the dot of Anstey's fag drift back and forth in the dark beneath the barracks, the red flare of it as he took a drag. It made him think of Mercedes' father stretched out on his daybed in the back kitchen, an arm behind his head, night closing in on their conversation. The man four years buried now. And all the absent and dead of Wish's life—his parents, Lilly and Hiram and Mercedes, Tom and Billy-Peter Keating—suddenly folded into his memory of that figure across the room, fading to a voice and the dark ember of a cigarette.

As if he would never come closer to them again than this.

There was no staying clear of the interpreter.

In the weeks after his arrival he set about claiming the camp, making impromptu inspections of the barracks, the hospital, the workstations, like a dog pissing to mark the corners of his territory.

He interrogated prisoners and guards to glean details of camp life, making a map of the place in his head. Which POWs worked in the shipyard, which in the coalmines and which in the kitchen, which guards were selling cocoa and beef and medicine from the Red Cross supplies kept in the storeroom. Wish saw him chatting with Osano, offering the civilian guard a cigarette.

In the middle of April the interpreter walked through the barracks handing out file cards and pencil stubs. "Each prisoner will be allowed a maximum of forty words," he shouted. "All letters will be screened and censored if necessary. You have five minutes." He went to the door and stood waiting.

Harris said, "You think these will actually be sent anywhere?"

They'd been permitted to send a note home only the once, when they first arrived at #14, in 1942. And the letters from Mercedes gave no indication she'd seen it. "Even if they are," Wish said, "I got me doubts about the logistics of the British Army."

Anstey and Harris stretched out on their berths, writing carefully in block letters, counting words on their fingers. They looked like children at their homework. Harris's huge feet hung over the edge of the bunk. Wish printed his name, rank and serial number across the top. That was all the soldiers were meant to include, but he and the two Canadians included the addresses they were writing to as well. *Mercedes Parsons, c/o Hiram Keeping, Georgestown, St. John's, Newfoundland,* he wrote, underlining the last word three times. *Enjoying sunny Pacific but hospitality a bust, home as soon as vacation over. Health continues good. Starved for fish cakes and sight of you. Have your letters, pls. keep writing. Wait for me.*

The cards were collected after precisely five minutes.

"They'll never make it out of camp," Wish said.

The next morning after roll call, the interpreter stood before the line. He took filing cards from his uniform pocket and looked down at them. "Corporal James Harris," he said.

Harris stepped forward and stood at attention.

The interpreter turned the card over. "Halifax, Nova Scotia," he said. "Canada."

"Yes sir," Harris said.

"Private William Anstey."

"Sir."

"Antigonish, Nova Scotia. Canada."

"Yes sir."

"Canadians."

"Yes sir," they both replied.

A node of discomfort started buzzing in Wish's stomach.

"Sir," Harris said, "is there a problem with those cards?"

The interpreter stepped up and slapped him across the face. He looked from one man to the next. "Canadians," he said again.

Both men said, "Yes sir."

The interpreter smiled at them. "I am very pleased," he said, "to meet you."

He turned away then, having marked the two of them, and Koyagi dismissed the entire company.

They talked among themselves that evening, lying in the barracks after the suppertime cigarette, waiting for roll call.

"You should steer clear of us," Harris told Wish. "Eat with some of the other fellows."

"He've already seen us ganging around together," Wish said. Although the thought had crossed his mind.

Anstey said, "He got some special kind of dislike for us, that's sure enough."

"Maybe he had a run-in with the Canadian troops in Hong Kong."

The man lying nearest the door through to the officers' berths called across to them. "Interpreter," he said. All the prisoners got to their feet and bowed as the soldier walked down the room, accompanied by another guard. He stopped in front of Wish.

"Private Furey."

Wish straightened up to look at him.

"That is your name?"

"Yes sir. Aloysious Furey, sir."

The interpreter ordered the other prisoners out of the barracks and the guard herded them toward the exit. When he and Wish were alone he said, "I have been speaking with Mr. Osano."

"Who, sir?"

The interpreter backhanded him across the face. "I have been speaking with Mr. Osano." He waited a moment before going on. "Your business venture will continue. But there will be a"—he pretended to be searching for the correct word—"a new tax," he said.

"I have no idea what you're talking about, sir."

The interpreter produced a box of matches from his pocket. He called the guard back into the barracks and waved the matches around, shouting and pointing at the berth and then at Wish. The guard butt-ended Wish in the stomach with his rifle, then kicked and shoved him outside, past the prisoners gathered around the entrance.

He was ordered to stand in the square with his arms outstretched, and a box filled with water was placed in his hands. He tried to guess the weight of it, ten or fifteen pounds he thought, a medium-sized codfish. The interpreter standing at his shoulder as the minutes ticked by. The seconds were leaden and seemed to drop into the box as they passed, his arms beginning to waver as the heft of it grew. After twenty minutes it was as if he'd fallen back into a malarial fever. His entire body shook, his hair and shirt drenched in sweat. The second the box dipped the interpreter laced into his back with a bamboo stick, forcing him to keep it raised to shoulder height. The rush of adrenaline holding it there a few more minutes.

They repeated the steps of this dance half a dozen times, and for a while Wish was able to take in details of the event. The interpreter used his left hand to swing the bamboo stick, which explained the name Lefty. He wore his pistol on the right, which meant he was right-handed and simply unable to swing with enough force from that side to satisfy himself. So the injury likely had something to do with his back.

That was the last rational thought he could manage. By the time the interpreter ordered him to set the box down, he couldn't think of his own name. He laid it as gently as he could manage and stood straight again, sucking air through his nostrils.

The interpreter said, "I could have you shot for this violation."

He was handsome in a way that made his arrogance more obnoxious. He had a mole high on the left cheekbone that seemed curiously precious, as if it had been drawn there with an eyebrow pencil. His eyes steady behind the wire-rimmed spectacles, a smile on his face.

He said, "I trust we have an understanding."

Wish bowed in front of him. Every muscle in his body quivering as if he were plugged into an electrical outlet. He held the bow, acquiescing, and at the same time he was placing the interpreter on the chart in his mind, on the far edge of a ring among the outer planets. Somewhere beyond human.

"I see you are a friend of the Canadians," the interpreter said, still smiling. "They are associates of yours."

"We're in the same outfit, sir."

The interpreter shouted an order to the guard, who singled out Harris and Anstey among the prisoners pretending not to watch the punishment. The three of them were marched to a line of individual cells made of bamboo, the ceilings too low for even Anstey to stand upright inside. The guard beat them across the backs and shoulders with a bamboo stick as they hustled inside, their heads covered with their hands.

They spent four nights in the cells. They were each given one ball of rice a day, laced with salt. Half of one cup of water each morning. The interpreter visited regularly to look in on them through the bamboo slats and to ask how they were enjoying the accommodations. He drank tall glasses of water where they could see him, a display of such childish cruelty it was difficult to credit. He seemed cartoonish to Wish, as if he had picked up his manner from watching crooks and hooligans in Hollywood films.

Talking was strictly forbidden, but they managed whispered conversations at night.

Anstey said, "He's off his head, that one."

"I don't know if it's that simple," Wish said.

"What is it, then?"

"There's something in him don't seem real."

"The bastard seems real enough to me," Anstey whispered.

Harris said, "He's the Jap to beat all Japs, for certain."

That was more or less what Wish meant. There seemed something made up in everything about the interpreter.

They spent hours talking about food, recalling the meals they'd eaten in their lives, daydreaming the dishes ahead of them. It was a kind of mental torture not much different than the interpreter's gulping water just out of their reach. But they couldn't help themselves.

"Tell you where I'd like to go I gets out of here," Anstey said. "One of those garden parties in Renews Wish goes on about."

"Don't torture me," Harris said encouragingly.

Wish panned across those tables in his mind, every square inch laden with plates and trays and bowls. He listed the dishes aloud. Salt fish and fresh. Roast chicken and pork and salt meat. Pease pudding and cabbage and turnip. Onion pudding. Big crystal bowls of potato salad and jelly salad and coleslaw. Fruitcakes and pound cakes and figgy duff for dessert. Partridgeberry pie and custard pudding. "A dime to load up your plate as high as you like," he said.

"Jesus," Anstey whispered.

They were quiet a while then, their hunger sharpened by the thought of all the food they'd passed up in their lives.

Anstey said, "You and your missus, Wish." He seemed to be trying to move on to something less provoking to his stomach. "You didn't have much time together before you joined up, did you."

"Not much, no."

"You had her before you come over, I hope."

"Fuck, Ants," Harris said. "Who put the hole in your manners bag?"

"I'm only saying, Harris. It'd be a shame if he didn't and never. You know," he said, "got the chance."

"Shut your mouth, would you? Jesus. Don't mind him, Wish."

He didn't respond, and that was the end of the conversation. But he spent some time afterwards thinking of the night he'd knelt in front of Mercedes out behind the house in the Cove. There was nothing sexual in the memory for him. He was too exhausted, too parched and hungry for that. But the thought he might never get the chance to properly lay down with her tormented him. *Consummation*, the Monsignor called it. Wish never understood why priests always wanted a grand word for ordinary things and came to think it was just a way of putting people in their place. But it was the priest's word he reached for when he tried to explain to Mercedes why they should wait. There was something high-minded and pure in it that seemed necessary in the circumstances. And he was afraid now, lying on the dirt floor of a bamboo cage halfway around the world, that it would never be his and hers together.

He shouldn't have hooked up with Harris and Anstey in that bar, the two of them drunk and no real idea what England was or the army or where they'd end up. If one useless bastard in Halifax had given him sensible directions to the enlistment office. He shouldn't have listened to Hiram and run off to Halifax in the first place. If he hadn't hauled Hardy down the stairs, none of this. If he hadn't knelt to say the rosary over poor drowned Aubrey Parsons. Hadn't chased after a Protestant girl whose mother would never have him. He shouldn't have hooked up with Hiram at all, was the truth of it, shouldn't have left Renews.

He lay awake through hours of this kind of suffering at night while the camp was quiet and Harris and Anstey slept or lay silently running over their own lists. There was a sickening sense of inevitability to the rain of incident and circumstance when Wish looked back on it. He started to feel that even the subtlest shift—if he'd woken earlier on the day he first saw Mercedes, if he'd drunk one beer more or less in the Halifax bar—even the most inconsequential change would have been enough to alter the chain of events and his life now would be completely different. God's hand was there in the details, Lilly always said, turning you left or right. And there was some vague comfort in thinking God was to blame.

After he and Tom and Billy-Peter off-loaded the statue of Jesus on the St. John's waterfront, they had a few glasses of shine on deck. From where they were moored they could hear the Salvation Army street service. A young man waving the *Good News* and shouting over the noise of commerce on the docks.

Tom went below to sleep as soon as it got dark and the two younger men set off to see what they could of the town. They found a tavern by the spilled light and noise as a door opened into the road, the room crowded with soldiers. They were Canadians, 1st Battalion of the Black Watch. They were drinking with a reckless intensity, every one of them gregarious and expansively friendly. They stood drinks for the two Newfoundlanders. A soldier named Kent leaned across the table, pointing a finger at them both. He had a head that looked like it had come in a box, flattop haircut, a bizarrely square jaw.

"You fellows going to join up?" he said. He wiped at the line of perspiration across his upper lip and smiled. "Nothing like a uniform to the ladies, I guarantee." He shook his square head. "A whiff of overseas and they want to make sure you get a proper send-off. I'm chafed sore."

After the tavern closed they were invited along to a house party on George Street. Soldiers again and a dozen local girls, the air blue with smoke. A gramophone in a corner was scratching out show tunes. Bottles of Old Sam on a rickety card table. "Bees to honey," Kent said, indicating the mix of uniforms and young women.

Hours later, Billy-Peter leaned over Wish where he sat in a chair by the gramophone. "It must be close to light," he said. "The old man will want to be setting for home."

The girls in the room were just starting to surrender items of clothing, the soldiers had stripped down to their undershirts. It seemed the wrong time to be leaving. But he said, "All right," and got to his feet to follow Billy-Peter out. They had to step back against the wall at the door to let a handful of arrivals go past them. Wish barely glanced at the newcomers, and he and Billy-Peter were halfway to the harbour before the face of the man with the waxed moustache registered. Hiram Keeping.

He made some lame excuse—he'd left his handkerchief behind, he said—and told Billy-Peter he'd catch him up. Already with it in his head to see about hooking up with Hiram. To stay behind in St. John's for good.

If they hadn't happened into that tavern full of soldiers. If Kent hadn't invited them along to George Street that night. If Hiram hadn't come through the door at that precise moment. If not for that goddamned moustache. There was no pattern or design to it all that he could make out. But he picked at the patchwork of seams in the fabric until he managed to fall asleep.

By the fourth night he was severely dehydrated and his head was ringing with the lack. The inside of his eyelids felt like sandpaper. He worked his mouth unconsciously, trying to manufacture a little saliva. Could hear the dry-leather sound of Harris and Anstey at the same activity, even when they slept. He dreamt of water in all its forms, rivers and rattling brooks, rain guttering through city streets, lakes and deep black-water ponds on the barrens. He filled his cupped hands and dream glasses and dream tankards, drinking them down one after another and no relief to be had from the exercise. Each time he woke from those dreams he broke down and wept in a low, dry wail that seemed somehow unconnected to him. As if it was the night itself that was keening.

Hunger was a physical strain, a weight he had dragged around for years now and sometimes managed to forget he carried, drunk or asleep. But four days of thirst just about undid him.

Sometime before light Wish woke to find someone crouching outside the cell. He pushed himself up on his elbows. "Who is it?" he said.

"Osano."

"Water," he said. "*Mizu*." He crawled to the bars. "*Mizu*."

Osano shook his head. "*Asa*," he said.

"Fuck *tomorrow*," Wish whispered. He tipped his hand to his mouth repeatedly. "A drink. *Mizu*."

"*Asa*," Osano repeated apologetically and he stood up then and left.

They were released after the morning roll call and none of them could manage to stand straight. A distant drone of aircraft passing overhead, American bombers far enough away that no one in the camp even glanced up. Anstey had been delirious through most of the previous night, talking gibberish to himself. Wish and Harris put their arms around him as they crossed the square, the heat of the fever burning through his shirt. They hobbled unsteadily back to the barracks in a hunch, like three decrepit old men. The sound of the explosions reaching them from miles off as the planes dropped their ordnance on targets around Nagasaki.

"The Yanks better get a move on now," Harris said. "Or we're done for."

Wish was still thinking about Osano's visit. The civilian had managed to parlay his involvement in the moonshining into some influence over the interpreter. Which had been enough to keep them from being killed outright or left to die in the cells. He tried to say something reassuring along those lines to Harris but his tongue was too dry and swollen to form the words.

MERCEDES

—

THEY LEFT THE CROWDS behind on the downtown streets, walking up past the Battery to Signal Hill. Passed Dead Man's Pond on the right, the dank smell of standing water just off the road. Trucks filled with soldiers laboured by them occasionally, the men singing drunkenly or shouting as they passed, the truck slowing beside them and the soldiers reaching their hands to offer a ride. But Mercedes preferred to walk.

Church bells had pealed out over the city mid-morning, the ships in the harbour sounding their whistles and sirens, cars driving through the streets with their horns blaring. Hiram closed up his shop and ran outside with only one arm of his coat on and his hat in his hand and he left Mercedes behind when she stopped at the Bashas' store. The front door was already locked and she went around to the back entrance, let herself into the kitchen, where a celebration was under way. The Basha family and most of the other Lebanese in the city crammed into the space, several huge pots simmering on the stove, a bottle of rum open on the table. Rania hugged Mercedes and kissed her on both cheeks

and everyone in the kitchen—men, women and children—stood
to take their turn.

They left the house in the afternoon and set off down
Prescott toward the waterfront, where thousands of others lined the
streets. Flags and bunting were hung from the buildings and
people leaned out the open windows above the sidewalks. Long
cheers rippled through the crowd, spontaneous renditions of "God
Save the King" and the "Ode to Newfoundland." But Mercedes
felt strangely subdued for all the commotion and fuss.

In the early evening she slipped away from the Bashas and
wandered up toward the Kirk. At the top of Long's Hill she
caught sight of another gathering on the pavement, traffic
backed up in both directions. She walked halfway up the hill
before she heard the sound of his trumpet. Easily a thousand
people surrounded him to listen. Mercedes had never gotten
used to the crowds in St. John's, the anonymous crush on the
streets, the physical intimacy of it. Even walking among so many
strangers was an unpleasantness for her. She covered her mouth
and nose with her hand to mask the smell of them as she jostled
her way toward the open circle of pavement where Johnny
Boustani stood.

He wore his uniform but his head was bare. The evening
was unusually warm and beads of sweat stood out on his face. He
played "If Stars Could Talk" and "Breezing Along with the
Breeze," the crowd raising their hands in the air to applaud
between numbers, and he bowed twice without taking the instrument from his lips, already moving into the next song. The
concave arch of his spine like a strung bow when he reached for
the upper register. He turned slowly as he played, so the music
travelled to all points of the compass. He caught sight of
Mercedes finally and broke off to drag her into the open space,
kissing her full on the mouth as people cheered him on. She
could smell alcohol on his breath, which surprised her, she had

never known Johnny to take a drink. She backed off quickly, shouting at him to keep playing.

The impromptu concert continued another twenty minutes until two policemen pushed into the centre, waving the crowd on their way to clear the street for traffic. Johnny packed up his trumpet and stood looking at Mercedes. He shrugged awkwardly, embarrassed to have made a spectacle of himself or to be caught drinking or to have kissed her so brazenly.

"I felt like playing," he said.

"Take me up to Signal Hill, would you?"

It was nearly dusk and as they walked east they had to work against a swelling crowd heading to the railway station to meet members of the 5th Regiment arriving on the night train. People shook Johnny's hand as they passed, stopped to offer the soldier a snort from a bottle or flask. Mercedes could tell from the reckless way he threw his head back, the way his Adam's apple pistoned the alcohol down his throat, that Johnny was drunk. But he was her guarantee she'd get access to the Hill.

They found rowdy groups of American soldiers at the foot of Cabot Tower, singing together, laughing. Total strangers embraced them as they arrived, pressing drinks on them. The men slapped Johnny's back so hard he almost pitched forward onto his face, recovering his feet in time to brace for the next blow. Mercedes stepped out past them all into the dry grass and picked her way down the hill to the Battery standing on a promontory directly above the Narrows.

This had been a favourite walk of hers in the summers, after she'd discovered that Johnny Boustani's company was enough to satisfy the patrols of military police who might question her presence on the Hill. She'd stayed up here for hours sometimes while Johnny sat in the grass and sang softly to himself, the subterranean thrum of the city drifting up to them from the dark below. Distant traffic, voices shouting in the streets, laughter. Weak stains of light leaking through the hooded headlamps of cars.

She heard footsteps coming through the grass toward her but didn't turn away from the view.

"Thought I'd find you here," Johnny said.

"I was sure they'd have the lights back on. Why are they keeping it dark?"

He put an arm over her shoulder to point out the lights near the west end of the harbour. "They've got the railway station lit up for the 5th Regiment."

She'd come up here hoping to see the city shimmering, incandescent, like a creature restored to health after a long, devastating illness. The war in Europe was over. There should have been deck lights blazing on the ships at anchor and lights terraced up the bowl of hills surrounding the harbour, like berries clustered on a bush of darkness. "This must be the only place in the Commonwealth still blacked out," she said. The disappointment made her chest ache.

"This place is nothing," Johnny said. "You should see Boston at night. New York."

"I bet they're beautiful," she said softly.

"They are." He paused. "Though not so much next to you."

Mercedes eased a step away from him. "How much have you had to drink, Johnny Boustani?"

"Can't a man have a little fun, Mercedes? The war's over, for Pete's sake."

"It's not over for everybody," she said. "Not yet."

She had been living above Hiram's shop since the early fall of 1942, in the same rooms Wish had occupied before lighting out for Halifax and then England. She moved in around the same time he was steaming toward the tropics aboard the *Wakefield*. There was something in not knowing where he was headed that made her feel she was losing him, and she took the rooms at Hiram's to offset that sense. For the comfort of sleeping in the same bed he'd slept in, of sitting in the same chair at the same window while she read his letters, of looking out on a view he knew by heart.

She worked days in the shop to pay her rent, keeping accounts at first and other small matters of paperwork, eventually learning to run a projector, making five dollars in an afternoon showing movies at children's birthday parties in the merchant homes on Circular Road. She assisted Hiram in taking portrait photographs when he was working in town, although he would never allow her into the darkroom where he developed the prints. It was a converted sewing room, the window blacked out and the doorframe sealed against light from the hall.

"It's unseemly," he said, "for a man of my position to be in such close and closed quarters with a girl of your station."

"What does my station have to do with your quarters?"

"You know how people talk."

It was the same argument he'd made when she'd proposed renting the rooms. "You aren't afraid of living alone here?" he'd said. "With me?"

"You're harmless enough."

Hiram's face went dark. "You don't know a goddamn thing about me, little miss," he said. "Don't forget that."

She knew from Wish that Hiram lost his "nature" to alcohol long ago. His sense of propriety was all show, but she'd hurt his pride. She said, "My father taught me how to look after myself around your kind."

Hiram's residence was passed on to him by his parents and was large enough to house a dozen or more in a pinch. Thousands of people had moved to the city since the start of the war for the jobs on the army bases and the docks, and accommodations were nearly impossible to come by. There were those who suggested Hiram's living alone in the circumstances was somehow unpatriotic, and Mercedes guessed he let her move in partly to blunt that criticism. But he held firm on keeping her out of the darkroom and she was happy to let him have this smaller, symbolic victory.

As he predicted, people talked. She was Hiram's illegitimate child from some ancient outport affair, come to track down her father. She and Hiram were secretly married. She was pregnant with Hiram's child. "There's no imagination to gossip," Hiram said when he reported the rumours to her. "It's the same old thing, over and over again."

She was surprised to discover she enjoyed Hiram's company, not least because he had an endless supply of anecdotes about the Southern Shore and many of those involved Wish in some way. When he was sober Hiram had little to say about him, as if he was afraid he might contradict some story Wish had already told about himself. But he was rarely sober and never for long.

Hiram's favourite story about Renews: The first night he showed a movie at Kane's store he set up the projector and went off to Tom Keating's after a drink. When he wandered back two hours later, the room was packed with people sitting on the chairs and lobster pots and boxes they'd carted with them for seats. And every last person in the audience sat facing the projector at the back of the room. "Wish too," Hiram said. "It made sense in a way, I guess, that's where the *machine* was. That's where you'd expect it all to happen."

There was a note of condescension in Hiram's opinions of everyone and everything from the outports, even when it was admiration he felt. As if he was praising a slightly retarded child.

His one real pleasure besides drink was gambling. He wagered bets on anything he could find a taker for. When the spring ice would block the harbour and how long it would stay. The date of the first snowfall of the year. In March, horse races were run on the ice at Quidi Vidi Lake, the animals who hauled groceries and coal and milk through the city pitted against one another and occasional challengers from the outports. Hiram was rumoured to have won hundreds of dollars on the outcomes. Easy money, he called it. "The Protestants won't be seen to bet against a Protestant horse, not to save their lives. And the micks are the same. But I got no qualms either way," he said. After taking a bet from an easy mark he rubbed his palms together and whispered, "The Lord hath delivered him into my hands."

Mercedes didn't understand this addiction of his and told him so.

He cocked his head at her. "You're a gambler," he said. "Same as myself."

She could feel her ears go red. "I am *not*," she said. According to her grandmother, gambling was worse than drinking or dancing.

"You picked your horse," Hiram told her. "And you put everything you have on him."

And she recognized what he said as the truth.

He said, "One time out of a hundred, a bet will call you. Rest of the time it's just guessing, but that one time. It's like the hand of God settling on you, pointing you this way or that. Any normal person would Jonah and run, for fear of looking a fool if it turns against them. Not me," he said. "And not you."

"What happens if you end up looking like a fool?"

"Faith is all we gamblers have going for us."

She asked Wish to take his shirt off one morning. Just to have a look at him.

This was the day after young Willard Slade's funeral. Two mornings after Wish had come to find her at the riddle fence, when he'd buried his head under her skirt and held it there like a man trying to drown himself in a bucket of water. She thought he must be drunk to act that way and tried to haul him off her, pulling harder at his hair as she felt something unfamiliar building in the distance, bearing down on her like some tidal wave of the senses, picking up speed and heft as it approached. It felt like a violent thing and she was terrified at first, her right calf seized up in a cramp halfway through the first orgasm of her life and she fell onto him, writhing like some evangelical in a trance.

It was only in the aftermath that she was able to sort it all into manageable categories, parsing the surge of pleasure from the fear, from the knot of pain in her calf that was still aching. She'd lain awake all night then, tormented by the memory of his mouth down there. She couldn't imagine a soul in the Cove having any truck with the like, and decided it must be a Catholic thing. Her face burning at the thought of anyone in the house knowing she'd allowed it to happen.

"Lie *still*," Agnes pleaded.

Wish knelt up, shrugging his shoulders free of the suspenders, unbuttoning the shirt. Not a hair on his chest. The hollows behind the collarbone deep enough to hold a tablespoon of water. Pale, puckered nipples like an infant's. She put her arms around his bare torso and held him, running a hand up and down the pronounced keyboard of his spine. She started at the nape of his neck, at the birthmark, and counted all the way to the tailbone, her fingers slipping under the band of his trousers. Sixteen vertebrae. She repeated the number in her head, to remember it.

It was as if she knew she had to take him in as quickly as possible, set enough of him to memory to carry her through.

"What else would you like to have a look at?" he asked.

She glanced up at his face. There was nothing lewd in the question. Or the lewdness was twined so delicately with something else, with a shy seriousness, that she never thought to be insulted. She said, "Everything."

"Now Mercedes," he said. "Don't be greedy."

"Everything," she said again.

He smiled at her and stood up out of the grass, reaching for the clasp of his trousers. And paused with his hand there.

"Have you ever seen a man naked before?"

"No."

He took several steps back toward the water.

"Where are you going?"

"You stay settled where you're to," he told her. He slipped his pants down his legs and stepped out of them, standing before her in only his socks. The skin so pale she could see a tracery of blue veins at the pelvis. Pubic hair a bush of tight curls, as if it was carefully tied up in rags at night. His *thing*. She had nothing else in her head to call it. It was hard and stood rigidly at attention. The dark mushroom cap of a head, the length of it quivering as the blood pulsed through. It was a ridiculous article to look at and for a moment she thought the urge to laugh might undo her.

She sat up on her knees, touching her mouth with the fingers of one hand. Things came over you, she thought. That's what it meant to be in love. Unimaginable things came over you and you were a different person and wanted different things than the world suggested you could be or want. She had no idea how to tell Wish what was in her mind. It was a Catholic thing and there were no words for it in the world that was hers before she found him. He was standing too far away to touch and she extended one hand toward him. She said, "Wish." He was already reaching to put his clothes back on and she wanted to stop him. She said, "I want to do for you."

He looked up at her quickly. Knowing exactly what she meant, she could see that. But he turned away to pull his pants up around his waist. The angry red mark at his neck. He hauled on his shirt, buttoned it with his back turned.

It was the wrong thing somehow. Suggesting it out loud was wrong, maybe even thinking of it was wrong and he was rushing away from her. "You must think—" she said.

"No. No, I don't." He knelt beside her and kissed her face, kissed her mouth and eyes. "Of course I don't," he said. "It's only . . ."

"Only what?"

"There's lots of time, is all. To do it right. When we're married."

"And what was that the other night, then? When you?"

He said, "That was just a taste"—he smiled at this little unintended joke and Mercedes smiled with him—"of things to come."

It made her more sure of him at the time, the unexpected restraint, his insistence on putting off the consummation, as he called it. But she regretted that now, agreeing to wait as if there was all the time in the world. She wandered through his rooms, touching this piece of furniture or that fixture he would have touched, and all the time choosing or discarding children's names or planning the cut of a wedding dress or the colours in a quilt sewn for an imaginary bed.

She was struck by Hiram's description of her as a gambler and had to admit there was something of a gambler's fancy in it all—that having wagered so much there was no other way for her to feel, no other outcome to hope for. It was intangible and shadowy and as real as anything she'd ever felt. She was like a person born blind, with no experience of sight except that every remaining sense insinuates the lack of it.

Hardy came to see her at Hiram's shop shortly after she moved in.

Mercedes was behind the counter and stood looking up at him when he came in, his hair bleached almost white by a summer on the water. She glanced down at Hardy's hands on the counter, saw his wedding band. "Are you and Ruthie married now?"

"Day after Christmas, when the minister was over to do a service at the church."

He told her that Clive Reid had taken a fever just before Christmas and nearly died but was on the water as soon as the weather was civil enough to fish. That the church hall had caught fire and burned to the ground, though they'd managed to save the church.

It struck Mercedes how she'd thought of the Cove and the people in it as frozen in time somehow, that their world had been suspended when she left and would remain unchanged, as they were in her mind. She felt those lives set in motion now, as if she was revising a film, the celluloid pacing through her thumb and forefinger, days and seasons, loves and illnesses and deaths. The sensation of it made her light-headed and she put both hands to the counter to steady herself.

"Sadie," he said.

"She's gone, isn't she."

"Before Christmas," he said. "She went peaceful."

Mercedes thought of her grandmother's certainty, her dogged-ness. The only book the old woman had ever read was the Bible. Five verses every evening and she'd crawled through both Testaments half a dozen times in her life. *Peaceful* didn't suit the woman.

"What have you got done to your hair?" Hardy asked her. "You looks some grand."

Mercedes only shrugged. "How's Ruthie?"

"You could offer me a cup of tea, Sade."

She took him to one of her two rooms on the second floor and put the kettle on an electric hot plate.

"How did you know to find me here?"

"It was the only place I knew to look." He picked up the tin of evaporated milk she'd set beside the cups. He said, "I thought this stuff was rationed for children."

"Hiram knows some people," she said and she motioned Hardy to a seat. She could hardly believe he was next to her, within an arm's length. They hadn't touched one another since he'd come in the door and she felt the absence of it suddenly, the way hunger sometimes ambushed her after sneaking up unnoticed for hours.

Hardy had never seen a contraption like the hot plate and he asked her a string of questions that Mercedes had no answers for.

And then just as casually he said, "How's things with your man? You two are still fixed for each other?"

"Is that Mother you're asking for?"

He didn't answer right away and she could tell he was trying to choose his words carefully. "Mother isn't—" he said. "She doesn't talk about it. About you." He nodded at her hands with his chin. "You're not married."

"I will be," she said. "When he gets home from overseas."

"Overseas?"

"He's gone to the war," she said. "Unlike some."

Hardy watched her awhile. The kettle shook on the hot plate and Mercedes got up to make the tea.

"You ever coming back home, Sadie?"

"Home?" she said angrily. She kept her back to him. "Home?" she said again.

When her grandmother fell ill, Helen or Mercedes read the evening's five Bible verses aloud for her whether she was lucid enough to take them in or not. The Book of Ruth they were reading from at the last. *The Almighty hath dealt very bitterly with me. I went out full and the Lord hath brought me home again empty.*

"Agnes misses you," Hardy said.

He was near tears and she couldn't bear to look at his face. "Don't," she said. She stirred a spoonful of milk into the cup.

"You're some hard bit of gear," he whispered. "You got no feeling for us at all, do you?"

"There's your tea," she told him and she rushed across the hall to her bedroom, closing the door behind her. After a few minutes he called her name, but she stayed where she was until she heard him go down the stairs and out the door to the street.

Johnny Boustani was assigned to the Intelligence office of the United States Army after Fort Pepperell was established, although he always said the word *Intelligence* as if it was some kind of joke.

In the months after Wish went missing he made a number of informal inquiries and offered Mercedes an educated guess on the whereabouts of Wish's company—Kyushu in the southwest, somewhere in the vicinity of Nagasaki—although whether Wish was still alive and with them there was no way to know. And he did his best not to answer Mercedes' questions about conditions in the camps during those early days. When she pressed him for details he said, "I'm just the guy who moves the flags around on the table maps."

"Someone must know something."

"We haven't heard much about it, Mercedes. Honestly."

"It's that bad, is it?"

"There's some things," he said, "you might be better off not knowing."

She continued writing to Wish all through the war, sending a letter out into the long silence every month, addressing them care of his unit's base in England. Even to Mercedes it felt like a useless exercise. But the alternative was giving him up for dead.

Mercedes said, "Hiram, what do you know about his aunt Lilly?" This was early on, when she was teasing out every scrap of information he had about Wish. "Why have they got her locked up at the convent?"

"She speaks Latin," Hiram said.

Mercedes stared at him.

"She learned on her own, they say. When she was a girl." He made a face. "She started speaking to the priest in Latin before she was ten, is the story on the shore. And no one could explain where she'd picked up the language. She says she was given messages from God in books that appeared out of nowhere and disappeared after she read them."

Mercedes thought of the woman's arm around her waist, the heat of it.

"She was living on her own for years out there until the day Wish found her," he said.

"Found her where?"

"Haven't Wish told you any of this?"

"No."

"Aren't you ever afraid of hearing too much?" Hiram grunted, as if he'd decided against going any further. But then he said, "Wish found her lying on the floor of that little shack she lived in. She had her arms stretched out like they were nailed to the cross. And she was bleeding from the palms of her hands."

"What do you mean, bleeding?"

"That's when they took her into the convent," Hiram said. "Wish was more or less living with the Keatings by then anyway. Him and Billy-Peter and Tom fished together and salvaged. And they were into the shine, running it along the shore. You can hardly blame him not wanting to live under the same roof."

"No," she said. "You can't."

It surprised her to see that knowing someone wasn't just a matter of accumulation, of simply adding details together to arrive at some coherent whole. It was obvious why Wish had told her next to nothing about Lilly. God spoke to her directly and she slept in the room next to his. He found her lying on the floor, blood seeping from her palms. She belonged to another world than this one, Patty Keating said.

Every detail Mercedes heard about Lilly made her seem more unreal. And pushed Wish a little further off at the same time. It seemed unfair that there were things you could learn about a person that meant you understood them less.

She learned to revise Hiram's films after his trips along the coast, rewinding the movies slowly, her fingers registering each nub of broken celluloid. She stopped the machine and snipped one or two frames clear, fastened the clean ends together with a glue she brushed on. Let it set a minute and began running the film through her fingers again. People would barely notice the hiccup in an actor's voice where these small repairs were made, the slight stutter in the picture's motion. But if she was forced to cut out long strings of damaged film whole words or phrases disappeared. When Mr. Gruffydd stopped short of kissing Angharad in *How Green Was My Valley*, saying he had no right, when she chased him to the door and said, "If the right is mine to give," no one in the audience but Mercedes would know she once added, "You have it." It was like having the gift of second sight, being privy to some secret part of the world invisible to other mortals.

But something in the process disturbed her. How easily skeins of conversation and gesture disappeared from the life of a picture. She lay awake nights thinking what would happen if she forgot those words, the brief significant glances. How the shape of those stories would be altered for good.

Her last visit from Hardy came early in the fall of 1943. Mercedes was playing a game of checkers on the counter with Johnny Boustani when he came into the shop and took his cap from his head. "I was in town," he said.

She introduced the two men and after a few moments of small talk Johnny gathered up his coat and hat and left them. Hardy watched after him and then gave Mercedes a questioning look.

"You want a cup of tea?"

"I was just wanting to set eyes on you. See you were all right."

"I'm all right."

He stood with his cap in his hands and he bent his head slightly, taking a long look at her. "You look a little nish, to me," he said. "Are you getting enough to eat?"

She'd had no word from Wish since before the fall of Singapore, fourteen months previous. "I'm eating fine," she lied. "Is someone dead, Hardy?"

"Everyone's the best kind. Ruth had a youngster after Christmas. A girl. I wanted you to know." He motioned his head toward the door. "This one, Johnny," he said.

"He's just a friend."

It made her so lonely to see him she felt sick and she wanted him out of her sight. He seemed to feel the impatience in her and it rattled his thoughts. He was carrying a winter's worth of news but he simply looked at her, not knowing what to say. He went to the door finally, stopped there before stepping outside.

"You can always come back to the Cove," he said, "if things go badly down here."

"You know the difference of that, Hardy."

He threw his cap to the ground. "God*damn* it, Mercedes." He bent over and swiped it. "You and Mother," he said. "I don't know which one of you is more mulish." He fixed his cap and went out the door.

Early in 1944 Mercedes finally received a note from Wish. The card typed and signed at the bottom in his hand. It had been written eighteen months earlier, just after his arrival in the Japanese POW camp. She went straight to the Bashas' store and jumped around while she shook the card in the air. Sammy watched her with a wide grin on his face, completely mystified. Amina grabbed Mercedes by the wrist in order to take the card and she read it aloud. Mercedes bit the skin on the back of her hand. Hearing Wish's words in another's mouth almost like hearing him speak himself.

The Bashas held a special meal that evening to celebrate. Johnny Boustani sat quietly in a corner and joined the toasts and sang along when the music began but he never looked in Mercedes' direction through the evening. Amina sat beside him, in a kind of silent commiseration that went on under the noise of the entertainment. Every time she caught Mercedes' eye her expression seemed to ask, "What about *him?*"

Mercedes had thought that moving out of the Bashas' house would mean seeing less of Johnny Boustani, but the opposite was true. It loosened the constraints that Rania's surrogate motherhood had imposed. Twice a week Mercedes and Johnny went to the movies at the base theatre. The Basha Orchestra played dances at the USO and Club Commodore and the Old Colony Club, and when Johnny wasn't sitting in with the band he and Mercedes danced or chatted with the Basha women or loitered outside for a cigarette.

"You treats him like a dog," Amina said, "letting him follow you around like that."

"I can't help how he acts."

"You're inviting it."

"Johnny Boustani falls in love with everyone," Mercedes insisted. "Didn't you tell me that?"

Judging by her father's advice, Mercedes thought Johnny had one thing on his mind when they first met and had tried his best to sweet talk his way into it. He gave up on talk eventually, accepting the borders she'd set for him and walking the limits of them repeatedly, like a prisoner taking exercise in the yard. She thought it was enough to have told him where things stood in her heart and let him make up his own mind about his chances.

They could see the single headlight of the locomotive rounding the curve at the trestle and chugging slowly into the brightly lit station. The roar of the crowd rolling out over the harbour as the soldiers of the 5th Regiment stepped onto the platform. The brassy strains of the CLB Armoury Band striking up.

Mercedes said, "How long do they think it'll last in the Pacific?"

"Eighteen months, some say. But it could go faster now we can throw everything at them." And a moment later Johnny said, "I guess they'll be shipping us out of here soon enough."

MICHAEL CRUMMEY

She could hear the regret in his voice. "Why do you waste so much of your time on me, Johnny Boustani?"

"I'll be the judge of how much time I'm wasting."

"You know my mind."

"Everyone knows Mercedes Parsons's mind," he said. "Mercedes not the least."

"You been good to me. Don't think I don't appreciate that."

He lurched away drunkenly before righting himself, heading back toward Cabot Tower. "Go to hell, Mercedes," he said.

She tried to call him back but he ignored her. She looked out at the lights of the welcoming ceremony below and stood with her arms folded, sure he'd come for her when remorse got the better of him. Half an hour later she was walking among the groups of soldiers around Cabot Tower, asking after him. Several people had seen someone wander off onto the headlands and she debated heading home on her own. But he was drunk and staggering around in the dark and in the end she couldn't leave him. She spent what felt like hours picking her careful way among the walking paths out there, calling his name until she heard him shouting "Johnny's not here." She kept calling and followed the sound of his denial, found him lying in the furze, staring up at the stars.

"Never had a bed so comfortable," he said when she knelt beside him in the moss.

"You're drunk."

"What if I am?"

"I don't trust drunk men."

"You?" he said. "Living with Hiram Keeping?"

"Hiram's different."

"I'm not drunk."

She shifted sideways to sit on the ground. The night was colder on the hill than in the city and she folded her arms around herself. "I'm froze to death, Johnny Boustani. Let's go home."

Johnny never took his eyes from the stars. He said, "I love you, Mercedes."

She looked up at the sky herself then, picked out the Big Dipper, Orion. Concentrated hard on them.

"I'm in love with you, Mercedes," he said again.

"You're drunk," she said.

He sat up suddenly to look across at her. "I know it's not what you want to hear. But it's a fact. I love you," he said. "I *loves* you."

"Don't make fun."

He lay back again, spreading his arms high at his sides. "Johnny Boustani," he said, "second lieutenant, U.S. Army Intelligence Office. Casualty of war." He started giggling. "Crucified by the love of a girl from the bay."

"How many times do I have to tell you?"

"He'll never come out of it alive, Mercedes."

"Johnny."

"It's going to go bad for those fellows when we invade."

Mercedes got to her feet and began walking away.

Johnny raised himself to his knees and shouted after her. "They're going to fight to the last woman and child. That's what the Japs are saying, Mercedes. And they're not going to waste a morsel of food or a drop of water or a single man to keep any prisoners alive."

"You're making that up."

"They're dead men, Mercedes. Every one of them."

"You *bastard*." She had never spoken a word like it aloud.

"I'll take care of you, Mercedes. I want you to know that."

"Shut up, Johnny."

"You could learn to love me, if you let yourself. If you let me take care of you."

She was only a few yards away but the dark made the distance seem immense and she screamed across at him. "You're a bastard, Johnny Boustani. Why are you telling me this?"

He leaned forward on his hands as if he was about to throw up. "I'm drunk," he said.

She came back to him and took him by the ear, lifting his head to talk directly into his face. "Say it isn't true," she said.

"I'm sorry, Mercedes."

She twisted his ear. "*Say* it."

He looked at her a moment, his eyes slurring slowly back and forth. "It isn't true," he whispered.

"You don't love me," she said.

"Never did. Never will."

She let go of his ear and his head sagged below his shoulders. He laid himself back on the ground, one joint at a time.

"I'm going home," she told him.

He didn't answer her and she walked off over the uneven ground. The wind had come up and she pulled her jacket tight at the throat with one hand. She looked back over her shoulder but there was no sign of movement in the dark. She stopped and tried out a number of other things she'd never spoken aloud before. "Goddamn it," she said. She looked up at the sky again. "For the love of Christ Jesus." She walked back to Johnny a second time and took him by the lapels of his jacket, dragging him to his feet. He put his arm over her shoulder and she half carried him across the headlands and down the road toward the lights of the city.

There was a new indoor pool in English Bay.

He happened on three boys he knew from the Japanese Language School, all members of the League of Divine Wind. They wore shorts and sandals, towels hung around their shoulders. They weren't friends of his but they invited him along because they were pessimistic about their chances and wanted the comfort of numbers.

The manager was apologetic, shrugging helplessly as he explained the facility's policy. The caustic smell of chlorine drifting out to them from the pool. He was an older man with a moon face under a straw hat, grey pants held high by suspenders. "Sorry, boys," he said, and it seemed to make him lonesome to turn them away. It was almost possible to feel sorry for him. They walked all the way to a swimming hole near Steveston instead. Putting the place out of their minds.

But the refusal ate at him and the following Saturday he went back to the pool on his own. The old man shook his head again. "No Japs," he said.

Nishino leaned against the doorframe while swimmers came and went and they chatted aimlessly awhile. He watched for a chink, a trap door, an open window in each word exchanged, in every casual detail. He told the manager he was living on a farm beyond Kitsilano and the old man smiled.

He said, "I lived in Kits for years before I moved into the city."

The next week, Nishino brought a container of fresh strawberries from the farm. They ate the fruit together while the manager spoke about this and that, happy for the audience. He had an uncle who'd worked as a shift boss in a sawmill in the valley years before, and Nishino told him it was the very same sawmill where his grandfather first found work when he moved to British Columbia. It was a bald-faced lie but a safe one—the English had trouble telling one Japanese worker from another—and the manager seemed delighted by the information.

"You're a clever little nip, ain't you," he said. And he apologized again, as he did regularly, for the pool's policy. "People just won't stand to share the place with your kind," he said.

And then Nishino made his proposal. The pool opened at ten each day. The manager agreed to let him and his friends come down for a swim at seven-thirty in the morning, as long as they promised to be gone before it opened to the general public. "I won't have enough paying customers to buy myself a quiff, they finds out I'm letting Japs in the water," he warned.

The air in the poolroom was humid, as dense with moisture as the rainforest. They cannonballed and belly-flopped off the diving board in the deep end until their skin stung. Just after nine, the manager poked his head through the change-room door and shouted at them to finish up. They swam into the shallow end toward the stairs leading up to the deck. The other boys were halfway out of the pool when they glanced back to see him standing splay-legged with his hands on his hips, only his head above the surface. A look of stilled concentration on his face.

It came to them all then without discussion or plan. They walked back down the stairs and stood at arm's length from one another. And after a few moments of willing it, all four boys pissed into the clear water of the pool.

WISH

—

HARRIS WAS ALREADY SITTING beside Anstey when Wish walked
down the row of berths in the hospital barracks. He'd soaked some
of the bread supplied to the sickest men in broth and was trying to
spoon it into Anstey's mouth.

Anstey tilted his head. "That you, Wish?" he said.

"Thought you were going blind, Ants."

Anstey was lying under two blankets, his head propped up on
an overcoat rolled into a pillow. "I could smell you coming," he said.

"Better or worse today?"

"Just colours still. And shapes. Coloured shapes."

"Open up," Harris said, holding the spoon to his mouth.

Anstey shook his head.

"Two more spoonfuls."

"Waste of your time," he whispered, "fussing over a dead man."

"Shut up, Anstey."

"Wish will be trucking me out to the French Temple before
long."

"Shut your mouth, I said."

"Open or closed, Harris. You can't have it both ways."

Harris put the bowl on the floor between his feet. "Closed then, you miserable bastard." He looked across at Wish. "Every man in this camp hungry enough to eat the leg off the Lamb of God and this little prick too contrary to drink a bit of soup."

It was hard for them both to watch the life bleed out of Anstey like air seeping from a balloon. He'd never recovered from the time they spent in the cells in April, suffering repeated bouts of fever and dysentery. McCarthy made several requests to have him assigned to the hospital, but the interpreter intervened to keep him at work. Until Anstey's vision started to fail. He'd lain in the hospital barracks the last two weeks of July and was no better for it. There was no medicine. Being excused from work and the bit of bread were the only allowances made.

Harris picked up the bowl again. "Come on, Ants," he said. "Don't make me beg."

Anstey opened as wide as he was able and Wish could see the grey-greenish tinge to the roof of his mouth. The same as his mother's before she died. Anstey's breathing was shallow but rapid and he accidentally aspirated the spoonful of broth, launched himself into a coughing fit. Harris lifted him forward, holding him up as the wasted body convulsed. Anstey's back studded by its chain of vertebrae, so prominent through the skin Wish could have counted them from across the room.

Harris eased him onto his back once the coughing ended and they all sat in silence while Anstey collected himself. It should have made Wish feel some kind of sadness to see his friend in that condition. But it was only a confirmation of helplessness that came over him and the useless bit of rage that accompanied it. Anstey let out a long breath of air and lifted his hand at the elbow to say he was all right.

Harris stiffened suddenly, his eyes flicking past Wish toward the door. "Lefty's coming," he whispered.

The interpreter walked the length of the barracks, looking neither left nor right. Wish and Harris stood, along with every patient capable of getting to his feet. Wish and Harris bowed as he approached, silently willing him to pass by. Knowing he would not.

The British doctor who provided most of the care to the sick men was out at the mess. Which was the reason the interpreter chose this moment to drop by, they knew. He stood at the foot of Anstey's sickbed and carried on a conversation with the Japanese orderly at the far end of the hospital.

"I'm told you are quite capable of standing," he said to Anstey.

Harris said, "He haven't got energy enough to *eat*."

"You act like women, you two."

"He's gone blind," Harris said uselessly.

"Get him *up!*"

Harris bowed and then pulled the covers away from Anstey's torso. Emaciated legs, knees the size of coconuts. "Come on, little buddy," he said. "Come on."

Wish moved to help but the interpreter raised a hand to stop him.

Anstey leaned heavily on Harris when he stood. He bobbed his head deferentially in the direction of the guard's voice. He was having trouble keeping his feet even though Harris was holding most of his weight. The interpreter stood watching them awhile. He took out a packet of cigarettes and lit one. He waved the package at Wish. "Smoke?"

Wish kept his eyes on the floor, ignoring the question.

The interpreter waited until he was satisfied the sick man wasn't about to collapse and continued down the aisle to the door at the opposite end.

Harris eased Anstey back into the berth. He said, "That fucker is number one on my hit list when this is all over. If I can still stand, so help me Christ."

Wish and Harris went straight to their bunks after the evening roll call. Their barracks had room enough for eighty men and had been full when they arrived at the camp in '42. Even with the arrival of the prisoners from Mushiroda, only a third of the beds were still occupied.

Wish said, "I wouldn't give Ants much more than a few weeks."

"You a doctor now, are you?"

"You seen the roof of his mouth, Harris, same as me. And that cough."

"He sure as hell isn't going to live on that maggot soup."

"We'll have to make a little midnight visit to the Red Cross storeroom, see if they got any more of those tins of beef stashed away."

They lay in their berths until the barracks had settled. It was perfectly still outside and pitch black. Even the lights in the guardhouse over the gate were blacked out to avoid leading American planes to bombing targets. They walked to the back of the building and Wish crawled into the space underneath. He felt around until he found the stash of bottles and crawled back into the open air with two. They walked along the back of the barracks, beside the ten-foot fence topped with rolls of razor wire. They went past the hospital to a smaller storehouse beside the headquarters.

"I spose we're dead men if it's Lefty in there tonight," Harris whispered.

Wish uncorked a bottle of shine and took a mouthful, then passed it to Harris. "No sense dying sober," he said.

He whistled at the door, and they heard footsteps inside, the door opening a crack.

"White Lightning," Wish said, shaking the bottle. "*Aruko-ru.*"

"*Ikahodo?*"

"*Ni,*" Wish said, holding up two fingers in the dark. "*Ni hon.*"

"Which one is he?" Harris whispered.

"Can't tell. But he sounds thirsty enough. *Yoi aruko-ru,*" he said, shaking the bottle again.

The door opened wide, an arm extended and waving them inside. The guard closed the door behind them and flicked on a flashlight, turning it to the ceiling to give a faint glow of light in the windowless room. His mouth and nose were covered with a kerchief. Wish and Harris bowed to him and handed over the bottles. He set them on the floor against the wall and walked to a padlocked door at the back of the room. After he opened it he waved them inside.

The storeroom was stacked floor to ceiling with Red Cross parcels, most of which had already been rifled through and pilfered from. In one corner sat a large white metal box with the Red Cross symbol on the cover. It was strapped closed and clearly hadn't been touched.

"Wish," Harris called and he nodded toward the container. "Medical," he said.

Wish turned to the guard and pointed at it. "*Kono,*" he said. Wish held up his hand, the fingers splayed. "*Go hon.*"

"No," the guard said.

"*Yoi aruko-ru,*" he said. He held up both hands. "*Juu.*"

The guard shook his head. He pointed at the box and said, "Nishino."

"*Nani?*"

"Nishino," the guard repeated angrily. "*Intapurita.*"

"The interpreter?"

"*Hai.*"

Harris turned away. And with his back to the guard he said, "We could take him right now, Wish, you and me."

"Don't be stunned, Harris. Just look for a few tins of beef."

The guard barked at them, suddenly furious, impatient to have them out of the room and gone.

Wish raised his hands. "Okay," he whispered. "Okay. Hurry the hell up, Harris, before he loses his head."

"I don't know why they bother covering their faces," Harris said. "Every single one of the bastards looks alike to me."

Wish used to think the same thing when they were first taken prisoner in Singapore. That sense only lasted a few weeks. But he had to admit that there was an absurd sameness to how they thought and acted that he couldn't penetrate. Half the time he didn't understand how their minds worked at all. There were obvious things, greed and pettiness and ridiculous little daily kindnesses as if they were all normal neighbours in a normal town. As often as not, though, he couldn't guess how they arrived in those obvious places, the streets their minds travelled to get there.

During their second winter in the camp he and Anstey had gone to the cookhouse to collect a stash of rotten sweet potatoes hidden for them by the Dutch soldiers. They left Harris outside as a watch, but in the darkness of the kitchen they stumbled over Osano, already inside as if he had been tipped off and was waiting for them. He shone his flashlight directly into their eyes and ran at them, screaming obscenities. He slapped them both with his open hand.

Wish tried to calm him down. "*Aruko-ru*," he kept repeating. "We alcohol," he said. "Partners."

Osano backed off finally and lectured them for several minutes, his face so contorted with emotion that it seemed he was trying to hold back tears. He reached into his shirt pocket and for the first time showed them that washed-out picture of his daughter or wife or mother, it was impossible to tell from the woman's face how old she was. "*Mitte*," he said, "*mitte*," shining the flashlight on the picture.

"What is it he wants?" Anstey said softly.

"The fucker's retarded," Wish said. "Just keep smiling." He looked at the photo, then smiled at Osano. "Some beautiful," he said, pointing. "*Kirie*."

He thought of Mercedes then and reached into his own pocket, bringing out the photograph to show the guard. He pointed at it and slapped his chest. "*Okami*," he said. "*Watasha no okami*."

Osano nodded and bowed to Wish and all three men felt a ridiculous wave of relief pass over them, as if some awful misunderstanding had been cleared up and the delicate line of civility and cooperation between them was re-established. They smiled and bowed to one another repeatedly.

"We go now," Wish said. *"Tachisaru."* He and Anstey backed slowly out of the room, still bowing.

Harris had bolted for the barracks when the shouting started and he was pacing the aisle when they got back. "What in Jesus' name happened in there?" he said.

"You should have heard this one go on," Anstey said, pointing to Wish, and he spoke a mouthful of gibberish that was meant to sound vaguely Japanese. "You learn to talk any more yellow," he said, "and your skin is going to turn."

It wasn't until he had a chance to think it through that Wish realized they'd walked in on Osano stealing food. There had been a rare delivery of meat that afternoon, thirty kilos of beef for the prisoners. A couple of kilograms on the black market would bring a tidy little windfall. Which made sense to Wish. Even Osano's yelling and striking them to cover his own indiscretion he could understand. But the guard's perpetual sheepishness and deference around him afterwards was a mystery. As if Wish might still be able to hurt him somehow.

Harris was rustling through Red Cross parcels at the back of the room. "Got three tins," he said. "And a quarter pound of chocolate."

"That'll have to do. *Domo,*" Wish said, bowing to the guard, who responded by holding his pistol tight to Wish's temple all the way to the door.

Mid-afternoon Saturday the truck arrived with the urns from area POW camps. Wish and McCarthy and the Dutch officer walked out into the parade square to meet it. There was no sign of Osano.

Wish looked into the box and counted eleven urns, besides the three from their own camp.

"Busy time," van der Meulen said.

"Attention!" a voice called behind them.

The interpreter stood a few feet behind them. All three of the men bowed.

"Climb in," he said.

There was no conversation at all as the truck drove up out of the valley. The interpreter stood facing out over the road ahead as if he was driving. Once the truck turned onto the open road and picked up speed, he sat against the cab, out of the breeze.

McCarthy said, "Where is Mr. Osano today?"

"The civilian guards have been relieved of their duties," Nishino said. "How is your Canadian friend?" he asked Wish.

Wish refused to look at him and pretended he couldn't hear the question over the noise of the engine and the wind.

"Private Anstey," McCarthy said, "is in desperate need of medicines."

"It's unfortunate that they are in such short supply."

"One round of M&B pills would be enough to keep him from dying."

"As I said. Very unfortunate."

The Dutch officer surprised them all then, saying, "We are not animals, you know."

Nishino paused, as if he was seriously considering this notion. "Then you should act like men," he said.

They drove on in silence until they pulled up beside the church. They carted as many of the urns inside in one trip as they could and Wish went back to the truck for the last two accompanied by the interpreter.

Lefty had become increasingly unpredictable as the summer progressed. There was a logic to his cruelty at first, parcelled out to advance his position in the camp or to carry out his peculiar vendetta against Harris and Anstey. But as rumours of American advances reached them in recent weeks, he seemed viciously unhinged. Wish thought there was a chance the interpreter might simply shoot him where he stood if he said anything now. Claim the prisoner was trying to escape. He felt surprisingly calm about it. There was even a blush of relief at the thought of everything ending right there in the church parking lot with Mary standing over him. His Mercedes. The Ocean Star.

"Your name," Wish said. "Nishino, right?"

The interpreter's head snapped back.

Wish bowed low to him, kept his eyes on his feet. "I'd love to get my hands on some of that Red Cross medicine you've got stashed away, sir." Wish took the interpreter's silence as encouragement to continue. "I'll get you whatever you want for it."

He was still looking down when the interpreter slapped him across the face. He fell back against the truck, juggled the urns in his arms to keep from dropping them. Pushed himself upright with his shoulders, bowed a second time.

"Get those urns inside the church."

Wish was about to start past the guard, but stopped. *You should act like men*, the interpreter had told them. He said, "Where did you learn to talk like that, sir?"

"Like what? Like a Canadian?" The two men watched one another until Nishino said, "Inside."

"Anstey is going to die without that medicine."

"Soldiers die," the interpreter said.

On Monday morning, Wish and Harris and a detail of other POWs were seconded from their work clearing debris at the shipyard. They were provided with picks and shovels black with coal dust from the mines worked by POWs at other camps in the area. The work detail set about digging a series of trenches inside the camp, five feet deep and three feet wide, that they covered with concrete. McCarthy and the ranking Dutch and American officers had been harassing Koyagi about the lack of bomb shelters to protect POWs for months. His capitulation on this point suggested the air raids were expected to continue. And treating prisoners as something more than expendable slave labour, however marginal the improvement, seemed a veiled admission by the Japanese of the possibility of defeat.

They worked alongside an American named Spalding who talked endlessly while he dug, as if speaking was a prerequisite for drawing breath. Wish couldn't begin to guess where he got the energy for it. The heavy work winded him. He had to lean on his spade and push words from his mouth. The effort felt no different than shovelling dirt.

Spalding was one of the few Americans Wish met in the camps who didn't have all his teeth. His skin tanned dark as leather. "You're the liquor boy," he said to Wish that first morning.

Wish held a finger to his mouth.

Spalding made a dumb show of zipping his lips shut. "Where you from?"

"Newfoundland."

Spalding gave him a look. "Newfun-what?"

"Newfoundland. Same as you says understand."

"Sounds made up."

Wish smiled. "God's country."

Spalding snorted. "That's what my father used to say about North Dakota. *God's country*. Don't know what kind of a God he believed in to be talking so much bullshit." He hefted a spadeful of dirt and tossed it up over the edge of the hole. "This ain't so bad," he said. "I spent all of nineteen years in Sherwood before I joined the army. I dragged a sled of milk around town in minus-forty when I wasn't old enough to smoke. Bottles of milk froze solid. And then all summer pitching hay in a hundred-ten. Shit," he said. "I always said I'd work in hell if the wages was right."

Harris said, "So what *do* you think of the wages?"

Spalding shrugged as he tamped the spade head into the ground. "I ain't complaining," he said. And he grinned a gap-toothed grin at them both.

They visited with Anstey in the evenings, swapping gossip and rumours and talking aimlessly about home. At some point in the conversation the sick man would fall asleep or lie listening silently, too tired to carry on talking himself. If a lull carried on long enough he would say, "Tell me a story," and Harris or Wish would scrounge some pointless recollection from their lives to fill the empty time.

Wish told Anstey about birding with Billy-Peter near Renews one late-fall afternoon when they were boys. They'd taken Patty's dog along with them. She was fed scraps and maggoty fish and never enough of either, which made her a fitful retriever. She gorged on two or three downed birds before she was satisfied to bring the turrs back to them whole. But the boys were hunting for a lark more than for food. They used lead-pellet shotguns to shoot turrs on the wing. Wish brought one down near the boat and the dog went over the side, Billy-Peter rowing along behind her. Wish saw the dog's head snap at the water and she turned to come back to them. Those peculiar orange eyebrows of hers. They hauled the dog aboard but there was no sign of the turr. "It must've sunk quick as that," Billy-Peter said. It was a queer thing but there were plenty of other birds to shoot at and they thought nothing more about it.

The dog went to lie behind the stove as soon as they got home and she was still lying there next morning and all through the day. Refused to eat or move. Growled when anyone came near. Stayed in that state three days and everyone had given her up for dead. She gave a low moan the afternoon of the third day and went slowly to the door, an odd stutter in her hind legs. Wish let her out-side and she went to the edge of the woods where she circled, whining the whole time, her tail up high and squatting awkwardly as she turned. It would have been comical if the animal wasn't in so much torment. He didn't know what was happening or how to help and simply stood there as the dog passed the turr, beak first and all of a piece. Every feather in place and not a mark on it, looking strangely serene and composed for something so defiled.

Anstey fell asleep at some point in the story and he and Harris sat quiet awhile when he was through. He glanced down at the sick man, lying there motionless and half blind. Like something the world had swallowed whole and shat out.

By the following Wednesday they had completed a bomb shelter for every two barracks. On Thursday, the detail was marched through the gate to a flat stretch of land two hundred yards outside the fence and ordered to dig again. Six feet deep this time and twenty yards square, a length of twine tied to wooden posts set out to mark the boundary. In the hospital barracks that evening Harris mentioned the dimensions as he was spooning morsels of beef from a tin into Anstey's broth.

"What's that for?" he asked.

"Another shelter, I guess."

"Too big for a concrete roof. Give like glass if it was hit."

"Okay," Harris said. "What is it, then?"

Anstey lay still a long time while the two men waited for an answer. He was almost completely blind now and stared blankly at the ceiling. It unnerved them not to be able to read his eyes.

"I don't know," he said, in a way that made them think he had ideas he wasn't willing to offer.

The next morning when they were marched back out to the site, a handful of civilian carpenters were already at work, laying posts fifteen feet from the hole. They stole glimpses of the raised wooden platform taking shape as they spaded deeper into the ground, the sound of hammers driving nails echoing off the camp walls behind them.

"What the hell are they putting up over there?" Wish asked finally.

Spalding stopped to glare at him. Went back to work, slamming the spade into the dirt furiously, as if he was falling behind in a digging competition.

"So?"

"That's a machine-gun platform, is what that is," he said, still shovelling.

Wish and Harris stood on their tiptoes to watch the carpenters at work and then looked around themselves at the hole they were standing in. Seeing it for what it was for the first time.

"Fuck," Spalding was whispering. "Fuck, fuck, fuck." He dropped his shovel and started laughing suddenly, his hands on his hips. He said, "Things must be looking pretty bad for the Imperial Japanese Army."

A Korean guard walked to the lip of the dig, yelling at him to get back to work.

"Well what's the difference?" Spalding said loudly. He held his arms wide. "Now or later. No goddamn difference at all, is there?"

Harris stepped a few feet farther away from the American. Refusing even to look at the man. The guard was almost hysterical, the surge of words incomprehensible until Wish heard him start counting backwards from five.

"Three," he repeated in English. "*Two*, Spalding."

The American stooped to pick up his shovel. "Shit," he said. He flicked a spadeful of dirt up near the guard's feet. "This ain't so bad," he said.

Anstey gave up eating before they ran out of the meat they'd bought to feed him. Harris stubbornly fortified the soup each evening, sneaking a tin into the hospital to slip tiny chunks of beef into his bowl, passing it on to other patients when it was clear that Anstey wouldn't be able to eat. Wish was surprised at himself for letting it go to others so easily. But they were all dead men, if the machine-gun platform was any indication. Food seemed beside the point.

They talked back and forth to one another, and to Anstey, although they couldn't say if he heard a word most of the time. It was all rumours of the war's progress and the desperate condition the Japs found themselves in. Something bizarre and monumental had occurred the day before, *Hiroshima* was the word they kept hearing, something unprecedented. There was a change in the demeanour of the guards at the camp, a peculiar glassy fragility had come over them.

"The Yanks are going to burn the fucking country to the ground when they get here, Ants," Harris said. "The Japs know it too."

There was a subdued sense of anticipation about them as they spoke, a viciously nihilistic hopefulness. They were resigned to dying in the lead-up to any American invasion and they lived for nothing but that inevitable event.

Ronnie Matthews came into the sick bay, walking quickly. "Lefty's about," he said.

"He's coming in here?"

"Directly."

Harris and Wish looked up and down the aisle. The doctor was sitting at one end with a Japanese orderly.

"What's wrong?" Matthews asked.

"Beef tin," Wish whispered.

The interpreter stepped inside and started straight for them. Matthews kept moving for the door at the opposite end of the building.

"Under the bed," Wish said.

Harris dropped the tin as he got to his feet, kicked it out of sight.

The interpreter shouted, "What was that?"

Wish and Harris bowed but said nothing. The interpreter pushed them aside and reached under the bed, came up with the tin.

"This man," he said, pointing to Anstey, "has stolen from the Red Cross supplies."

The British doctor was coming down the aisle toward them. He said, "This man can't sit up in his bed."

"He will be moved to the cells until the commandant recommends appropriate punishment."

"No fucking way," Harris said, stepping between the interpreter and Anstey's bed. "I stole it," he said. "I stole the damn beef."

Wish looked away from them.

"Wait here," the interpreter said, and he went back toward the door.

"Jesus, Harris," Wish said. "He'll beat the hell out of you over this." Wish looked to the doctor. "Tell him, for chrissakes."

"Tell me what?" Harris said.

"Anstey's already gone, you stupid cunt. He's a dead man."

"Not by that bastard's hand, he's not."

There was an accusation in Harris's voice that made Wish go calm, his skin crawling cold.

"We're all dead men," Harris said.

The interpreter came back down the aisle flanked by two guards. "You," he said, pointing at Harris with the beef tin. "You stole this."

"Yes sir."

"No," Wish said.

"Fuck off, Furey."

"It wasn't him, sir."

"He's a liar," Harris shouted.

The interpreter held up his hands, displaying uncharacteristic composure until both men went quiet. "Who stole this ration?" he asked Wish.

"I did, sir."

The interpreter waved the tin at Harris. "Did you steal this?"

"Yes sir," he said. "I did."

The interpreter looked back and forth between the two. His face was blank, neither surprised nor pleased nor offended. Just that peculiar glassiness. "Very well," he said finally. "You will both come with me."

All of the feeling had gone out of Wish's legs and he couldn't make himself move. Harris stepped past him to start for the door. Whispered "You stupid cunt" as he went by.

At the evening roll call both men were brought before the assembly on the parade square, where Captain Koyagi interrogated them through the interpreter and they confessed again to stealing from the Red Cross supplies. Wish and Harris were stripped to the waist and forced to their knees with their backs against a post, their arms lashed behind them.

Koyagi gave a lecture on the evils of petty theft, explaining that the Red Cross materials belonged to the prisoners as a collective and they hurt only themselves by stealing from one another. Then he nodded to the interpreter.

Wish watched the interpreter and a second guard coming toward them, bamboo sticks in their hands. All of Nishino's faux cheerfulness was gone, only a sullen resoluteness to the face, a bleak sincerity. Wish thought of Mercedes suddenly, realized she'd been all but absent from his mind for weeks now. As if there was no place for her in the certainties he'd accepted for himself.

He said, "You'll let Mercedes know for me, Harris." Knowing Harris had no better chance of surviving than he did. But taking some comfort in the fiction, regardless. "You'll tell her."

"All right," he said.

Wish stared off into the middle distance, thinking of her face the morning he'd stood naked for her out by the Washing Pond. It looked as if she was about to laugh but she lost herself suddenly, watching him. It was a strange act of love, he thought, his standing apart from her naked, she simply taking him in.

He pictured that look on her face now. Lost himself inside it for a moment.

After the morning roll call, Nishino watched the prisoners shuffle off to their workstations or to the vehicles waiting at the gate to take them to the shipyard or one of the coal mines farther out the harbour. There had been a dozen mistakes in the numbering off because of prisoners missing from their habitual spots in the line, and Nishino beat each man as he shouted their correct number. It seemed a deliberate strategy, to garble the language or claim not to know it. His back lit up with spasms every time he swung the stick.

When he left the parade square he went to his barracks and lay down to rest. The nightmarish details out of Hiroshima still running through his head. Every living thing in the city, they were told, human and animal, seared to death. It was barely conceivable, too surreal to credit. He'd never felt angrier or more helpless. Thinking about it exhausted him.

He had no idea how long he'd been asleep when the commandant's staff assistant shook him by the shoulder. Captain Koyagi wanted to see him. Bad news, Nishino knew. The sun was high as he crossed the square, mid-morning already. The commandant's office was in the building nearest the camp gate, underneath the watchtower. Nishino had been alone in the room with the officer only once before, on the day he arrived from Mushiroda camp, when he presented Koyagi with a letter of introduction from Lieutenant Sakamoto. The furnishings were spare, a single wooden table along one wall, a filing cabinet, two straight-back chairs before the desk. The only opulent touch was the officer's chair, an English-style wingback finished in green leather. Koyagi had read the letter standing behind the desk, glancing up from the paper occasionally. He folded it away immediately after finishing it and bowed perfunctorily to Nishino before dismissing him. Nishino had no idea what the letter from Sakamoto contained, but it hadn't been welcome information to Koyagi. The commandant was professional but cool in his dealings with his new interpreter, giving him the run of the camp and never offering any criticism of his conduct, though Nishino could sense a deep-seated disapproval in his manner.

Koyagi rose from the leather chair when the interpreter came in. They bowed to one another.

"Sit down," Koyagi said, pointing to the straight-back chairs.

Nishino glanced at them and then back at the officer. Koyagi was almost a head shorter than he was. He said, "I would prefer to stand."

"As you wish."

Nishino kept his eyes focused on the top of the desk.

"Do you know why I've asked to see you?"

It could be anything, he thought. To tell him the Americans had invaded the country. That the prisoners were to be executed and buried, the camp torched. Events were moving toward some final, apocalyptic resolution and it seemed to Nishino that his fate and the fate of Japan itself were about to be set before him.

Koyagi walked past Nishino to the single window looking out on the parade square. They stood nearly back to back, like two men about to fight a duel.

"How long have you been with the Imperial Army, Private Nishino?"

"Almost six years, sir."

"You did your field training with Lieutenant Kurakake."

"Yes."

"He is a good man. A good soldier."

"Yes."

"But soft. This is his one weakness. Softness."

"I don't agree, sir."

Koyagi made a noise in his throat. "Your loyalty to him is commendable. He taught you to kill, Nishino?"

"Of course."

"How did he do this?"

"We were—" Nishino paused—"with prisoners," he said.

"Each soldier was ordered to bayonet a prisoner?"

"Yes."

"Did any soldiers in your unit refuse?"

"Some hesitated."

Nishino could hear Koyagi turn from the window behind him.

"Tell me, how did Lieutenant Kurakake deal with these soldiers? The weak ones?"

"He beat them with the flat of his sword."

"And did this suffice?"

"For the most part."

"For the most part?"

"There was one soldier who was unable, even then."

"This soldier was named Ogawa. Chozo Ogawa."

Nishino turned his head to look directly at the captain. He pulled himself more rigidly to attention, shifting most of his weight to his left leg. "Yes sir."

"Ogawa wept, is this true?"

"He did."

"And?"

"After the beating failed to move him, Lieutenant Kurakake ordered me to assist."

"How?"

"We stood side by side and charged prisoners together."

"How often?"

"Five, six times. Until Ogawa stopped crying."

"You didn't despise him for this?"

"Of course I did. He was unfit. He was unfit to be a soldier."

"Did you know of his connection to Lieutenant Kurakake?"

"Not at the time," he said. "I did not."

Koyagi came back around his desk and sat in the leather chair. "Please," he said, "be seated."

Nishino's back was slick with sweat. He felt light-headed. Koyagi motioned to the chairs again and he sat finally.

"I went to officer school with your former commandant at Mushiroda Camp, Lieutenant Sakamoto," Koyagi said. "We were both sent to Manchuria from military school to take up our assignments with the infantry. Our company commander was a certain Colonel Ogawa."

"Chozo's father?"

Koyagi nodded as he lit himself a cigarette. He leaned across the desk and offered one to Nishino. "There were twenty-two raw officers there at the time. We knew nothing about war that wasn't learned in a classroom. So we were given a weeklong field-operations training session. Do you know who our instructor was, Private?"

"Lieutenant Kurakake?"

"Exactly right. Lieutenant Kurakake." Koyagi stared at the interpreter, a strange look on his face, a look of mystification and glee. "A lieutenant then and he remains so even now."

"He prefers to fight."

"Perhaps," he said, "perhaps that is the reason. He was certainly a good soldier, a good teacher. Those first days he took us around the scenes of earlier battles, showing us what had gone well, what had failed. Asking us to transfer our book knowledge to the field of war. Discussing strategy, tactics. All around us the carnage of the real thing." He smiled at Nishino. "I was twenty-two years old, you understand. I had never done more than slap a face in my life. I was afraid I lacked the stomach to make that transition." The officer drew on his cigarette. "On the next-to-last day, Kurakake took us to the detention centre. There was a room full of Chinese incarcerated there and he pointed to these men. Civilians mostly. Villagers. Peasants. Kurakake said, 'These are the raw materials for your trial of courage.' And then we were dismissed.

"In the morning we were taken to the site of our *trial*. There were seats set out for the regimental commander, the battalion commanders, the company commanders, all arranged near the edge of a pit three metres deep. And twenty-four prisoners were there as well, bound and blindfolded. That is when it came clear to me, Nishino, what our trial would be. Kurakake bowed to the regimental commander and ordered a prisoner brought to the pit. The Chinese man was carried to the spot and forced to kneel there. Kurakake looked us each in the eye. He said, 'Heads should be cut off like this.' There was a bucket of water beside him. He unsheathed his sword and scooped up a dipper of water, pouring it over both sides of the blade. He stood behind the prisoner and steadied himself, legs wide, the sword raised behind his head."

Koyagi had barely begun his cigarette, but he leaned forward to tamp it out in the ashtray. "I was eighth among the raw officers. When my turn came my only thought was, 'Don't do anything unseemly.' One of the others had lost his nerve and simply slashed the prisoner's head. He had to strike again and again to kill his man with Kurakake shouting at him, calling him a fool. I didn't want to disgrace myself. I bowed to the regimental commander and unsheathed my sword. I wet it down as I was instructed and stood behind my prisoner. I held the sword above my shoulder and then swung down with one breath, *Yo!*" Koyagi made the motion with the flat of his hand. "I washed my sword and wiped it down with paper. When I sheathed it I noticed the blade was bent slightly from the force of the blow. And I was changed too, Nishino. As all soldiers are. When I returned to my unit that night I was stronger somehow. I was ready to serve. I felt without a doubt it was my *destiny*." The officer used the English word, mispronouncing it in an old-fashioned way,

Nishino said, "I still don't know why you wished to see me, Captain."

"Your friend Chozo," Koyagi said, "he was rejected by the officers' academy. His father made several attempts to enrol the boy before he died, but it was an impossible fit. It was a great shame to the family, even though he was the youngest. Ogawa's oldest brother asked Lieutenant Kurakake to take him on, to make a man of him. At the least, to give him a good death. But you know this already."

"Some of it I know."

"Lieutenant Kurakake should have refused the request."

Nishino's eyes widened. "He could not."

"Having accepted, he should have let the matter die with Ogawa. But this is Kurakake's weakness. His softness. He allows too many of the formalities of civilian life to govern in the time of war."

There was a long pause between them, each man baldly watching the other.

"He has taken good care of you for your service, Private Nishino. Through Lieutenant Sakamoto. Through me."

"I am not ungrateful."

Koyagi took a key from his breast pocket and unlocked the desk drawer to his right. He removed a single sheet of paper and set it on the desk where Nishino could see it. "One last gesture of thanks," he said, "from Lieutenant Kurakake."

The note had been sent from the *Kempaitai* Chief of POW Camps in Tokyo, addressed to the chiefs of staff of the army in Korea, Taiwan, Kwantung, North China and Hong Kong, and to the

commanding officers of all prisoner-of-war camps. It was headed
POW *Camps Radio #9 Top Military Secret.*

*Personnel who mistreated prisoners and internees or who are held
in extremely bad sentiment by them are permitted to take care of the
situation by immediately transferring or by leaving without trace.*

Nishino glanced up at Koyagi. The officer was studying his
hands. There was more to the message about destroying documents
that would be unfavourable in the hands of the enemy, but he
couldn't take it in.

"What does this mean?"

"It means," Koyagi said, "the time is coming soon when we
soldiers may well be judged by the formalities of civilian life."

"We will never surrender." Nishino's voice broke and he spoke
louder to tamp the emotion down. "Japan will never surrender."

"I once believed the same," Koyagi said quietly. "But this . . ." He
searched for an appropriate word. "This *event* in Hiroshima."

Nishino said, "I wish to be transferred."

"There is nowhere to be sent, Private. The army is no longer any
use to you."

"I will not desert."

"The choice is yours, of course. You have made many enemies
among the prisoners here and at Mushiroda. There is blood on your
hands."

"I did not join the Imperial Army to make friends."

"I'm certain, as well, that you did not join the Imperial Army to
become a prisoner." Koyagi stood from his leather chair as he spoke,
not allowing time for a response. He said, "You are dismissed,
Private Nishino. Good luck to you."

Nishino went straight to his barracks. He lifted his kit onto his berth
and went through it quickly. He fumbled open a small brown
envelope at the bottom of the trunk and shook the medal into his
hand. Blue ribbon with red and white stripes. A silver medallion

embossed with the head of King George. He had kept it with him through the war. As if he could shame his father this way.

He returned the medal and put the envelope into his breast pocket. He packed the clothes into a shoulder bag and reached under his bed, hauled out several bottles of Osano's liquor. He packed these into the bag as well and marched straight out into the sunlight. He was blinded for a moment by the brilliance of the day and he closed his eyes against it, heard engines droning above him. He shaded his eyes and looked up to see four vapour trails heading south. As he watched they turned slowly and made their way back toward Nagasaki. The prisoners still in the camp began rushing toward the underground shelters, but Nishino stood and watched the planes pass overhead toward the city. He couldn't understand why they weren't bombing. Something dropped from them, three small parachutes, he thought.

And then it seemed another sun came out all at once above the hills around Nagasaki, a second sun shining darkly blue and consuming the world it shone upon.

MERCEDES

—

SHE WAS SITTING BESIDE JOHNNY BOUSTANI in the music listening room at the USO.

They'd been meeting there every Thursday lunchtime for two years now, playing jazz and classical records on the hi-fi. Cole Porter and Louis Armstrong, Debussy, Beethoven, Chopin. Dizzy Gillespie, Benny Goodman. King Oliver's Creole Jazz Band.

Every drop of summer warmth had been wrung from the sunlight through the windows and it lay in pale squares on the floor. Two full months had passed since the Japanese surrender. Mercedes knew from Johnny and from accounts in the local paper that POW camps on the Japanese islands were liberated when the Americans landed at the end of August. And she still had no word from Wish.

Johnny had been making informal inquiries through friends and knew that the prisoners who survived the camps on Kyushu, including those nearest Nagasaki, were evacuated on American navy ships, most of them passing through San Francisco on their way to being decommissioned. But there was nothing he could learn from the British army to say that Wish had returned from overseas or died there before the liberation.

"Everything's in a shambles," Johnny said. "There's still hundreds of British POWs in Germany unaccounted for."

"If Wish was alive," she said.

"Letters get lost, Mercedes."

"Not telegrams. Not phone calls."

They were listening to a recording of the Brandenberg Concertos. In the weeks after the Japanese surrender it had been all Duke Ellington for them and they sometimes cleared a space of chairs to jitterbug. But as the time without news of Wish dragged on, Mercedes lost her taste for the nicotine buzz of big band jazz and insisted on classical music instead.

"Any official word would probably have gone to Renews. To his aunt."

"Lilly knows how to reach me."

They were quiet for a while, billowing cigarette smoke to the ceiling.

She said, "Hiram is betting on the week of November fifteenth for the first snow this year."

"That would suit me just fine. I hope never to see another day of winter in this place."

"What are you going to do when you get home, Johnny Boustani?"

"Don't know. Find a girl. Start a family." He cleared his throat to stifle the stupid giggle.

It occurred to her she would never come back to this room. That it was likely she'd never hear most of the music she'd fallen in love with here again. Movies at the base theatre, the dances for American servicemen. All of it was coming to an end, her life about to change completely for the second time in her twenty-one years.

"I hope you're happy," she said.

Johnny looked at her with a sour face and went across to the hi-fi to flip the record. The hiss and pop of the needle before the music started up again like the sound of a fire in a kitchen stove. He turned to Mercedes. "I'm going to tell you this," he said. "And you won't say a word until I'm done telling you." He waited to give her a chance to protest and when she said nothing he carried on. "I know you don't feel," he said, "you don't feel for me what I do for you." He took a breath. "But if things go bad for you. If you hear what I expect you'll hear. I want you to consider." He looked down at his feet.

"You're some smooth talker, Johnny Boustani."

He smiled at his shoes and shook his head.

"Sure can play that trumpet, though. I'll give you that."

"You'll know where to find me," he said. "That's all I'm saying."

She hid her face behind her hands and Johnny looked away from her. He turned up the volume on the hi-fi so she wouldn't have to worry about anyone in the hall hearing her while she bawled.

The farewell meal for Johnny Boustani took place the following Saturday. Mercedes spent most of the day with the Basha women in the kitchen, chopping and stirring and cleaning pots. They made *tabouleh* and *kibbee,* and Mercedes diced handfuls of the season's last wild spearmint that she and Amina had picked on the banks of the Waterford River.

Dozens of people crammed into the house that evening, spilling out of the kitchen into the single aisle of the storefront, where chairs and tables were set up for guests. All the Lebanese families in town and Johnny's closest friends in the Intelligence office were there. Mercedes sat between Johnny and a Major Dumbrowski. They chatted aimlessly about the weather and what would become of the U.S. servicemen still in town now that the war was done. There was a burst of laughter down the long table and Sammy called Johnny to him, waving both arms. Johnny excused himself and Mercedes turned to the major. She said, "I've been reading about these atom bombs." The language in the newspapers a mix of comic book hyperbole and the biblically apocalyptic. *The Allies' new super weapon. A rain of ruin from the air, the like of which has never been seen on earth.* Mercedes had asked Johnny what more he could add to the accounts in the *Evening Telegram*, but he pleaded ignorance, which simply fed her desire for details.

"It really is astonishing," the major said. "Nothing like it in the whole of human history." He lowered his voice, leaned a little closer to Mercedes. "This is all classified information, you understand." He tapped her hand with his index finger. "And there's a lot still to learn over there. They estimate the temperature at the hypo-centre reached somewhere between fifty and a hundred million degrees. Blast winds of six hundred miles an hour. Everything at ground zero flattened in a matter of seconds. There's one particular area in the hypo-centre called the vaporization point, everything within that area, the buildings, the people, they would have simply disintegrated." He made a magician's motion with his hands, as if to say *poof*. "Not a trace left behind."

Mercedes had been playing out scenarios in her mind for weeks in a kind of harrowing make-believe. It was obvious that nothing she'd imagined came close. But she felt curiously detached from the truth of it, watching the major's mouth as he spoke. His teeth seemed too big and too white to be real.

Dumbrowski said, "Just over two miles away from ground zero in Nagasaki there was an office building staffed by five hundred women, and the force of the blast catapulted most of them through the windows. They were laid out in the grass like dolls, not a bruise or a burn mark on them."

He noticed the expression on Mercedes' face then and checked himself. "It's the end of war we're talking about, Miss Parsons. All wars. What the world has been through the last five years will never happen again. Think about that. The demise of warfare. What a *feat*," he said.

"You all right?" Johnny asked when he came back to his seat.

"Fine," she said. "Best kind."

She helped clear the tables and took a turn with a dishtowel while the men set up their instruments in the store, but she slipped out the back door before the music started. She walked slowly over to Hiram's and more slowly up the stairs to her room. She didn't turn on any lights. The house was cold from standing empty all day but she lay on top of her blankets and seemed not to notice the chill at all.

She had never truly doubted him, not in all her time in St. John's. She was convinced she would know if Wish was dead, that she'd sense it. That he would appear to her, the way her father's fetch had, sitting in the chair outside her bedroom. But that notion seemed quaint and pathetic suddenly. Even her memory of seeing her dead father dripping water in the hall struck her as ridiculous, given the world she found herself living in. People disappear without a trace. She thought of the motion the major made with his hands. *Poof.*

Wish was dead. And she'd lost the strength or the will to believe otherwise.

She was somewhere between sleep and waking when a knock at the door startled her. It took her a moment to pick out the familiar shapes of her dresser, a wooden chair in the corner. She heard keys in the lock, the thunk of the bolt sliding. She lifted her head off the pillow. Hiram was on the Southern Shore, his last trip of the fall, and he wasn't due back in St. John's for days.

"Mercedes," a voice called.

Johnny Boustani came up the stairs, calling her name again. She lay where she was and waited for him to find her. He went into the sitting room, flicking a light on and then off.

He opened the door of the bedroom. Mercedes said, "Don't turn on the light."

He stood in the doorway, looking in at her.

"Where did you get those keys?"

"Rania got them from Hiram. Just in case. She sent me over to check on you."

"What time is it?"

"I don't know." His shape was coming clear in the darkness, leaning against the doorframe. "After midnight. No one knew where you went."

She didn't say anything more and he came across the room to sit beside her on the bed. She could smell alcohol on him.

"You're missing the dancing."

"He's dead, Johnny."

"Who?"

"Wish."

"You don't know that."

"He's dead, Johnny."

She slapped her open hand against his chest, grabbed the material of his shirt. Pulled him down and raised herself to meet him at the same time, their teeth knocking together. She could taste blood as she kissed him and the taste of it set her head ringing. They sloughed out of as much of their clothes as necessary and Mercedes hauled him between her legs. Felt that first sharp tug like a stitch being tweezered from a wound. She bit into Johnny's neck, bucking her hips against him.

She was never so furious in all her life.

He came quickly and lay still on top of her while she squirmed and pushed against him. "Come on," she hissed. "You bastard."

He arched up to look at her. "Mercedes," he whispered.

She pushed him off before he could say another word. She rolled out of bed and stood up, fixing her underwear and hose, straightening the skirt and blouse.

Johnny sat behind her with his pants around his ankles, his shoes and uniform jacket still on. "Mercedes?"

"You have to go now," she said. "Tell Rania I'm fine."

Johnny Boustani left St. John's on an American troop transport ship the following Wednesday on his way to a posting at Fort Lowell near Boston. He and Mercedes barely spoke when they met to say goodbye. Johnny gave her an envelope with his contact information at the base, and the address and phone number of his parents in Pennsylvania. They didn't hug or kiss, only shook hands.

"I'll be seeing you," he said.

"I won't leave here until I get word," she said. "One way or the other."

"You know where to find me."

It snowed for the first time on November 19. Hiram collected seven dollars in winnings and handed it all to Mercedes. "Buy yourself something nice," he said.

She used the money for a ticket on the coastal boat to Renews. She travelled there alone and made her way directly to Tom Keating's house, where Patty sat her down with tea and the same molasses buns larded with pork fat.

"My lord, you've grown up since the last we saw of you," she said. "You're a proper woman now."

"How are things with Lilly Berrigan?"

"She's back in her own place. The Sisters keeps an eye on her there."

Mercedes knew all this from Hiram, who carried the gossip from the Southern Shore home to St. John's. "Have she had any news?"

"Not a word, as far as I know."

Mercedes said, "Where does Lilly live?"

The building was as small as she imagined a goat barn would be. In the room that served as kitchen and parlour, a daybed was set along the wall beside a Maid of Avalon stove salvaged from a wreck by Tom Keating that the Sisters had talked off his hands. The only ornamentation was a Sacred Heart hung on the wall beside the stovepipe. One square of window opposite the bed, over a barnboard table. The only other room, a tiny space large enough for a cot and a chair that served as a nightstand, was Lilly's bedroom. The place was empty but they could hear the sound of an axe thocking wood out behind and they walked around the shack to find her.

Lilly Berrigan was as thin and white as Mercedes remembered. She was wearing a pale okra dress and a scarf tied around her head and she stood watching them with the axe at her waist. A pile of birch and spruce junks around a chopping block.

Patty said, "Lilly, I told you to let that wood be and I'd send Billy-Peter over to split it for you."

Lilly ignored her. "Hello, Mercedes," she said. She let the axe head down to the ground and leaned on the handle, catching her breath. She watched the younger woman in a way that made Mercedes feel her face was transparent and everything beneath it visible to her. Lilly said, "You're looking well."

"I thought you might have news for me."

Lilly walked over to her, touched Mercedes' face and let her hand trail down across the front of her coat. "I think," she said quietly, "you have the news you need."

It was the waiting that infuriated Mercedes, the knowing and being forced to wait for proof. She felt that anger rising in her again and had to choke it off to speak another word. "You'll let me know, Lilly? If you hears anything?"

Lilly went back to the chopping block and set up a junk of birch, split it evenly with the axe, the cleft halves falling away to either side. "I'll let you know," she said.

Mercedes went off on her own afterwards, wandering out over the headlands above Aggie Dinn's Cove. She wrapped herself in her coat and sat watching the ocean until near dusk and she was stiff with cold when she finally got back to her feet. She made her way by the church and walked behind it to the grotto with the statue of Mary. The Ocean Star. A rosary hanging from her left wrist, a brass halo over her head that read *The Immaculate Conception*.

In all the times she'd gone to the Basilica with the Bashas, Mercedes had never prayed to the Virgin, and she was surprised to feel the need to offer one now. She started to repeat the verse from the Book of Ruth she'd memorized while reading aloud to her grandmother. *Intreat me not to leave thee, or to return from following after thee.* But she wasn't able to go further than that.

She prayed for forgiveness instead. Though she wouldn't allow herself to think on what she was asking forgiveness for.

There was no sign of Hiram when she came back to the shop the next day. He sometimes slept in the afternoon if he'd had too much to drink, and Mercedes went up the stairs to her sitting room as quietly as she could. Heard him calling from the darkroom at the back of the house. "That you, Mercedes?"

She went back down the stairs and stood at the door.

"Any news?" he asked.

"No," she said. "Nothing."

She heard him potter around for a few minutes before he came out into the hall. His face was pale and there were beads of sweat at his temples. He said, "I've been thinking." He was wiping his hands on a rag and he looked down at them as he spoke. "Wish thought Hardy was dead when he left here, Mercedes. When he enlisted. He might have thought he needed to hide some things."

"He used his real name. My letters wouldn't have gotten to him if he lied about that."

"He might have said he was from somewhere else than Renews, though. There was nothing on paper to say one way or another. He could have lied about kin."

"So any official word from the army . . ."

"Could have been sent anywhere." He let out a long sigh. "I've made a shag of all this."

She touched his arm and then went up to her room, stayed there the rest of the day.

In the week before Christmas a small parcel arrived for Mercedes, addressed by an unfamiliar hand. Hiram was alone in the shop when the mail arrived. There was no return address, but it was postmarked in Halifax. He shook it side to side and guessed there was another envelope inside the larger one. He set it on the counter and pretended to work away at other things, glancing at it periodically while he waited for Mercedes.

She had sent a telegram to Johnny Boustani at the beginning of December and through subsequent phone calls had arranged to fly to Montreal before the New Year, where Johnny had been told it was easier to get an entry visa into the U.S. It was also a reasonable train ride from Boston, and Johnny was going to come up to meet her if she had any trouble at the consulate. In that case, they planned to get married in Montreal and travel together into the States on the train.

She hadn't said a word about the reasons for these arrangements but it was obvious to Hiram that Mercedes was pregnant. And the package from Halifax caused him so much discomfort that he made regular retreats to the back office for a shot of whisky. It could only be one thing, he knew, and the envelope fairly glowed on the counter where he set it. It would catch his eye as he turned, as if it had jumped like a trout gasping on a rock. And that would send him to the office for another drink.

He was soused by the time Mercedes got home, sitting in the back office with his head on the desk, half asleep. Came to his senses enough to see her in the doorway and said, "Hello, Mercedes, my love."

"Why don't you go have a lie-down for yourself, Hiram?"

"Couldn't chance the stairs." He leaned back in the chair, his torso at an odd angle that he seemed helpless to correct. "Can't hold the liquor like I used to."

"What's going to become of you after I leave?"

"I'll get by." He waved his hands theatrically. "Everyone manages, hey? Everyone carries on. Won't even miss you, I wager. Barging in and waking me in the middle of a grand little nap."

She turned to go out to the shop but he stopped her.

"Mercedes," he said. "A question." He placed both hands on his knees to steady himself. "If there was a way. . . ."

"Yes?"

"A way to know what happened to Wish. If someone said he knew and could tell you. I'm just curious, you understand. None of my goddamn business, certainly. But, given your circumstances."

"What are you going on about?"

"Would you want to know, is my question. One way or the other."

She studied him then, the face swollen with alcohol and drunken sleep, the purplish nose veined like a tree leaf, a dark red welt on one cheek where he'd lain on the desk. The ridiculous moustache. "What's this about, Hiram?"

"Just answer the goddamn question, would you?"

"No."

"No?"

"No."

He rubbed his face with both hands and looked at her again. "No, you won't answer the question?"

"No," she said. "I wouldn't want to know."

He tipped his head to one side. "Why not, Mercedes?"

"I think," she said. "I know he's dead." She stumbled there and bit her lip. "But let's just say he's alive and changed his mind about me. About us. That he was alive and decided he wouldn't come looking for me. I'd rather not," she said. She made a little motion with one arm. "I know he's dead," she repeated.

Hiram rubbed his face again, scrubbing hard.

"Your head bothering you, Hiram?"

"Killing me."

She said, "I'll get you a cold towel."

Hiram waited until he heard her footsteps on the floor overhead and then went out to the front counter. He picked up the envelope and looked around, trying to decide where to put it. Scurried to the office when Mercedes started back down, stuffed it away in a drawer.

"Here you are," she said.

"Thanks, my love."

He leaned back in the chair and draped the towel over his face.

"Hiram?"

"Mm?"

"Do you think I'm doing the right thing?"

He took the towel away slowly but wouldn't look at her. "I hope you and Johnny are happy together, Mercedes. He's a good man. He's a lucky man."

"Right or wrong, Hiram."

"There's no right or wrong," he said, "only better odds or worse. I like your odds." And he put the towel back over his face.

Two more tidal waves came into Lord's Cove that night, Wish told her, though neither was as massive as the first. They waited up in the hills until they were certain it was over with and then walked back down to the shoreline, picking their way through the wreckage. His mother carried him on her back, to keep track of him. It was dark by then but the sky was clear and enough moon to have a sense of the devastation. Their house was gone, as were most of the houses near theirs. Down on the shoreline the stages and boats and every bit of equipment had been picked up and smashed, the beach a field of wooden debris. The carcasses of a dozen drowned cows lay half submerged on the landwash.

A few buildings had been swept right off their foundations and washed into the water. They could just make them out, hulking darkly on the surface, most of them tilting hard and halfways to going under. But there was one house, almost out of the harbour altogether. It was standing high up, Wish said, like she was built to float. The sea dead calm. There was a fire in the stove when the house was carried out to sea and the chimney came free from the wall or the stove itself had tipped onto the floor in the commotion. One side of the kitchen was on fire, the window lit up with a red and yellow glow that seemed to be pulsing, dimming and flaring like a massive heart beating inside the room. Not another spark on the shore, just that one light devouring the house out on the water. Wish said it was the loneliest looking thing he'd ever laid eyes on.

Before first light Mercedes climbed out of bed and dressed in a rush. She went up to the third floor, banged on Hiram's bedroom door. She kept hammering, even after she heard him up and shuffling around the room, searching for his clothes.

"Jesus, Mercedes," he said. "What is it?"

"You have something," she said. "A letter or something. Where is it?"

He leaned his forehead on the doorjamb.

"Hiram," she said. "God*damn* it."

They went down over the stairs in the dark and Hiram lit a lamp in the office. He took the envelope out of the drawer but before he handed it over he said, "This is a mistake, Mercedes. You said so yourself."

She held out her hand and he passed the envelope across to her. "I want to be alone," she said. "When I open it."

Hiram pushed past her, muttering under his breath, and she waited until she heard his footsteps on the stairway before she sat next to the lamp and looked at the envelope. A woman's hand she thought at first, judging by the delicate lines. But there was too much of a scrawl to the letters for that and she decided it was a man, an elderly man or someone ill. Postmarked in Halifax. She turned up the lamp before she opened the package.

Another sealed envelope inside and a single loose square of paper. She unfolded the note. The same fragile hand as the address on the outside.

Dear Mercedes Parsons.

She stopped there and folded over herself in the chair, her head on the desk. She stayed that way for a long time, breathing shallowly, her teeth set. When she sat back up she brushed the note flat with the palms of her hands.

Dear Mercedes Parsons,

My name is Jim Harris, I was in the service with your Wish. Before we shipped out for the Pacific he entrusted the enclosed to me and asked that I send it to you in the unfortunate instance that he not make it back to you. I am very sorry to be sending it to you. He spoke of you often and only ever wanted the best for you. With deepest regrets, JH.

Mercedes moved from the note straight to the second sealed envelope, not allowing herself to pause, to let the unambiguous finality of those words stop her. Her hands were shaking and she had trouble hooking a finger under the seal to rip it open. There was no paper inside, no letter or note. Only one item, coiled at the bottom of the envelope that she shook out onto the desk. It was a length of knotted string.

Her last sight of Newfoundland was from the window seat of her flight to Montreal. Morning and a grey day, sunlight occasionally breaking through the overcast. The noise of the motors so thick in the cabin it was nearly impossible to speak to the passenger beside her and she was grateful for that. The plane climbed steeply out over the fields at Torbay and banked hard to starboard, angling above the city. She could see the dark nipple of Cabot Tower on Signal Hill and southwards the lighthouse at Cape Spear. The ships at anchor in the harbour, the spires of the Basilica rising above the flat tarpaper roofs of the houses. And just as quickly they were beyond the city and still climbing over the snow-covered barrens of the Avalon. All that showed through the acres of white was granite ridges or shale and black spruce and scrub brush the colour of rust.

They were so high above the ground by then that she thought it would be impossible to make out the shapes of individual people if any were down there to be seen. And she decided she would remember the place just that way, an empty white landscape dotted with craggy rock and the black circles of ice on the ponds, all of it bordered by the cold blue of the ocean. She stared and stared, as if she might be able to burn that picture permanently into her mind to the exclusion of any other.

And then they were above the clouds.

1994

—

MERCEDES

—

1.

THE HARBOUR WAS WRONG.

It was a beautiful June day over the Avalon. Mercedes staring out at the ragged coastline with its ruffle of white surf as the plane banked for its approach. She'd reached into the shoulder bag and taken out her sunglasses, putting them on over her eyeglasses against the glare. Cabot Tower above the Narrows. She touched her finger to the window. She said, "The harbour looks . . ."

Her daughter leaned across to peer past her. "What are you saying?"

"The harbour doesn't look right somehow."

Isabella eased back in her seat. She said, "It's been nearly fifty years, Mercedes." She called her mother by her first name when she was angry, to add that distance. And Bella still hadn't recovered from the early start to the day.

Mercedes had insisted on getting to Logan International three hours ahead of time to be sure of a window seat during the last leg of the trip, hoping for a clear day and this view, the plane looping out over the ocean on its approach and swinging in low

233

above the headlands, the Narrows, the harbour. Isabella tried to talk her into a more sensible departure time until Mercedes suggested she might drive the thirty-five miles to the airport herself. It was five in the morning when she picked up Mercedes, and Bella had never been a morning person. They sat for hours in the departure lounge, Bella sullenly sipping at a coffee while planes taxied down the runway. Mercedes ticking off each flight on the departures board as it left. "American Airlines Flight 11," she'd say. "Los Angeles." "Flight 175, United." Isabella got up eventually and moved to sit out of hearing.

They'd changed planes in Halifax en route to St. John's and after take-off Mercedes brought her black canvas shoulder bag out from under the seat, peered into it for the fifteenth time.

Bella said, "He's not going anywhere, Mom."

Mercedes ignored her, reaching a hand inside to touch the metal container. "Boustani in a box," she said. Sat back with her eyes closed, listening to the voices around her. The first time in fifty years she'd heard a Newfoundland accent other than Agnes on the phone. She nodded off several times to the leisurely rustle of Bella flipping the glossy pages of a magazine, kept shifting her position to ease the ache in her hips and back, to take her swollen feet out of her shoes.

"Would you settle?" Bella said.

"Wait till you're old," Mercedes said. "Then talk to me."

She used to say the same thing to Bella about motherhood. "Wait till you have children. Then talk to me." Now she threatened her daughter with age. Maybe Bella would never get old either, she thought.

Mercedes stared down at the city. The south side looked abandoned, the rows of wartime barracks, the houses and outbuildings and wharves wiped away. An elevated four-lane highway set along the Waterford River valley. The tiers of fish flakes along the Battery torn down and gone though the houses were still there, set higgledy among the rockface. On the north side of the harbour she could see the twin spires of the Basilica, the Kirk below it. New office buildings on the waterfront, ugly red brick and glass. For miles beyond what she'd known as the city, the countryside was parsed and sectioned by subdivisions and strip malls.

And the harbour had changed somehow, she was sure. The contour of the thing was different. Like a face pushed into an odd shape by the hands of the shoreline. And that obvious but unidentifiable difference lit the slow burn of anxiety that she'd managed to keep at bay up to then. She would have to find a bathroom, she knew, first thing. "What *is* it?" she said.

Bella said, "Think in your head, Mom. Not out loud."

After the plane taxied in, they walked down the portable stairs and across the tarmac into the terminal. A crowd of people waiting in the dimness beyond the open Arrivals door. Mercedes looked among the faces as she approached them but couldn't pick out a single feature. It was almost pitch dark inside, as if the windows were blacked out. "What in God's name?" she said aloud. She held the straps of the shoulder bag with both hands and walked so close to Isabella their shoulders touched.

A woman stepped up to her, took her by the shoulders. "Sadie," the woman said. "What have you got those things on for?"

"Oh Jesus," Mercedes said. She took off the sunglasses. "I forgot I was wearing them." She looked at her sister, saw a glimpse of their mother beneath the grey curls, beneath the puff and sag of the cheeks. Deep creases in the earlobes the same as their father. She leaned into her. "Hello, Agnes," she said. A blur of powder and perfume obscuring the smell she was looking for. She straightened quickly and said, "I'm busting for a pee, Aggie. Where are the bathrooms in this place?"

They drove to the White Hills and down through Pleasantville, the rows of flat-roofed military quarters converted to civilian apartments

235

and offices after the Americans left St. John's in the 1960s. They went along the shore of Quidi Vidi Lake and turned up King's Bridge to Military Road, driving into Georgestown. Mercedes sent them around the same block half a dozen times but she couldn't say for sure where Hiram's shop had been among the rows of houses. They drove down Duckworth Street and back along Water, Mercedes pointing out the location of every storefront and shop on the strip during the war. At the end of Water Street, Agnes turned left again onto Harbour Drive, a street that hadn't existed when Mercedes left St. John's. Tons of stone quarried from the south side hills and dumped into the harbour with old concrete and debris, the surface paved, a cement dock running the length of it.

"I could tell something was different," Mercedes said. She craned her head toward Isabella in the back. "Didn't I say something was different, Bella?"

"Yes, you did, Mercedes."

Agnes said, "Did you want to go up to Signal Hill?"

"Bella?"

"Be a shame to waste the good weather."

They found a spot in the Parks Canada parking lot below Cabot Tower. The wind blowing hard when they got out of the car and walked to the low stone wall to look over the city.

Agnes had her arm in Bella's and was studying her. "She don't look at all like you, Sade. She must be the spit of her father."

Mercedes glanced at Isabella. An unfortunate face, she thought, pear shaped and all the features tightly clustered at the centre, it made Bella look permanently offended. She was twenty-nine years old and disappointed in life in some way. As if it had all been rehearsal so far and she was uncertain about ever making it to opening night.

Mercedes looked out at the city. "Never thought I'd lay eyes on this place again."

Bella said, "Did you want to do it now?"

"I'm not ready," she said. "Not yet."

"He's been dead three years, Mom."

"I want him with me tomorrow," she said. She let out a long breath of air. "Johnny never really thought much of this place. I don't know why he'd want to be set out here for evermore."

"He was just looking for a way to get you home," Agnes told her. "That's what I think."

Mercedes saw the truth of it right away, though it had never occurred to her before that moment. "You always were the one with the brains, Agnes," she said.

"I'd have traded them for looks any day."

Mercedes laughed. "You see what can happen to looks."

Agnes slipped off her sister's sunglasses and touched the injured side of her face. "Where's the plate?"

Mercedes drew a line from her left eye socket down across her cheek, then put the sunglasses back on. "I think myself and Johnny are going to take a little walk out past the tower," she said. But she didn't move from the spot where she was standing.

Agnes lived in an apartment building just off Torbay Road, across the street from a strip mall. A kitchenette and boxy living room downstairs. Photos of her three children over the television. Half a dozen pictures of her and David through the years and in every shot his lame hand was hidden in a pocket or behind Agnes's back. Ag had married Clive Reid's youngest boy while they were still living in the Cove, where David taught kindergarten through Grade 11 until the school was closed in 1964. Once their own children left for universities and jobs on the mainland David retired, and they moved to St. John's from Fogo. David dead nearly a year now.

After their supper Agnes brought out a bottle of sherry. Isabella drank only a few mouthfuls before she went upstairs to bed. It was barely coming on to dark.

"Is she all right?"

"She had an early morning," Mercedes said. Though in her mind the simple question rippled out into every nook of her daughter's life.

Bella had been the most unexpected of unexpected children. Born almost twenty years after Marion, their *only* child as Mercedes had come to think of her. She had been calling her husband One-shot Boustani for the better part of two decades. And then Isabella.

"I can't believe she's not married yet," Agnes said.

Mercedes rolled her eyes. Through Bella's twenties half a dozen men came and went without making a dent in her aimlessness, her detachment. Mercedes rarely met the people she dated, sometimes knew nothing more than a first name. Which made her suspect some of them, at least, were married. Each unsuccessful affair left her daughter a little more contrary, a little sadder. There was an abortion when she was twenty-six, Bella talking about it as if it was nothing more than a toothache. Her nonchalance in matters of the heart was too practised to be sincere, Mercedes thought. The listless world-weariness in her bordered on self-hatred.

"Wasn't she seeing someone just now?" Agnes asked.

Mercedes made a *pffft* sound through her teeth and lips.

"What a sin. She's a sweetheart."

"To you maybe." Mercedes raised her glass of sherry. "To the rest of us she's cold as a witch's tit."

Agnes put a hand to her mouth, appalled. "*Sadie*," she whispered.

Mercedes' face went suddenly serious. She said, "No one's called me Sadie since I moved to the States."

They looked at one another awhile longer.

"Welcome home," Agnes said.

A crowd of several hundred gathered at the war memorial on Duckworth Street the following morning to commemorate the fiftieth anniversary of D-Day in Europe. Wreaths were laid under a steady drizzle of speeches and prayers. Mercedes and Isabella and Agnes stood across the street from the ceremonies, keeping to the outskirts of the crowd. She still disliked large groups, the mauzy whiff of them, how they made it impossible to isolate any individual smell. It was like white noise to Mercedes, an irritating hum.

Earlier that morning she had hugged her sister at the sink, before either of them had dressed for the day. She wanted to get to her before she powdered up, pushed her face into Agnes's neck to breathe her in. "You smell exactly the same as I remember," she said.

"Oh Jesus," Bella said. "The Nose has found you out, Aunt Agnes."

"What do I smell like?"

"Like you."

"And what is that, if you don't mind?"

"It's—" she paused, "it's a bit like toasted homemade bread."

Bella threw her head back and laughed. "Buttered or not buttered?" she asked.

"Oh be quiet, Bella."

Agnes smiled up at Mercedes, embarrassed by the peculiar intimacy. "Toast?" she said.

"I took her to a movie once, Aggie. And she kept moving her head back and forth, like a dog sniffing the air. 'Do you smell that?' she said. 'Do you smell that?' I thought she was losing her mind. 'Baby poo,' she said. 'It smells like baby poo in here.'"

Mercedes stood with her arms tightly folded. Agnes looked from Isabella to her sister and back again. "What was it?" she asked.

"*Popcorn*." Bella threw her head back again. "She thinks theatre popcorn smells like baby caca."

"While they're *breast*feeding," Mercedes insisted. "It *does*."

239

"What do you want for breakfast?" Agnes asked, desperate to change the subject.

"Have some toast, Mom," Bella said.

Agnes gave her niece a look. "I could make you some oat-meal, Sadie."

"Just tea," Mercedes said coldly.

It was nearly impossible to see what was happening at the base of the war memorial from where they were standing. "Why don't we try to get a little closer," Agnes suggested.

Mercedes said, "Johnny would have wanted to stay a little out of the way. He was always embarrassed about serving here. Not making it overseas."

"There was all kinds of ways to serve, Sadie. He was one of the lucky ones." Agnes lifted her glasses to wipe at her eyes.

Isabella said, "It was the merchant marine Hardy was with, was it?"

Agnes nodded. "Ruthie wouldn't let him—that was his wife, Ruthie—she wouldn't let him join the forces. Merchant marine was the closest she'd let him get to overseas. Last part of 1943 he signed up." She took a breath and let it out slowly through her nostrils. "He told some stories when he was home on leave," she said.

"Like what?"

"Isabella," Mercedes said.

"Like what, Agnes?"

"They went across in these huge convoys, you know, mer-chant marine and navy ships together. When a boat was torpedoed the convoys just kept moving. Even if there were survivors in the water, they couldn't stop for fear of losing more ships. His first time across, two boats went down. The calmest kind of weather, not a breath of wind. Hardy saw a fellow out in open water, he had his life jacket on and was watching the convoy sail past him. A Brit he was. And he had his hand in the air, waving it around, and he was yelling 'Taxi! Taxi!' Making a joke of it."

"Jesus," Bella said. "He told you that?"

"He never said a word around us women. He was up drinking with Clive when all this came out. I heard it from David, after we got married." Agnes paused there, and Mercedes steeled herself, gripping the straps of her shoulder bag and hanging on. "I keep thinking of Hardy out there like that," Agnes said, "watching the boats sail by."

"We don't know," Mercedes said. "We don't know what happened to him except his ship went down." She was trying to keep the anger from her voice. "Don't torture yourself."

"Leave her alone, Mercedes."

"Can we just be quiet and watch what's going on?" she said.

Bella looked away and hugged her aunt's arm tighter. And no one said another word.

Mercedes didn't know that Hardy was on his way to join the merchant marine the last time she saw him in St. John's. Johnny insisted she write a letter home after Marion was christened and she included a picture of the baby in her silk shantung gown. Agnes wrote back, sending a copy of Hardy's obituary. Dead more than a year before Mercedes heard, a year that he'd been living on in her head. Fishing, she thought, where her father had spent his life fishing, raising his own children with Ruthie. It made her feel like a fool to have imagined him happy all that time and finding some measure of happiness in imagining it.

The speakers went on and on, she didn't know why a memorial service had to be as interminable as the war it commemorated. A cold rain began to fall just as a young cadet lifted a bugle to play "Taps" and Mercedes felt gut-foundered suddenly, so greedily hungry that the world seemed to drop under her feet. A whiff of ammonia flooded her nostrils and she grabbed uselessly at Aggie's coat before she hit the sidewalk.

2.

TWO PEOPLE WERE STANDING at the foot of her bed when she came to herself, Isabella and a young man in a white lab coat who was saying, "Most of the effects of a concussion are temporary. It all depends on the severity." He looked barely old enough to drive a car. "And things are complicated in this case by the concussion sustained in her earlier accident. Some of these effects are cumulative. And with someone as elderly as your mother."

"I'm right here," Mercedes interrupted. She closed her eyes again. "I can *hear* you."

"Mrs. Boustani," the doctor said cheerfully.

"How long have I been here, Bella?"

"Since yesterday, Mom."

"Yesterday?"

"Do you remember any of our conversations, Mrs. Boustani?"

Mercedes looked at the doctor. "No," she said angrily.

"Do you know my name?"

"I've never laid eyes on you in my life."

He smiled at her. "I'm Dr. Mullaly. I'll be looking after you while you're here. You gave yourself a nasty knock. We're going to keep an eye on you for a few days."

She tried to sit up. "Where's Johnny, Isabella? Where's your father?"

"He's right here, Mom." She pointed to the shoulder bag in a chair by the bed.

Mercedes slumped back against the pillow. "I hate hospitals," she said. "They have such a . . ." A look of confusion and fear crossed her face.

"What is it?" the doctor said.

She took a breath of air through her nostrils, searching for the ubiquitous medicinal smell she detested. But there was only a stark blankness.

"You were going to say something, Mrs. Boustani."

"No, nothing. Never mind."

"Mrs. Boustani," Mullaly said. "Did you have a word in your head that you weren't able to get ahold of just then?"

"No," she said.

He was about to ask something else when Agnes came into the room carrying a Tupperware container and waving a copy of the *Evening Telegram*.

She said, "You made the paper, Sadie."

"Oh *fuck*."

"Mom," Bella whispered.

Agnes placed the Tupperware container on the table tray and opened the paper across the bed. "Here, here, here," she said. "'The commemoration was interrupted briefly when Mrs. Mercedes Boustani (nee Parsons) collapsed.'"

Mercedes' eyes rolled back in her head.

"'She was attended by St. John Ambulance workers at the scene,'" Agnes read, "'and transferred to the Health Sciences Centre where she is being treated for a concussion. Mrs. Boustani, a Newfoundland native originally from Little Fogo Island, is the widow of Lieutenant Johnny Boustani (ret.) who was stationed in St. John's during the Second World War.'"

"How do they know all that?"

Agnes looked up at her sister, her mouth open. "They asked me."

"*Jesus*, Agnes."

"All right," Dr. Mullaly said. "That's enough excitement for now. You need to rest, Mrs. Boustani."

Bella opened the Tupperware and offered it to her mother. "Have a muffin, Mom."

"Just out of the oven," Agnes said.

Mercedes picked one from the container and brought it to her mouth. The heat was still in it, but she couldn't smell a thing. She felt as if her head was stuck inside a box of Styrofoam. "I'm not hungry," she said. There were tears in her eyes and she looked away out the window.

"Maybe it would be best," Dr. Mullaly suggested, "if we gave your mother some time alone to rest."

And the three of them stepped out of the room together.

By the third day Mercedes was able to sit in a reclining chair beside her bed and watch the tiny television set for an hour at a time before her head started throbbing. Bella went downstairs to the cafeteria for a coffee while Mercedes was watching a husband and wife throw chairs at one another on a daytime talk show. She heard her name being called softly and turned to see Amina holding a black leather purse in both hands, looking expectantly at the woman asleep in the bed beside her own.

"She a friend of yours?" Mercedes asked.

"Someone I knew years ago. During the war. I didn't even know she was in town."

"She don't look well."

"She was in the paper. They said she hit her head."

Amina was colouring her hair jet black. She wore a dark sleeveless blouse, a black skirt above the knee and high-heel shoes, as if she were on her way to the USO for a dance. The legs of a thirty-year-old.

"Is she in a coma?"

"Amina," Mercedes said, smiling.

The woman darted a look across the room. "Mercedes?" she said. "Mercedes? You *witch*."

"My God, girl, you haven't changed in fifty years."

Amina came across the room and leaned into her, kissing

both cheeks. She sat on the edge of the bed and held her hand. "How long are they going to keep you here, Mercedes?"

"If I don't wet the bed tonight or go on a raving streak, I'm a free woman."

"You're not in a hotel, are you? You have to come stay with me when they let you out."

Mercedes smiled and squeezed her hand, to put off disappointing her. She thought of the first time she went to the Waterford River with Amina and her mother to pick spearmint. She didn't know how to tell it from grass. "You Newfoundlanders," Rania had said. "There is more to taste in the world than salt." She picked a blade and crushed it in her fingers, held it to Mercedes' face. "You see?" she said. "It grows everywhere and not a soul on this island can see it for what it is." The locals called the Lebanese *grass-eaters* for this peculiar habit of theirs, picking and cooking weeds from the riverbanks. The scent of it still brought Mercedes back to that kitchen at Rawlin's Cross, to those loud, ridiculously beautiful women. It was the cleanest smell she'd ever encountered, so intense and vibrant and clear it was almost a place of its own. It occurred to her she might never experience it again.

Mercedes said, "You're alone now, Amina?"

"I have the two boys, they keep an eye on me."

"What about your Mom and Dad? And Maya and Sammy?"

"They're dead now, of course. Maya and Sammy went back to Lebanon in the fifties." And a moment later she said, "Were you going to call me while you were in town?"

Mercedes looked up at the television, where the husband and wife were being held at bay by men in blue T-shirts with the word SECURITY stamped across the backs. The audience on their feet and cheering. The husband and wife were pointing at one another, shouting.

"I'm sorry to hear about Johnny, Mercedes."

She said, "Were you happy, Amina? In your marriage?"

245

"I've been alone ten years. I hardly remember being married. Most of the time, I guess I was."

"Me too," she said. "I keep forgetting how lucky a thing that was."

"And how is Marion? She must be nearly fifty herself now."

Mercedes turned from the television. She hadn't intended to call her or anyone else in town. To avoid this one inevitable conversation.

Amina put a hand to her mouth. "Oh," she said.

"It was a lifetime ago," Mercedes said. "She wasn't eighteen."

"What happened?"

"Just one of those things," she said. She left it there, and the two women looked about the room, like suburban neighbours who'd run out of things to say about the weather. Mercedes' head ached.

"Do you remember Lilly?" Amina said finally.

"Wish's aunt Lilly?"

"She's living in town. At St. Pat's Mercy Home."

"She's still alive?"

"She was a few months ago. Turned ninety. I saw the birthday announcement on the suppertime news. They showed a picture and everything."

Mercedes touched her forehead with the tips of her fingers. "Would you turn off that television for me? I've got such a headache."

"I should go and let you rest."

Mercedes looked at Amina but couldn't recall her name. "Where's Isabella?" she said.

"You should have a little lie-down," Amina said, and she took Mercedes' arm and helped her up from her chair. She settled her in bed, kissed both her cheeks again. "I'm in the phone book," she said. "You call me when you feel better."

Mercedes was asleep before Amina was out the door.

———

Marion took her mother to find the cotton candy on the midway while Johnny went into the tent where the afternoon program was about to begin. Mercedes didn't really care for cotton candy, sickly sweet and that clot of matted tissue dissolving in her mouth. But it was preferable to the small-time rodeo that her husband had come for. Women in cheerleader outfits circling the ring to start the events, cowboy hats and spangled boots, American flags set in leather holders in front of the stirrups. She wasn't sure if the girls or the horses were less appealing to her.

They'd spent the last half of the summer travelling across the Midwest and the prairies. Marion had just finished high school and was going to a small art college in California in the fall. They drove through the Black Hills of South Dakota and up into Montana, planning to head south then through Idaho and Nevada on the way to dropping her at the college. All the way from Forsythe to Custer they passed signs advertising the rodeo, each one featuring a scantily clad cowgirl smiling on horseback. And after each sign, Johnny became more insistent. "A ro-*day*-o, Mercedes," he said. "When will Marion get another chance to see one?"

"Maybe Marion doesn't want to see a ro-*day*-o at all, Johnny Boustani."

"Why don't we ask her?"

They both looked back over the front seat to their daughter.

She said, "Watch the road, Dad." And then, "Would there be cotton candy?"

She had her father's dark hair and Mercedes' eyes and she had grown taller than either of her parents, so that at first glance she seemed much older than her years. They both doted on her, more and more as it became clear she was going to be their only child. Marion had a certainty about her that reminded Mercedes of her grandmother, though it didn't lead to any smallness in the girl. When she was eleven her class went on a field trip to the Isabella Gardner Museum in Boston, and she came home with her mind made up to paint. They scraped together enough money to give her private art tutorials, driving her into Boston on weekends for life-drawing or watercolour classes. They spent part of each Saturday at public galleries, and once or twice a year went back to the Gardner to allow Marion to revisit her favourite pieces. An opera singer by Degas in a high-necked black dress. A Botticelli of the Virgin and Child attended by an angel. *The Concert* by Vermeer. Mercedes had no idea what was in them to hold her daughter's interest. "You know, Marion," she'd say, leaning in close to the Rembrandt self-portrait, "he hasn't aged a day since we were here last."

Marion took a dollar from her coat pocket. "Cafeteria," she said. "Go. Give me an hour."

She often felt as if Marion was the adult in their relationship, that the girl tolerated her parents' foolishness with the kind of bemused forbearance a mother offers her children. Distracting her with cotton candy on the midway to allow Johnny to watch cowgirls circle the ring in Custer, Montana. They wandered through the crowds away from the main tent as the music struck up inside, picking at the pink clouds of cotton candy as they went. The thrum of the horses' hooves making the ground shake underneath them.

At the heart of the incident, she learned afterwards, was the flag.

The gelding was spooked by something, a noise in the crowd, a flash of light. The cowgirl was bucked from the saddle but the flag jammed tight in its holder near the stirrup. The horse bolted from the tent, the pole slapping at its flank like a whip. A surge of movement on the midway, a wave of voices roiling toward them and Mercedes turned in time to see the horse's head shearing above the crowd. She put a hand on Marion's arm before she was knocked aside by the animal's shoulder, before her daughter was pulled down and dragged along by the undertow of the hooves pistoning the packed dirt.

She had no memory of her visit with Amina when she woke, only a heaviness in her chest that she recognized as Marion. Agnes was sitting in the reclining chair, asleep in the light of the television.

From the moment Bella was conceived, Mercedes thought of the pregnancy as a kind of compensation, as if the world was out to make amends for her loss. But on the night her water broke she lost her nerve. When Johnny carried her suitcase out to the car she refused to leave the house. "I can't face it," she said. "I can't go through losing another." She leaned into a contraction, sucking air through her teeth.

Johnny knelt in front of her, using both hands to wipe the tears from her face. "It's not like you've got a toothache, Mercedes. For the love of Christ," he said.

Once she'd come through the labour, the sense of reparation that accompanied the pregnancy returned stronger than it had been at the outset. She went so far as to forget the moment of doubt entirely and disputed it every time Johnny told the story.

Mercedes had gone to the Isabella Gardner Museum on the anniversary of Marion's death each year, to look up at those ancient pictures as her daughter had. She meant Bella's name as a quiet memorial to the lost child, a prism she thought might refract some of Marion's light into the arrival of their second. Johnny had reservations about drawing such a direct line between the two but he could see Mercedes would have her way and let it be.

"Ag," Mercedes whispered. "Agnes. Where's Isabella?"

Her sister stirred in the chair.

"Where's Bella?" she said again.

"I sent her home for a rest."

"What time is it?"

She brought her watch up close to her face. "Eight-thirty. You slept through supper."

Mercedes nodded to herself. There was something pricking at her mind, some unfamiliar pea niggling beneath the depth of Marion's loss.

Agnes stood beside the hospital bed and took Mercedes' hand. "Well now," she said. "Here we are."

"What the hell does that mean, Ag?"

"I don't know," she said, suddenly defensive. "Just. Here we are."

"Two widows, you mean."

"Yes."

"Alone in the world."

"That's what I mean."

"Abandoned by everyone they ever loved."

Agnes said, "Were you always as saucy as this, Sade?"

She smiled. "I guess I always had it in me."

"You haven't mentioned him since you come home."

"Mentioned who?"

"Don't play stupid."

Mercedes glared at her sister, trying to warn her away from the subject.

"He must be in your mind. Coming back here."

"Johnny was a good husband to me."

"I'm not saying anything about Johnny."

"What are you saying, then? That I haven't got over something that happened when I was sixteen?"

"Now, Sadie."

"I barely knew him, Agnes. I can hardly remember . . ."

"If you were over it you'd have come home for long ago."

They were quiet for a while, and that persistent niggle worked at her, Mercedes trying to pin it down. It came to her suddenly then, like a voice from the stars. "When I get out of here," she said, "I want to go visit St. Pat's."

"Where?"

"St. Pat's Mercy Home. There's someone there I need to see."

The Mercy Home was built on a small rise of land just north of Elizabeth Avenue. Mercedes talked Agnes and Bella into dropping in there as soon as she was discharged.

"Well who is it?" Agnes wanted to know.

"A woman I met while I was in St. John's."

"What kind of woman?"

"Just be quiet and drive, Ag."

They spoke to a nurse at reception and then Mercedes asked her daughter and sister to wait in the lobby.

Bella lifted her arms and let them fall back against her sides. Agnes took her by the elbow and led her to a bench beside the window. "Your mother was always like that," Mercedes heard her saying.

"Like what?"

Bella turned her head and said, "We're waiting, Mercedes."

She took the elevator to the fourth floor, repeating the room number in her head. She went along the corridor slowly, looking in at each open door. It was like passing lighted windows at night, she couldn't help herself. Gnarled creatures asleep in front of television sets or nearly buried under quilts in their beds. The home had a feel similar to the hospital, the same unnatural state of cleanliness and order. But an undertone of quiet resignation in place of the frantic bustle, the apprehension.

She hadn't been able to think of anything but Lilly since her name and location had mysteriously come to mind. She thought of the last time she'd laid eyes on the woman, standing behind her shack with an axe in her hands. Walking up to Mercedes with her preternatural stare, touching her face and her belly. *You have the news you need*, she'd said. It was years later before it occurred to Mercedes she was pregnant at the time, though not even she knew it then.

251

A candystriper stood in Room 417 with her back to the door, tucking a shawl around the lap of a resident, blocking Mercedes' view. She knocked gently on the door.

"Come in," the girl said. "Show's just about to start."

"Hello?" Mercedes said.

The girl looked over her shoulder. "Thought you were some-one else," she said. "I'm just setting up Ms. Berrigan for her show."

"Lilly Berrigan?" Mercedes said.

"That's the one. Come in and have a seat."

The candystriper went across to a tiny colour television on a dresser and adjusted it so the screen faced Lilly more directly. The old woman watching the girl with her tongue protruding from her mouth and a bemused look on her face, as if she hadn't wanted a shawl tucked on her lap or the television adjusted and was simply humouring her.

"Hello, Lilly," Mercedes said, coming into the room.

She looked up and nodded. "Hello," she managed, barely above a whisper.

"I'm Kathleen," the candystriper said, holding out a hand. She was over six feet tall.

"How long has Lilly been here?"

"Since before I got here, and I've been volunteering for seven years now. She was transferred over from the Waterford back in the eighties sometime."

"The mental institution?"

"That's right."

Mercedes looked past her to Lilly, who was ignoring the two women altogether. *Wheel of Fortune* was just coming on, waves of tinny applause rippling into the room.

"She's harmless enough," Kathleen said. She turned to Lilly and raised her voice. "Aren't you, my love?" She smiled at Mercedes. "Those sorts of things tend to go into a kind of remis-sion as people age. Although she still has her moments."

The candystriper's cheerfulness was so overwhelming it made Mercedes feel tired, as if she'd spent too much time in full sun.

Kathleen glanced down at her watch. "He's usually in before the show starts."

Mercedes said, "Who?" It was an innocent question altogether. "Her nephew."

A ridiculous sense of being called flooded through her, the hand of God turning her this way or that. She felt calm and hollow and ready to be filled. "Her nephew?" she said.

"Yes," the girl said on her way out the door. "Do you know him?"

The old woman was staring at the television, clapping the heels of her palms together as the wheel spun on the screen. Mercedes turned around twice in the middle of the room and then left without bothering to say goodbye to Lilly.

"Well," Agnes said, getting to her feet when Mercedes came toward them. "Was she not there?"

"I want to sit for a few minutes," Mercedes said.

"Are you okay, Mom?"

"Fine," she said. "Fine. I just need a minute."

Agnes said, "I'll go get the car." And she left them to sit in silence, Mercedes watching the front door, sitting up slightly each time it opened.

"What's wrong with you?" Bella asked.

A man in a tan raglan and brown slacks came through the door. He was carrying a large Tim Hortons cup. A bald pate so dark and smooth it looked polished, a ring of white, white hair like a laurel around his head. A small constellation of age spots at the temples. The same peculiarly long, peculiarly handsome face. Mercedes watched him wait at the elevator and caught his eye briefly as he turned inside to punch the floor number. She watched the lights indicate the elevator's rise to the fourth floor.

253

"Who was that?" Bella asked suspiciously.

"Someone I used to know," Mercedes said. "A long time ago." She got up from her seat. "I'm ready now," she said, still impossibly calm.

When they got into the car she said, "Take me up to Signal Hill."

She'd intended to scatter Johnny's ashes out on the headlands, as near the spot where he'd first drunkenly declared his love for her as she could remember. From the parking lot at Cabot Tower a wooden staircase angled down a hundred feet into a valley and a series of staircases stuttered up the opposite side. Isabella wouldn't allow her mother do that much climbing so soon after her fall, and Mercedes decided to go down to the Battery above the Narrows instead. Bella went with her, refusing even to let her carry the shoulder bag herself.

It had been a calm day in the city but up on the hill the breeze was blustery and insistent, a faffering wind that jerked at their clothes from all directions. They stopped in the lun of the small stone building and Bella took out the urn, handed it to her mother.

Mercedes walked into the open, holding the container against her breast. She turned to all points of the compass to find a spot downwind but gave up finally, shaking out the container of ashes with her eyes closed. The grey dust kicked up into a swirl around her before flying off into the meadow grass and out over the water of the Narrows. She had to shake ash from her hair, brush it off her clothes.

Through it all she was unemotional, businesslike, as if she was fulfilling the terms of a contract on behalf of strangers. She found it impossible not to think Johnny had arranged all of this, that he planted Lilly's name and location in her head somehow, knowing who would cross her path there. Her head a pinwheel of sparks every time Wish came into her mind and she pushed the thought of him aside. For fear of falling where she stood. To leave one more day to her husband before her life changed for good, one last time.

WISH

—

HARRIS DIED IN HALIFAX just after the war, and Wish headed west again, travelling up through Quebec and into northern Ontario, where he worked a number of years in the gold mines of Cobalt and Kirkland Lake. Eight relentless months of winter but the weather never touched him. Riding the cage down the shaft, the temperature rising as the cables lowered them half a mile underground. Minus forty on the surface and the mine like a greenhouse, the air hotter and more humid the farther into the earth they travelled. It made him think hell was down there some-where, as the Monsignor always claimed, if they could only manage to dig deep enough.

He kept to himself as much as possible. Found a bed among Québécois crews so he wouldn't be burdened by the expectations of small talk, of casual conversations, arguments. He had a gaunt, ascetic look about him, and the Frenchmen called him *le moine* for his lack of interest in poker or dancing or the religiously observed weekly visits to local brothels. He worked as much over-time as the mines would give him and drank on his own when he wasn't working. He kept his pay in a tobacco tin, along with Mercedes' letters and picture and a few souvenirs from the war. Harris had pressed the Military Medal on him just before he died and Wish sometimes sat with it, drunk and alone in the bunkhouse, running a finger over the detailed profile of King George. The carefully kempt beard, the epaulets and collar of the military jacket. The king's own row of medals on his chest.

In the early fifties Wish worked beside a man who'd lost an eye in the Korean conflict, and he got it in his mind to go back overseas. He jacked up in Kirkland Lake and travelled by train into the States. He was still twenty pounds underweight and failed the military physical, a possibility that had never occurred to him. He drifted aimlessly across the American Midwest then, taking odd jobs and handouts before he settled for a time in Chicago. He worked days as a rail mechanic in the Armour and Company Stockyards and six nights a week running the projector in a fifty-seat theatre on the outskirts of Canaryville, several blocks west of Bronzeville. He rented a single room in a boarding house near the theatre, furnished with an army cot, a table and two wooden chairs, a hot plate and a radio. On the walls he taped up half a dozen old posters he'd found in the projection booth. *Godzilla* and *Earth vs. The Flying Saucers.* Jane Russell lying back on a bed of hay in *The Outlaw*, one saucy stalk of straw in her mouth. *The Red Shoes. Force of Evil.* Rita Hayworth in *The Lady from Shanghai* wearing a backless black dress beside the tagline "You know nothing about wickedness."

He was living at the edge of what was known as the Black Belt on the city's South Side. Hundreds of Negroes passed through Canaryville on their way to and from the stockyards where they worked beside Poles and Lithuanians on the killing floor of the slaughterhouses. The only black person he knew by name was Magnolia Cooksey, who came to the theatre after the last show of the night to sweep up the spilled popcorn and scrape bubblegum off the bottoms of the seats. He didn't know how old she was. A youngish face, but there were rich veins of grey threaded through her black hair. She sang to herself as she worked her way along the aisles. She had the most prodigious behind of any person he'd ever encountered.

Wish drank from a flask throughout the evening shows, sitting opposite the projector until it was time to change reels, watching the grey V of light flicker into the hall, the muffle of dialogue outside the room barely decipherable. He was quietly drunk by the end of the night and he took exaggerated care in shutting down the projector and putting away the reels. Before leaving, he put the room into meticulous order, straightening chairs and film canisters and the trash can, like a man trying to conceal evidence of a struggle.

He looked in on Magnolia on his way to the exit. She was never more than a third of the way to the front of the room by then, always the last to leave the building. She'd started work at the theatre around the same time he had and was just as new to the city. Her southern accent gave that much away. He felt some affinity with her for that, for the sense he had of her place on the outskirts of the world they found themselves in.

"Goodnight, Magnolia," he called to her.

"'Night, Mr. Furey, sir," she said. *Mistuh* and *Suh* is how it sounded in her mouth. "Y'all have you self a good one now," she said, without raising her head from the aisle.

The accent was completely foreign to him and at the same time there was something in her soft-vowelled drawl that reminded him of the way people spoke home in Newfoundland. An ease with words, an effortless deviation from the straight and narrow. He loved to hear her talk, even though it brought on a ragged homesickness he hadn't felt since his first days in the camps.

"Thanks, Magnolia," he said.

———

He woke in the mornings without an alarm and fixed himself tea and a breakfast of beans warmed on the hot plate, eating from the can as he stood at his window, looking down on the early traffic. If the weather was halfways decent he walked to his job at the stock-yard, otherwise he took the El.

In the evenings he ate at a diner across the street from the theatre, sitting alone at the counter with a handful of newspapers he'd taken at random from a stack the waitresses piled on the shelf over the coat rack. He drank three or four cups of coffee along with a plate of steak and eggs while leafing aimlessly through the papers. There was nothing in particular he was interested in, other than distraction. He started with the sports section when he could find it and from that moved on to entertainment pieces, movie reviews, gossip columns. The front section was always a last resort and he did little more than skim the headlines or the captions when there was nothing else to read.

It was always the same waitress working the counter, a woman at least twenty years his senior. The blue nametag pinned over her breast said *Ingrid*. Her accent was German or Austrian and he guessed she'd arrived in the States as a teenager, sometime between the wars. She wore a wedding ring and he assumed she had hooked up with an Irishman to be working so far from Lincoln Square. But he never asked her for details and never offered so much as his name to her. She called him and many of her other regular customers Joe. She never let his cup go dry. At 6:20, he placed a twenty-five-cent tip under his plate and walked across the street to set up for the early show.

On Sundays he had one afternoon matinee to run and the rest of the day to himself. Most often he spent it lying on the cot while darkness fell, the radio tuned to a ballgame at Comiskey Park, bur-bling away to itself like a child left alone in its crib. He hated the dead time and smoked away the hours, lighting one cigarette off the other, counting them aloud in Japanese. He'd forgotten almost everything else of the language, but the numbers still came to him effortlessly.

Nishino caught him and Anstey smoking a few weeks after their time in the solitary cells. They were lying underneath the barracks near the still when the interpreter called them out, ordering them into the push-up position. Nishino sent a guard to find Osano and they waited there, holding themselves arm's-length above the ground by their fingertips. When Osano arrived he was ordered to beat Wish while the interpreter went at Anstey. Bamboo canes across their backs and upper thighs, the sound like a bat striking the baseball squarely in Comiskey Park. Line drives. The civilian guard swinging with the intensity of a man who lived in fear of finding himself on the ground with the prisoners. It was the end of whatever Osano could do for Wish. That was the message the interpreter was sending.

When Nishino stepped back from the job, Osano let up as well. Wish allowed himself to relax enough to draw a full breath and the interpreter caught him with the toe of his boot, just below the ribs. He dropped to the ground, trying to breathe around the foaming knot of pain, rolled onto his side to vomit. It was a week before he was able to pass urine after that kick. A month longer before he could piss standing up.

Wish blew smoke rings at the ceiling, watching the tight circles drift and break apart. He drank beer all Sunday evening as well, keeping them cool in a bucket of water beside the cot, lining the empty bottles along the windowsill above the bed. When he finished his twenty-sixth smoke of the night he got up to turn off the radio and strip out of his pants and shirt.

He woke first thing on Monday morning without an alarm.

In the summer of 1955 Wish fell in with a woman named Jane Adams. They met at the theatre before a Friday-night showing,

Jane waiting in line at the concession stand as he passed on his way to the toilet. She waved enthusiastically when she caught sight of him and then stood with her hand held awkwardly in the air, as if she had mistaken him for someone else. She was wearing a turquoise-blue dress with crinoline under the wide skirt. Dark red lipstick and mascara and her brown hair was done up in curls. It seemed overly elaborate for the place, he thought.

"Armour and Company, right?" she said to him.

She worked on the line at the stockyard, packaging lard and smoked meats, one of the few jobs in the entire process reserved for women. She had seen him on the El several times and they had gotten off at the same stop.

"Do you come to the shows often?" she asked him.

"No," he said, and then smiled. "Yes," he said. "I work up in the projection booth. I haven't seen you here before, have I?"

"I was going up to the Aragon Ballroom. Supposed to meet some of the girls on the line."

He watched the colour coming into her face.

"First time in years for me," she said. "Since before the war. When I got up there I was a nickel short the admission. Too late to get all the way down here on the El and back. But I was all dressed up." She lifted her arms away from her body. "Didn't want to waste the effort."

"Well," Wish said. He was dying for a piss, shifting back and forth on his feet. "Enjoy the show."

He saw her on the El twice in the next few weeks, her brown hair straight and hauled back into a severe ponytail. She was widowed by the war, a mother of two boys. Her husband had been killed in Italy, she said. She asked him if he liked to dance.

"I don't mind a scuff," he said, and she looked at him blankly. "Yes," he said. "I likes a dance."

They went to the Ballroom on a Sunday evening. She wore the same turquoise-blue dress, her hair done up in the same curls.

The Tiny Bradshaw Orchestra was on stage, playing swing and big band tunes rooted to a heavy backbeat that packed the dance floor. Wish knew only jigs and square dances and he felt lost in the anthill of motion. Jane took him off into a corner, away from the busyness, to teach him how to jitterbug, how to do the Lindy Hop. It was the grip of her hand in his as she swung away, it was how she caught his eye over her shoulder before looping back like a fishing line between casts. It was the sway of her breasts beneath the fabric of the dress. It was her hand at the small of his back turning him this way or that.

They went back to his single room and Jane waltzed him across the tiny space toward the army cot. They'd both been sneaking nips from his flask through the evening and they nearly tipped into the table as they went. Jane reached behind her back to unhook the dress without taking her mouth from his, letting it drop to the floor around her feet. The room was illuminated by the streetlight outside the window and he leaned back to look her up and down as she stepped out of the ring of material, turning away from him to drape it over the back of the chair.

Jane looked over her shoulder. "You all right, Wish?" she asked.

He nodded as she came across the room to him and slipped her arms around his back. She put one leg through his and lifted her thigh into his crotch as she kissed him.

She caught her breath when he pushed inside her the first time, as if she'd been cut, and he raised his head to look at her.

"Did I hurt you?"

"I want it to hurt a little," she whispered, rocking her hips to urge him on.

Before he came she reached down to his ass, slid a wet finger inside him, and the unexpected burn of it set him off. The afterglow simmering all the way to his toes.

He lay awake a long time afterwards, trying to understand

what could possibly have kept him from this sweetness for so long. And he could hear the voice in his head warning him off it even now, repeating its single word of advice: *Run, run, run.*

In September, something happened to Magnolia Cooksey. When she came to the theatre she was grim and withdrawn. She didn't sing to herself as she worked through the aisles and when Wish stopped in to say goodnight she only said, "Yes sir," curtly. She seemed angry with him personally, although he couldn't imagine what might have prompted it.

One evening he said, "Is everything all right, Magnolia?"

She was halfway down the aisle and stood upright, one hand on the back of a chair. "Mr. Furey," she said. "Do you know where I'm from? Where I belong?"

"Down south, is it?"

"I am from Mississippi," she told him. "From the Delta."

"Did I do something?" he asked her.

She bent back to the aisle to say she was through talking.

Wish mentioned Magnolia to Jane on the El the next morning as they rode into the stockyard, thinking maybe it was a woman's problem of some sort that plagued her, something another woman would be able to explain to him.

Jane turned her head away from him slightly and blew air through her lips. She had been hinting broadly at marriage since their first night together and was becoming increasingly frustrated that Wish ignored her on the matter. When Jane said she loved him, he nodded into her hair or squeezed her hand, incapable of returning the sentiment. It was just a matter of time, he told himself. She had the two boys to think about and wasn't about to wait around forever.

Jane said, "Who's to say what goes on in a nigger's mind." There was almost a wistful tone in her voice. She looked across at him. "I got more important things to worry about," she said.

He fell asleep over the table in the projection booth after the show ended that Friday night and for the first time in years he dreamt of the wake for Willard Slade's boy, Mercedes walking into the room where the corpse sat up in the coffin, leaning in to kiss the empty space that had been a mouth.

Magnolia Cooksey woke him as she came in to sweep and empty the trash can. She started to back out of the room as soon as she saw him there. "Sorry, Mr. Furey, sir," she said. "Thought you was gone for the night."

"It's all right, Magnolia," he said. His head felt sluggish, he could almost hear the liquid rock to one side as he looked up. He got to his feet and grabbed the edge of the table to steady himself. She had interrupted the dream before Mercedes turned to him to speak but he heard the words in his head, like a line of dialogue he'd snipped from a reel of film. *Don't make a whore of me.*

Magnolia said, "I'll come back when you finish up in here." *He-ah.*

"Come in, come in, my love," he said, looking around for his coat. "Come in, I'm just on my way home out of it."

She was partially hidden behind the door. He looked up to see the whites of her eyes huge in the blackness of her face.

"What is it, Magnolia?"

She said, "Where you all from, Mr. Furey, sir?"

He said, "My name is Wish, Magnolia."

"You Irish, Mr. Wish, sir? You sounds about Irish."

"No," he said.

"You're not from nowheres around here."

"Nowheres. No, I'm not."

"I'll come back when you finish up," she said again.

"Magnolia."

She had almost closed the door completely and peered in through the crack. She didn't trust him, he realized. Had never trusted him, a drunken white man, the theatre all but empty.

"It's a nice name," he said. "Magnolia. I had a friend from home," he told her. "Mercedes, her name was. You ever hear tell of someone else with that name?"

"No, sir. Not as I can recall." And then she said, "I'll come back when y'all finished up here."

On Monday he sat flipping through newspapers, waiting for Ingrid to bring him a slice of pecan pie. He'd grabbed a handful of dailies, and near the bottom of the pile was a week-old copy of the *Chicago Defender*, a Negro paper he'd never seen in the diner before. He shook it out and laid it across the counter, scanning the headlines. The entire front page dedicated to the story of Emmett Till, a teenager from the South Side who had gone missing while visiting an uncle in Mississippi that summer. Wish had heard talk about it around the stockyards but hadn't paid much attention. A photo of the crowds from the Black Belt who gathered to file past the boy's open casket after his body was shipped home to Chicago dominated the page. Hundreds upon hundreds of them on the sidewalk and spilling out onto the street.

Another photograph showed the dead boy in his coffin. Wish stared at the image, just to the left of his coffee cup. He traced the black-and-white square, his hand shaking. The corpse had been found in the Tallahatchie River three days after the disappearance, a gin fan tied to the boy's neck with a loop of barbed wire to weight him down. The fourteen-year-old had whistled at a white woman, the paper said, and the woman's husband and brother-in-law had taken him from his uncle's house at gunpoint. He turned back to the photo of the crowd. He knew Magnolia Cooksey was in that mass of people, waiting her turn to see the boy.

"They got off," Ingrid said. She was standing opposite him, looking down at the paper.

"Who?"

"The men they say killed that boy. It was on the radio today."

"They got off?"

"Not guilty."

Wish glanced back down at the paper. The face in the picture was not a face. It had been beaten so severely that there was only a blank, featureless pulp above the shirt and tie. The nose was missing. A dark spot above the ear where a bullet had entered the skull. Wish wouldn't have been able to say even that the dead child was a Negro if the caption hadn't named him. A sheet of glass had been fitted over the corpse to shield mourners from the worst of the smell.

"I bet we won't ever hear the end of this one," Ingrid said. She had one hand on her hip and the pie in the other. She dropped the plate in front of him with a disgusted shrug.

Wish folded the paper and stood up. He took two dollars from his pocket and set them beside his plate.

"You want this pie?" Ingrid called as he went to the door.

He walked out into the evening air, gulping it in, trying to settle his stomach. He looked up and down the street and then started back to his room.

He took his one suitcase from under the army cot and packed as much of his clothes as would fit, leaving the rest in the tiny closet. He took the back off the radio and pulled out a small envelope and Mercedes' picture and a roll of bills he'd been adding to since his arrival. Twos and fives and tens mostly, a few twenties. He slipped a fiver from the roll and set it on the table with his key and a note to say he wouldn't be needing the room any longer. He put fifty dollars in each of his shoes and pocketed the rest of the money. He filled his flask and stuffed a full bottle of whisky into the suitcase. He opened the small envelope and shook out the Military Medal into his hand. He stood holding it a moment, testing the weight. He considered leaving it behind but put it back in its envelope, stuffed it into his coat pocket. He set his copy of the

Chicago Defender on top of his clothes, the faceless face staring up at him before he closed the lid and fastened the snaps. He flicked off the lights on his way out the door.

He took a train out of Chicago to Madison, travelling north across Wisconsin through Sauk City and Baraboo, Black River Falls and Wisconsin Rapids before stopping at Eau Claire in the Chippewa Valley. He stayed a couple of months there, renting a room by the week on Runway Avenue, living off his savings and casual work with a trucking and moving company.

He walked down to the railway station every Sunday morning and asked the agent where the day's trains were headed. The station agent came to know his face. "East or west?"

"Don't matter," Wish said. "West."

"Listen here," the agent said one Sunday, "I told you last week and the week before. Train headed west today goes into St. Paul, Minnesota. From there you can go on just about anywhere you like. Are you travelling or not?"

"I'm just curious," Wish said. "Where I'd wind up if I went."

The agent was a tall, sallow man who in Wish's mind was the very picture of a mortician. Lank black hair combed flat and perfectly manicured hands. He was wearing a striped shirt and wire cuffs above the biceps. "You want a for instance?" he asked.

"All right."

He brought out a map. "Look here," he said. He used a pen to point to towns and cities along the rail line. "You can take the 57 out of St. Paul to Monticello, Albany and Glenwood. Past Glenwood, you run through Wahpeton and Detroit Lakes and then on into North Dakota."

"North Dakota?"

"That's right."

Wish studied the map a few minutes. "You got Sherwood on there somewhere?"

The agent glanced up at him. "You want to get to Sherwood?"

"I'm just curious."

"Take a train north out of West Fargo on the Burlington Northern Line. Take that as far as Great Falls and head west from there." He dotted the map with his pen. "Devil's Lake. Rugby. Granville. In Granville the BN line turns north and that'll take you all the way. You can sleep until they kick you off the train, if you like. Sherwood's the end of the line."

The last time he'd crossed the prairies by train was with Harris on their way to the Atlantic coast from San Francisco after the war. Mile after mile the same placid surface of turf sectioned and squared. He saw something of the ocean on its most serene days in the landscape that made him lonesome for home at first. But it began to feel surreal soon enough, artificial, like the scenes painted as movie backdrops. It was almost as if the prairies had been scraped flat by hand, a carpet of greens and browns and ochre rolled across it. North Dakota reminded him of a hospital for some reason, the acres of farmland scoured smooth, the endless antiseptic blue of the sky. It filled him with the same vague sense of panic.

He ate a meal of minute steak and eggs at a diner on the main street and the waitress jotted down the address of a widow who let rooms by the day or by the week. He thought of Mrs. Gillard in the Cove.

"Why's it always widows let rooms, I wonder?"

The waitress shrugged. "They got room, I imagine."

It was dark by the time he went back out onto Main Street, carrying his one suitcase. The wind was blowing hard and he turned up the collar of the Navy coat he'd picked up in Eau Claire. He walked till he found the three-story farmhouse and rang the bell.

He slept in till mid-morning and found his way back to the diner for breakfast. The temperature was near freezing, the windows of the restaurant running with condensation on the inside. Apart from two men huddled together at the counter, the place was empty. Orange vinyl seats, the cracks sealed with tape.

"How'd you sleep?" the waitress asked.

"Best kind, my love."

She was wearing the same mustard-coloured acrylic uniform. Her eyebrows were plucked clean and drawn back in with an eyebrow pencil. She brought the coffee pot across to his booth along with a handful of newspapers. He put his hand over the mouth of his cup, asked for tea with a drop of fresh milk.

"As opposed to sour milk?" she said.

He glanced up from the papers. "What's that?"

"You asked for *fresh* milk."

"Out home," he said. "You get tin milk or fresh." She kept staring and he said, "Never mind."

"You don't want steak and eggs again this morning, do you?"

He considered it and shrugged. "Why not."

He leafed through the papers, noting the scores of hockey games played a week and more ago, until she brought him his breakfast.

"Have everything you need?"

"I'm looking for a friend of mine," he said.

She raised one of her carefully drawn eyebrows. "What kind of friends you got need to be looked for?"

"We were in the army together."

She stepped away from him, the coffee pot dangling from her hand. "Whatever you are," she said skeptically, "you ain't American."

"I was with the Brits."

"You don't sound British, either."

He shrugged.

"What's your friend's name?"

"Spalding."

"Lucas?"

"I never got his first name."

"He's not in trouble or nothing, is he?"

"I was just passing through. Thought I'd look him up."

"Have a gander around you, mister," she said. "No one just passes through Sherwood."

"Do you know where I can find him?"

He walked back and forth in front of Spalding's house half a dozen times, looking for some indication someone was home. He stood on the front porch, thnking about what he was doing there in Sherwood, North Dakota, trying to track down a stranger. What it was he was looking for. There wasn't anything he could put words to, though it wasn't less real or less perilous for that. He hadn't had a drink since he left Eau Claire two days before and he felt the lack of it at the core of himself suddenly, his legs trembling underneath him.

"You going to knock or just stand there all day?"

Spalding stood at the side of the house, wiping his hands on a rag.

"Hello, Lucas."

"I know you?"

"Been a while." Wish came down off the step. "Nagasaki #14," he said.

"Well Jesus," Spalding said. "Jesus, Jesus. Liquor Man."

Wish smiled at him, although it was impossible to say whether the American was happy to see him or not.

"You put on weight," Spalding said.

"I was just passing through. Thought I'd look you up."

Spalding smiled then, a little warily.

"Got your teeth all fixed up, Spalding."

"Army paid for it after I got home," he said. "Felt like I had a mouth full of rocks for the longest time. Missed all them open spaces." He was still wiping grease off his hands with the dirty cloth. "Had to learn how to spit all over again. How've you been . . . ?"

"Wish Furey."

"Right, right. And your buddy," Spalding said. "Harris, was it?"

"He's dead."

"That right?" Spalding said. "You want something to drink?"

They walked along a concrete path to a shed at the back. A small wood stove throwing heat in the corner and a workbench covered with the disassembled parts of a hunting rifle. "Just getting her cleaned up for the season," Spalding explained. "You a hunter?"

"Not since before the war. Used to go after a caribou in the fall, a few partridge." He put out a hand to the workbench to steady himself. "You got that drink, Spalding?"

He pulled down a bottle of Canadian Club and an extra mug from a shelf over the bench, poured them both two fingers of rye. He passed the mug across. "You still making that rotgut of yours?"

After he swallowed a mouthful, Wish said, "Cheaper to buy it in the stores these days." He looked around the shed, a single small window over the workbench, a bare bulb hung from the ceiling. A radio on the shelf beside the whiskey bottle whispered a static-laden version of "The Streets of Laredo."

"Sit down," Spalding said, gesturing to the only chair in the room, next to the stove.

"You don't get a lot of company."

"Not much for it." Spalding hopped up to sit on the workbench. "Married?"

"Well," he said. "Technically. Hitched up after I got out of the service. Seemed like the thing to do after spending all that money to get the teeth fixed." He grinned, as if to show them off.

"Where is she?"

"Gone to live with her people in Bismark. Years ago now."

"You didn't have youngsters at least."

"A girl. She must be going on seven or eight now."

"She come out all right?"

"Ten fingers, ten toes. If that's what you mean."

"You ever see her?"

He looked into his glass. "Like I said. I'm not much for company." He picked up the bottle of rye and handed it across to Wish. "Help yourself," he said.

Wish poured his mug half full and then drank off another mouthful. He said, "You don't mind me being here, do you, Lucas?"

Spalding got down off the workbench and turned away from him without answering. He set about assembling the rifle, clicking the oiled parts together in smooth, practised motions. Wish watched him closely. The years had made little difference in the man, the same flattop army haircut, the same fiercely gaunt face. Though the nearly manic air he'd had about him was gone.

"What happened to Harris?" Spalding asked suddenly.

"He got sick."

"Sick how?"

"Cancer, I spose. He put a bit of weight back on after we got out but he lost it all again and more besides. He was already halfways to gone when we got off the train out east. His hair all fell out. We weren't home two months."

Spalding nodded, wiping the cloth along the length of the rifle barrel.

"He finished it himself in the end," Wish said.

Spalding went still. "He killed himself, you mean."

Wish said nothing, and Spalding reached up a hand to switch the radio off.

"That what you came out here for, to tell me that?"

"I'd have come a long time ago if that was it," Wish said. "I don't know what I come here for."

Spalding picked up the rifle and cracked the barrel, slid in two shells and snapped it shut. "When I had my medical done on ship, heading home, the doc told me I'd be lucky to see the other side of forty."

"Me too."

Spalding held the gun across his hips. "So far so good for the two of us, I guess."

"I guess."

"I'm going out after a buck tomorrow. You're welcome to come along if you like."

They watched one another awhile.

"All right," Wish said finally. He drained the whisky in his mug. "I'll come along."

Spalding pulled up outside the widow's place the next morning before daylight. Wish was at the front door waiting, stepped outside when he saw the headlights turn the corner at the bottom of the street. They headed east on 107 and the sun came up in their faces as they drove. "Got a thermos of coffee," Spalding said, passing it across the seat.

Wish unscrewed the top and bent his face to the dark, acrid smell.

"Just coffee in there. Don't drink when I'm hunting."

They drove east as far as Cut Bank Creek and parked on the side of the road. "Hoofing it from here," Spalding said. He'd brought an old pair of boots and a hat for Wish along with a hunting vest to wear over his Navy coat. They gathered the rifle and gear from the truck bed and started walking south along the river. The sun was above the horizon by this time but the day was crisp and dry with cold.

They were making for a thin stand of trees at a bend in the river that seemed to move away from them at the same rate they were walking. It was mid-morning by the time they finally stopped there and shared a white-bread potted meat sandwich washed down with mouthfuls of the lukewarm coffee.

"They come in through the trees to the river," Spalding whispered. He was crouched with the rifle across his knees and looked directly at Wish. "You going to take the shot, we see one?"

"I'll see how I feel, if that's all right."

Spalding looked off toward the river and watched the slow black current moving past them. "You ever make it back to God's Country?"

"Not so far."

"Thought you had a girl waiting for you out there?"

"It didn't work out that way."

"She wasn't waiting or you didn't go looking?"

"We going to hunt today, or just sit here jawing?"

"I'm going to finish this sandwich." Spalding glanced up at the blue. "Fine day," he said. "Days like this are almost enough to make me think the old man was right about North Dakota." He said, "I never did tell you how I wound up in #14, did I."

"No."

He shifted on his haunches to make himself more comfortable. "We were in a camp in Thailand before we got shipped over. And there was a rumour going around before the transfer that it was a kind of holiday camp in Japan. But only the healthy POWs would be allowed to make the trip. And there were a bunch of tests done to determine who was healthy and who wasn't, the last of which was a stool test." He swore under his breath. "Army's the same all over the world, I guess. Word was you had to produce a healthy stool to get out of there, present it on parade. Something firm enough to hold in your hand, let's say. And half of us were still pissing out our asses, we never did get used to that dirty rice they gave us to eat. But we made up our minds we weren't going to be disqualified on that account. The way we heard it they were planning to shoot the ones left behind."

Spalding grinned. Wish still hadn't gotten used to the full set of teeth. They made him wary of the man.

"The latrine in that camp was set over a running stream that carried everything off into a field outside the fence. And the day of the stool parade there was a couple hundred of us hanging around the far side of the johnny, waiting for a healthy soldier to take his morning constitutional." He started giggling uncontrollably then, pressing his chin into his chest to try to restrain himself. "Grown men," he said. "Fighting over turds." He wiped at his eyes with the back of his hand. "And that's how I wound up in #14. Got my hands on a solid one. Presented it at parade like it was the company colours." He took a deep breath. "Fucking hell," he said.

"You're going to scare off the deer," Wish told him.

"We didn't do anything we have to be ashamed of, is all I'm saying. However it might look from here." Spalding was staring off toward the river.

"You don't think maybe some of us went above and beyond the call?"

Spalding spat into the grass. He lifted the rifle off his lap and held it in both hands, as if considering the weight of it. "You sure you don't want to take it?" he asked.

Wish only watched him.

"I'm not going to do it for you," Spalding said. "If that's what you come out here for."

Wish stood up slowly. "We should get a move on."

"I guess we should," Spalding said.

They never caught sight of a deer, first or last, though they were out all day. They went straight to the diner to eat when they drove back into Sherwood. They both ordered the special—liver and fried onions with mashed potato and mixed veg—and drank beer while they waited. They'd barely spoken to one another after their conversation that morning and for a while it looked like they might

275

carry on that way, sitting in silence until the plates were brought to their table, and quiet while they ate, both men ravenous and concentrating on the food in front of them. After they were through they ordered more beer and lit cigarettes.

Spalding said, "I've never got over the food thing. Can't leave a morsel on the plate. It's all I can do not to pick it up and lick it clean."

Wish leaned on the table toward him. "What else have you not got over?"

"Living here now," he said. "It's like sleeping in the bed I slept in when I was a youngster. It don't fit me like it used to. It's not how I remembered it over there at all." Spalding lifted the bottle to his mouth. "What about you?"

"What about me?"

"Was she not waiting or did you not bother to look?"

Wish didn't say a word.

"Never mind," Spalding said. "None of my business."

Wish picked up his coat where it lay on the seat and rifled through the pockets until he found the envelope and the front page of the *Chicago Defender*. He unfolded the newspaper and turned it so Spalding could see the picture, but the American hardly glanced at it.

"Remind you of anyone?"

Spalding drank a mouthful of his beer.

Wish shook the medal out on the table. Horizontal stripes of blue, white and red on the ribbon. A silver medallion. "Harris gave it to me before he died," he said. He turned the medal over and pointed at it. "There's something engraved on the back there. Do you see that?"

"Don't look like much to me."

"It's Japanese, is what it is. Whoever owned this medal had something engraved on it in Japanese. Why would they do that?"

"How the hell would I know?"

"He learned to speak English in Canada." Wish looked up at Spalding. "Nishino," he explained. "The interpreter."

"He told you that?"

"In so many words. That must be where he got his hands on this medal."

"So what if he did?"

"I don't know. I don't know. Fuck," Wish said.

Spalding tamped out his cigarette in the ashtray. He said, "What were you out there at the river for today?"

"Hunting deer, I thought."

The American folded the newspaper in half to hide the muti-lated face and leaned back in his seat. "Why are you carrying that thing around with you?"

Wish tucked the medal back in its envelope. "I don't know."

Spalding let that hang in the air, then said, "You can't let that fucker get under your skin."

Wish offered a strained smile. "What if he was always in there?"

"Well in that case." Spalding paused. "I guess you'd have to see a priest about that," he said.

"Priest fuck," Wish said quietly. He reached into his pocket for a five-dollar bill, laid it on the table between them.

"Don't crucify yourself with it, is all I'm saying."

"Fill up the truck with the change," Wish said and he got up from the booth. He took the sheet of newspaper and walked to the exit.

"Hey, Furey," Spalding called after him.

He turned back with his hand on the door.

"Those are my boots."

Wish looked down at his feet. "I'll leave them in the truck," he said.

2.

THE DOOR TO THE SHOP in Georgestown was open and he let himself in without knocking. There was no sign of Hiram in the main room. Equipment was scattered about behind the counter and along one wall, a heavy coat of dust on the surface of the cameras and projectors and all along the counter. He went through to the darkroom, the door standing open. The developing trays were stacked on the floor, an acid stink of disuse to the room. The tiny office was as dishevelled as he remembered it, receipt and log books stacked among pulp novels and yellowing newspapers from a dozen years past. A scatter of empty glasses that smelled of alcohol.

He went up the stairs to the second floor, walked through the rooms he'd lived in, but they were choked with an untidy array of boxes and old furniture and outdated film equipment and felt completely foreign to him. He stood at the foot of the stairs leading to the third floor. "Hiram," he said. It was warmer as he went up and there was a dank, closed-in smell of unwashed clothes and sleep. The bedroom was dark with a blanket hung over the window but there was enough light to see that the unmade bed was empty and clothes lay strewn about the floor and over the back of the single chair inside. A rank smell coming from behind the closed door of the wash closet. Hiram stretched out on the floor inside like a creature stranded on a beach by the tides. His face purple and bloated, a stench of piss and vomit. Wish took a shaving mirror from the washstand and held it under the man's nostrils. Mist on the glass. He grabbed Hiram by the lapels of his coat, dragged him out the door to the bedroom where he manoeuvred the dead weight of him up onto the mattress one appendage at a time. "You fucking cow, Hiram," he said.

In the tiny kitchenette he found a kettle and a package of tea bags. A bag of hard bread, Purity jam-jams. He put the kettle on to boil and sat on a milk crate near the window. He turned on a white radio sitting on the sill, plowing the dial through heavy banks of static without ever finding a station signal. Looked down at the street finally, trying to picture it as it was when he'd lived above it twenty years earlier.

The kettle whistled as it boiled, pulling him back to the kitchenette, to the smell of the present. 1960. His first time home to Newfoundland since he'd left to go overseas. He couldn't say why something as meaningless as the turn of a decade would bring him here when so many other things had failed. It was a Catholic thing, he decided. Twelve disciples. Forty days and forty nights. The numbers were talismans, no different than a crucifix or rosary beads. Logic didn't come into it.

From the line of empty bottles on the wash closet floor, from the state of the business affairs downstairs, Wish guessed Hiram was somewhere close to drinking himself to death and was dedicated to it now with a single-mindedness that precluded everything but the drinking. He had no idea if the man would even recognize him. He carried two mugs of tea into the bedroom and took the blanket down off the window. He propped Hiram up against the headboard and pinched his earlobes, shouting his name.

A gurgle in response, one limp hand trying to bat him away.

"Some fight left in you yet," Wish said. "Hey, Hiram?"

Fifteen minutes later he'd spooned half a cup of tea into Hiram's mouth and managed to get the man to speak in monosyllables. But there was still no sign of recognition from him.

"You know me, Hiram?" he shouted. "You know who I am?"

He fixed Wish with a heavy-lidded stare. "You're dead," he slurred.

Wish said, "I come back to haunt you, you bastard." And something like a smile flickered across Hiram's face.

———

"Did I ever pay you that fiver I owed you, Wish?"

They sat at a desk in the kitchenette that Hiram had been using as a table. Dark outside, the room lit by a small lamp on the desk. Hiram had slept a few hours more and was drinking another cup of tea, liberally laced with whisky.

"You gave me five dollars before I got off the coaster. You don't remember that?"

Hiram bit into a stale jam-jam and talked through the gummy mess of it in his mouth. "I don't remember half what I seen in my lifetime." He raised his mug. "The drink catching up with me."

"Where is she, Hiram?"

He looked down into his mug. "She left just after the war. Went to the States and married a Yank. Good fellow."

Wish could see him considering how much more he should tell. "What?" he said.

"I think she was pregnant when she left here, Wish. I expect she was, anyway. And she went off and married him."

"Where to?"

"Somewhere near Boston. Lovell or something kin to that. Lowell? Jesus," Hiram said. "Wish Furey. Like Lazarus from the grave. You heard any news of Lilly?"

"No."

"She was in here to the Waterford for a while."

"The mental?"

"That was a year and more ago. She had one of her spells, a bad one by all accounts. No one knew what to do with her out in Renews so the priest had her sent in here. She's probably gone home by now."

"She's mad?"

"What did you think?" the older man asked. He looked genuinely curious. "You thought she was a saint or some goddamn thing?"

Wish didn't know for certain what he thought. "*Capo per-duto*," he said. A kind of relief raising goosebumps on his skin.

Lilly was long ago discharged from the Waterford, as Hiram predicted. Wish hitched a ride on the new road to the Southern Shore as far as Aquaforte and walked the rest of the way into Renews. Dark by the time he arrived. The highway passed directly in front of Tom Keating's house, electric lights illuminating the rooms on the ground floor. Wish turned up the path that ran along the north side without stopping. He passed the cemetery and walked down behind the church across the brook. He stopped outside the low fence at the grotto, looking up at Mary. The Ocean Star. The bare rock walls half covered now in some kind of vine.

He'd touched the feet of the Virgin for luck the last time he went through the doors of the French Temple in Nagasaki, the day after the commandant surrendered the camp to Major McCarthy. The stained glass windows were blown out but the building was far enough outside the city centre that it stood relatively intact besides. It had been turned into a kind of refugee camp, the pews hauled from the floor and stacked on one side of the church to make room. Oil lamps were lit and hung along the walls with litters of the injured and dying laid beneath them. Several hundred people taking shelter in the open space. The smell of seared flesh.

"He's camped out in the basement," Wish said. "Down with the urns."

The heads of those still awake in the church turned toward them but no one spoke or made a motion.

Harris said, "Let's get this show on the road."

The three of them picked their way toward the door to the left of the altar that led downstairs, stepping over people as they went. After the surrender of the camp they had access to handguns and they each carried one. But they had other plans for the interpreter. Wish and Harris recruited Spalding for the expedition because they were afraid they wouldn't have the strength between them to give the man what he deserved. There was no light in the stairwell. Harris had a flashlight but didn't turn it on for fear of giving themselves away.

"You sure he's down here?" Spalding whispered.

"I seen him."

"Suppose he's scuttled off somewheres since then?"

"Shut up, Spalding," Harris said.

Wish used a hand against the wall to follow along the corridor, counting doorways as they passed. He stopped outside the door next to last from the end. "Got that flashlight ready, Harris?" he asked.

Wish stepped around the low concrete wall at the front of the grotto and knelt in the grass below the statue of Mary. He said, "*Ave Maria, gratia plena, Dominus tecum. Benedicta tu in mulieribus, et benedictus fructus ventris tui, Iesus.*" But he couldn't bring himself to go any further.

Lilly's shack was abandoned and someone was using it to store firewood, piling the split junks in rows against the wall. He thought for a minute about looking for her at the convent but walked back down through Renews instead, taking the path along the water to avoid the grotto. At the Keating house he let himself into the light and stood in the doorway to the kitchen. The room was as crowded as ever and no one took much note of him at first. Tom Keating was sound asleep on the daybed with two youngsters sitting on the edge of the cot, picking at one another. Billy-Peter was dealing a hand of cards at the table and glanced up at the doorway. He set the cards down beside the crib board.

"Jesus in the Garden," he said.

Wish lifted his arms away from his body for a second, a gesture that was almost apologetic.

Patty Keating came in from the pantry with a pitcher of water that she dropped on the floor when she saw him. She ran across to grab him, alternately hugging him and beating at his chest with her fists, screaming all the while. Tom sat up on the daybed, shouting questions with a hand cupped to his ear, trying to figure what all the commotion was about.

Wish spent the rest of the evening in the kitchen, drinking beer and talking to Tom and Billy-Peter about the fishing and the fate of everyone he knew in Renews and how things had changed on the shore since Newfoundland voted to join Canada in 1949.

"We all voted against it around here," Tom Keating said. He had an air of surprise about him, as if he'd never expected to wake from his sleep again. Not a single tooth left in his mouth and he gummed his words like they were made of paste. "The Monsignor as much as told us to vote against it."

"I didn't vote against it," Patty insisted. She was sitting in her nightgown with her grey hair done up in braids, her arms folded under her breasts.

"She's going straight to hell anyway," Billy-Peter said.

"We got the road out of it," she said. "And a cheque from the government every month for the youngsters. I got no regrets."

Billy-Peter's wife sat off to one side, crocheting. Geraldine Bavis. A girl Wish had walked out with himself a few times before he left Renews. Deen she was called. The priest came on them down at Aggie Dinn's Cove, hardly into anything by then, just holding hands and the shyest bit of necking. Father Power drove them out of it, shouting hellfire and whacking Wish across the shoulders with a birch walking cane as he hobbled after them. At mass that Sunday the Monsignor laid into Deen's parents for the lack of spiritual direction in her life. The girl never so much as looked at Wish again.

The two youngsters sitting beside Tom Keating on the daybed were Billy-Peter's and Deen's. "What's their names?" Wish asked.

"This one's Billy," Billy-Peter said. "And the little one is Peter. Got another one upstairs asleep."

"You been busy," Wish said and Deen smiled down at the doilie she was crocheting.

The oldest of the two was nearly ten, a high pook of hair at the crown and a quick way about him that made the boy seem birdlike, cautious and brazen by turns. "You was in the war," he said.

No one else had mentioned the subject. "Hardly at all," Wish said. "The Brits gave up Singapore just after I got over there. I didn't get a chance to fire a shot."

The boy screwed up his face. "You never even killed no one?"

Wish took a swig of beer. "I never said that now, did I?" He turned to Billy-Peter. "Where is Lilly to these days?"

"She's up at the convent," he said. "You heard she was in town for a while?"

"I heard."

"She got the run of the convent these days. The nuns dotes on her like she was a newborn lamb."

"She'll be tickled to death to see you," Patty said. "She never would believe you was gone for good."

Wish glanced across at Tom, who seemed to have dozed off again where he sat. "I'm keeping you crowd up," he said.

"Take him up to bed, Mother," Billy-Peter said.

It was hours still before the last of the people in the room made their way upstairs to bed or out the door to their own houses. Wish and Billy-Peter sat with their beer for a while then, smoking cigarettes to have something to do with their hands.

They were altar boys together when Wish first arrived in Renews, following Father Power around with the crucifix, ringing the bell, kneeling, genuflecting. Repeating the Latin prayers sleepily, until a phrase caught their pubescent attention. *Aufer a me,*

Domine, cor lapideum, aufer cor coagulatum, aufer cor incircum-cisum. Take away my heart of stone, my hardened heart, my uncircumcised heart. Even in Latin that notion was enough to induce a fit of the giggles in them both. Father Power cuffing the backs of their heads to snuff the laughter before it got out of hand.

They hunted for a rare glimpse of cleavage as women came to the altar for communion. Rated the girls after mass as they removed their vestments, ranking them in order of desirability. The Wish List, he called it. "If I ever gets my hands on that Geraldine Bavis," he said. "By the Jesus."

Billy-Peter gave him a two-handed shove. "You needs to get your heart circumcised," he said.

"You and Deen looks fine together," Wish said now.

"We're managing all right. You don't look none the worse for wear."

"Not a scar." Wish held his hands out at his sides, that same apologetic gesture.

"You're not sticking around, are you."

"I'm going to leave you some money to look after Lilly."

"She don't want for nothing up there."

Wish took out a billfold and counted out a hundred dollars. "All the same."

"I'll put it by. Just in case."

"There's more of this if you needs it. I'll drop you a note when I settles somewhere."

Billy-Peter said, "Your woman come out here during the war, you know."

"Mercedes?"

"She was with another girl and a Yank soldier. She come look-ing for you, she said." He paused there. "What become of her?"

"She married the Yank."

Billy-Peter's head jerked back slightly. "Is that right?" he said. That fact alone seemed enough to answer any questions he might have had about what happened to Wish after the war. "Where you planning on going from here?"

Wish shrugged. "I thought I might try my luck in the Boston States."

3.

HE WOKE EARLY WITH AN ERECTION. Stared down at it when he got to his feet, surprised. He didn't feel aroused in any sexual way but he could have hung a coat on the knob. "Hello, stranger," he said. Tried to think of when he'd last found himself in that condition. He'd been living alone so long he'd hardly noticed the lack and couldn't fix the time or place with any certainty.

He'd moved back to Newfoundland for good in the early 1980s, when Billy-Peter wrote to tell him Lilly had been readmitted to the Waterford. He was working as a mechanic at a roadside service station in New Mexico at the time, living on his own after the implosion of the latest in a long line of relationships with women no better at holding their liquor or their tongues than himself. He did oil changes and muffler replacements and pumped gas. Creeping up on sixty then and ready for a change himself.

Billy-Peter stopped in around ten and made himself at home at the kitchen table with a coffee. Since Deen passed on, Billy-Peter came up to Calvert for a regular visit. Drove in on Thursdays to put on a pot of stew or cook up a French fry of potato and bologna while Wish was visiting Lilly at St. Pat's. The two men sitting with plates on their laps in the evening, watching some ball game or old movie pulled in by the satellite dish that Billy-Peter's oldest boy had wangled up on the roof.

"What's news?" Billy-Peter asked, lifting the cup to his mouth. He wore a blue baseball cap high on his head, as if there was a raft of cotton batting stuffed between the hat and his hair.

Wish said, "I woke up with a hard-on this morning," and Billy-Peter spit a mouthful of coffee up his nose. "I know," Wish said, incredulous.

Billy-Peter wiped at his mouth. "Signs and wonders," he said, "before the end of time."

Wish laughed along with him. But he couldn't help feeling there was something vaguely and ludicrously apocalyptic about it. A resurrection so unexpected, so inexplicable, it was bound to carry some significance beyond the simple physical fact of itself. He was still mulling it over while he took Lilly down to the common room after *Wheel of Fortune*. Someone was spelunking old hymns and show tunes on the piano as he set her up at a table near the window and Lilly hummed along tunelessly to them. He brought a deck of cards and the plastic crib board that he kept in her room and dealt them a hand. Maybe he was losing his mind as well, he thought, maybe he was spending too much time in the company of madness.

Lilly was able to lift the cards off the table and hold them but Wish had to point to them one at a time to know which she wanted put in the kitty and which to lay down as they played a hand. Her aptitude for the game surprised him. There were days she didn't know where she was, couldn't call up Wish's name, but the simple arithmetic of the cards, the rules and patterns of the game never left her. He counted out her points on the board, moving the matchsticks they used as pegs to keep score. He played to lose and most often did. "*Laurus*," Lilly announced after every win, clapping the heels of her palms together. Wish held his head in mock despair, repeating "*Fundo, fundo, fundo*," under his breath. Defeat, defeat, defeat.

When he'd arrived home in Newfoundland and spoken to the doctor assigned to Lilly's file at the Waterford, he was told she'd been dressing up in an approximation of the vestments of a priest, some stolen from the church, others improvised from her own clothes. Wandered through Renews offering the sacrament to gulls and dogs, performing Latin exorcisms on sheep and rocks and the rusted-out remains of a washer someone had dumped on the side of the road. There was just the hint of a smile on the doctor's face.

"You finds this hilarious, do you?" Wish said.

The doctor shrugged. He had a slight foreign accent, something eastern European. "It is a rather harmless delusion," he said. "Much less distressing than her previous episodes. And she has stabilized. There's no reason she couldn't be discharged."

"Well what is she doing here, then?"

"She has nowhere to go, Mr. Furey. The convent in Renews has been closed. We have nowhere to send her."

He bought an abandoned house in Calvert, between St. John's and Renews, for the cost of a second-hand car. He bought a second-hand car besides, shuttling into St. John's from the Southern Shore twice a week to visit Lilly and make arrangements to get her into a home. For the better part of a decade afterwards he made a weekly pilgrimage into St. Pat's to watch television and let her beat him at crib beside a window in the common room.

Fundo, fundo, fundo.

He set the matchstick pegs back into their starting positions on the crib board after his third loss in a row. "You're a hard ticket, Lilly," he said. "A damn good thing I don't have any money riding on these games."

Lilly was looking past his shoulder and smiling when he glanced up. And then he felt a hand on his neck, just the slightest touch. He turned his whole body to avoid straining his back. The woman had drawn her hand away quickly as if she'd scalded herself. She was portly and grey haired and there was something wrong with her face, a long, barely visible scar on one cheek surrounded by a patch of deadness. He shifted further in his chair to face her more directly and she took a step back, not out of any uncertainty but to have a better view of him.

She said, "I was just wanting to make sure." She gestured at him. "That birthmark."

Something in the woman stepped forward then, as if she moved out of a shadowed doorway into sunlight. As if the girl he'd known leaned out from the high window of what fifty years could do to deface a person. Eyes as green as sea-glass.

"Holy fuck," he said. "Mercedes Parsons."

"I thought you were dead, Wish."

Delayed was the word that came to his mind but he couldn't manage to get it out. Mercedes watched him as calm as you please, not a feather out of her. And her composure fed the panic rising in him. She'd expected to find him here at this table, had tracked him down somehow. "My God, Mercedes," he said.

She pulled out a chair to sit at the table. She said, "Hello, Lilly."

Lilly bowed forward in her wheelchair.

He felt light-headed, almost drunk, smiling stupidly to cover his surprise, the rush of fear. *There'll be no stopping her now,* was his thought. He fumbled with the box of matches, placed two more on the crib board and looked across to her as a question. They sat in silence while Wish shuffled and dealt. Through the course of that game and the next they spoke only what was required to play the hands or tally their points. He took refuge in the arbitrary fall of the cards, the simple patterns layered one on another as each hand played out, trying to guess what she was doing here, to figure out what he could get away with telling her. Mercedes seemed content to sit there as if they'd sat across from one another all their lives, as if nothing between them awaited answers or explanation or apology. Every time she smiled at him Wish felt much the same as he had that first afternoon in the Cove when he'd been waiting for her and she managed to surprise him anyway, standing in the doorway of the church hall. Expectant and caught out. Fearful, childish, impatient. All at sea.

On the far side of the room, the piano player stuttered out a song Wish knew from the war, the words called up in his head by the music: *We'll meet again, don't know where, don't know when.* The tune seemed impossibly ancient to him, almost as old as light.

Lilly nodded off in her wheelchair. Wish considered taking her back to her room but was afraid of breaking the spell of the cards, of setting things between him and Mercedes off on another road. He dealt Lilly out of the game instead and they carried on with a two-hander. Wish knocking the cards for luck when he cut the deck. Kathleen came by to wheel the old woman down the hall to her bed and they played a while longer. But Lilly's absence unsettled them, as if it pointed up a raft of other absences. Mercedes dealt a hand and looked up at him over her cards.

"What are you doing home?" he asked.

"My husband asked to have his ashes scattered up here."

"He's dead?"

"Three years now."

He thought he should offer condolences but managed only to say, "How did you know to find me here?"

"I came by to see Lilly last week. Kathleen told me you were a regular visitor."

"The fucking mouth on that one," Wish said. He picked up his cards and moved them around aimlessly in his hand. "How did you know to find Lilly?"

He could see her hesitate as if she had concocted a lie and held it back at the last minute. She shrugged. "Just luck, I guess."

The numbers and faces on the cards were meaningless to him, the light-headedness creeping back.

Mercedes said, "Tell me about Jim Harris."

He glanced up quickly.

"Jim Harris," she repeated. "He sent me a note and that length of string after the war. To say you were dead."

It was an accusation she was making and he could feel the colour flooding his face. "You were already knocked up by then, weren't you?" he said.

The uninjured side of her face startled, as if he'd slapped her.

"According to Hiram you were," Wish said, trying to sound like less of an arsehole.

She said, "I waited for you until I—" She stopped and ran her hands along the length of her skirt. "I never heard a word from you," she whispered.

He took out his handkerchief and wiped at his eyes. *Old man*, he thought. He cried at the drop of a hat these days, as if someone was turning on a tap in his head. He'd gone to the war memorial on the anniversary of D-Day and wept before the ceremony even started, wiping away snot with a handkerchief. *Pathetic old fucker.* He cleared his throat and looked away out the window.

"Jim Harris," she said again.

"Jimmy Harris," he said and he cleared his throat again. "He was with me in Nagasaki, him and Anstey. Anstey never made it out. And Harris got sick on the train home from San Francisco. Just racked up with cancer, wasted away to nothing." Wish leaned forward to stare at his feet, one elbow on the table, the other on the back of the plastic chair.

"You were with him," she said. "On that train home."

"I was with him the whole time, Mercedes. I was with him when the bomb was dropped. And picking through the ruins afterwards." He glanced across at her. "What made him sick was in me too, is what I mean. The doctors told me as much." He shook his head. "No one should have to go through that," he said. "To watch someone die like that."

She picked up her cards. "I kept that note for a long time," she said. "That and the string." No sign of tears. A cold, calm fury.

"I made him write the note," Wish said, straightening in the chair. "He wouldn't do it at first. Said it was—" He tipped his head to one side, as if listening to a conversation across the room. "I told him," he said. "I'd let him die alone if he didn't."

She rearranged the cards in her hand. Weighing things up in her mind, he could see, trying to redistribute the facts of her life in light of his sitting there in front of her. He expected she'd despise him before it was done and he couldn't blame her for that.

Before the Japanese surrender, the POWs at Nagasaki #14 were divided into work groups and taken into the city to collect the dead and burn them. Hundreds and thousands lying about the ruins, some barely recognizable as human. Blackened bones—spine and pelvis, femurs, skulls—still warm to the touch days after the explosion. They salvaged bodies from beneath the rubble, torsos and arms and legs, like bizarre deep-sea creatures brought up into the light of day. They gathered the corpses into piles, dousing the pyres of flesh with gasoline before setting them alight. A piece of cloth tied over their faces against the dense, drifting stench. A blue, mineral twilight persisting all hours of the day. Wish saw a woman sitting on a concrete step that first morning, her neck and face and one side of her head scorched raw, the dull-white of her skull visible in spots through the tattered scalp. She was nursing an infant, the skin of the baby's back bubbled by the heat of radiation. It looked to Wish like pork rind just out of the oven. The woman seemed barely aware of her surroundings, of the child in her arms. *Dead to the world*, was his thought. But he felt nothing for her or the infant. He was only a day out of the cells, every movement excruciating, and he struggled through the heavy work of hauling bodies with a grim satisfaction. Praying for as much again on every yellow bastard in the country.

Mercedes said, "Would you really have let Harris die alone?"

A hard little smile crossed his face. "I don't know," he said. "It was a long time ago."

"The Wish I knew," she said.

He shrugged.

She put her hands and her cards in her lap. "You never come looking?" she said. "Did you ever even think?"

"It was a long time ago, Mercedes."

They walked together down the hall to Lilly's room. Mercedes took his arm and he couldn't think how to get clear of her hand until they stood back against opposite walls to let a resident go by in her wheelchair. He kept well to his side then so she couldn't touch him without having to reach.

In Lilly's room a young woman Wish didn't know was sitting in a chair near the television. Mercedes said, "Hello, Bella."

"I got tired of waiting downstairs," the woman said. She was looking him up and down.

"This is my daughter," Mercedes told him.

Wish stared at her and Mercedes in turn. "She's too young," he said.

Mercedes slapped him with the back of her hand. "I'm not *that* old."

He caught himself and laughed, as if he'd intended only to make a joke, and introduced himself.

"Isabella," she said, eyeing him warily.

He had no idea how much she knew of who he was.

Mercedes said, "How did you find Lilly's room?"

"Ran into the Amazon as I came off the elevator."

"Kathleen?"

"She told me I could wait for you here." Bella stood up. "Are you ready to go, Mom?"

Mercedes looked around the room quickly. She seemed caught off guard by the question. She glanced at Wish but he refused to meet her eye. "All right," she said. "I guess so, yes."

Isabella walked out to the hall, where she waited for her mother. Mercedes was looking around the room again as if it had been her home for years and she was about to leave it for good.

"Mom," Bella called.

"All right," she said. "Goodbye, Lilly." She turned to Wish and then went to the door. She stood there with her back to the room for a moment. "I'm going to visit the Cove," she said. She looked back at him and Wish was struck by the length of the scar, the odd lifelessness on that side of her face, as if a stroke had paralyzed the muscles there. "Going to drive up to Fogo and see if I can't find someone to take me across. You wouldn't like to come, would you?"

"No," he said. "No. Thanks. Couldn't get away."

He could see she was hurt by the curtness of his refusal and he had to bite his tongue to let it lie. He stood listening to Mercedes and her daughter walk down the hall to the elevator, taking in one long breath after another. Thinking, *That's done.* And feeling no relief with the thought.

Billy-Peter's truck was still parked in the gravel driveway when he arrived home in Calvert. Lights on inside as dusk came down, smoke rising out of the chimney, a fire laid in the wood stove to cut the evening chill. Wish sat in the car outside the house awhile. He was surprised to see Billy-Peter's truck for some reason. He was surprised to see the house itself. He couldn't remember the drive home, thinking about Harris, about losing Anstey just before the Japanese surrender.

In the last two days of his life, Anstey fell into sleeps so deep it was a kind of unconsciousness. He was oblivious to any movement or noise around him, to pain or discomfort, to his own hunger and thirst. They knew the war was all but over by then and somehow it made Wish feel more profoundly impotent that there was nothing they could do to help. The British doctor lifting the blankets to examine Anstey's blue feet, the progress of the mottling as it crept to his knees. Anstey surfaced occasionally to ask what day it was, what time of day. He asked for Wish and Harris by name and nodded almost imperceptibly when they answered him. Then he went under again, for hours at a time.

There were spasms of inarticulate panic at the end, Anstey's head ratcheted off the bed, the blind eyes wide, his jaws working as if the air was emptied of oxygen. Harris with an arm around his shoulders to ease Anstey down, whispering to quiet him though there was no indication he could hear a sound. Anstey slipped back into a dead calm within seconds, but the useless urgency of those moments made Wish nauseous. It was like being forced to witness an execution over and over again. Harris brushing Anstey's forehead and cheeks with his fingers, his shoulders shaking. "That lousy fucker" was all he could choke out. "That miserable cunt." And there was no question who he had in mind.

They cremated the corpse as soon as Anstey died, and Wish smuggled his ashes out of the camp the following night. Carried the urn and a flashlight in a cloth satchel, wheeling a bicycle he'd found propped against the wall of the main guardhouse. He half expected to be shot but no one paid him any mind. Some of the guards had deserted in the days since the explosion, the interpreter among them. Those who remained oversaw the camp with a blankness akin to that of the woman he'd seen nursing her child in the city. As if nothing visible to the naked eye held any significance.

He was too weak to ride the bicycle uphill, leaning on the seat and the handlebars as he struggled up the inclines, catching his breath as he coasted down the other side. At the French Temple he touched the Virgin's feet before picking his way through the crowds taking refuge inside. He'd planned to say the rosary but civilians in various states of injury and distress were camped around the altar and he went straight to the basement.

He wandered the corridors, pushing doors ajar, shining the flashlight along the walls. Eyes staring back at him in every one of them. When he finally located the crypt, someone was stretched out asleep on the floor there as well. He picked his way over the man and played the beam of the flashlight over the shelves until he came upon a handful of names and units he recognized. He placed Anstey's remains beside them and turned to leave, the light flicking over the sleeping figure. Wire-rimmed glasses folded and placed on the floor near the man's head. Wish's scalp prickled and he stood still until the dizziness passed. He crouched beside the man then. A smell of alcohol rising off his breath. The dark mole high on the left cheekbone.

Nishino had made himself at home in the room: a scatter of clothes, a mug, several bottles of the alcohol Wish had brewed at the camp, half a dozen votive candles for light. A bucket in one corner that stank of shit. He'd abandoned his uniform for civilian clothes but the kit bag still sat in a corner. Wish stepped over him carefully, raising the flap to look inside. The handgun in its leather holster. He glanced over his shoulder at the sleeping man and tried to think, think, think. Considered shooting him right there, a bullet to the head to finish him. He didn't know if any other soldiers were camping out in the church or if they'd bother to come after him if there were. He took the holster from the bag and crept out the door. He emptied the chamber of ammunition, slipped the bullets into his breast pocket. Stepped back inside, replaced the gun and holster in Nishino's kit bag.

He knelt before the Virgin outside the church, whispered a quick prayer. Pulled the bicycle out of the bushes where he'd stashed it and started back to the camp, euphoric, resolute. The phrase *The Lord hath delivered him into my hands* running through his head as he went.

Billy-Peter came to the door of the house. "Supper's ready," he called.

Wish opened the car door and shifted his legs out, using his hands to help move the dead weight of them. He didn't know if

he'd be able to stand and he hung on to the doorframe a few minutes to be certain. He leaned into the car to grab the coffee he'd
picked up for the trip home and carried it with him. He staggered
slightly as he came into the kitchen, caught himself on the
kitchen table.

Billy-Peter said, "Jesus, Wish, that's not the hard-on throwing
you off your stride, is it?"

"Got a headache," he said, walking by Billy-Peter toward the
back bedroom.

"I'll lay your supper in the oven, will I?"

He didn't bother to answer. Closed the bedroom door behind
him.

It was mid-morning the next day before he woke. He sat up on
the side of the bed and looked slowly around the room, trying to
guess the time by the fall of light through the window. The
bureau top scattered with loose change and coffee mugs. Empty
plastic hangers in the closet, a pile of dirty clothes on the floor
beneath them. He felt viciously hungover, low and uneasy,
though he couldn't for the moment place the cause. He picked
up the nearly empty Tim Hortons cup from the bedside table
and took a cold mouthful.

He hauled on the pants and shirt that were lying on the floor
by the bed and walked out to the kitchen in his bare feet, still trying to do up his fly. Found Billy-Peter sitting at the kitchen table
with Mercedes and her daughter and another woman he didn't
know. All of them drinking tea like it was any old morning. And
the whole of the day before breached the surface of his mind.

"Morning," Billy-Peter said. He got up from his chair. "I'll
put on some coffee."

"What the hell are you doing here?" Wish said.

"Stayed over," Billy-Peter said. "Thought I should keep an
eye on you last night."

"I wasn't talking to you. How did you know to find me here?" he asked Mercedes.

"Kathleen told me you were living in Calvert."

"Jesus fuck," he said. "The mouth on that one."

Isabella said, "He's a real charmer, Mom."

The third woman was Mercedes' sister, he could tell just from looking at her. She was holding a wallet-sized picture in her hand and he said, "Where did you get that?"

"I stepped in to see if you were awake earlier," Billy-Peter said. "Thought they might like to see it."

It was the photo taken in Hiram's shop during the war, Mercedes as a young woman, the ancient black-and-white creased and faded. Wish hadn't looked at it himself in years, had dug out the envelope the night before, alone in his bedroom. Just to remind himself of the physical fact of Mercedes' face. To set it against the face of the woman who'd ambushed him at the nursing home. He'd left the picture lying on the bureau and a hangover fog of emotion flooded him now, seeing it on display. A rootless, insidious sense of betrayal. He pointed at Billy-Peter. "You blood of a bitch," he said.

"Settle down, Wish."

"Get the fuck out of here. And give me back the key to the front door."

"There's no lock on the front door, you foolish prick."

He looked at Billy-Peter a moment. "Fuck," he said. He marched to the porch and pulled his shoes on his sockless feet.

"Where you going?"

"Over to Mercer's for a drink."

"Mercer's don't open before noon."

"I'll wait." He straightened up and reached for the door.

"Wish."

"*What*, goddamn it?"

Billy-Peter pointing with a smug little grin on his face. "Your fly is down."

"Fuck," he whispered. Isabella and the other one, what the hell was her name? Both of them laughing as he hauled at the zipper. He took a ball hat off a coat hook and went out the door with it, crunching down the gravel driveway. Realized at the car that he'd left his keys inside.

"She's almost brewed," Billy-Peter said, nodding to the coffee maker when he came back into the house.

Wish shouted something then, a wordless guttural syllable. He whipped the ball hat across the kitchen and it tailed sideways before it fell to the linoleum, halfway to the counter. Something in his chest tailing sideways and dropping in much the same fashion.

Mercedes turned her teacup slowly on the table, watching as the two men contemplated the cap on the floor.

Wish said, "What's the sense of me going up to the Cove with you, Mercedes?"

"I don't know."

"You don't know a goddamn thing about who you're talking to. You really don't."

"Maybe that's why I'm asking."

"You might as well sit down, my son," Billy-Peter said. He set a cup of coffee on the table. "She got the nerve of a mule."

Wish looked up at the ceiling with his hands on his hips. "Sweet flying fuck," he said.

Mercedes' sister got up to drag a folding chair over to the table for him. He felt completely defeated. Run to ground. He walked over and sat beside her. *Agnes*, her name was. "Thank you, Agnes," he said. "Thanks."

4.

THEY DROVE IN THROUGH the country in Agnes's car, four hours to Gander, where they turned north to follow the coastline through Notre Dame Bay. It was cold and wet the whole way, socked in with fog along the shoreline. "Capelin weather," Wish said.

Mercedes and Agnes kept up a ping-pong conversation over the seats, pointing out the changes on the northeast coast since they were girls together on Little Fogo Island. Pavement and power lines. Schools and rinks and baseball diamonds. Split-level bungalows. Manicured lawns. 7-Elevens.

The Cove itself had been abandoned around the time the Americans left the Pleasantville base in the 1960s. The provincial government had forced dozens of small, isolated communities to relocate to towns with schools and medical services. People loaded their boats with what could be carried away and left behind what couldn't. Homes and storehouses and wharves. The web of cart tracks and walking paths to the stages and fishing rooms, the slide paths through the backwoods where winter fuel was cut and hauled. The berry fields, the Washing Pond, the Spell Rock. The generations buried one next the other in the graveyard.

Most of the larger islands in the bay had been strung together with causeways in the years since the war, so you could drive onto New World Island from the mainland and straight across from there to Twillingate. But the ferry was still the only way out to Fogo. They sat with the engine running to keep warm while they waited in line above the dock in Farewell.

"Bella's never been on a boat before," Mercedes said. "Have you, Bella?"

"Can't wait," she said.

The two-dozen cars in line pulled onto the lower deck of the ferry. Wish set the handbrake and they all climbed up into the fog, walking across to the guardrail as the vessel inched away from the dock. A fresh wind was blowing outside the harbour and the ferry began to kick sharply port and starboard as they moved into the open water of Notre Dame Bay.

Bella put both hands on the rail and stared out over the whitecaps. "How long is this trip?"

"Forty-five minutes, give or take."

"Are you all right, Bella?" Agnes asked her.

The colour was already seeping out of her face. "I think I'll go back to the car and lay down awhile."

Agnes followed after her and they both disappeared down the stairs.

Mercedes said, "Her father was useless on the water too."

"She seems out of sorts altogether."

"She's been out of sorts her whole life." Mercedes looked down at the rail. "Not a bit like Marion."

"How old is Marion now?"

"Marion's dead, Wish."

"Oh," he said. He leaned out over the rail. Mercedes told him about the rodeo, about the runaway horse and the scar on her face, and all the while she talked he nodded down at the waves, as if he'd heard the story before and was just indulging her need to tell it.

"I was wondering," he said, "where that scar came from."

"Lost five teeth on this side and the cheekbone was shattered. I didn't know Marion was gone till I woke up in hospital. They put in a plate," she said. "It sets off the metal detectors at the airport." She touched her cheek with her fingertips. "Most of the nerves are dead."

"You got plenty of that to spare."

She put her arm into his. "I blamed you for a long time," she said.

He leaned away to get a good look at her.

"That birthmark of yours, you know. And losing her the way we did. It felt made up. Like there was some kind of design in it." She laughed a little at her own foolishness.

Wish could see it would be hard to dismiss the conclusion out of hand. The world threw enough bullshit into a life that some of it was unreasonably persuasive.

They were quiet a long time then, watching the wake furl away from boat until the shudder of the engines reversing came up through the decks. Mercedes said, "What happened to you over there, Wish?"

"How much do you want to know, Mercedes?"

"Everything."

"Now my love," he said, "don't be greedy."

"Everything," she said again.

They spent the night at a bed and breakfast run by a couple from Ontario. The Hendersons served scallops wrapped in bacon, a salad with tomatoes and olives and goat cheese for their supper.

Mrs. Henderson said, "We get the cheese sent in from St. John's. Richard drives over to Gander twice a week for the produce and even then there's no guarantee of anything fresh."

"The air's always fresh though," Mr. Henderson said. The joke felt practised and awkward at once. "That's why we moved here in the first place," he said, and laughed again.

The Hendersons knew of a man up in Tilting who'd been carting his sheep across to the Cove on Little Fogo Island for years, letting them graze free over the summer. He was due to make the trip any day, they said.

Agnes picked over her salad, leaving behind as much of the cheese as she could without being rude. When the Hendersons were out of the room she said, "Only people who never grew up around goats would eat the like of that."

Late the next morning, they stood watching Gerry Foley tie the feet of twenty-five sheep, lifting them one at a time aboard his longliner. A squat, broad-shouldered man, a full beard tufted with grey.

"Haven't been a soul living out at the Cove this thirty years almost," he said. "What is it you wants with going out there?"

Mercedes said, "I grew up out there."

"Is that right? What's your name, then?"

"Parsons, I used to be. Sadie Parsons."

He repeated it under his breath as if he were rubbing a lamp. "Sadie Parsons, Sadie Parsons." He hefted another sheep aboard and looked back at her suddenly. "You're not the one run off after that Catholic fellow during the war?"

"What, did it make the paper or something?" Isabella asked.

"We didn't have a paper," Gerry Foley said. "Kept a good many gums flapping around here, though. That fellow got killed overseas, didn't he?"

Mercedes looked at Wish.

"Is this him?" Gerry Foley said. "Well, Jesus comforted Mary. She found you after all? Surprised we never heard that up this way. Is this your youngster?" he said.

"No," Isabella said. "I'm not."

Bella looked uncertain about getting aboard. The sheep bleating and rustling underfoot, as if the floor of the boat was a living, breathing thing. The smell of shit rising off them. She sat in the stern, as far from the animals as she could manage. Mercedes picked her way past the cuddy to the bow. It was another cool day but the fog had cleared off. Little Fogo Island a speck in the distance.

Agnes decided at the last moment not to go with them. "When I closed the door of that house in 1966 it was just the same as when Mother and Father lived there," she said. "That's how I want to keep it in my mind." She watched them pull away from the dock. "Say me to everyone," she shouted.

They were hardly clear of the harbour when Bella put her hand over her mouth and leaned forward over her knees.

"She's going to be sick," Wish announced to no one in particular.

Gerry shouted at her from the wheel. "Over the side, missus. Don't throw up in the jesus boat."

She leaned out over the gunnel and vomited into the ocean.
"Get it up, my love," he said. "Good for the fish."

Wish leaned his back against the cuddy. "Seems an awful lot
of trouble," he said, "hauling the animals out this far every year."

"Got to keep them fenced in home. Eating up people's
flower gardens, council says. Everyone with carpet on the floor
and they're afraid of tracking a bit of sheep shit into the house."
He rolled his eyes. "You take this boat now. Out after the cod in
her since nineteen and seventy-two. Till the government closed
the fishery two years ago. They got nothing better to do but make
my life miserable with their by-laws and decrees and moratori-
ums." He smiled across at Wish. "That's why we fought the war,
I spose."

An hour later the boat shimmied up to a pier in a shallow
area on the north side, below the Spell Rock. It was the only wharf
in the Cove still standing and it was obvious that Gerry Foley had
gone to a fair bit of trouble to keep it up. They stepped off as he
began carrying his sheep out onto the dock by their feet. Bella was
pale and shaking and she sat down at the Spell Rock, saying she'd
catch up with them later.

Mercedes and Wish walked along the path, which was hard-
packed by Gerry's sheep. Mercedes pointed to each building they
passed and named the people who'd lived in it, as if they were still
eating and sleeping under the staved-in roofs. There was no sign of
the church hall, and Mercedes told Wish it had burnt to the
ground during the war. The church was still standing, though the
doors were gone, and they walked in through the open archway.
The sanctuary had become a kind of barn, the pews uprooted and
stacked along one side of the building, the open floor space covered in straw and old sheep shit. A breeze of wind blowing through
the glassless windows. The plain wooden cross gone from the wall
behind the altar. Mercedes walked across to a window and looked
up at the cemetery behind the church.

"You ready to go up there?" Wish asked.

"Not yet. No. Let's head over to the south side first."

They walked slowly down the bowl of the harbour. A dozen sheep had begun making their way along the path toward them but there was still no sign of Bella. On the shoreline all the fishing rooms and twine lofts and drying flakes were gone or lying in a shambles of grey wood. The remains of half a dozen stone cages that had been the bases of wharves rising out of the water.

Wish picked his way through a pile of lumber, lifting sticks aside to clear away a criss-cross of rough-hewn beams, running his hand along the length of them.

"What are you looking for?"

"This was someone's twine loft. Thought maybe." He straightened from the beams and went along a ways, clearing boards from another. "Here you go," he said, running his hand along letters carved into the beam with a knife. Ledger, calendar, diary, the entries made haphazardly over the years. He started reading aloud.

Put out the trap 24 June 1953
Making a window March 17 1959 wet day no ducks
Size of coffin 5ft 9in
    22 ins from head to shoulders, depth 12 ins
    21 ins wide on shoulders
Came home May 12 1946
Snowy day April 4 1962, finished planking punt
The Hood in the harbour landing salt
June 17 not a fish yet
29'th of June took up a trap from a piece of ice
    set it out again July 1'st 1953
Down in the store June 17 1961
Sep 7 Clive Reid drowned this morning

The familiar name brought him up short and he stopped there, straightening from the beam. Mercedes was already walking away from him, back up to the path. Wreckage all around her.

Wish sat on the beam he'd been reading from, facing out toward the harbour. He could hear the sheep complaining as they roamed in over the paths. Looked up toward the Spell Rock to see Bella coming toward him.

"Where's Mom?"

"She headed up the south side."

They both looked in that direction and could see her moving slowly toward the house where she was born.

Bella sat near him on the beam and watched the harbour a few minutes. She said, "You were the reason she left here, is that right?"

"Did Mercedes tell you that?"

"My father. He said Mom left her life behind for you."

Wish smiled at her, surprised. He couldn't imagine why the man would tell her such a thing. "Me and your mother were just kids then, both of us."

"Huh," she said, in a way that suggested dissatisfaction or doubt. Deciding whether or not to say something more on the subject. She looked up and down the beach. "It's like someone dropped a bomb on this place."

"We should follow your mother up," he said.

He led Bella along the wall of the house, the branches of spruce and alders scraping at their arms and legs as they went. They leaned in the back-kitchen doorway, an odd smell of rain and wet grass inside. There was no sign of Mercedes. The riddle fence around the backyard had disappeared and the outbuildings were gone as well. Only a two-seater outhouse with the doors off the hinges stood among the trees that had grown tight to the back kitchen. Wish excused himself and made his way over the bramble, picking out the rough squares of shale that had been used as foundations for the cold room and storehouses.

The outhouse was farther back than any of the other buildings had been and it was almost buried in brush. He pushed through the branches to step into the doorless stall. An incongruously sweet smell of moss rising up to him as he pissed into the darkness. He stepped out and sized up the tiny building as he zipped his fly. Not the outhouse that stood there in 1940 obviously, but he was ambushed by the thought of leaning young Mercedes against the sidewall, of kneeling under her raised skirt to kiss the sweet of her. Felt an uncanny echo of what he'd felt at the time. Ridiculous and reckless and completely certain. Realized he'd forgotten that. He could always recall fabrics and colours and tastes but he'd forgotten what it was to suddenly decide he was in love with Mercedes. That he would love her. He leaned a hand against the rotting frame, looked up at the grey sky. Even the memory of it made him unsteady.

Bella had already gone inside when he came back to the house. The floor uneven and fragile with rot under his feet. The ceiling rafters almost touching his head. The frame of the daybed still in its corner, a board table in the same spot under the window. Dark squares on the walls where the two pictures used to hang, Queen Victoria and King Billy crossing the Boyne. He was about to tell Isabella that he and Mercedes had kissed for the first time in this room when he heard footsteps overhead.

Wish walked down the hall to the foot of the stairs. "Mercedes," he shouted. The steps were tilted on a severe angle, as if they were on a boat that was taking on water and listing heavily to one side. He used a hand against the wall as he went up, not trusting the rail to hold his weight. He stepped carefully along the hallway. In places he could look through the floor straight into the rooms below. "Mercedes," he said.

"In here."

She was in a bedroom wrestling with the head of an old iron bed frame. A bureau with two missing drawers stood against the wall. A blind over the window, glass still in the frames.

"I can't get it free," she said. "Have a go at it, will you?"

He jimmied the post back and forth, inching it out. He stopped when he had it halfway to catch his breath, the palms of his hands stained red with rust. He went back at it, grunting as he twisted and pulled, the ancient bed frame squealing.

Bella called from downstairs: "Should I leave you two alone up there?"

"Oh be quiet, Bella," Mercedes said and she smiled at Wish. "I spose you can't even get it up any more." She put her hand to his shoulder. "Poor old Johnny was limp as a rag for years before he died."

Wish reefed angrily at the post, struck by the easy affection in her voice, the years of uncomplicated intimacy it implied. When the post came free, Mercedes leaned past him to stare down into the frame, reaching a single finger into the open space to fish at something inside. She brought up a small parcel wrapped in cloth, shook it gently to rattle the coins. The string was brittle and broke in her fingers as she untied it. She unrolled the cloth on the dresser. She said, "This is where I got the money to go to St. John's."

He picked up a bill and held it up to the window. Two dollars. 1931. Newfoundland tender.

Mercedes picked out a plain gold ring among the coins, held it in her palm.

"Nan's wedding band," she said. She rewrapped the package and set the fold of muslin into her shoulder bag. "She tried to give it to me before I left the Cove to come after you."

The wistfulness in her voice stung him, and he moved several steps away from her. He said, "You remember I almost ran off before your father drowned?"

She nodded.

"Agnes said there had to be something to bring me back, remember?"

"When did she tell you that?"

"You told me," he said. "It was something she said to you."

"All right."

He could see she had no memory of those conversations but was willing to go along, to find out what he was getting at. "I came back to make something up to you. Something to do with the night you kissed me downstairs. You remember that."

She smiled. "I'm not dead yet, am I?"

"Do you remember what you said? When I touched you?"

"I went to look in on Nan and then everyone came in the door, back from church. And you left before I got to say a word to you."

"Before you went to look in on your grandmother," he said. "You pulled away from me."

"I never." A look of disbelief on her face.

He smiled at his feet. "You pulled away and you said, 'Don't make a whore of me.'"

She shook her head, but he could tell from her expression that it was coming back to her. Her hesitation and the way those words set him on his ass in the chair. She said, "I never."

"Hiram had money on it all, did he ever tell you that?"

"On what?"

"Don't be stupid, Mercedes."

"On *what*?"

Wish leaned his weight against the bed frame. "Every little place we went into with the movies, he'd give me odds on bedding some missus. Usually someone with a husband off on the Labrador for the season."

"You bet with him?"

"I was a youngster, Mercedes. I was pissed at your mother, is most of it. The bet was just an excuse."

She adjusted the straps of the shoulder bag, as if it was falling away from her.

"I was just a youngster," he said again. "I would have screwed a knothole in a fence post for fifty cents."

She smiled and didn't smile and smiled again. She drew her head back to take in a breath of air. "A knothole," she said. Every breath seemed to be striking her like a slap in the face.

"Mercedes."

She went out the door with both hands clutching the straps of the shoulder bag.

He went as far as the rail, calling after her, but she ignored him and he let her go. He walked into the bedroom and stood at the window, swearing under his breath. The window was so old that the glass had settled and pooled near the bottom, the striated panes distorting everything he could see out across the Cove, sheep appearing and disappearing like pennies in a water glass. The two women came around the side of the house below him and started down the path, their figures wavering like a mirage through the ancient glass.

He hadn't felt anything for Mercedes in so long he assumed it had leached from him somewhere in his travels, in the years of itinerant work and drinking, in the long string of temporary relationships. But he was wrong about that. He felt as if he was exhuming a creature preserved in a peat bog for centuries: the body intact, the face leathery and tanned black by the bog but still identifiable. The material of the clothes retaining its original colour under a camouflage of wet turf.

He left the camp after the tidal wave of wind and heat ripped through, the single spectral pulse of it and the violent recoil, as if it was cast out on a line and jerked back to the place it was thrown from. Windows shattered. Anything movable tumbled first in one direction and then the opposite. Utterly, utterly silent afterwards as he picked himself up from the ground and walked out the gates. Some kind of cloud rising over the hills in the distance, a grey bloom exfoliating steadily, a long central column towering like the stalk of a plant. The cloud was eerily symmetrical, as if it was the product of intelligent design, and it chilled him to watch it expanding moment by moment as he walked up out of the valley, the sky darkening over him.

When he crested the hill above the camp he could see what was left of the shipyard in the distance. Buildings and warehouses, destroyers and carriers reduced to piles of scrap metal. Beyond that, more devastation than it was possible to catalogue. He turned away from the city, walking for more than an hour in the opposite direction without a plan, until he passed the French Temple. The building was still intact and empty when he stepped inside and he walked toward the altar, brushed a pew clear of shattered glass.

Others began arriving shortly afterwards. He didn't acknowledge them and no one spoke. It was as if they were gathering for some prearranged service. By late afternoon the sanctuary was crowded and people had already begun dislodging pews to shift them out of the way. Some of the survivors had made their way from neighbourhoods near the city centre and most of those were badly burnt. One boy lay against the wall near Nishino, shaking with some kind of fever. His upper body was naked and the skin appeared to have been torn away in one long strip from his torso, raw muscle over the rib cage, the wound outlined in vermilion and black. His mother sat near his head and the boy was asking her for ice cream, repeating the question relentlessly without pausing for an answer. Nishino could feel the mother watching him, realized finally it was his uniform that drew her gaze, that she was expecting some sort of direction or assistance from him. It seemed then that the eyes of everyone in the church were on him and he began to shake under that weight, a tremor running through his shoulders, his teeth chattering.

He gathered up his kit bag and went through a doorway beside the altar. Took the set of stairs to the basement and wandered through the dark corridors until he found an unoccupied room. It had no windows and there was only enough light from the hall to confirm it was empty. He pushed the door shut and lay against it in the pitch, trying to quiet his breathing, to stop his teeth knocking. The muffled sound of the people on the floor above him filtering into the darkness.

He would have to get rid of the uniform. He began emptying the pockets, making a small pile of items to one side. He fished out the medallion last and sat holding it, tracing the outline of the king's head with a fingertip, his hands still shaking.

It was his sister who had brought it to him. She was only ten at the time but had inherited all of their mother's responsibilities short

of managing the family's money. She cooked for the men, worked
the farm and kept the house, cleaning, washing and mending
clothes. On Saturdays, when his father drove produce to the market
and spent the night with his mistress in New Westminster, she
stripped sheets, washed the bedroom floors, straightened closets.

"Where did you get this?" he asked her.

"I was putting away his clothes," she said. She looked down at her
feet, embarrassed by the obvious snooping she'd done. "There's
something written on the back."

He reached for the medal. "You should be ashamed to be looking
through his things."

"The first part of it is Father's name. I don't understand the rest."

"You should be ashamed to know so little of your own language."

"What does it say, Noburo?"

"Mind your own business," he said, putting the medal away in his
pocket.

His father's mistress was a white woman, a childless widow who
ran a market stall established by her husband before the First World
War. He had been killed in action in France and in the years since
she had taken to wearing the dead man's clothes and knee-high
rubber boots. Nishino met her when he was still a boy, when he and
his father drove the vegetables to New Westminster, and he was
fascinated by the woman at first. She smoked cigarettes and swore a
blue streak and drank whisky. She seemed not to care what anyone
said or thought about her. After the truck was unloaded they drove a
few miles outside of town to a river, where his father spent the late
afternoon fishing for trout while Nishino swam a little ways
upstream. Some afternoons the woman came out to meet them
there and she and his father would wander off into the trees for half
an hour.

The affair wasn't a closely guarded secret but it was carefully
shaded and bordered, operating so far beneath the surface of the
family's days it was possible to ignore it completely. It was only after

his mother's death that it started to seep into their lives in a public way. His father began spending nights with her in New Westminster and the woman occasionally came to the house in Kitsilano for meals, although there was never a suggestion of anything as brazen as having her sleep in the dead wife's bed.

The increasingly open nature of the relationship meant that plenty was said about it in the community. On two occasions small gangs of white men drove out as far as their farm to break out the windows and warn his father away from the woman. They were all drunk. They threatened to burn the farm to the ground if Nishino's father refused to screw his own kind.

The engraved symbols on the back of the medal his sister found read *Hisatsune Nishino. Private First Class. The Somme. Ypres. 1917–18.* His father would have met the woman through his acquaintance with her husband in the New Westminster Regiment. When she came to visit the farm in Kitsilano she carted an armful of newspapers and magazines with her, *The Vancouver Sun* and *The New York Times* and *The Washington Post, Atlantic Monthly, Anvil, New Masses,* and she spent the evening poring through them angrily, editorializing as she went. There was no world event beneath her opinion. Chancellor Hitler recognizing Manchukuo and publicly supporting a Japanese victory in China. The expropriation of American oil companies by President Cardenas in Mexico. Nishino's father sat smoking and nodding slowly, never contradicting or arguing with the woman. Austria and Hungary recognizing Franco in Spain. The League of Nations adopting a resolution to investigate the use of poison gas by Japanese troops in China. "Poison gas," she said. "And the god-damn League of Nations adopting resolutions. Is that what you and George fought the war for?"

Nishino left the farm in Kitsilano at three in the morning after one of these visits, walking all the way into Vancouver. He left a note addressed to Hisatsune Nishino, Private First Class, to say where he was headed. Boarded a ship bound for Tokyo, his father's medal still weighting his pocket.

The traffic in and out of the church continued steady for days. Nishino rarely left his room in the basement for fear of losing it to other squatters, waved his pistol around when necessary to keep it to himself. He ate almost nothing. He slept most of the day and night and dreamt often of his mother, the woman always at work in the farmhouse or out in the fields, smiling up at him as she finished each task. Or lying on her deathbed and breathing strangely, each inhalation abrupt and mechanical and so widely spaced one from another he felt panicked, holding his own breath, waiting for the next.

He jolted awake in the darkness, sucking in a lungful of air. Shimmied his way toward the wall and leaned his weight against it. It was late, he guessed, not a sound from the church overhead. He searched around with his hands until he located the bottle he'd been drinking from. He was almost through the last of the alcohol. He tried to count the days since he'd arrived but couldn't even say whether it was day or night outside the room. He felt like a prisoner in the crypt, berated himself for leaving the camp, slinking off like a coward to hide in the bowels of a Catholic church. Even Chozo Ogawa had been granted a soldier's death and he found himself envying the boy.

It was the thing he despised most in the POWs, how they clung to life even when there wasn't a shred of respect to be gained in it. And it was clear to him now that he was no different, that the country where he'd become a man had infected him with the same weakness. He lacked the courage to turn the gun on himself, whatever the weight of shame he carried by living.

He drifted into sleep again, was woken by the sound of footsteps on the stairs at the end of the corridor and he listened to them approaching. Voices too muffled to make out. The *sss ssss sss* of English.

He tried to find his glasses where he'd laid them on the floor, sweeping his hands in wide arcs. The footsteps slowed in the corridor and came to a stop outside his door. He scrambled for his kit bag and took the handgun from the holster, moving back to the farthest corner of the room. He heard the word *flashlight*.

The door slammed open and a single beam flicked over the room before coming to rest on him. He couldn't see anything beyond the blurred circle of light. He placed the gun against his head and squeezed the trigger repeatedly, long after it was clear the weapon was empty of ammunition. Only a cold clicking sound jarring his temple.

"I am very pleased," a voice behind the light said, "to meet you."

MERCEDES

———

1.

BEFORE THEY WENT LOOKING for Wish's house in Calvert that morning, they'd driven all the way down to Renews. They stopped in front of the church and walked across to the grotto. The statue of Mary in the same alcove but everything else was barely recognizable from the first time Mercedes had seen it. She took off her sunglasses.

"This was all bare," she said. "There wasn't a green thing for miles."

A thick coat of vines covered the stone walls, the knoll behind it overgrown with a cultivated copse of trees. The Stations of the Cross laid out along a path shaded by spruce and fir, cypress and hawthorn and mountain ash. The state of the place surprised her in a completely predictable, prosaic way. To see she'd been away long enough for those trees to be planted and mature, that a lifetime had passed in her absence. It made the time left her seem meagre, insufficient to what she wanted of it.

Wish clearly wasn't going to offer anything easily. There was a practised deceit in his manner, a vulnerability that seemed false,

317

that was meant to disguise real damage. He confessed just enough to hide the truth, went only as far as she could push him. The calculation of it all infuriated her, the guile.

Bella said, "What's wrong, Mom?"

"Nothing," she said. "It's just." She took a deep breath. "What do you smell here, Bella?"

"Nothing."

"Try, for God's sake. Take a whiff."

Isabella rolled her eyes and started sniffing at the air. "Nothing," she said again.

Agnes said, "Spruce. Salt water."

"I haven't been able to smell anything since I woke up in hospital."

"Why didn't you mention this to the doctor?"

"They wouldn't have let me out if I told them, would they?"

"Well you're going back," Bella said, "first thing."

"Not till we get back from the Cove."

"Don't argue with me, Mom."

"I'm not arguing. I'm telling."

"Don't be so goddamn stubborn."

"Wait till you get old," Mercedes said. "Then talk to me."

"Jesus *Christ*," Bella said.

Mercedes watched Isabella stalk off past the old convent and down toward Aggie Dinn's Cove. Agnes gave her a look and Mercedes nodded in Bella's direction to say go after her. When they were out of sight she looked up at the statue of Mary, at the woman's blank gaze. She brought a hand up to her cheek, felt the hard metal plate under the dead skin. How stone would feel to the touch under a layer of cloth. She took another breath through her nostrils. Nothing. It was as if she was in the process of leaving the world one sense at a time.

She crossed herself and said, "Hail Mary, full of grace, the Lord is with thee. Blessed art thou amongst women."

She hadn't said the rosary or the Ave since she'd converted to marry Johnny Boustani in 1946. He insisted they raise Marion in the church and took a hand in what he called her spiritual instruction. She'd always ridiculed Johnny for his little ritual observances, saying the rosary in the living room while she cleared the supper dishes, lighting candles at the feet of the saints, saying novenas to St. Theresa. When they put their first house in Lowell up for sale in 1959, he buried a figurine of St. Joseph upside down in the garden for luck. "A goddamn grown man," she'd said, "praying to dolls."

He gave up the church after Marion died. They had Isabella baptized but never darkened a church door afterwards. Mercedes hadn't so much as overheard the rosary for decades. She didn't know which mysteries were meant to be recited on which day and had forgotten the order they were laid out in, but she pressed on below the statue of Mary, throwing them out in a jumble as they came to her. Crossed herself when she was done. If she'd known what saint to bury for luck, she'd have done that as well.

When they left the wharf in Tilting, Mercedes made her way out past the cuddy of Gerry Foley's longliner to sit in the bow. Her eyes tearing up in the breeze. She fished her sunglasses out of the shoulder bag, put them on against the wind. Little Fogo Island looming on the horizon, growing steadily. It felt almost as if she was the one sitting motionless, that the place was coming to meet her finally, after all these years of waiting.

Rounding the headland and a first view of the Cove. Most of the buildings fallen in on themselves, the lumber stripped of paint and ochre, gone grey with the weather of thirty years. The church still standing, though she could see that every last window was gone, the large double doors off the hinges. And up the south side the house she'd grown up in tilting awkwardly, like a child's drawing of a house.

"That's our place," she said, calling back to Wish and pointing.

"Which one?"

"There," she said. "The last one on the south side."

He shaded his eyes.

"You don't remember?"

He shook his head apologetically and she called past him to Isabella.

"Our house," she shouted.

Isabella nodded miserably, without bothering to look.

All the way up the path to the house she was thinking of Clive Reid, his name whittled into the beam under a pile of rubble on the landwash. She knew from Agnes that he'd drowned years before, trying to take up his trap in rough weather. But seeing his name carved into the beam brought him back whole. "The Tennessee Waltz." That first unexpected kiss. The rush of it clinging to her for weeks, even after she decided she had no interest in Clive himself. And the guilt, like the pale underside of a leaf flying up in a wind. A married man and she'd done nothing to protest or stop him.

Her grandmother was just beginning her slide into illness at the time and the delicacy of her constitution made her more observant somehow, more wary. She was the only one who noted any change in her. Mercedes insisted her grandmother was imagining things, but the old woman's certainty wore her down.

"I kissed a man," she admitted finally.

They were separating cream from the milk in the cold room and the old woman set down the pan she was holding. "What man?" she said.

Mercedes wouldn't look at her.

Her grandmother raised Mercedes' chin with one hand, then drew back and slapped her face with all the force her ancient body could muster. "This is a godly house you live in," she said. "You would do well to remember that."

320

Wish arriving in the Cove then, all limbs and long face, a conspiratorial smile that made you think he had something important to say to you later on, when he could get you alone. Crossing himself at the sight of crows. She'd heard her grandmother prattle on about his kind enough to know what the old woman would think of him. And something in Mercedes found that an irresistible draw.

From a distance the house seemed solid enough, but she could almost feel it waver once she was inside. Pitch dark until she remembered her sunglasses and took them off. The walls peeling and water-stained, the floors rotting out. She went along the hall to the parlour, which was empty, the hand-built chairs and settee, the hutch and end tables gone now, sold or stolen by antique dealers who scoured the outports to supply shops in Quebec and Ontario and New England. She tried to recall the close, polished scent that had defined the room when she was a girl, but even her memory of smell seemed to have left her.

Mercedes turned from the door to the staircase behind her. Went up one step at a time, testing her weight on each one. The naked bed frame still in her parents' room. She pictured her grandmother lying there after Mercedes' father was buried. When she offered Mercedes her wedding ring. She gripped the left post at the head in both hands but couldn't budge it. Decided to wait there until Wish came up from the shoreline.

The path from the house back down to the harbour was uneven and she had to concentrate to avoid stumbling as she went.

She was taking long slow breaths and each one made her head ring. Spruce gum and new grass, the scoured-clean smell of salt water in the wind. It was like an air bubble popping in the inner ear cavity, a distant muffle of sound instantly dialled sharp and clear. Juniper and rotting lumber, the sour odour of alder bushes. She could smell Isabella's shampoo wafting back to her, honey and yeast, and beyond that the barely perceptible smudge of the sheep taking over the Cove.

A wager with Hiram, Wish told her, standing in the old bedroom, his hands filthy with rust. I'd have screwed a knothole, he said. She started to feel dizzy as he spoke and she gripped the straps of her shoulder bag with both hands. She was suddenly and for the first time afraid of the man, of what he could do to her memory of him. A whiff of ammonia in her nostrils and she thought she might faint until the smell of the house came rushing past it, mildew and old iron and the punky odour of rooms shut up with themselves for years, mouse droppings and mothballs. The cheap aftershave Wish was wearing, alcohol and leathery mint, and something awful beneath that. Sweat and old age and fear. Corruption. She wanted open air and she left him there, walking too quickly down the wonky stairs.

Isabella was getting farther and farther ahead of her on the path. "Bella," she said. She felt like lying down where she stood, stretching out in the grass beside the path and sleeping. "I need a second," she said.

Bella came back to her. "You okay, Mercedes?"

"I just need a second." She lifted the dark glasses with one hand and wiped at her eyes.

"What happened up there, Mom?"

"Nothing. Nothing much. It's just," she said. "Everything."

"Can we go now?" Isabella said. "Are we done here?"

"I want to see the graveyard," Mercedes said. "Then we can go."

The cemetery fence was down, the remains of the palings almost lost to the high grass and spruce that circled the clearing. A handful of Gerry Foley's sheep had made their way into the graveyard and were grazing among the headstones, which were sunken and tipped, or cracked at the base and fallen into the grass where they were being swallowed by a slow green tide of moss. The oldest marble stones were worn bare by age and the elements, the carved lettering of names and dates stripped away and lost. Mercedes wandered around the space, trying to recall where her father was buried. She stood in the centre of the graveyard and turned a slow circle.

Isabella pointed to a squat black marker of polished stone. "That's got to be recent," she said.

They walked over together and found her father's grave, her mother and grandmother laid to rest on either side. A small plaque at the foot of the plot in memory of Hardy.

Bella ran a hand over Helen's marker, the black stone as smooth as glass. She said, "You never considered coming back for her funeral, Mom?"

"Johnny tried to talk me into it. Said I'd always regret it if I didn't."

"And?"

"What's one more regret?" She waved a hand in the air. "I have to sit down."

Isabella helped her onto the grass and sat beside her. The sheep had congregated on the opposite side of the clearing, and they watched the animals work over the ground. They were lackadaisically methodical, the sound of them cropping the new growth on the graves like a glimpse of life at work in some secret place, the world's subterranean appetite on display.

Bella motioned her chin toward the church, where Wish was making his way along the path. "Prince Charming at six o'clock," she said.

"Call him up for me, would you?"

Bella watched her mother a moment longer before she stood and called to Wish.

"I'll meet you over at the boat," he shouted.

"Tell him to come up," Mercedes said.

"Mom wants you a second."

Wish laboured into the clearing, out of breath and limping. He rubbed a finger under his nostrils. "Almost too old for this," he said.

Mercedes looked up at him, thinking he might be talking about more than the walk.

He gestured toward the headstones. "This is your crowd, is it?"

"It is."

"Your mother," he said, pointing to the black marker.

"What's left of her."

He leaned toward Isabella. "Her mother never thought much of me, first or last."

"I'm not sure I blame her," Bella said.

Mercedes smiled at her daughter. *Saucy as the black.* It was the one thing Mercedes was certain had passed directly from her.

Wish said, "I think it was more along the lines of a philosophical difference with me and Helen."

"That's what I always thought," Mercedes said. "No one told us youngsters anything in those days."

Wish crouched and leaned awkwardly on one arm to settle on the ground. "What do you mean?" he said. He seemed relieved to be talking about something other than what had gone on in the old house.

"Mom got sick the year before she passed away. She was living with Agnes by then. Had a fever so high she was out of her mind half the time, didn't recognize anyone, didn't know where she was. Kept asking for the priest."

"The priest?"

"Ag thought it was just the fever, you know, foolish talk. But she went on and on about it and it looked like they were going to lose her. Ag sent David across to Tilting and he carried the priest back. Left them alone in the room awhile." Mercedes looked across at Wish, his mouth working hard. She said, "Mother's people were from somewhere in Conception Bay but they had nothing to do with her once she came here with Father. I always thought it was just her being pregnant before she married."

"She was Catholic," Wish said.

"No one said a word about it all those years."

Wish made an attempt to get to his feet but began drifting awkwardly sideways. Bella jumped up to grab his arm.

"You okay?" she said.

He pulled his arm free. Used both hands to smooth the white hair ringing his head. "Mercedes," he said, as if he was trying the word out for the first time. Tried to recall McCarthy's phrase, Nuestra Señora de las Mercedes.

"It must have been hard for her, all those years. She told Ag that Nan sat her down with a hymn book the first week she was here and said, 'You learn them, missy. Because there's no micks in this house.'"

Wish was still unsteady on his feet and Bella waited beside him, her hands ready. He was staring down at the black headstone. "Well, missus," he said. He seemed about to say something more but turned away to look at Bella and then at Mercedes. He started toward the church and they watched him go, nodding to himself as he walked along the path toward the Spell Rock.

Bella said, "Is that what you brought him out here to tell him?"

"I guess so."

"She was afraid of losing you. Your mother."

"She wanted to spare me what happened to her, I imagine. She was afraid I'd lose my family altogether."

"She wasn't far wrong there, was she."

Mercedes looked up at Bella, at the angry smile on her face. She could smell the chlorophyll of the freshly cropped grass drifting across the clearing. She reached for a hand. "Let's go," she said.

2.

BELLA DROVE THE FIRST LEG of the trip back to St. John's. Mercedes heard Agnes whisper across to Wish in the backseat, "What happened over there?" But he didn't say anything in response that she could make out.

In Clarenville they stopped for gas and ate fried chicken at a Mary Brown's that was empty but for them. Dusk when they walked back to the car, and they pushed on into the night, Wish driving, the tide of darkness settling over them as they travelled east. By the time they crossed the isthmus onto the Avalon Peninsula it was pitch outside, their world reduced to thirty feet of road in the headlights, no stars overhead. Agnes and Isabella nodded off in the back and Mercedes glanced across at Wish to make sure he wasn't drifting. He seemed to feel her watching.

He said, "The things the Monsignor used to tell us about you."

"Who?"

"Your people. Protestants. Threw you all in together, Billy Sunday and Christian Science and the Quakers and Alexander Dowie, the Sally Ann. Trial marriages and prison reform and prohibition. A diseased imagination, he used to say, at odds with the genius of Catholicism."

"The what?"

"The genius of Catholicism. Funny how I spent all my time at mass daydreaming about some girl's tits and I can still quote him, chapter and verse." Wish took a breath. "Father Power didn't think much of you crowd," he said.

She could see he was furious.

He said, "It's Spanish, did you know that?"

"What is?"

"Mercedes. It means compassion or mercy or some goddamn thing."

"No," she said. "I didn't know that."

Wish wagged a finger in her direction without taking his eyes from the road. He said, "You wanted to know everything, is that right?"

"That's what I said."

"You haven't changed your mind about that?"

She hesitated, wondering if she wasn't too tired for it. But in the end she said, "I'm too old to change."

He flexed his fingers on the steering wheel as if to get a better grip. He said, "There was a guard at the camp I spent the war in. He was an interpreter there the last six months. Nishino, his name was."

She shifted in her seat to watch him as he talked, his face lit by the dashboard lights. He went on for the better part of an hour, speaking levelly and without emotion, as if he was providing an affidavit, listing dates and events, victims and perpetrators and bystanders, answering questions to clarify, interpreting phrases, naming names when he remembered them. Osano, McCarthy, Spalding. Koyagi, van der Meulen. Nishino. Nishino. Nishino.

He told her about losing Anstey and carrying the urn to the French Temple, happening on the interpreter asleep in the crypt. Like a gift. He said, "We busted in on him there the next night. Me and Harris and Spalding. He was sitting with his back against the far wall and the gun in his hand. Put it up to his head and pulled the trigger. Click, click, click, like that. Just kept pulling the trigger. Click, click, click. We all stepped in, me and Harris and Spalding following behind. And Nishino knelt up to meet us, his hands down by his side. He just give up. We had these wooden clubs the guards at the camp used on us and we started right in. He stayed upright a long time. Pushed himself up off the floor once or twice. Never made a sound."

327

She could tell he was fighting not to go under and she said, "It sounds to me like maybe he got what he deserved."

"I was called there, is how I saw it at the time. It was a right-eous thing." He cracked his window open, as if he was afraid of being overheard and wanted the noise of the wind to cover his voice. "But right and wrong never come into once we got going. It was just . . . His little piggy eyes, you know. It could have been any-one of his kind, is what I think now."

Mercedes reached a hand across but he shrugged away from her. Through the window lay the invisible sprawl of barrens and brush land she'd flown over leaving the island fifty years before. She could feel the massive splay of it ravelling through the darkness to either side of them, as if the countryside itself were shadowing his words. It seemed malevolent somehow, she thought. Or simply indifferent, which amounted to the same thing.

Wish said, "It was hard work given the shape we were in. We had to take it in shifts, just to have breath enough to keep at it. We'd brought a couple of handguns and Spalding said we should finish him off and get out. But that's not what we wanted."

Mercedes looked out at the road, at the stretch of pavement coming at them. They were less than half an hour outside St. John's, a sallow glimmer of city lights reflected under clouds on the horizon, as if the place had been set afire when they left the day before and the ruins were still smouldering.

Wish said, "Do you know what we wanted, Mercedes?" She didn't answer, and he said, "You can change your mind if you like."

"Just finish it, Wish."

He nodded but didn't say anything more for a while, as if he'd changed his own mind about it.

"Wish?"

He said, "We were on our way out the door after we were through and Harris grabbed my arm, told me to hold the flash-light. I turned the light on Nishino and Harris went through his pockets. He had some American money, an old medal. When Harris was done I flicked the light over the corpse one more time. Over the face. There was blood running out of his ears and the eyes swollen shut."

"*Jesus*, Wish."

"I'm almost through," he said. "We were all just standing there then, looking at what we'd done to him. And Harris. I don't know. Harris stood over him and opened his pants and he—" Wish looked out the side window, then back at the highway. "He pissed on him. Right where I had the light shining. He was saying, 'How do you like that, you yellow bastard.' And then Spalding stepped up and joined him."

"That's enough," she said.

"*That's* what we wanted, Mercedes."

She rolled her window all the way down, leaning her head out into the roar of it so she wouldn't have to hear another word. She filled her head with the cold and the noise until Bella woke in the back and told Mercedes to roll the window closed.

WISH

—

HE TURNED OFF THE HARBOUR arterial just outside the downtown core, taking the exit for the Southern Shore highway out to
Calvert. Keeping a close eye on the speedometer. All the while he
was talking to Mercedes he'd caught himself picking up speed and
had to ease off the accelerator. They hadn't said another word after
Mercedes rolled up her window but he kept losing himself in the
basement of the French Temple and the needle would climb
above 100, 110.

He'd driven in and out the Southern Shore highway in a similar state of distraction when he came home to Newfoundland to
settle things for Lilly. He was in hard shape at the time, drunk most
of the day and not able to function in any sensible way when he was
sober. He often had no memory of the trip to St. Pat's when it was
done, on autopilot the whole way. He stopped for a coffee and a
doughnut in Churchill Square and ate half a container of Tic Tacs
before going in to see Lilly, but there was no hiding the condition
he was in. She could see it in the slovenly way he dressed, in his
rheumy eyes and the sallow colour of his skin, in the perpetual

three-day whisker. One afternoon she leaned toward him out of her chair and said, "You have to ask God for help with this." She tipped her hand to her mouth to show him what she meant.

He'd just that week spent half his life savings on a car and the house in Calvert and had no idea how he was going to get by. He was in a foul enough mood to argue with a crazy woman. He said, "There is no God, Lilly."

She said, "*Adjutorium nostrum in nomine Domini qui fecit coelum et terram*. Without Him," she said, "we can do nothing. You have to say the prayer of a special intention to Our Blessed Lady, every day for thirty days, to ask for her intercession."

"I brought a crib board," he said. "Interested in a game?"

He'd quit drinking half a dozen times in his life, always to appease women who left anyway once they saw that sobriety made him no easier to live with. It had never occurred to him to quit when he was alone. But he poured a bottle of Screech down the sink when he got home from St. Pat's that night. In the morning he brewed a pot of coffee and made a fresh pot every hour. Did the same every day afterwards, morning to night, black coffee strong enough to stand a spoon up straight. Drank it as fiercely as the rum. Just to prove Lilly wrong in the matter, to settle something for himself. He stumbled a few times, spent an evening at Mercer's hammering back dark-and-dirties until he puked. Each slip goading him sober for longer periods. It had been years now since he last took a drink. And there was some small comfort in staying dry of his own volition.

He'd hoped to receive some of the same comfort in telling Mercedes his story, some sort of release or relief, but there was none. It felt like an act of cruelty, almost a violent thing in the aftermath, to carry through as far as he did when he could feel Mercedes pulling away. And even then he was holding back, refusing to give up the one detail not even Harris or Spalding knew.

When the two men were done pissing on the corpse, they wanted Wish to take a turn. "Have a go there, Liquor Man,"

Spalding said, waving toward the dead man. "Let 'er rip," Harris insisted. They were both angry when he refused, as if they felt his reluctance was a judgment on them. But the truth was more pedestrian and bizarre: his cock, Wish realized, was stiff as a poker. He'd gone months in the camp without a gig, without a single sub-terranean niggle to suggest he'd ever manage an erection again. Then this freakish, inexplicable hard-on. "Let's go," he said to them. "We're done here, let's go."

Mercedes reached out to touch his arm and the road came back to him suddenly, a winding stretch near Tors Cove. The speedometer just shy of 120 kilometres an hour. He eased off, touched the brake.

Bella spoke up from the backseat. "Maybe I should drive awhile."

"Calvert's just up the road," he said. "I'll be fine." He glanced across at Mercedes but she had gone back to staring out her window into the dark. Trying to piece it together, he guessed, trying to see where and how she fit into the mess. Or just wanting to get clear of the whole goddamn works, to put it out of her head for good.

The house was dark when they pulled up. Bella took his seat behind the wheel and he walked up the steps. He watched through the screen door as the car backed down the driveway, Mercedes staring straight ahead as they went, refusing to meet his eye. They stopped at the bottom of the drive and he could see Mercedes talking with Bella, an animated little exchange that con-tinued for a few moments after Bella put the car into park. They seemed a long way off to him.

Mercedes stepped out of the car and walked up the driveway. She stopped at the foot of the bridge and looked up to him behind the screen.

"You have to give me something," she said.

"What?"

"You can't leave it like that," she said. "Give me something, anything at all. Make something up if you have to."

"What are you saying, Mercedes?"

"I'm telling you right now," she warned him.

He pushed the screen door open and took one step down onto the bridge. She looked directly at him and he thought she might actually be counting to ten in her head. He raised both hands to smooth down his little ring of hair. Tried to talk himself into letting her go, letting it end where it was.

She started back to the car.

He said, "For fuck sake, Mercedes," but she ignored him.

"*Mercedes.*"

She turned around, walking slowly backwards down the drive. She looked tired and worn, the dead side of her face completely expressionless, which made the wear seem permanent, irredeemable.

He said, "I met Marion."

She stopped where she was. "You what?"

"I came down to Lowell once," he said. "Years ago. You were living in a duplex, a yellow two-story that backed onto a park. You and the girl were sitting in the backyard."

He'd had no trouble tracking them down. He sat on a park bench in a fedora and sunglasses, throwing breadcrumbs to ducks at the pond's edge. The path around the water looped within three feet of their back fence and he circled it occasionally, to have a closer view. Mercedes drinking lemonade beside the girl, who was curled up in a deck chair with a sketchpad. The phone rang in the house periodically and one of them would disappear inside to answer it. Mercedes flipped through magazines and fell asleep with her arm over her eyes. As if she'd never known him.

Mercedes said, "What was she wearing?"

"Jesus, Mercedes. It was thirty years ago."

"*Think* for a minute."

"Shorts," he said. "I don't know what colour. She had nothing on her feet. A white blouse, the sleeves rolled to her elbows. She had a big pad of paper on her lap. Barrettes to keep her bangs out of her face." He motioned toward Mercedes. "She was about the age you were the first time I laid eyes on you."

"What do you mean, you met her?"

"You were gone inside to answer the phone and she . . . Marion . . . she was sitting there alone. I strolled by the fence. Said hello as I passed by. She didn't know me from Adam. I said what a day it was, or some such thing."

"What did she say to you?"

"Only hello back and it was a fine stretch of weather. Just talk. She had one foot up on the chair and she was swinging the knee back and forth right lazy like. Not a care in the world."

Mercedes had a hand against her mouth and he stopped there. He said, "That's all I got for you."

He went in the door again and closed it behind him, walking through the dark to his bedroom and closing that door as well, without waiting to see whether it was enough to satisfy her.

The rest of the weekend was coffee and satellite television. The Expos leading the NL East and on their way to the pennant if there was no strike, as the papers kept predicting. *Mary Poppins* and John Wayne in *The Searchers*. Reruns of *The Dukes of Hazzard* and *Three's Company*. Billy-Peter showed up on Monday evening and he went straight for the kettle, put it on the burner, set about making himself a cup of tea. Wish was sitting in the living room, flicking aimlessly through channels. Australian-rules football. Country and western videos. "Some fucking friend you are," he said. "I could have been lying dead up here this days."

"You'd be better company dead," Billy-Peter said. "How was the trip to Fogo?"

America's Most Wanted. A southern evangelist sweating on a stadium stage in Brazil. A black man in a suit and tie shadowing the preacher's every move, translating each sentence into Portuguese. Braves and the Phillies, no score in the second.

Billy-Peter came and sat in an easy chair while he waited for the kettle to boil. Wish set the remote down and looked across at him. Relieved to see he didn't expect an answer to his question, all his attention on the ball game. When the kettle whistled in the kitchen Wish waved Billy-Peter back into his seat, got up to see to it.

"Any word from Mercedes?" Billy-Peter shouted.

"Not since they dropped me home Saturday."

"Do you know where she's staying in St. John's?"

"With her sister, up in the Torbay apartments." He brought the mug in and set it on the coffee table.

"You going to track her down?"

"She knows where I am."

Billy-Peter smiled to himself and picked up the mug.

"What?"

"Nothing, forget it."

"Forget what?"

Billy-Peter took a sip and made a face. "Jesus, Wish. Didn't anyone teach you how to make a sensible cup of tea?" And he went off to the kitchen for more milk and sugar.

Wish turned up the volume and stared blindly at the television. *Aufer a me, Domine, cor lapideum*, he thought. Take away my heart of stone. Wiping his eyes clear of tears before Billy-Peter came back to his seat.

And neither man mentioned Mercedes again.

Tuesday afternoon there was a knock at the door. He was asleep on the chesterfield in front of the television and wasn't sure at first what had woken him. Stumbled to the porch when the knock came again.

"You look surprised," Isabella said.

"Jehovah's Witness are the only crowd that knocks at a door around here." He looked past her to Agnes's car in the driveway.

"Just me," she said. "Mind if I come in?"

He backed away from the door and she went by him to sit at the kitchen table.

"Tea or coffee?"

"Just some water would be fine."

He rooted through the cupboard for a glass, ran the tap to let the water cool. Pulled out a chair and sat down next to her. "What can I do for you, Isabella?"

"I just thought I'd drop in."

"Your mother know you're here?"

"Let's just say I'm trying to satisfy my own personal curiosity."

He laughed. "About what exactly?"

She put both her hands around the glass of water on the table, shrugged her shoulders. She didn't seem to know what to say now that she was there beside him. Her right wrist was crowded with woven bracelets, a dozen or more in a rainbow of colours. Wish felt sorry for the woman, there was a lostness about her that suggested a bystander at the scene of a fatal accident. Her obvious discomfort made him fidget in his chair.

He said, "Mercedes ever tell you about my birthmark?" He leaned forward. "What does that look like to you?"

"I don't know," she said. "An animal, maybe. Dog? Horse?"

"Exactly right," he said. "Your mother wouldn't admit it. But that's what it is."

She sat back in her chair with her arms folded, her expression meant to say, *Do you have a point?*

He told the story of his pregnant mother walking in over the slide-hauling trail, the burning horse barrelling past them, his mother falling and clutching at her neck.

"Someone actually, literally, set a horse on fire, is that what you're saying?"

He nodded.

"That's some fucked-up shit."

"I never did tell your mother what that was all about."

"There was a *reason*? Jesus."

"It was a fellow out in Renews owned the horse, she was black as a night without stars but for a white mark on her forehead and built to run. He used to take her into St. John's every March for the races on Quidi Vidi Lake and there wasn't a horse in town could touch her. She was the pride of the Southern Shore."

Bella started laughing. "Wasn't this a movie of the week or something?"

He glared at her but caught himself. "Never mind," he said.

She started back-pedalling, as if a voice in her head had reprimanded her. "No, come on. You may as well finish it."

"Doesn't matter," he said. Every bit of his sympathy drained away.

"All right, *fuck*. I'm listening. Tell me about the goddamn horse." She watched him a while longer until it was obvious to her that he was done. Sipped at her water. She said, "Mom tells me you served in the Pacific."

"I did." A low buzz of nausea starting up, like the first hint of seasickness.

"You were in Japan when they dropped the atom bomb?"

"In Nagasaki."

"What was that like?"

"What was it *like*?"

"Yeah," she said uncertainly.

"Jesus, I don't know."

"You were there, weren't you?"

He laughed to himself. Shook his head. Thought of how he'd tried to describe Nishino's mutilated face to Mercedes, clawing after a few words that wouldn't obscure or falsify or mislead, managing only to diminish the reality of it. The ineffable fact of it, lying there at his feet. He didn't have the stomach for

337

another failure of that sort now. Talking seemed just another way of forgetting.

Bella could see the hesitation in him. She said, "You don't think it was right."

"They did it because they could," he said and shrugged, as if to withhold judgment. "I'll tell you what I thought at the time. I thought the Americans were the only ones in the world had the guts to drop those bombs and God bless them. I prayed for more, is the truth of it. Even after I saw what it did."

"Is that why you didn't come looking for Mom after the war?"

"I don't see how that's any of your business, Isabella."

"She could have set things right, you know."

"Set what right?"

"Whatever it is that went wrong with you over there."

He looked away.

"I'm being serious."

"I know you're being serious," he said. He shook his head. "You crowd are all alike, every last one of you."

"What's that supposed to mean?"

"I'll tell you what I think now, Isabella," he said. He spoke without raising his voice. "There isn't another country in the world could have dropped those bombs and then carried on claiming love is the cure for all that ails the world. What a feat that is. Hallmark and Disneyland and Hollywood and whatever the fuck else makes you believe such bullshit. What a *feat*," he said again. He could feel his legs quivering under the table.

Bella held up her hands. "Okay," she said. "Forget it. I didn't come out here to fight."

"Why did you come out here, Bella?"

She craned back in her chair, her arms wide, her eyes on the ceiling. Folded into herself again. "There's a museum in Boston, an art museum Mom likes to go to."

"Art?"

"It's my namesake, this place, the Isabella Gardner Museum. Mom used to take Marion there. You know my sister, Marion?"

"I know her."

"They never talked about Marion, my parents. Her name was never mentioned in the house. But Mom used to take me to the museum when I was a girl, before I was old enough to know the difference. There was one picture there she used to spend a long time looking at, something by Vermeer called *The Concert*. You know it?"

He raised his hands helplessly.

"There's a girl at a harpsichord, a piano-type thing, and another girl singing from a score. And there's a man in the centre of the painting, a big man with shoulder-length hair and a sash over his coat. All you can see is the back of him, he's staring straight ahead as if the whole scene is something he's imagining. He always creeped me out, that guy, I could never figure what he was thinking. Felt like he was about to swallow those girls whole."

Wish scratched at the tuft of hair over his ear. "Bella."

"Never mind," she said. "Doesn't matter. The thing is, the painting was stolen a few years ago."

"Stolen how?"

"Right off the wall is how. I don't know the details. There were a couple of other pieces went missing with it. It was in the papers for a while, the Vermeer was worth millions, they said."

Bella's voice was calm enough although Wish could see her face changing, colour coming into the cheeks. It was anger, he thought, some ancient grudge so familiar to her she hardly recognized its presence.

"They've got a blank frame on the wall now where *The Concert* used to hang. And Mom still goes in every year on the anniversary of Marion's death to see it." Isabella stared across at him. "That's Mercedes," she said. "In a nutshell."

He looked past her, thinking hard. "So what you're saying," he said.

"What I'm saying is, me and Dad were always her number twos. That empty frame is where Mercedes spends her quality time."

He had to hold back a smile, not expecting something as simple or as sentimental from Isabella. He said, "That hardly seems fair to your mother."

"Then you don't know her."

The thought seemed to embarrass them both and they were quiet awhile.

"So," she said finally. "You felt guilty to be alive. Is that why you didn't go looking for her? You didn't deserve a happy, normal life?"

He got up to pour himself a coffee at the counter, took a mouthful. It had been sitting in the pot for hours and it was brackish and grainy. He leaned against the counter, took another sip. Stared into his cup.

"Don't be so fucking coy," she said.

He glanced up, surprised at the emotion in her voice, the raw disappointment. Saw the simple equation. It wasn't anger he'd seen in her face at all. He said, "Maybe I'm not the one feels guilty to be alive."

Bella settled back in her chair, trying to keep her face carefully blank.

"There's nothing can happen between your mother and me that will bring Marion back, Isabella. Or change how she is with you."

Bella said, "Jesus." She gave an angry little laugh to dismiss the notion. She picked up her glass and drank off half the water and got up from her chair. She walked to the porch and stopped with her hand on the door. She said, "Tell me something, Wish. Were you as ruthless a prick before the war?"

"I imagine I always had it in me," he said. "Yes."

———

After Isabella left he sat in the car in the driveway, trying to talk himself out of heading over to Mercer's for a drink. Thought of the medal with the head of King George in his dresser drawer and slipped back into the house, tucked it away in his shirt pocket like a saint's medallion. For the heft of it. He went over his conversation with Bella as he drove, trying to repeat some of the things he'd just said, but the words seemed absolutely foreign to him. It was like trying to recall the details of a drunken argument after sobering up. He couldn't even say if he understood what the words meant, let alone whether or not he believed them.

There was no one else at Mercer's but Gail behind the bar, a white T-shirt pulled tight over her generous breasts that read *Itty Bitty Titty Club*. She looked at him suspiciously as she opened the beer but took his money without a word.

"Keep the silver," he said when she handed him his change.

He sat alone at one of the small square tables and drank the beer in three long mouthfuls. He ordered a dark-and-dirty and another beer to chase it. Looked around as he finished them off. A row of small windows up high along one wall, a neon Labatt sign and a television on over the bar. The rest of the room in a cool, damp dark like the church and fishermen's halls where they'd showed movies on the coast.

The horse was called Ocean Star, for the Virgin Mary and for the white mark on her forehead. A household name on the Southern Shore, even when he was a youngster, though she was dead and gone by then. In his parents' day anyone travelling through Renews would stop in to watch her grazing in the open fields and feed her half an apple or a handful of tobacco. Priests up and down the shore offered special prayers to bring her luck in the March races. On the Feast of St. Francis there was an outdoor service near Mass Rock to bless her, the Monsignor making the sign of the cross over her forehead. Until the year she was sold to a merchant in St. John's, a man born into more money than God gave Solomon, a man who already owned a dozen horses. The merchant was a Protestant and the story going around said he planned to shorten the animal's name to Star.

His mother woke to Wish kicking and she went out into the moonlight with Lilly to walk through the discomfort. They passed three men on the path by the cemetery, local men they recognized by their voices as they said hello in the dark. They carried on out over the mash, thinking nothing of the encounter other than it was late for anyone to be about. One of the three would have held the bridle and whispered to calm the horse while the other two doused her back with kerosene. Led her to the open door where they set the perfect black coat aflame and let her run straight to hell.

Wish didn't feel a goddamn thing from the drinks. He ordered a double dark-and-dirty and sat nodding in the gloom. He'd taken out the box of matches he used to score Lilly's crib games and he was lighting one after another as he sat there, letting them burn down till they scorched his fingertips. Waiting for the alcohol to kick in.

By eight o'clock he'd surrendered his table to stand at the bar, telling war stories to Gail and a handful of other solitary drinkers on the stools. He was showing around the medal to make up for the lack of visible scars.

"What did you get this for?" someone asked him.

"Buddy of mine took it off a dead Jap."

"Where did the Jap get it?"

"Stole it, I'd say." He swallowed back half his drink. "He was a mean prick, that one. Almost beat me to death."

Gail said, "That was in the camps, was it, Wish?"

"Just before the big one hit Nagasaki. He had me locked up in a bamboo cell when the bomb dropped." His half-smile was so reluctant he looked like he was in pain. He and Harris were both thrown in the cells after the beating and missed their shift at the shipyard, three miles closer to ground zero. They'd trucked past it on their way to collect and cremate bodies in the city and there was nothing left of the place but scrap metal.

"What does this mean?" a man at the opposite end of the bar asked. He held the medal up. "What's this written on the back?"

"Give it here," Wish said. "You fucking pricks," he shouted. He walked the length of the bar and grabbed it, shoved it into his breast pocket. "Can't trust you fucking crowd with anything."

"You should have something to eat," Gail said to him. "A bag of chips or something."

"Chips, fuck," he said. "Fuck. Who wants a drink?" he said.

Hours later he went to the bathroom, found the stall and single urinal occupied. He shifted back and forth on his feet, waiting. Looking around the tiny room. Unzipped his pants and pissed into the sink. The door squealed open behind him and a man's voice said, "Jesus Christ, Furey."

"Get in line," he shouted over his shoulder. And laughed to himself.

Gail refused to serve him another drink. He argued with her until she picked up the phone and threatened to call her husband to throw him out. He sat in his car then, too drunk to get the keys into the ignition. Thinking Nishino, Nishino, Nishino.

That erection was what tipped him, the man dead on the floor at his feet and his own shins wet with blood. He meant to cable a message to Mercedes as soon as they landed in San Francisco and couldn't bring himself to send it. Sick with the thought all the way back to the East Coast, dreaming of her every night and that phrase he'd briefly forgotten was the only thing she said to him. The train passing through Montreal before he saw it whole, the details lining up one next the other so he could almost hear the pieces snap into place. Harris and Spalding yelling *slant-eyed prick* as they pissed over the mutilated face, *yellow bastard,*

343

MICHAEL CRUMMEY

and Wish standing there with a hard-on, Jesus fuck. His hand between the legs of the little Protestant girl too good for the likes of him, her superior cunt of a mother off saying her prayers and his cock as stiff as a poker.

He'd taken the bet with Hiram on their trip back from Twillingate to harden his resolve in the matter, to make sure he wouldn't falter. Five dollars to bed Mercedes and though there was no way the mother would know about the wager, he liked to imagine her hearing it said aloud. That furious little engine churning inside him. His hand wet and no sign of reluctance in the girl until the moment she pulled away. *Don't make a whore of me,* she said. He was bewildered by that moment of prescience. It sounded like someone else's words in the girl's mouth, the accusation so plaintive and shrewd it felt as if some angel or saint had intervened to shame him with his own intentions.

He took up with Mercedes almost as a kind of penance then, an act of attrition, as if loving her would prove the accusation wrong, as if he could erase his own sense of guilt by offering the girl some comfort in the wake of her father's death. Convince himself he was a different person than he was. It was an elaborate lie that even he was taken in by, a fiction that comforted him through the length of the war as if it were real.

Harris stretched out across the seats opposite as the train shuddered toward Halifax, clumps of hair coming away from his scalp. He said, "You'll stay with me when we get there, Wish. You won't let me die alone."

It was near dawn when he woke, slumped in the front seat. He was still drunk but managed to start the car, backed slowly out onto the deserted highway. Gail had shaken him by the shoulder when she was closing up, asking if he was all right, and he'd pushed her away. Passed out again after she closed the door. Dark-and-dirty, he remembered as he drove, all afternoon and night, the bile coming back on him.

344

The woman nursing her infant among the desolation of
Nagasaki filtered out of that haze, as she often did in the long
hangover of his adult life. How he felt nothing for her or the baby
as he salvaged and torched corpses like so much driftwood. It was
what he'd prayed for at the time and there was no remorse in him.
It would be years still before he came to see that wishing such a
fate on them had made it so. His wish alongside the wish of others
like him. He might as well have stripped the skin from the
woman's scalp with his own fingernails, held the baby over the
fires cremating the city's dead until the skin bubbled black.

More than any other it was his memory of those two nameless figures that made a place for him among the outer planets.
Somewhere beyond human. The mother's eyes dead and the
infant sucking listlessly at the breast. Madonna and child. Halfway
up the road to his house he pulled over and opened the door,
leaned out to vomit onto the pavement.

Billy-Peter's truck was in the driveway and Wish found him
asleep on the chesterfield, the television still on. He went to the
kitchen and put on a pot of coffee. Sat at the table, waiting for it
to perk, his two hands trembling like an engine idling high.

Thursday afternoon he drove in to St. Pat's.

He was showered and freshly shaven and wore the only
decent white shirt he owned, buttoned to the throat. He stopped
for coffee in Churchill Square and picked up an apple fritter as a
treat for Lilly. Walking down the corridor to her room he could
make out the singsong Latin of a priest celebrating mass, could
hear the formal timbre of it in her voice. He stood in the doorway
a minute, watching. Lilly was draped in towels to approximate a
priest's vestments. She had a mug in her hands and a toothbrush
she was using to anoint the room with holy water. Kathleen was
standing near Lilly in her flowered uniform, a towering altar boy.

"Jesus, Kathleen, would you stop humouring her with this?"

"Sure what's it hurting?"

"You got her made up like a circus freak."

"It's only a few old towels, Mr. Grumpy-pants."

He stepped into the room and set his coffee down on the bed-side table, took off his raglan.

Kathleen said, "Look at you, done up like a stick of gum."

"How long's she been at this?"

"Sometime this morning." She checked her watch. "Duty calls. She's all yours." She touched his arm on her way past. "You do look nice," she said. "What's the occasion?"

"I'm sober," he said. He leaned over Lilly to look into her face and raised his voice. "No cards for you today, Father?" he said. "No *Wheel of Fortune?*"

Lilly ignored his questions, handing him the cup to be set on the tray beside her wheelchair. She dipped her fingers and crossed herself and started the Pater Noster.

It struck him funny suddenly, watching the old woman with her vestment of towels and holy water toothbrush. Nishino inadvertently saving his miserable little life in Nagasaki. Mercedes' mother a Catholic like himself. Everything that had ever happened to Wish seemed part of some mad joke designed to be the end of him. He started giggling stupidly at the thought that so far it had failed. That he clung so fiercely to his coffee and pirated satellite television and Billy-Peter's pots of stew, to the second-hand car he kept alive with spit and tape and a prayer. As if some impossible moment of redemption was bound to materialize out of that fog. He tried to catch Lilly's eye. He said, "It's a good life if you don't weaken, hey, Father?"

He pulled a chair up close, started reciting the prayer along with her. Pinching his arm savagely to stifle the laughter.

MERCEDES

—

Johnny Boustani took care of Mercedes, as he promised. And Mercedes had learned to love him, as he predicted. Even now that simple arithmetic surprised her.

Johnny quit the army two years after she arrived in Lowell to avoid a transfer, started offering music lessons, tuning pianos across Massachusetts, ran a store for a while that sold second-hand instruments and sheet music. Through most of the fifties and early sixties he played with a jazz quartet at clubs around Boston. With Marion to look after, Mercedes only saw him perform on occasion and found it increasingly disconcerting to see him so unselfconscious, so at ease. The world never quite fit Johnny, except when he played. The music altered something in him, like an engine revving in neutral suddenly dropped into gear. Velocity and torque. A mechanical thrum so smooth it was nearly inaudible. It was like watching a stranger inhabit the face and hands of her husband.

She fell in love with the man she'd dismissed completely during the war, the earnest maladroit. The same artless, gawky innocence she found so jarring when they met became the thing

347

she relied on most in him. His endearing ineptness in the world of ordinary things.

She was struck by the loss of that again now, turning from Wish at the door of his house in Calvert and making her way down the driveway to the car. Bella watching through the windshield as she came. No one spoke a word all the way into St. John's. Johnny wouldn't have been able to stand that. He would have sung something, attempted an off-colour joke and spent several minutes trying to explain the humour after he screwed up the punch line. He would have told one of his infamously mortifying stories of personal embarrassment to distract her, and Mercedes would have felt safer to hear him talk. It would have made her feel more human.

They went to bed as soon as they arrived at Agnes's apartment, and Mercedes fell immediately asleep. Woke early the next morning, lay listening awhile to the traffic on Torbay Road. The steady swish and fade almost as soothing as the sound of ocean surf on the beach. She loved those first few minutes of the morning, the brief amnesia of it, before her life filtered through the calm.

Wish came back to her first, the dark corridor of his voice only an arm's length away in the front seat of the car. *Everything*, she'd asked for and she felt glutted to the point of nausea now. Blood on his shins, he said. The two men pissing on the mutilated face of the corpse. She'd stopped him there, rolling down the window to avoid hearing him confess he'd done the same or something worse.

It was no wonder people needed God to talk to, she thought. No one else could stand it.

She sat up on the side of the bed, waited a moment for the habitual dizziness to pass before getting to her feet. And then Marion struck her. Wish saying he'd met her, strolling by their house beside the park. Mercedes sat back down, letting the fact of it roam in her head. That Wish could have come within a stone's throw and Mercedes not know it, not have the slightest inkling.